Dear Rea

It is so nic   with
you. Fortu   ave to shovel snow,
shiver as y   p through the woods looking for the
perfect Christmas tree or worry about your vehicle sliding
off the road.

Some of my favorite Christmas holidays were spent in the
Gallatin Canyon. The cabin my dad built was small and
rustic. The outhouse was a short run out the back door.

Since the cabin was on the side of a mountain, there was
always sledding. Dad built a skating rink out front. Friends
would come up to sled and skate. Mom always baked and
had something warm waiting for us when we'd rush inside
to get by the fire. My dad was a masonry contractor so we
always had a fireplace. In the cabin, there was a stone one
in the living room and a brick one in the kitchen. It was the
only heat.

My best memories are of my brother and I playing in the
snow—there was always lots of snow—and of course
opening presents on Christmas morning.

Like Tanner "Tag" Cardwell in *Christmas at Cardwell Ranch*,
there is no better place to be at Christmas than in this
winter wonderland—until he stumbles over a body.

For Chance Walker in *Keeping Christmas*, he needs to
get Dixie Bonner out of Montana and back to Texas by
Christmas. But Texas might not be in the cards this holiday
for either of them—with a killer on the loose.

Glad you could stop by. So curl up with a mug of hot
chocolate and enjoy Christmas in Montana. I believe it's
beginning to snow.

B.J. Daniels

ABOUT THE AUTHOR

USA TODAY bestselling author B.J. Daniels wrote her first book after a career as an award-winning newspaper journalist and author of thirty-seven published short stories. That first book, *Odd Man Out,* received a four-and-a-half-star review from *RT Book Reviews* and went on to be nominated for Best Harlequin Intrigue that year. Since then, she has won numerous awards, including a career achievement award for romantic suspense and many nominations and awards for best book.

Daniels lives in Montana with her husband, Parker, and two springer spaniels, Spot and Jem. When she isn't writing, she snowboards, camps, boats and plays tennis. Daniels is a member of Mystery Writers of America, Sisters in Crime, International Thriller Writers, Kiss of Death and Romance Writers of America.

To contact her, write to B.J. Daniels, P.O. Box 1173, Malta, MT 59538, or email her at bjdaniels@mtintouch.net. Check out her website, www.bjdaniels.com.

Books by B.J. Daniels

Other titles by this author available in ebook format.

USA TODAY Bestselling Author

CHRISTMAS AT CARDWELL RANCH

&

KEEPING CHRISTMAS

B.J. DANIELS

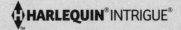 HARLEQUIN® INTRIGUE®

ISBN-13: 978-0-373-83794-6

CHRISTMAS AT CARDWELL RANCH &
KEEPING CHRISTMAS
Copyright © 2013 by Harlequin Books S.A.

The publisher acknowledges the copyright
holder of the individual works as follows:

CHRISTMAS AT CARDWELL RANCH
Copyright © 2013 by Barbara Heinlein

KEEPING CHRISTMAS
Copyright © 2006 by Barbara Heinlein

Recycling programs
for this product may
not exist in your area.

Printed in U.S.A.

www.Harlequin.com

CONTENTS

In memory of Rita Ness,
who will always be remembered as the bright
ray of sunshine she was. She is dearly missed.

CHRISTMAS AT CARDWELL RANCH

CHAPTER ONE

HUGE SNOWFLAKES DRIFTED down out of a midnight-blue winter sky. Tanner "Tag" Cardwell stopped to turn his face up to the falling snow. It had been so long since he'd been anywhere that it snowed like this.

Christmas lights twinkled in all the windows of the businesses of Big Sky's Meadow Village, and he could hear "White Christmas" playing in one of the ski shops.

But it was a different kind of music that called to him tonight as he walked through the snow to the Canyon Bar.

Shoving open the door, he felt a wave of warmth hit him, along with the smell of beer and the familiar sound of country music.

He smiled as the band broke into an old country-and-western song, one he'd learned at his father's knee. Tag let the door close behind him on the winter night and shook snow from his new ski jacket as he looked around. He'd had to buy the coat because for the past twenty-one years, he'd been living down South.

Friday night just days from Christmas in Big Sky, Montana, the bar was packed with a mix of locals, skiers, snowmobilers and cowboys. There'd be a fight for sure before the night was over. He planned to be long gone before then, though.

His gaze returned to the raised platform where the band, Canyon Cowboys, was playing. He played a little guitar himself, but he'd never been as good as his father, he thought as he watched Harlan Cardwell pick and strum to the music. His uncle, Angus Cardwell, was no slouch, either.

Tag had always loved listening to them play together when he was a kid. Music was in their blood. That and bars. As a kid, he'd fallen asleep many weekend nights in a bar in this canyon listening to his father play guitar. It was one of the reasons his mother had gathered up her five sons, divorced Harlan and taken her brood off to Texas to be raised in the Lone Star State.

Tag and his brothers had been angry with their dad for not fighting for them. As they'd gotten older, they'd realized their mother had done them a favor. Harlan knew nothing about raising kids. He was an easygoing cowboy who only came alive when you handed him a guitar—or a beer.

Still, as Tag watched his father launch into another song, he realized how much he'd missed him—and Montana. Had Harlan missed him, as well? Doubtful, Tag thought, remembering the reception he'd gotten when he'd knocked at his father's cabin door this morning.

"Tag?"

"Surprise."

"What are you doing here?" his father had asked, moving a little to block his view of the interior of the cabin.

"It's Christmas. I wanted to spend it with you."

Harlan couldn't have looked any more shocked by that—or upset.

Tag realized that surprising his father had been a mistake. "If this is a bad time…"

His father quickly shook his head, still blocking the

door, though. "No, it's just that…well, you know, the cabin is a mess. If you give me a little while…"

Tag peered past him and lowered his voice. "If you have someone staying here—"

"No, no, it's nothing like that."

But behind his father, Tag had spotted a leather jacket, female size, on the arm of the couch. "No problem. I thought I'd go see my cousin Dana. I'll come back later. Actually, if you want, I could get a motel—"

"No. Stay here. Bring your stuff back later. I'll have the spare room made up for you. Your uncle and I are playing tonight at the Canyon."

"Great. I'll stop by. I haven't heard you play in a long time. It'll be nice."

Tag had left, but he was still curious about his father's female visitor. He knew nothing about his father's life. Harlan could have a girlfriend. It wasn't that unusual for a good-looking man in his fifties.

Tag tried not to let Harlan's reaction to him showing up unexpectedly bother him. Determined to enjoy the holiday here, he had made plans tomorrow to go Christmas tree hunting with his Montana cousin Dana Cardwell. He'd missed his cousins and had fond memories of winter in Montana, sledding, skiing, ice-skating, starting snowball fights and cutting their own Christmas trees. He looked forward to seeing his cousins Jordan and Stacy, as well. Clay was still in California helping make movies last he'd heard, but Dana had said he was flying in Christmas Eve.

Tag planned to do all the things he had done as a boy this Christmas. Not that he could ever bring back those family holidays he remembered. For starters, his four brothers were all still in Texas. The five of them had started a barbecue joint, which had grown into a chain called Texas Boys Barbecue.

He would miss his brothers and mother this Christmas, but he was glad to have this time with his cousins and his dad. As the band wound up one song and quickly broke into another, he finished his beer. He'd see his father back at the cabin. Earlier, he'd returned to find the woman's leather jacket he'd seen on the couch long gone.

Harlan had been getting ready for his gig tonight, so they hadn't had much time to visit. But the spare room had been made up, so Tag had settled in. He hoped to spend some time with his father, though. Maybe tomorrow after he came back from Christmas tree hunting.

As he started to turn to leave, a blonde smelling of alcohol stumbled into him. Tag caught her as she clung to his ski jacket for support. She was dressed in jeans and a T-shirt. Not one of the skiers or snowmobilers who were duded out in the latest high-tech, cold-weather gear.

"Sorry," she said, slurring her speech.

"Are you all right?" he asked as she clung to his jacket for a moment before gathering her feet under her.

"Fine." She didn't look fine at all. Clearly, she'd had way too much to drink. "You look like him."

Tag laughed. Clearly, the woman also didn't know what she was saying.

She lurched away from him and out the back door.

He couldn't believe with it snowing so hard that she'd gone outside without a coat. Hesitating only a moment, he went out after her. He was afraid she might be planning to drive herself home. Or that she had been hurrying outside because she was going to be sick. He didn't want her passing out in a snowdrift and dying of hypothermia.

Montana was nothing like where he lived in Texas. Winter in Montana could be dangerous. With this winter storm, the temperatures had dropped. There were already a couple of feet of snow out the back door of the bar before this latest snowfall. He could see that a good six inches of new snow had fallen since he'd arrived in town.

He spotted the woman's tracks in the snow just outside the door. As he stepped out to look for her, he saw her through the falling snow. A man wearing a cowboy hat was helping her into his pickup. She appeared to be arguing with him as he poured her into the passenger seat and slammed the door. The man glanced in Tag's direction for a moment before he climbed behind the wheel and the two drove off.

"Where did she go?"

He turned to find a slim brunette behind him. "Where did who go?"

"Mia." At his blank expression, she added, "The blond woman wearing a T-shirt like the one I have on."

He glanced at her T-shirt and doubted any woman could wear it quite the way this one did. The letters THE CANYON were printed across her full breasts with the word *bar* in smaller print beneath it. He realized belatedly that the woman who'd bumped into him had been wearing the same T-shirt—like the other servers here in the bar.

"I *did* see her," he said. "She stumbled into me, then went rushing out this door."

"Unbelievable," the brunette said with a shake of her head. Her hair was chin length, thick and dark. It framed a face that could only be described as adorable. "She didn't finish her shift again tonight."

"She wasn't in any shape to continue her shift," he said. "She could barely stand up she was so drunk."

For the first time, the brunette met his gaze. "Mia might have had one drink because a customer insisted, but there is no way she was drunk. I saw her ten minutes ago and she was fine."

He shrugged. "I saw her two minutes ago and she was falling-down drunk. She didn't even bother with her coat."

"And you let her leave like that?"

"Apparently her boyfriend or husband was waiting for her. The cowboy poured her into the passenger seat of his pickup and they left."

"She doesn't *have* a boyfriend or a husband."

"Well, she left with some man wearing a Western hat. That's all I can tell you." He remembered that the blonde had been arguing with the man and felt a sliver of unease embed itself under his skin. Still, he told himself, he'd had the distinct feeling that she'd known the man. Nor had the cowboy acted odd when he'd looked in Tag's direction before leaving.

"Lily!" the male bartender called. The brunette gave another disgusted shake of her head, this one directed at Tag, before she took off back into the bar.

He watched her, enjoying the angry swing of her hips. Then he headed for his father's cabin, tired after flying all the way from Texas today. But he couldn't help thinking of the brunette and smiling to himself. He'd always been a sucker for a woman with an attitude.

LILY McCABE CLOSED the front door of the Canyon Bar behind the last customer, locked it and leaned against the solid wood for a moment. What a night.

"Nice job," Ace said as he began cleaning behind the bar. "Where the devil did Mia take off to?"

Lily shook her head. It was the second night in a row that Mia had disappeared. What made it odd was that she'd been so reliable for the three weeks she'd been employed at the Canyon. It was hard to get good help. Mia Duncan was one of the good ones.

"It's weird," Lily said as she grabbed a tray to clear off the tables. In the far back, the other two servers were already at work doing the same thing. "The man who saw her take off out the back door? He claimed she was *drunk*."

James "Ace" McCabe stopped what he was doing to stare at her. "Mia, drunk?"

Lily shrugged as she thought of the dark-haired cowboy with the Texas accent. Men like him were too good-looking to start with. Add a Southern drawl... "That's what he said. I believe his exact words were 'falling-down drunk,'" she mimicked in his Texas accent. "Doesn't sound like Mia, does it? Plus, I talked to her not ten minutes before. She was fine. He must have been mistaken."

Admittedly, she knew Mia hardly at all. The young woman wasn't from Big Sky. But then most people in the Gallatin Canyon right now weren't locals. Ski season brought in people from all over the world. Mia had shown up one day looking for a job. One of the servers had just quit and another had broken her leg skiing, so James had hired Mia on the spot. That was over three weeks ago. Mia had been great. Until last night when she'd left before her shift was over—and again tonight.

"Well, tonight was a real zoo," Reggie Olson said as she brought in a tray full of dirty glasses from a table in the back. "The closer it gets to the holidays, the crazier it gets."

Lily couldn't have agreed more. She couldn't wait for Christmas and New Year's to be over so she could get back to her real life.

"Did Mia say anything to either of you?" she asked.

Reggie shook her head.

Teresa Evans didn't seem to hear.

"Teresa," Lily called to the back of the bar. "Did Mia say anything to you tonight before she left?"

Teresa glanced up in surprise at the sound of her name, her mind clearly elsewhere. "Sorry?"

"Someone's tired," Ace said with a laugh.

"More likely she's thinking about her boyfriend waiting for her outside in his pickup," Reggie joked.

Teresa looked flustered. "I guess I *am* tired," she said. "Mia?" She shook her head. "She didn't say anything to me."

That, too, was odd since Teresa was as close to a friend as Mia had made in the weeks she'd worked at the bar. Lily noticed how distracted the server was and wanted to ask her if everything was all right. But her brother was their boss, not she. His approach during her short-term employment here was not to get involved in his employees' dramas. Probably wise since once the holiday was over, she would be going back to what she considered her "real" life.

"Maybe you should give Mia a call," Lily suggested.

Her brother gave her one of his patient smiles, looked up Mia's number and dialed it. "She's not home," he said after he listened for a few moments. "And I don't have a cell phone number for her."

"If she left with some cowboy, she must have a boyfriend we haven't heard about," Reggie said. "He's probably the reason she was drinking, too," she added with a laugh. "Men. Can't live with them. Can't shoot them."

Ace laughed. "Reggie's right. Go ahead and go on home, sis," he said when she brought up a tray of dirty glasses. "The three of us can finish up here. And thanks again for helping out."

She'd agreed to help her brother over Christmas and New Year's, and had done so for the past few. Since it was just the two of them, their parents gone, it was as close as they got to a family holiday together. The bar was her brother's only source of income, and with this being his busiest time of the year, he had to have all the help he could get.

Ace had learned a long time ago that if he didn't work his own place, he lost money. With Lily helping, he didn't have to hire another server. She didn't need the money since her "day" job paid very well and working at the Canyon gave her a chance to spend time with the brother she adored.

"I *am* going to call it a night," Lily said, dumping her tips into the communal tip jar at the bar. Her Big Sky home was a house she'd purchased back up the mountain tucked in the pines about five miles from the bar—and civilization. The house had been an investment. Not that she could have stayed with her brother since he lived in the very small apartment over the bar. Christmas would be spent at her house, as it was every year.

When she'd bought the house, she'd thought Ace would move in since her real home and work was forty miles away in Bozeman. But her brother had only laughed and said he was much happier living over the bar in the apartment.

Lily loved the house because of its isolation at the end of a road with no close neighbors—the exact reason

Ace would have hated living there. Her brother loved to be around people. He liked the noise and commotion that came with owning a bar in Big Sky, Montana.

But as much as she yearned to go to her quiet house, she couldn't yet. She wanted to make sure Mia made it home all right. Mia lived in an expensive condo her parents owned partway up the mountain toward Big Sky Resort.

Lily noticed Mia's down ski jacket where she'd hung it before her shift, her worry increasing when under it she found Mia's purse hanging from its shoulder strap. She left both there, thinking Mia might return to retrieve them. As she went out the back door of the bar, she saw that it was still snowing. She glanced toward Lone Mountain, disappointed the falling snow obliterated everything. She loved seeing the mountain peak glistening white against the dark winter sky. It really was a magnificent sight.

Thinking of the skiers who would be delirious tomorrow with all this fresh powder, she had to smile. She understood why her brother loved living here. The Gallatin Canyon was a magical place—especially at Christmas.

The Gallatin River, which cut through the steep, granite bluffs in a breathtaking hundred-mile ribbon of river and winding highway, ran crystal clear under a thick blanket of ice. Snow covered the mountains and weighted down the pine boughs, making the entire place a winter wonderland.

Before the ski resort, the canyon had been mostly cattle and dude ranches, a few summer cabins and even fewer homes. Now luxury houses had sprouted up all around the resort. Fortunately some of the original cabins still remained and the majority of the canyon was national forest, so it would always remain undeveloped.

The "canyon" was still its own little community made up of permanent residents as well as those who only showed up for a week or two in the summer and a few weeks around Christmas and New Year's for the ski season.

Outside, her breath expelled in cold white puffs. She hugged herself as she looked through the driving snow and saw Mia's car. Mia was always so protective of her car. It seemed strange that she would leave it. But if she really had been drunk... Maybe she was planning to come back.

Who had she left with, though? Some cowboy, the Texan had said. That, too, didn't sound like Mia, let alone that the cowboy had "poured her into the passenger seat."

Everything about this felt wrong.

Unable to shake off the bad feeling that had settled over her, Lily headed for her SUV. The drive up to Mia's condo didn't take long in the wee hours of the morning after the bars had closed. There was no traffic and few tracks in the fresh snow that now blanketed the narrow paved road. Her windshield wipers clacked noisily trying to keep up with the falling snow, and yet visibility in her headlights was still only a matter of yards.

Lily was used to driving in winter conditions, having been born and raised in Montana, but just the thought of accidentally sliding off the road on such a night gave her a chill. Why hadn't she told her brother where she was going?

She'd heard tomorrow was supposed to clear, the storm moving on. With a full moon tomorrow night, maybe she would go cross-country skiing. She loved skiing at night in the moonlight. It was so peaceful and quiet.

Through the falling snow, she got glimpses of Christmas lights twinkling on the houses she passed. She'd already done all her Christmas shopping, but she was sure her brother would be waiting until the last minute. They were so different. She was just thankful they were close in spite of their differences, even though Ace was always trying to get her to loosen up. He saw her orderly life as boring.

"You need to have some fun, sis," he'd said recently when he'd given her a ski pass and the ultimatum that she was to use it on her day off. "It will do you good."

She didn't need Ace to tell her what else he thought would do her good. She'd forbidden him to even mention her former fiancé Gerald's name. Not that it often stopped him.

Distracted with her thoughts, she saw that she'd reached her destination. But as she pulled up in front of Mia's condo, her earlier bad feeling turned to dread.

Mia's front door stood open. A drift of freshly fallen snow had formed just inside the door.

CHAPTER TWO

THE HAIR STOOD up on the back of Lily's neck as she got out of her SUV and walked toward the gaping front door.

"Mia?" she called as she carefully peered in. She could hear music playing inside the condo. Mia's unit was on the end, and it appeared that whoever was staying in the adjacent one wasn't home.

Lily touched the door. It creaked the rest of the way open. From the doorway, she had a view of the stairs. One set went up, the other down.

"Mia?" she called over the music. No answer as she carefully stepped in.

She'd only gone a few steps up the stairs when she saw what appeared to be a fist-size ball of cotton roll across the floor on the breeze coming in the open door behind her.

One more step and she saw dozens of white balls of cotton. Her heart began to pound. Another step and she saw what was left of the living room sofa cushions.

The condo looked as if it had been hit by a storm that had wreaked havoc on the room. The sofa cushions had been shredded, the stuffing now moving haphazardly around the room. Lamps lay broken in pieces of jagged glass shards on the wooden floor. A chair had been turned over, the bottom ripped out. Nothing in the room looked as if it had weathered the storm that had blown through here.

Who would do such a thing? Why would they? Lily fumbled out her cell phone as she backed down the stairs, her heart hammering against her rib cage. What if whoever had done this was still in the condo?

"I need to report a break-in," she said the moment she reached her SUV and was safely inside. She kept her eyes on the open doorway. When the dispatcher at the local marshal's office answered, she hurriedly gave her name and the address.

"Is the intruder still there?"

"I don't know. I only went just inside the door."

"Where are you now?"

"I'm outside. I don't know where the owner of the condo is. I'm worried about her."

"Can you wait in a warm place?"

"Yes. I'm in my vehicle and watching the condo."

"Please stay there until law enforcement arrives."

MARSHAL HUD SAVAGE was on duty when the call came in. He'd just been up on the mountain on a disturbance call. All day he'd felt as if he were moving in a fog. A cop friend of his from the academy had been killed two nights ago. He was still in shock.

Paul Brown's death, on top of what had happened to Hud's family last spring, had left him shaken. In April, he'd let a dangerous woman come into his home. Hud's wife and children had almost been killed.

He was a *marshal*. He should have seen what was right in front of his eyes. He would never forgive himself. Worse, the incident really had him questioning if he had the instincts anymore for this job.

When he'd heard that his friend Paul had been murdered just forty miles away in Bozeman, he'd been ready to throw in the towel.

"I'm running scared," he'd told his wife, Dana.

She'd hugged him and tried to persuade him that none of what had happened to their family was his fault. "I was the one who was so excited to have a cousin I'd never met come stay with us. You saw that I was happy and ignored things you wouldn't have under any other circumstances."

"I'm a *marshal,* Dana. There is no excuse for what happened last April. None."

Now as he turned into the condo subdivision in the pines, he tried to push everything but this latest call out of his mind. More and more, though, he wasn't sure he deserved to be wearing this star.

As he pulled up, a young brunette got out of her SUV and stood hugging herself against the cold snowy night. A break-in this time of year was unusual. Normally this sort of thing happened during off-season when there were fewer people around.

"Are you the one who made the call?" he asked as he got out of his patrol pickup.

She introduced herself as Lily McCabe.

"Ace's sister," he said with a nod.

"Sometimes I forget how small a community Big Sky is," she said, not looking in the least bit happy about the prospect that everyone knew her business.

Gossip traveled fast in the canyon. Hud had heard something about Ace's sister being left at the altar. He couldn't imagine any sane man leaving this woman.

"Wait in your vehicle while I take a look inside," he told her. But as he headed for the open front door, he saw that she was still standing outside as if too nervous to sit and wait.

At the door, he pulled his weapon and stepped in, even though he doubted the burglar was still inside. The condo had been ransacked in a way that surprised him. This was no normal break-in. Nor was it a simple case of vandalism. Whoever had done this was looking for something and was determined to destroy everything in his path if he didn't find it.

He moved carefully through the upper floor, then the lower one, before he returned to the woman waiting outside.

"Is she…"

He shook his head. "No sign of anyone. I've called for backup. Until they get here, can we talk in your vehicle?"

She nodded and climbed behind the wheel. She'd left the SUV running, so it was warm inside. He couldn't help noticing how neat and clean the interior was as he pulled out his notebook. "Whose condo is it?"

"I don't know their name. Mia told me that her parents own it. She is the one who's been staying here."

"Mia?"

"Mia Duncan. She went to work for my brother at the Canyon three weeks ago. I'm here helping out over the holidays, as you apparently know."

He nodded. He'd heard Ace's sister had bought a house about four years ago up the mountain—about the same time her brother had opened the Canyon Bar.

"Were you meeting Mia here after work?"

Lily shook her head. "She left before her shift was over. I was worried about her, so I decided to drive up and check on her."

"Did she say why she left?"

"No. That's just it. She didn't say anything. One of

our patrons saw her leave with a man. The patron said he thought she'd been drinking."

He sensed that she didn't see how any of this helped and hated talking about Mia behind her back. "Could the man she left with have been a boyfriend?"

"She'd said she wasn't seeing anyone, but I can't swear to it."

"Did this patron describe the man he saw her leave with?"

"Just that he was wearing a cowboy hat and driving a pickup."

"That doesn't narrow it down much. What is this patron's name?"

She shook her head. "I've never seen him before. I'm sorry that I can't offer much in the way of details. He had a Southern accent, if that helps."

"You're doing fine. Did you see anyone leaving as you drove into the condo complex tonight?"

"No. But as soon as I pulled up here, I saw that her door was partially open. I only went a few steps inside before I called you."

He'd seen her footprints in the snow. Unfortunately, the footprints of the intruder had been covered by fresh snow. Someone who knew Mia's hours at the bar and knew she wouldn't be coming home until the bar closed? But she left early. So where was she?

Hud wrote down Lily's cell phone number and closed his notebook as another patrol rig drove up. "I'll call if I have any more questions."

"I don't know Mia well, but I'm worried about her. This is the second night she's left in the middle of her shift without telling anyone. Before that she was our most reliable employee."

He nodded. If it wasn't for the ransacked condo, he

would have just figured the woman had met some man and fallen hard. People in love often became less reliable employees.

Hud assured Lily he'd let her know when he heard something. But he could tell nothing he might say would relieve her worry. After seeing the inside of the condo, he shared her concern.

WITH HER SHIFT finally over, Teresa Evans opened the back door of the bar and looked out at the falling snow. She had mixed feelings about seeing her boyfriend after the fight they'd had earlier before she'd left for work.

But she didn't have to worry about it. The main parking lot was empty. No Ethan sitting out here in his old pickup, the engine running, the wipers trying to keep up with the falling snow. No Ethan at all.

The only vehicles were Reggie's SUV and Ace's old Jeep. Both were covered in snow.

"Do you need a ride?" Reggie asked behind her, making her jump. The other server stopped to frown at her. "Are you all right?"

"I'm fine," she said a little too sharply.

Reggie raised an eyebrow.

"Didn't Lily say Mia left with someone else earlier?" Teresa asked. "Her car's gone."

Reggie glanced to the spot where Mia had parked earlier. Teresa followed her gaze. There was a rectangular spot in the snow where the car had been.

"I guess she must have come back for it," Reggie said with a shrug. "I hope she wasn't as drunk as that customer thought she was. Bad night to be driving as it is."

"Yeah," Teresa agreed. "Or to be working."

Reggie took hold of her arm and gently squeezed

it through Teresa's coat. "Hey, accidents happen. Ace knows that."

It took her a moment to realize that Reggie was referring to the tray of glasses she'd dropped earlier in the evening when she was clearing one of the tables. "Clumsy," she said to cover the truth. "I think I'm coming down with something."

"Is everything okay with Ethan?" Reggie asked, lowering her voice, as they stood under the shelter of the small landing just outside the bar. Reggie didn't look at her when she asked it. Instead, she pretended more interest in digging her keys out of her purse.

Teresa stared through the falling snow, trying to conjure Ethan and his old pickup. "We're good." That wasn't exactly true, but it was too cold to get into it out here in the wee hours of the morning. "I appreciate you asking, though."

"Hey, we're friends. You sure you don't want a ride?" Reggie said, looking around as she found her keys in the bottom of her shoulder bag. "I don't see Ethan."

"He'll be along soon. He probably just fell asleep. I'll give him a call. If worse comes to worst, I'll walk. It's not that far."

Reggie looked skeptical. "You'd be soaked to the skin if you walked in this." But she let it drop, no doubt sensing that whatever was going on with Teresa, it wasn't something she wanted to talk about. "Well, then, I'll see you tomorrow. I just hope it won't be as crazy as it was tonight." With that, Reggie stepped off the covered landing and headed for her car.

Teresa found herself wondering when Mia had come back for her vehicle as she watched Reggie clean the snow from her car and finally drive away. She couldn't shake the memory of what Mia had said to her earlier.

Several cars went by, disappearing quickly into the falling snow. Still no sign of Ethan. Reaching into her pocket, she told herself he had probably fallen asleep and forgotten to set the alarm. Her pocket was empty. She tried the other one. Empty. With a groan, she remembered leaving her cell phone on the breakfast bar earlier. She'd been in such a rush to get out of the apartment and away from Ethan, she'd forgotten it.

Ethan wasn't coming. Had she really expected him to come after the fight they'd had? She considered going back inside the bar to wait, but she didn't want Ace to know Ethan had stood her up. As soon as Reggie's taillights disappeared in the snowstorm, Teresa started the walk home.

The fight earlier had been another of those stupid ones.

"I need to know you want to marry me and have this baby," he'd said while she was getting ready for work.

"Stop pressuring me." Ever since she'd told him she was pregnant, he'd been so protective that sometimes she couldn't breathe. He was determined they had to get married and settle down. His idea of settling down was moving closer to his parents, who lived down in Billings.

"I don't think your new friend Mia is good for you. I saw her talking to some guy the other day. I've seen him before. He's bad news."

Teresa stifled a groan.

"I don't want you getting involved in some drug deal, or worse."

She had turned to face him, unable to hide her growing impatience. Ethan had been like this ever since he'd gone to the law enforcement academy and was now working for the Montana Highway Patrol.

"I'm sure Mia isn't involved in any kind of drug deal."

"Your friend might not realize what she's getting herself into with a man like that."

It made her angry to hear him talk this way. "Mia's a big girl," she'd snapped. "She can take care of herself." When Ethan looked skeptical, she'd added, "Mia carries a gun." Instantly, she'd wished she hadn't added that part.

"She *what?*" he'd demanded.

"It's just a small one. She wears it strapped on her ankle."

Ethan had sworn and begun to pace. "You're hanging out with a woman who carries a concealed weapon? Does she even have a permit to carry it?"

"Damn it, Ethan. Stop acting like a narc."

He had stopped dead in his tracks. *"What?"*

"It's just that you used to be fun. Now you're such a…"

He had waited for her to finish.

"Cop."

Without another word, he'd grabbed his coat and left.

Still, she couldn't imagine him not picking her up. He was too concerned about her and the baby. Something must have come up with his job, she thought now as she walked through the deep snow toward the apartment they shared.

Ethan had been her high school sweetheart. She smiled to herself now as she thought of how they'd been back then. He had been adventurous, up for anything. His friends said he was crazy fun.

But a couple of years ago, he'd almost gotten into some serious trouble with some ex-friends of his. The incident had apparently scared him straight. He was no longer crazy fun. Far from it.

Teresa wasn't sure she wanted to be married to a cop. She wasn't sure she wanted to be married to Ethan. She wasn't even sure she wanted to be pregnant.

Shoving those thoughts away, she found herself worrying about Mia as she ducked her head against the thick falling snow. Tonight she'd seen Mia get into some kind of argument with a man who'd come into the bar alone. The conversation had looked personal—and definitely heated. At one point the man had grabbed Mia's arm. In the skirmish, the man ended up spilling his drink on her.

Teresa had quickly stepped in.

"Back off. I have it under control," Mia had snapped, wiping at her alcohol-soaked jeans.

Teresa might have argued differently, but the man had raised his head and looked right at her before getting up and leaving.

Mia had apologized a while later when they'd both gone up to the bar to get their drink orders. "I just didn't want you getting involved." Mia's gaze had met hers, worry in her eyes. "I might have already involved you too much. I'm sorry."

She'd been startled by her words. Even more startled when Mia had gone to the room where they kept their coats. Teresa saw Mia take something out of Teresa's ski jacket pocket and stuff it into her jeans pocket.

Teresa had confronted her, only to have Mia pull away. She'd stood helplessly as Mia grabbed her tray of drinks and headed off through the crowd toward one of the large tables at the back of the bar.

Not long after that Mia had seemed unsteady on her feet.

As Teresa had gone back over to the empty table where the man had been sitting, to clear his table, she spotted the hypodermic needle lying under his chair. Her heart had begun to pound. Was Ethan right? Was the argument over drugs?

It still gave her chills to remember the look on the man's face when he'd glanced up at her. Not long after that, she'd seen Mia stagger into some man before leaving through the back door. Mia had definitely appeared drugged. Had she left with the man?

She felt a chill now as she slogged through the deep snow, glad she wasn't that far from home. She'd left behind the cluster of buildings that made up the center of Meadow Village. Now there was nothing but snowy darkness. Pines, their branches heavy with snow, stood like sentinels at the edge of the mountain to her right. To her left, the golf course was an empty field of deep snow.

The storm hadn't let up for hours. She kept her head down against the falling snow, but it still clung to her face and eyelashes. With each step, she regretted not going back into the bar and calling Ethan. Sometimes she was her own worst enemy.

At the sound of a car approaching, she moved to the edge of the road. Probably Ethan, she thought. Was it possible he'd simply fallen asleep and on awakening, realized he hadn't picked her up?

She felt headlights wash over her. Chilled to the bone, she could feel the deep wet snow soaking into her jeans up to her knees. She was angry with him, but right now she didn't feel like fighting. Worse, she didn't want her own foolish stubbornness to make her end up walking the rest of the way home just to spite Ethan or try to make him feel guilty.

Once they got back to the apartment, she would take a nice hot shower. Maybe have a beer with him. Or a soda, she thought, remembering that she was pregnant. She might even be up for making love. Anything to take the edge off and forget for just a while that her life was a mess and had been as far back as she could remember.

Teresa shielded her eyes from the blizzard and the bright headlights as the vehicle caught up to her. A thought struck her in that instant. The engine sound was wrong. She knew it wasn't Ethan in his old pickup even before she saw the large black SUV slow to a stop next to her.

It was one of those expensive big rigs like ones she saw all over Big Sky. The windows were dark as well as the paint. She was trying to see inside, to see if she knew the driver, when the back door was suddenly flung open.

The man who jumped out was large and bundled up in a bulky coat. Her heart was already racing by the time he grabbed her. She tried to scream, but he clamped a gloved hand over her mouth and dragged her toward the large SUV. She fought, but he was too strong for her. Still, she got in a few good kicks and punches before he forced a smelly cloth over her mouth and nose, and everything went black.

CHAPTER THREE

HUD GOT THE call just after daylight the next morning. He'd been up all night with the break-in. He needed sleep and food badly, and was on his way home, hoping for both when the call came in.

"My fiancée didn't come home last night."

"Who am I speaking with?" he asked. The man sounded more than a little upset.

"Ethan Cross."

Hud knew Ethan, knew his record. A wild, good-looking kid who'd gotten into trouble a lot before going to the academy and becoming a highway patrol officer.

"Your fiancée is Teresa Evans?" he asked to clarify. Ethan had been with Teresa since high school. That was the nice thing about a small community. Hud knew the players, at least the local ones.

"She works at the Canyon. I was supposed to pick her up after closing, but I got called out on an accident down by Fir Ridge. With the roads like they were, I didn't get back in time. When I realized she wasn't home, I went looking for her. This isn't like her."

Hud took a guess. "Did the two of you have a fight earlier yesterday?" It was an old story, one he'd heard many times.

"Not really a fight exactly. Still, she wouldn't not come home."

"She probably just stayed at a friend's place to let

things cool down. Have you checked with any of her friends?"

"There's only one she's been tight with recently. I tried Mia's number, but she doesn't answer."

"Mia Duncan?" Hud asked, and felt his pulse quicken when Ethan said yes. "Have you tried Teresa's cell phone?"

"She forgot to take it when she left for work. I found it when I called her number looking for her."

"Let's give her a few hours and see if she doesn't turn up," Hud said, hoping he didn't have two missing women, since Mia Duncan hadn't turned up yet, either.

TAG COULDN'T BELIEVE how much he'd missed this. As he trod through the knee-high snow on the mountain the next morning swinging the ax, he breathed in the frosty air and the sweet fresh smell of pine.

"How about that one?" Dana called from below him on the mountainside. They had climbed up the mountain behind his cousin's ranch house Christmas tree hunting. Now she motioned at one to his far right.

He waded through the new-fallen snow to check the tree, shook off the branches, then called back, "Too flat on the back. I'm going up higher on the mountain."

"There's an old logging road up there," she called from down below. "I'll meet you where it comes out. If you find a tree, give a holler. Meanwhile, I'll keep looking down here." She sounded as if she was enjoying this as much as he was, but then Dana had always loved the great outdoors.

He felt a chill as he remembered what had happened to her and her family last spring. Some crazy woman had pretended to be a long-lost cousin, and having designs on Hud, had tried to kill Dana, her children and her best friend, Hilde. Fortunately Deputy Colt Dawson had found out the woman's true identity and arrived in time to save them all.

Tag couldn't imagine something so horrifying, but if anything, his cousin Dana was resilient and Camilla Northland was in prison, where hopefully she would remain the rest of her life.

The new snow higher up the mountain was as light as down feathers and floated around him as he climbed. He had to stop a couple of times to catch his breath because of the altitude. "You're not in Texas anymore," he said, laughing.

The land flattened out some once he was near the top, and he knew he'd hit the old logging road. As he started down it, he kept looking for the perfect tree. Dana's husband, Marshal Hud Savage, had warned him not to let Dana come back with one of her "orphan" trees. Hud hadn't been able to come along with them. He was working on a burglary case involving a condo break-in and a possible missing person.

"She'll find a tree that she knows no one will ever cut because it's so pitiful and she'll want to give it a Christmas," Hud warned him. "Don't let her. You should see some of the trees that woman has brought home."

Tag told himself he would be happy with whatever tree they found as long as it was evergreen. But he knew he was looking for something special. He hadn't had a real Christmas tree in years. Along with getting one for Dana's living room, he planned to pick up a small one for his father's cabin. He knew Harlan probably didn't decorate for Christmas, but he'd have to put up with it this year since his son was determined to spend Christmas with him.

Dana had said she would lend them some ornaments

and the kids would make some, as well. Tag couldn't wait, he thought, as he looked around for a large pretty tree for Dana and a smaller version for him and his father.

He hadn't gone far down the logging road when he picked up a snowmobile track coming in from what appeared to be another old logging road. Dana had told him that they often had trouble in the winter with snowmobilers on the property because of the catacomb of logging roads that ran for miles.

He remembered hearing one late last night, now that he thought about it. A lot of people got around that way in the wintertime. For all he knew, his father had been out and about after the bar closed. To visit his girlfriend? The thought made him smile.

"I found a tree!" Dana called from somewhere below him on the mountain. He couldn't see her through the thick, snow-filled pines.

"An orphan tree?" he called back, and heard her laugh. "Hud will have my head," he mumbled to himself as he started to drop off the side of the mountain, heading in the direction he'd heard Dana laugh.

He'd only taken a couple of steps when the sun caught on an object off to his right. Tag saw what looked like a branch sticking up out of the snow. Only there was something very odd about the branch. It was blue.

As he stepped closer, his heart leapt to his throat. It wasn't a branch.

A hand, frosty in the morning sun, stuck up out of the deep snow.

MARSHAL HUD SAVAGE arrived by snowmobile thirty minutes after he'd gotten the call from his wife. He found Dana and Tag standing half a dozen yards away from the body. It was the second time in the past six years that remains had been found on the ranch. Hud could see that Dana was upset and worried.

"It's going to be all right," he told her. "Go on down to the house and wait for the coroner. He'll need directions up here."

As soon as she left, he stooped down and brushed the snow off the victim's face. Behind him, Tag let out a startled sound, making him turn.

"You know her?" he asked.

Tag nodded, but he seemed to need a minute to find his voice. "She works at the Canyon," he said finally. "I think her name is Mia. I ran into her at the bar last night. Or more correctly, she ran into me. Was she… *murdered?*"

"Looks like she was strangled with the scarf around her neck," Hud said. He could see where the scarf had cut into her throat. "But we'll know more once the coroner and the lab does the autopsy."

"I thought it might have been an accident," Tag said.

Hud studied him. He seemed awfully shaken for a man who'd only just run into the woman the night before. "So, what exactly happened last night at the bar?"

He listened while Tag recounted the woman stumbling into him, apparently quite drunk, and how he'd gone out the back door after her to make sure she was all right. "I saw her getting into a pickup with a man."

"And you think her name was Mia?" Hud asked. Could this be the missing Mia Duncan? He had a bad feeling it was.

Tag told him that all he knew was what another server at the Canyon had told him. "She had apparently left in the middle of her shift."

"Do you know the name of the other server you talked to?"

"Lily. At least that's what the bartender called her."

Hud nodded. "Tell me about the man the victim left with behind the bar."

"Cowboy hat, pickup. It was snowing so hard I can't even swear what color the truck was. Dark blue or brown, maybe even black. That's about it. I only got a glimpse of the man through the snow," Tag said.

"But he got a good look at you?"

He saw that the question took Tag by surprise. "Yeah, I guess he did."

"I might need a statement from you later," Hud said. "If you think of anything else…"

"I'll let you know," Tag said as the coroner and another deputy arrived by snowmobile. The coroner's had a sled behind his snowmobile.

"Dana will have a pot of coffee on when you reach the house," Hud told him. He'd seen Tag's rented SUV parked in front of the ranch house.

Tag nodded and turned to leave.

Hud watched him go, worrying. Dana had just been disappointed by one "cousin." He didn't want her disappointed again if he could help it. But he couldn't shake the feeling that Tanner "Tag" Cardwell knew a lot more about the victim than he'd admitted.

He reminded himself that his instincts were off. He was probably just looking for guilt where there wasn't any.

TAG WAS GLAD he didn't have to talk to anyone on the walk down the mountain. His head was spinning.

He'd been shocked when he'd recognized the dead woman—even more shocked when he'd seen what she was wearing. A leather jacket like the one he'd seen lying over the arm of his father's couch just yesterday.

Since discovering the body, he'd kept telling himself it couldn't be the same woman. Just as his father couldn't be involved in this.

That was why he hadn't mentioned the jacket to the marshal, he told himself. He couldn't be sure it was the same one. But both his father and the woman had been at the bar last night. Tag knew how some women were about cowboy guitar players—even old ones.

A chill had settled in his bones by the time he reached the ranch house. He liked the idea of a hot cup of coffee, but he didn't want to talk to anyone—especially his cousin—about what he'd seen on the mountain.

As he climbed into his rented SUV, he told himself that the woman's death had nothing to do with his father. And yet Tag couldn't wait to reach the cabin. Harlan Cardwell had some explaining to do.

LILY TRIED NOT to roll her eyes at her brother. *"Ace."*

"Don't 'Ace' me. Lily, it's time you got back on the horse. So to speak."

She really didn't want to talk about this and now regretted stopping by her brother's tiny apartment over the bar this early in the morning. She'd come to talk about Mia Duncan—not her ex-fiancé, Gerald Humphrey.

"What chaps my behind is that Gerald was the wrong man for you in the first place," Ace said as he refilled her coffee cup. "That man would have bored you to death in no time."

She thought about how much she and Gerald had in common. Of course Ace thought him boring. Ace had never understood what she and Gerald had shared.

"But to pull what he did," Ace continued. "If he

hadn't skipped the country when he did, I would have tracked him down and—"

"I really don't want to have this discussion," she said, picking up her mug and moving over to the window. The world was covered in cold white drifts this morning. The sun had come out, turning the fresh snow to a blinding carpet of diamonds.

"Sis, I love you and I hate to see you like this."

Lily spun back around, almost spilling her coffee. She couldn't help being annoyed with the older brother she'd idolized all her life. But this was a subject they had never agreed on.

"You hate to see me like *this?*" she demanded. "Ace, I'm *happy.* I have a great life, a rewarding career. I'm… content."

He mugged a face. "Sis, you live like a nun except for the few times a year that I drag you out to help me with the bar."

"We really should not have this conversation," she warned him, wondering now if he had actually needed her help at the bar or if his asking her to work the holidays with him was part of some scheme to find her a man. If it was the latter… She said as much. "Ace, so help me—"

He held up his hands in surrender. "You know how much I need your help. And I didn't mean to set you off this morning."

But he had. "You should be more concerned about your *other* employees. If you had seen Mia's condo…"

"I *am* concerned. I put in a call to the marshal's office first thing this morning, but no one has called me back yet. I called the condo number Mia gave me, but not surprisingly, there was no answer there. I figure once she discovered the break-in, she probably stayed with a friend last night."

Lily wasn't so sure about that since she didn't think Mia had made any friends in the weeks she'd been working at the Canyon. The only person Mia had spoken to at the bar was Teresa. Which had seemed odd because of the age difference.

Mia was in her late thirties, while Teresa was barely twenty-one. Neither was outgoing, so that could be why they'd become somewhat friends, at least from Lily's observation.

So this morning, she'd placed a call to Teresa's cell, only to reach her boyfriend, Ethan. "Mia isn't the only one who's missing this morning," she told her brother. "That's why I came by so early. Teresa didn't come home last night."

Ace seemed only a little surprised, but then he'd been running a bar longer than Lily had been helping out. "Maybe Mia and Teresa are together. I'm sure they'll turn up. Teresa and Ethan probably had a fight. I noticed she was acting oddly last night." He frowned. "But then again, so was Mia, now that I think about it. I saw her get into it with one of the customers. Teresa came to her rescue, but Mia handled it fine."

"Why didn't you tell me about that last night?" Lily demanded.

"Because it blew over quickly. You and Reggie didn't even notice."

"Who was the customer?"

Ace shrugged. "Some guy. I didn't recognize him. Lily, people act up in bars. It happens. A good server knows how to handle it. Mia was great. I'm telling you, I wouldn't be surprised if they both show up for work tonight."

Lily hoped he was right. "Did you ask Mia why she left early night before last?"

"She apologized, said she'd suddenly gotten a migraine and hadn't been able to get my attention, but since it hadn't been that busy…"

Lily nodded. Had Mia been drinking the night before last as well as last night? If so, Lily really hadn't seen that coming.

But what did she really know about the woman? Other servers she'd worked with often talked about their lives—in detail—while they were setting up before opening and cleaning up after closing. She'd learned more than she'd ever wanted to know about them.

Mia, though, was another story. She seldom offered anything about herself other than where she was from—Billings, Montana, the largest city in the state and a good three hours away. It wasn't unusual for people from Billings to have condos at Big Sky. Mia's parents owned a condo in one of the pricier developments, which made Lily suspect that the woman didn't really need this job.

"What do you know about Mia?" Lily asked her brother now.

He shrugged. "Not much. She never had much to say, especially about herself. I could check her application, but you know there isn't a lot on them."

"But there would be a number to call in case of emergency, right?"

"I think that is more than a little premature," her brother said. "Anyway, if the marshal thought that was necessary, he would have contacted me for the number, right?"

"Maybe. Unless they have some rule about not looking for a missing adult for twenty-four hours. Still, I'd like to see her job application."

Ace got to his feet. "I've got to open the bar soon anyway. Come on."

In the Canyon office, her brother pulled out Mia

Duncan's application from the file cabinet and handed it to her.

He was right. There was little on the form other than name, address, social security number, local phone number and an emergency contact number. Most of his employees were temporary hires, usually college students attending Montana State University forty miles down the highway to the north, and only stayed a few weeks at most. Big Sky had a fairly transient population that came and went by the season.

So Lily wasn't surprised that the number Mia had put down on her application was a local number, probably her parents' condo here at Big Sky.

"No cell phone number," she said. "That's odd since I've seen Mia using a cell phone on at least one of her breaks behind the bar."

Lily didn't recognize the prefix on the emergency number Mia had put down. She picked up the phone and dialed it, ignoring her brother shaking his head in disapproval. The number rang three times before a voice came on the line to say the phone had been disconnected.

"What?" Ace asked as she hung up.

"The number's been disconnected. I'll call the condo association." A few moments later she hung up, now more upset and worried than before. "That condo doesn't belong to her parents. It belongs to a retired FBI agent who recently died. The condo association didn't even know Mia was staying there."

At a loud knock at the bar's front door, they both started. Lily glanced out the office window and felt her heart drop at the sight of the marshal's pickup.

CHAPTER FOUR

As TAG PULLED up in front of his father's cabin, he saw that Harlan's SUV was gone. He hadn't seen much of his father since he'd arrived and wasn't all that surprised to find the cabin empty. Harlan had been in bed this morning when Tag had left to go Christmas tree hunting. He had the feeling that his father didn't spend much time here.

Tag felt too antsy to sit around and wait. He needed Harlan to put his mind at ease. That leather jacket the dead woman was wearing was a dead ringer for the one he'd seen on the arm of Harlan's couch.

Fortunately, he had a pretty good idea where to find his father. If Harlan Cardwell was anything, he was predictable. At least Tag had always thought that was true. Now, thinking about the murdered woman, he wasn't so sure.

Just as he'd suspected, though, he found his father at the Corral Bar down the canyon. Harlan was sitting on a bar stool next to his brother, Angus. A song about men, their dogs and their women was playing on the jukebox.

The sight of the two Cardwell men sitting there brought back memories of when Tag was a boy. Some men felt more at home in a bar than in their own house. Harlan Cardwell was one of them. His brother, Angus, was another.

Tag studied the two of them for a moment. It hit him

that he didn't know his father and might never get to know him. Harlan definitely hadn't made an attempt over the years. Tag couldn't see that changing on this visit—even if his father had nothing to do with the dead woman.

"Hey, Tag," Uncle Angus said, spotting him just inside the doorway. He slid off his bar stool to shake Tag's hand. "You sure grew up."

Tag had to laugh, since he'd been twelve when he'd left the canyon, the eldest of his brothers. Now he stood six-two, broad across the shoulders and slim at the hips—much as his father had been in his early thirties.

After his mother had packed up her five boys and said goodbye to their father and the canyon for good, they'd seen Harlan occasionally for very short visits when their mother had insisted he fly down to Texas for one event in his boys' lives or another.

"I hope you stopped by to have a drink with us," Tag's uncle said.

Tag glanced at the clock behind the bar, shocked it was almost noon. The two older men looked pretty chipper considering they'd closed down the Canyon Bar last night. They'd both been too handsome in their youths for their own good. Since then they'd aged surprisingly well. He could see where a younger woman might be attracted to his father.

Harlan had never remarried. Nor had his brother. Tag had thought that neither of them probably even dated. He'd always believed that both men were happiest either on a stage with guitars in their hands or on a bar stool side by side in some canyon bar.

But he could be wrong about that. He could be wrong about a lot of things.

"I'm not sure Tag drinks," his father said to Angus,

and glanced toward the front door as if expecting someone.

Angus laughed. "He's a Cardwell. He *has* to drink," he said, and motioned to the bartender.

"I'll have a beer," Tag said, standing next to his uncle. "Whatever is on tap will be fine."

Angus slapped him on the back and laughed. "This is my nephew," he told the bartender. "Set him up."

Several patrons down the bar were talking about the declining elk herds and blaming the reintroduction of wolves. Tag half expected the talk at the bar would be about the young cocktail waitress's death, but apparently Hud had been able to keep a lid on it for the time being.

Tag realized he couldn't put this off any longer. "Could we step outside?" he asked his father. "I need to talk to you in private for a moment."

"It's cold outside," Harlan said, frowning as he glanced toward the front door of the bar again. Snow had been plowed into a wall of white at the edge of the parking area. Ice crystals floated in the cold late-morning air. "If this can't wait, we could step into the back room, I guess."

"Fine." Tag could tell his father was reluctant to leave the bar. He seemed to be watching the front door. Who was he expecting? The woman who'd been in his cabin yesterday?

"So, what's up?" his father asked the moment Tag closed the door behind them.

"I need to ask you something. Who was at your cabin yesterday when I showed up unexpectedly?" Tag asked.

"I told you there wasn't—"

"I saw her leather jacket on the couch."

Harlan met his gaze. "My personal life isn't—"

"A woman wearing a jacket exactly like that one was just found murdered on the Cardwell Ranch."

Shock registered in his father's face—but only for an instant.

That instant was long enough, though, that Tag's stomach had time to fall. "I know you couldn't have had anything to do with her murder—"

"Of course not," Harlan snapped. "I don't even know the woman."

Tag stared at his father. "How could you know that, since I haven't told you her name?"

"Because the woman who owns the leather jacket you saw at my cabin came by right after you left this morning. She is alive and well."

Tag let out a relieved sigh. "Good. I just had to check before I said anything to the marshal."

"Well, I'm glad of that."

"I had to ask because this woman is the same one who stumbled into me last night at the Canyon—the same bar where you and Uncle Angus were playing. After seeing that leather jacket at your cabin…well, you can see why I jumped to conclusions."

"I suppose so," his father said, frowning. "Let's have that beer now. We'll be lucky if your uncle hasn't drank them."

"The woman worked at the Canyon Bar," Tag said, wondering why his father hadn't asked. Big Sky was a small community—at least off-season. Wouldn't he have been curious as to who'd been murdered? "She was working last night while you were playing in the band. A tall blond woman? I'm sure you must have noticed her. Her name was Mia."

Harlan looked irritated. "I told you—"

"Right. You don't know her." He opened the door

and followed his father back to the bar. Angus was talking to the bartender. Their beers hadn't been touched.

The last thing Tag wanted right now was alcohol.
His stomach felt queasy, but he knew he couldn't leave
without drinking at least some of it. He didn't look at
his father as he took a gulp of his beer. He couldn't look
at him. His father's reaction had rocked him to his core.
A young woman was murdered last night, her body
dumped from a snowmobile on an old logging road on
the Cardwell Ranch. He kept seeing his father's first
reaction—that instant when he couldn't hide his shock
and pretend disinterest.

"You two doing all right?" Angus asked, glancing
first at Tag, then at Harlan. Neither of them had spoken
since they'd returned to the bar. Tag saw a look pass
between the brothers. Angus reached for his beer and
took a long drink.

Tag picked up his, taking a couple more gulps as he
watched his father and uncle out of the corner of his
eye. Some kind of message had passed between them.
Neither looked happy.

"I'm sorry but I need to get going," he said, checking his watch. "I'm meeting someone." He'd never been
good at lying, but when he looked up he saw that neither his father nor his uncle was paying any attention.
Nor did they try to detain him. If anything, they seemed
relieved that he was leaving.

Biting down on his fear that his father had just lied
to him, he reached for his wallet.

"Put that away," his uncle said. "Your money is no
good here."

"Thanks." He looked past Angus at his father. "I
guess I'll see you later?"

"I'm sure you will," Harlan said.

"Dana's having us all out Christmas Eve," Tag said. "You're planning to be there, aren't you?"

"I wouldn't miss it for anything," his father said. He hadn't looked toward the door even once since they'd returned from the back room.

Tag felt his chest tighten as he left the bar. Once out in his rented SUV, he debated what to do. All his instincts told him to go to the marshal. But what if he was wrong? What if his father was telling the truth? He couldn't chance alienating his father further if he was wrong.

On a hunch, he pulled around the building out of sight and waited. Just as he suspected, his father and uncle came out of the bar not five minutes later. They said something to each other as they parted, both looking unhappy, then headed for their respective rigs before heading down the canyon toward Big Sky.

Tag let them both get ahead of him before he pulled out and followed. He doubted his father would recognize the rented SUV he was driving. It looked like a lot of other SUVs, so nondescript it didn't stand out in the least. He stayed back anyway, just far enough he could keep them in sight.

His uncle turned off on the road to his cabin on the river, but Harlan kept going. Tag planned to follow his father all the way to Big Sky but was surprised when Harlan turned into the Cardwell Ranch instead. Tag hung back until his father's SUV dropped over a rise; then he, too, turned into the ranch. Within sight of the old two-story farmhouse, Tag pulled over in a stand of pines.

Through the snow-laden pine boughs, he could see his father and the marshal standing outside by Hud's patrol car. They appeared to be arguing. At one point, he saw Hud point back up into the mountains—in the direction where Tag had found the dead woman's body. Then he saw his father pull out an envelope and hand it to the marshal. Hud looked angry and resisted taking it for a moment, but then quickly stuffed it under his jacket, looking around as if worried they had been seen.

Tag couldn't breathe. He told himself he couldn't have seen what he thought he had. His imagination was running wild. Had that been some kind of payoff?

A few minutes later, his father climbed back into his SUV and headed out of the ranch.

Tag hurriedly turned around and left, his mind racing. What had that been about? There was no doubt in his mind it had something to do with the dead woman his father had denied knowing.

DANA STARED AT the Christmas tree, fighting tears.

"It's not *that* ugly," her sister, Stacy, said from the couch.

Last night, Dana, her husband and her two oldest children had decorated it. It hadn't taken long, since the poor tree had very few limbs. Hud had just stared at it and sighed. Mary, five, and Hank, six, had declared it beautiful.

Never a crier except when she was pregnant and her hormones were raging, Dana burst into tears. Her sister got up, put an arm around her and walked her over to the couch to sit down next to her.

"Is it postpartum depression?" Stacy asked.

She shook her head. "It's Hud. I'm afraid for him."

"You knew he was a marshal when you married him," her sister pointed out, looking confused.

"He's talking about quitting."

Stacy blinked in surprise. "He loves being a marshal."

"*Loved.* After what happened here on the ranch last spring, he doesn't think he has what it takes anymore."

"That's ridiculous." A woman pretending to be their cousin had turned out to be a psychopathic con artist. "Camilla fooled us all."

Dana sniffed. "Not Hilde." Her sister handed her a tissue. Hilde had tried to warn her, but she'd thought her best friend was just being jealous and hadn't taken her worries seriously. Not taking Hilde's warnings seriously had almost gotten them killed.

"Hilde's forgiven you, right?" Stacy asked as Dana wiped her eyes and blew her nose.

"Kind of. I mean, she says she has. But, Stacy, I took some stranger's word over my best friend's, who is also my business partner and godmother to one of my children!"

"You and Hud both need to let this go. Camilla is locked up in the women's state prison in Billings, right? With six counts of attempted murder, she won't get out until she's ninety."

"What if she pretends to be reformed and gets out on good behavior? Or worse, escapes? We're only a few hours away."

"You can't really think she's going to escape."

"If anyone can, it's her. Within a week, I'll bet she was eating her meals with the warden. You know how she is."

"Dana, you're making her into the bogeyman. She's just a sick woman with a lot of scars."

Dana looked at Stacy. Her older sister had her own scars from bad marriages, worse relationships and some really horrible choices she'd made. But since she'd had her daughter, Ella, Stacy had truly changed.

"I'm so glad you're in my life again," Dana said to her sister, and hugged Stacy hard.

"Me, too." Stacy frowned. "You have to let what happened go."

Dana nodded, but she knew that was easier said than done. "I have nightmares about her. I think Hud does, too. I can't shake the feeling that Camilla isn't out of our lives."

CAMILLA NORTHLAND WAS surprised how easy it was for her to adapt to prison. She spent her days working out in the prison weight room, and after a month of hitting it hard, figured she was in the best shape of her life.

She'd tuned in to how things went in prison right away. It reminded her of high school. That was why she picked the biggest, meanest woman she could find, went up to her and punched her in the face. She'd lost the fight since the woman was too big and strong for her.

But ultimately she'd won the war. Other prisoners gave her a wide berth. Stories began to circulate about her, some of them actually true. She'd heard whispers that everyone thought she was half-crazy.

Only half?

Like the other inmates, she already had a nickname, Spark. Camilla could only assume it was because of the arson conviction that had been tacked on to her attempted murder convictions.

She'd skipped a long trial, confessed and pleaded guilty, speeding up the process that would ultimately land her in prison anyway. It wasn't as though any judge in his right mind was going to allow her bail. Nor did she want the publicity of a trial that she feared, once it went nationwide, would bring her other misdeeds to light.

The local papers had run stories about the fire and Dana and her babies and best friend barely escaping. Dana and Hilde had become heroes.

It was enough to make Camilla puke.

So now she was Spark. Over the years she'd gone by so many different names that she was fine with Spark. She liked to think that whoever had given her the new moniker had realized she was always just a spark away from blowing sky-high.

She knew that if she was going to survive, let alone thrive here, she had to be in the right group. That, too, was so much like high school, it made her laugh.

The group she wanted to run with had to be not just the most fearsome but also the ones who ran this prison. She might be locked up, but she wasn't done with Hud Savage and his precious family. Not by a long shot.

Being behind bars would make it harder, though, she had to admit. But she knew there were ways to get what she wanted. What she wanted was vengeance.

So the moment she heard about fellow prisoner Edna Mable Jones, or Grams as she was fondly called, Camilla knew she would have it.

TAG HADN'T REALIZED where he was going until he saw the sign over the front door. The Canyon. As he pulled up in front of the bar, the door swung open and the barmaid he'd met the night before stepped out and headed for an SUV parked nearby. He figured that by now Hud would have talked to her and anyone else at the bar who'd known the victim.

Earlier, he'd told himself there was nothing he could do but wait for the marshal to catch the killer. That was before he'd talked to his father—and witnessed the meeting between Hud and Harlan at Cardwell Ranch. As much as he didn't want to believe his father was involved, he knew in his heart that Harlan was up to his neck in this. He was more shocked that it appeared the marshal was involved, as well.

As he watched the brunette head for her SUV, he realized he'd come here because he'd hoped Lily would be able to help him. She had worked with the dead woman. She also might know something about Harlan since apparently the Canyon Cowboys had played at the bar on more than one occasion.

She had started to climb into her vehicle, but when she saw him, she stopped. Frowning, she slammed the door and marched over to Tag's rental SUV.

"You," she said as he put down his side window. "I just told the marshal about you and how you were the last one to see Mia."

He laughed, clearly surprising her. "Other than the killer. Also, the marshal already knows about me. Hud Savage is my cousin-in-law. I'm the one who found her body."

Lily pulled back, startled. *"You?"*

Tag hadn't heard the bartender from last night come out of the bar until he spoke. "Lily, you're starting to sound like an owl," he said as he joined them.

"This is the man I told you about," she said to the bartender. "The one who said Mia was drunk." She narrowed her eyes when she looked at Tag again, accusation in her tone and every muscle of her nicely rounded body. "He *claims* he's related to the marshal."

The bartender shook his head at Lily and reached past her to extend his hand. "James McCabe, but everyone around here knows me as Ace. You must be one of Harlan's sons, right?"

"Tag Cardwell."

"Cardwell?" Lily said in surprise.

"This is my sister, Lily, but I guess you two have met." Ace seemed amused.

Then his sister said, "He found Mia."

Ace nodded somberly. "We're in shock. In fact, I just put a note on the door that we're going to be closed tonight. We didn't know Mia that well, but the least we can do is close for the night in her memory." He glanced at his watch. "I told the marshal I would stop by his office. I better get going." He squeezed his sister's shoulder and said, "Nice to meet you," to Tag before he walked over to an old Jeep and climbed in.

Neither Tag nor Lily spoke until her brother had driven away.

"Sorry about—"

Tag waved her apology away. "You don't know me from Adam. I would have been disappointed if you hadn't suspected me."

She narrowed her eyes at him again as she realized he was flirting with her. "Have you remembered any more about the man Mia left with last night?" she asked, all business.

He shook his head. "I wish I'd gotten a better look at him or paid more attention to the truck he was driving." But it had been snowing hard and he'd had no reason to pay that much attention.

"I can't believe anyone would murder her."

He nodded, thinking what a shock murder was in a place like Big Sky. Crime was so low people felt safe here. When he was young, he and his brothers were allowed to wander all over this country. Looking back, he knew there'd been a fair share of close calls while climbing rocks, swimming in the river, skiing and sledding off the side of mountains. But they'd never known the kind of danger the dead woman had run across.

"You said you didn't think she had a boyfriend, right? Did you ever see her talking with someone in the bar she might have had an interest in?" *Like a member of the band,* but he didn't say that.

"No one she seemed interested in. She just did her job. I never even saw her flirting with anyone. So maybe she did have a boyfriend. She didn't talk about her personal life." Lily sighed and started to walk to her vehicle again.

"Lily?" He liked the name and it seemed to fit her.

She turned to look at him over her shoulder, leery again.

"If you ever want to talk, or maybe…" He dug in his coat pocket, thinking he might have one of his business cards. When he felt something odd shaped, cold and hard, he frowned and drew it out. "What the…?"

Lily stepped back to his open window. "What's wrong?"

"This," he said, holding up the object he'd found. "I don't know what it is."

"It's a computer thumb drive," she said, then eyed him as if she thought he was messing with her.

"I know that," he said. "The question is, what is it doing in my coat pocket? I have no idea how it got there."

"When was the last time you checked your pockets?" she asked.

He shrugged. "I bought this ski jacket before I flew out here. Yesterday was the first time I've worn it."

She frowned. "Are you saying it wasn't in your pocket when you left Texas?"

"I don't know. I don't think so. All I can tell you is that it isn't mine." He tried to remember where his ski jacket had been. Last night at the cabin, his father had taken his coat and hung it up. Was it possible he'd put the thumb drive in the pocket? Why would he do that?

With a start, Tag remembered the dead cocktail waitress stumbling into him, grabbing his coat and holding on to him as he tried to help her get her feet under her. A chill ran the length of his spine as he remembered her words.

"You look like him."

Was it possible she meant Harlan?

Before he could shove the thought away, Lily said, "Is there any chance Mia put it in your pocket last night?"

CHAPTER FIVE

"I THINK WE'D better see what's on that thumb drive," Lily said. "There's a computer in the bar office." With that she turned and headed for the front door. She heard Tag Cardwell come up behind her as she inserted her key into the lock.

"Why would she put this in my pocket?"

Lily shook her head. She had no idea. Just as she had no idea why Mia had left early two nights in a row or why Tag had thought Mia was falling-down drunk. She said as much as she opened the door to the bar, locking it behind them, before leading him to the office.

"Isn't it possible she was pretending to be drunk?" Lily asked, although that seemed even more far-fetched.

"She wasn't pretending," Tag said.

"Then she got drunk awfully fast after I talked to her." Stepping behind the desk, she held out her hand for the thumb drive.

"She smelled boozy, but it could have been drugs."

Lily shook her head. "Not Mia." But even as she said it, she realized again how little she really knew about the woman.

"You know, I was just thinking," he said as he handed over the thumb drive with obvious reluctance. "It's possible one of my brothers put it in my pocket at the airport as I was leaving. We're in business together, so it could be tax information they wanted me to look at.

My brother and my nephew saw me off at the airport. In fact, my brother held my coat while I was looking for my ticket."

She could tell he wanted the thumb drive to turn out to be something simple and innocent. No one wanted to think they had any kind of connection to a young woman's murder. She figured he was probably right. The other was too much like a spy movie.

As she considered Tag, she had to admit he would make a great spy. He looked like the kind of man who could save the damsel in distress. He definitely was sure of himself. But a spy with a Stetson and a Texas accent? It had more appeal than she wanted to admit, and she quickly shook the image off.

Lately her mind had been wandering into the strangest places. She knew what her brother would have to say about it. He was determined she find another man after what she liked to think of as "the Gerald Era" with its straight-out-of-a-country-and-western-song bad ending.

She pushed in the thumb drive, and Tag came around the end of the desk to stand next to her. He smelled like winter, a blend of cold and pine. She ignored the masculine scent just below the surface as she ignored the way her nerve endings jumped with him standing so close. Maybe her brother was right and it was time to get back on that horse that had thrown her.

It was definitely time to quit the cowboy clichés.

The icon came up on the page. She hesitated only a moment before she clicked on it. A series of random letters appeared.

GUHA BKOPAR
CAKNCA IKKNA
BNWJG IKKJAU

HSQ SWUJA
YHAPA NWJZ
NWU AIANU

LWQH XNKSJ
IEW ZQJYWJ
YWH BNWJGHEJ
HWNO HWJZANO
DWNHWJ YWNZSAHH
DQZ OWRWCA

"It's just gibberish," Tag said with a relieved laugh. "It looks like some kid was playing on a computer."

Lily nodded, feeling disappointed. "It does look that way," she agreed. She checked, but this page was the only thing on the thumb drive.

She'd wanted answers so desperately about Mia that she'd latched on to the thumb drive, determined she could solve the mystery. It was the way she approached life, her brother would have told her. Full steam ahead—as long as it was logical. The thumb drive hadn't been the answer, nor had she jumped to the logical conclusion. It wasn't like her.

Tag stepped away, shaking his head. "Maybe it was something my nephew put in my pocket. Ford's five and is always playing on the computer. He was at the airport with his dad the day I flew out."

"You're suggesting your five-year-old nephew put this on a thumb drive for you?" she asked skeptically.

"It's probably his idea of a goodbye letter. My brother would have put it on the thumb drive for him. Jackson is a single parent," he said as if that explained it enough for him.

Lily wasn't as convinced. Admittedly, she'd been

so sure Mia had put it in his coat pocket last night that she hated to give up the possibility. How nice it would have been if whatever was on the thumb drive would provide a clue to the woman's murder. Unfortunately the world seldom worked the way she thought it should.

"I was wondering," Tag said. "Since the bar won't be open tonight…"

His words didn't register until much later. Lily was busy staring at the letters on the screen trying to make them into more than they no doubt were.

The fact that the letters were all capitalized substantiated Tag's theory that they were probably done by a child who had just happened to hit Caps Lock before he started typing.

What interested her was that the lines were so short—none more than fourteen letters. The columns were also short, one on top of the other, broken halfway down by an empty line, then an equal number of lines below that. Six each. Awfully neat for a child, she thought, but then it could have been random—just like the letters.

She mentioned this to Tag without looking away from the screen.

"You *counted* them?" He laughed, then sobered when she sent him a withering look. "Sorry, it just seems odd to me that you'd count them."

Lily tried not to let his comment annoy her. "I'm a mathematician. I tend to count things."

His dark eyes widened. "A *mathematician?*"

She could tell he was fighting a grin, hoping she was joking. "I teach math at Montana State University," she said simply. Lily had seen too many men's eyes glaze over when she'd tried to explain her love of mathematics or how important it was for solving economic, scientific, engineering and business problems. Few people realized they used math in so many ways in their daily lives. Nor did they care, for that matter.

"Oh," was all he said. Much better than the men who said, "So you're smart." After that, they quit calling.

"Would you mind if I kept this for now?" she asked, pointing at the thumb drive.

Tag shrugged. "It's all yours. I'll check with my brother, but I'm betting my nephew Ford is behind this." Clearly, he was no longer worried about it. "I could call you later and let you know."

Lily realized that earlier he'd been about to ask her something about tonight. Had he been about to ask her on a date? She hadn't dated since Gerald. The thought of going out with this cowboy—

"I'll need your number," he said.

"So you can let me know what your brother says about the thumb drive. Right."

"Right," he said, looking amused at how flustered she had become.

She scribbled her number on one of the Canyon Bar business cards and handed it to him. Then she saved the page to the computer, emailed herself a copy, ejected the thumb drive and stood holding it.

"You sure you don't mind me keeping this for now?"

He grinned. "No problem. If it is a letter from my nephew, well, I think I got the gist of it," he said with a laugh.

And if it wasn't? She pocketed the thumb drive before walking him to the door. Ace had made a sign he'd posted, saying because of a death, the bar would be closed for the day. It was taped to the door as she let Tag out.

He seemed to hesitate before heading to his SUV. "I'm sorry about Mia."

"Thank you. Let me know what your brother says about the thumb drive."

Tag nodded and looked as if he had more he wanted to say, but after a moment, he touched his cowboy hat and left.

TAG HAD ALMOST asked Lily McCabe out. Mentally he kicked himself as he climbed behind the wheel of the SUV. Lily had lost a woman she'd worked with. She probably wasn't interested in going out with the man who'd found the victim's body. Not tonight anyway.

There'd be another chance before he left, he mused. He just hoped she didn't think the reason he hadn't pursued it was that she taught math. Wouldn't she have to have a PhD to teach math at a university? He let out a low whistle that came out frosty white in the winter air. Beautiful *and* smart. Everything about Lily McCabe intrigued him.

The temperature was dropping fast, but he hadn't noticed until he sat down on the pickup seat. It was as cold as a block of ice, hard as one, too.

He got the engine going. The heater was blowing freezing-cold air. He turned it off until the engine warmed up, rubbing his hands together. Even with gloves on, his fingers ached. He really should have gone with the more expensive rental—the one with the heated seats. But he was a Texas boy who'd forgotten how cold it got up here in Montana.

When he reached his father's cabin, he saw that Harlan hadn't returned. He couldn't imagine where he might have gone, so he went inside to wait. Lily Mc-Cabe had taken his thoughts off his father and his growing suspicions. But now, standing in his father's empty cabin, they were back with a vengeance.

He desperately wanted to believe that Hud would find the killer and clear all this up. Unfortunately, he kept picturing his father handing the marshal the thick envelope. What the hell was going on?

At the window, he caught a glimpse of Lone Mountain looming against the cold blue sky and thought about going skiing. But he felt too antsy. Maybe his father had gone over to Uncle Angus's.

As he started to leave the cabin, he remembered his promise to call his brother. He dialed Jackson's number and was relieved when he answered on the third ring.

"How's Montana?" his brother asked.

Tag thought it telling that Jackson hadn't asked how their father was first. "It's beautiful. Cold and snowy. I'm thinking about heading up to the ski hill." Not quite true, but it sounded good.

Jackson laughed. "Glad I'm in sunny, warm Texas, then."

"As the youngest, you probably don't have the great memories I do of the canyon. But this place grows on you. Summers here are better than any place on earth."

"How's Harlan?" Jackson and their brothers had quit calling him Dad a long time ago.

Tag wasn't sure how to answer that. "I went down to this local bar last night and listened to him and Uncle Angus play in their band. He really is a damned good guitar player. Mom might have been right about him having a chance at the big time."

"Yeah, right," Jackson said, clearly losing interest in this part of the conversation. His brother had thought he was a fool to want to spend Christmas with their father—let alone surprise him.

"You know how he is," Jackson had said. "I just hate to see you get hurt."

"I'm not expecting anything," Tag had said, but he could tell his brother didn't believe him. As the eldest, he had the most memories. He'd missed his father.

He realized that he'd had more expectations than he had wanted to admit. He'd wanted Harlan to be glad to see him. He'd also wanted Harlan to act like a caring father. So far he was batting zero.

"I need to ask you a question," Tag said. "When you and Ford saw me off at the airport, did Ford put a thumb drive in my pocket?"

"You mean one of those computer flash drives?"

Tag felt his heart drop. "I thought maybe he'd written me a goodbye letter on the computer and you saved it to one since I found one in my pocket."

"You do know that Ford is five and doesn't know how to write goodbye letters, right?"

"Yeah, but what's on the thumb drive looks like a kid typed it, pretending he was writing a goodbye letter."

"Sorry, I had nothing to do with it, but I'll ask Ford if he knows anything about it." He left the phone, returning a few moments later. "Nope. Ford's innocent. At least this time," he added with a laugh. "So, when are you coming back?"

"I'm not sure." Earlier he'd told his uncle he was leaving right after Christmas. That was before he'd officially met Lily McCabe. "Probably after New Year's."

"Hope you solve the mystery of the thumb drive," Jackson said with a laugh.

"I'm sure it's nothing." He thought of Mia and his father. He hoped to hell it was nothing.

LILY PUT THE thumb drive into her laptop the moment she got to her house. The house was small by Big Sky standards—only three bedrooms, three baths, a restaurant-quality kitchen, a large formal dining room and an open living room with a high-beamed ceiling.

The structure sat back into the trees against the mountainside and had a large deck at the front with a nice porch area next to the driveway and garage. She'd chosen simple furnishings, a leather couch in butter-scotch, her mother's old wooden rocker, a couple of club chairs with antique quilts thrown over them.

The dining room table was large, the chairs comfortable. It was right off the kitchen and living room. That was where she kept her computer because she liked the view. She was high enough on the mountain that she could look out through the large windows at the front of the house and see one of the many ski hills and the mountains beyond. It felt as if she could see forever.

The moment she inserted the flash drive, the letters came up again on the screen. It looked like a foreign language, one with a lot of hard vowels.

She knew she didn't want the letters to be random and that she was going to be disappointed if Tag was right and they were just gibberish typed in by a child.

But as she pulled up a chair, she thought about Mia. What if she was the one who'd put this thumb drive in Tag's jacket pocket—just as her imaginative mind had suggested? He'd said that Mia could barely stand up she was so drunk. Or drugged. What if she'd needed to get rid of the thumb drive?

Her heart began to beat a little faster as she thought of Mia's condo. Was the thumb drive what the person had been looking for? She knew she was letting her imagination run wild and it wasn't like her.

Her earlier thoughts of Tag Cardwell as a cowboy spy were to blame, she told herself. And yet this could be the stuff of secret-agent novels. A spy who's been compromised and has to ditch the goods, an encrypted message and a mathematician who gets involved in solving the mystery.

And gets herself killed, she thought with wry humor.

But she couldn't help studying the letters. She knew a little about codes because they involved math and because she'd played around with them as a girl, sending "secret" coded messages to her friends about the boys she liked. Her friends struggled with the deciphering and tired of them quickly.

It had been years, but she remembered some of the basics. She began to play with the letters, noticing there were eighteen *W*s and sixteen *A*s.

The most common letters in the English language were *E, T* and *A*. So if these were English words, then *W* and *A* were probably one of those more frequently used letters. Though by the position of the *A* letters, they represented something other than *A,* she thought.

Her cell phone rang, making her jump. She was surprised to hear Tag's voice.

"I talked to my brother. He says the thumb drive didn't come from Ford."

"Really?" She was already pretty sure of that anyway, but she did like the sound of his voice. He had a wonderful Texas accent.

"I'm sure there's another explanation," he said.

She was, too.

"I'd better go. Just wanted to let you know." He seemed to hesitate.

She felt her heartbeat kick up even against her will.

"Okay," he said.

"Thanks for letting me know. Maybe I'll talk to you later."

"Yeah."

She hung up, a little disappointed he hadn't asked her out—if that was what he'd been about to do earlier—but now all the more determined as she studied the letters again. Codes often involved simple addition or subtraction. She should be able to break this one by trial and error, but it would take time.

If it really was a code. She was glad she hadn't mentioned her suspicions to Tag, though. He thought she was geeky enough as it was.

TAG SWUNG BY his uncle's cabin. Who better to get the truth from than Harlan's brother? Tag had seen the look pass between them. He had a feeling there were few secrets between the two of them. If his father had a girlfriend, Angus would know.

But when he knocked at the door, there was no answer. He glanced in the curtainless window. The cabin was small, just three rooms, so he could see the bed. Clothes were thrown across it, the closet door open as if he'd packed in a hurry.

At the bar earlier, Angus hadn't mentioned going anywhere, especially this close to Christmas. Tag thought about the way the two of them had acted as they were leaving the bar. All his suspicions began to mushroom.

He checked the makeshift garage and found Angus's rig gone. Maybe he'd gone over to his daughter's. Tag drove on down the canyon to the Cardwell Ranch. This time Marshal Hud Savage was nowhere to be seen.

"I went by your dad's cabin," he said after Dana answered the door and ushered him into the kitchen, where she was baking cookies. The babies were napping, she said, and the two older kids, Mary and Hank, were with their aunt Stacy.

"It looks as if Angus is going out of town. I thought you might—"

"He's been called away on business," Dana said. "He wasn't sure when he'd get back, but he promised he would try his best to be here Christmas Eve."

"He got called away on business?" Tag couldn't help his skepticism or the suspicion in his tone. He couldn't imagine what business his uncle might have other than buying new guitar strings. "Just days before Christmas? What kind of business?"

She shot him a questioning look. "He's never said. Why?"

Tag let out a surprised sound. "So this isn't unusual?" Dana shook her head. "And you've never asked him?" He hadn't meant for his tone to sound so accusatory, but he couldn't help it. How could she not know what her father did for this so-called business?

"In case you haven't noticed, our fathers do their own thing. I'm not sure exactly what they do, but occasionally it takes them out of the canyon for a few days, usually on the spur of the moment."

This news came as a complete surprise. "Harlan does this, too? I didn't think either of them ever left. So they're *both* involved in this *business?*"

She gave him an impatient look, then shrugged.

"Aren't you suspicious?"

She chuckled. "*Suspicious?* Dad could have a whole other family somewhere. Maybe more than one. But if that's the case, he seems happy, so more power to him."

Tag couldn't believe her attitude. "Has either of them ever had girlfriends locally?"

She thought for a moment. "Not really. Maybe a long

time ago. Like I said, they seem happy just doing their thing, whatever that is." She pulled a pan of cookies from the oven and deftly began sliding them onto a rack to cool.

As she did, she said, "Angus and I aren't that close. I'm busy with the kids and the ranch and Hud, and Dad's a loner, except for his brother...."

"I always thought that if I lived here, Harlan and I would be closer," Tag said as he took a seat at the table and watched her. He couldn't help feeling disappointed. He'd really thought this trip would bring him closer to his father. If anything, it seemed to be pushing them even further apart. "What is it about those two that they aren't good with their own kids?"

Dana sighed. "Or with their wives. They just aren't family men and never have been. But don't let that spoil your Christmas here," she said, and handed him a warm cookie. "We're going to have a wonderful time whether they make it Christmas Eve or not."

"Yes, we are," Tag said, sounding more upbeat than he felt. Right now, he felt as if the Grinch had already stolen Christmas.

After he left the ranch, he drove around aimlessly, hoping he might see his father or uncle coming out of one of the local businesses. Finally, he stopped for something to eat, but barely tasted the food in front of him.

When he came back out, he was surprised it was already getting dark. The sun had disappeared behind Lone Mountain several hours ago, and the deep, narrow canyon was shrouded in shadows. He'd forgotten how quickly it got dark this far north in the winter.

As he drove up to his father's cabin, he was relieved to see Harlan's SUV parked out front. He'd half expected that, like Angus, Harlan had taken off for parts unknown on some "business" trip.

Wading through the snow and growing darkness toward the cabin, he was determined to get the truth out of his father. No more lies. Either that or he would have to go to the marshal with what he knew. Nix that. He'd have to take his suspicions to the cops in Bozeman, since he wasn't sure he could trust Hud. Admittedly, he didn't know much about Mia's death—or about his father's possible involvement. Just a gut feeling—and a leather jacket.

Deep shadows hunkered around the edge of the cabin as Tag started up the steps. He'd shoveled the steps and walk early this morning before he'd left to go Christmas tree hunting. That now seemed like a lifetime ago.

There had been some snow flurries during the day close to the mountains. The snow had covered the shoveled walk. Tag slowed as he noticed the footprints in the scant snowfall.

His father had had company. Several different boot prints had left tracks up the walk. One had to be his father's, but there were at least two others. His brother? But who else? He'd gotten the feeling his father had few visitors. Then again, he hadn't thought his father had female visitors and he'd been wrong about that.

Only one light shone inside the house. It poured out to splash across the crystal-white snow at the edge of the porch.

He slowed, listening for the sound of voices, hearing nothing. From the tracks in the snow, it appeared whoever had stopped by had left.

He thought of Dana now. Unlike her, he had to know what was going on with his father. He wasn't buying that they had "business" out of town occasionally. Monkey business, maybe.

As he opened the door and looked in, all the air rushed from his lungs. The cabin had been ransacked. He stared, too shocked to move for a moment. Who would have done something like this, and why?

He thought of the thick envelope that his father had given the marshal. Was that payoff money to keep a lid on what his father and uncle were involved in? The envelope had been thick. Where would his father get that kind of money? Not from playing his guitar at a bar on weekends.

Drugs? It was the first thing that came to mind. Were his father and uncle in the drug business?

At the sound of a groan, he rushed in through the debris to find his father lying on the floor behind the couch. Tag was shocked to see how badly Harlan had been beaten.

He hurriedly pulled out his cell phone and dialed 911.

CHAPTER SIX

HATE IS A strange but powerful emotion. Camilla went to bed with it each night; it warmed her like wrapping her fingers around a hot mug of coffee. It was her only comfort, locked away in this world of all-women criminals. The place didn't feel much like a prison, though, since it was right in the middle of the city of Billings.

Only when she heard the clang of steel doors did it hit home. She was never leaving here. At least not for a very long time.

Of course the nightmares had gotten worse—just as the doctor had said they would. She'd known they would since they'd been coming more often—even before she'd been caught and locked up. She'd wake up screaming. Not that screaming in the middle of the night was unusual here.

The nightmare was the same one that had haunted her since she was a girl. She was in a coffin. It was pitch-black. There was no air. She was trapped and, even though she'd screamed herself hoarse, no one had come to save her.

The doctor she'd seen a few years ago hadn't been encouraging, far from it. "Do night terrors run in your family?" he'd asked, studying her over the top of his glasses.

"I don't know. I never asked."

"How old did you say you were?"

She'd been in her late twenties at the time.

He'd frowned. "What about sleepwalking?"

"Sometimes I wake up in a strange place and I don't know how I've gotten there." But that could have described her whole life.

He'd nodded, his frown deepening as he'd tossed her file on his desk. "I'm going to give you a referral to a neurologist."

"You're saying there's something wrong with me?"

"Just a precaution. Sleepwalking and night terrors at your age are fairly uncommon and could be the result of a neurological disorder."

She'd laughed after she left his office. "He thinks I'm crazy." She'd been amused at the time. Back then she hadn't been sleepwalking or having the nightmare all that often.

Unfortunately that was no longer the case. Not that she worried about it all that much. So what if she got worse? It wasn't as though she was going anywhere, and everyone here already thought she was half-crazy.

So, Spark. How would you say you're dealing with prison life?

In her mind's eye, she smiled at her pretend interviewer. "I exercise, watch my diet and, oh, yes, I have Hate. It keeps me going. Hate and The Promise of Retribution, they're my cell mates."

Tell inquiring minds. Who's at the top of your hate list and why?

"It's embarrassing actually." Camilla thought about the first time she'd laid eyes on Marshal Hud Savage. The cowboy had come riding up on his horse. "Do you believe in love at first sight?" she asked her fictional interviewer. "Then I have a story for you."

"Your father says he didn't get a good look at the intruders," Marshal Hud Savage told Tag later that night at the hospital.

"How is that possible? They beat him up. He had to have *seen* them."

"What makes you think it was more than one man?" Hud asked.

"The tracks in the snow. There were three different boot prints. I'm assuming one pair was Harlan's."

Hud nodded. He seemed distracted.

Tag felt that same sick feeling he'd had earlier today when he witnessed his father with the marshal. "Harlan didn't mention anything when the two of you talked just after noon today?"

Hud frowned. "Why would Harlan—"

"You didn't see my father earlier today? I thought he said he was stopping by your place to talk to you."

The marshal's eyes narrowed before he slowly shook his head. "Harlan told you that? Maybe he changed his mind."

Hud had just lied to his face. "I must have misunderstood him." Tag felt sick to his stomach. What the hell was going on? "I hope you're planning to find who did this to him and why."

"I know my job," Hud snapped. "Look," he said, softening his tone. The marshal appeared tired, exhausted actually, as if he hadn't had much rest for quite a while. "When your father is conscious, maybe he'll remember more about his attackers."

It angered him that Hud was trying to placate him. "*If* he comes to." Harlan had fallen into a coma shortly after the EMTs had arrived to take him to the hospital. What if he didn't make it?

"Harlan's going to be all right," Hud said. "He's a tough old bird."

Tag hoped Hud was right about that. His cell phone rang. He checked it, surprised to see that the call was from Lily McCabe.

"Excuse me," he said, and stepped away to answer it. "Hey."

"I think it's in code." Lily sounded excited.

"Code?"

"The letters on that thumb drive, I think they're two lists of names."

"Names?" A call came over the hospital intercom for Dr. Allen to come to the nurses' station on the fourth floor, stat.

"I'm sorry. Did I catch you in the middle of something?"

"I'm at the hospital. Someone ransacked my father's cabin and beat him up."

"Is he all right?" She sounded as shocked as he felt right now.

"The doctor thinks he's going to recover. He's unconscious. The marshal is here now." He looked down the hall and saw that Hud was also on his cell phone. Tag wondered who was on the other end of the line. Uncle Angus?

"Did he tell you that Mia Duncan's condo was also ransacked?"

It took Tag a moment to realize she was referring to the marshal—not Harlan or Angus. "No, he didn't mention that." Another reason not to trust Hud—as if he needed more.

"That's odd. First Mia's condo is ransacked and she's murdered, then your father's cabin and he gets beaten up. This is Montana. Things like that just don't happen."

Apparently they did. "That *is* odd," he said. First Mia's, now his father's place? Had Harlan come home and surprised his intruders? Or had they torn up the place *after* they tried to kill him?

"I'm sure there's no connection."

"Yeah." He didn't want to see a connection to his father and the murdered woman, but the coincidences just kept stacking up. "So you say those letters are actually names?" He knew he sounded skeptical.

"I have only started decoding them, but yes, they appear to be names. I can't really explain it over the phone. But I thought you'd want to know right away."

He glanced down the hall. Hud was still on his cell phone, his back turned to Tag. What if Mia had put that computer thumb drive in his pocket last night?

"I want to see what you've found." More than she could know.

"You're welcome to come up to my place when you're ready to leave the hospital."

"Give me your address. I'll come over as soon as I can, if that's all right."

She rattled off an address on Sky-High Road up on the mountain. "It's at the end of the road."

As he disconnected, he saw the doctor coming down the hall. "Harlan is conscious," he said to the marshal, then looked in Tag's direction. "He'd like to see his son."

Hud started to say something, but the doctor cut him off. "He said he'll talk to you after he talks to his son."

Tag walked down the hall and pushed open the door into his father's hospital room. Harlan looked as if he'd been hit by a bus, but he was sitting up a little and his gaze was intent as he watched Tag enter.

"You gave me a scare," Tag said as he stopped at the end of his father's bed.

"Sorry about that." Harlan's voice was hoarse. He was clearly in pain, but he was doing his best to hide it. "The marshal will catch the little hoodlums. How times have changed. They're targeting old people now for our prescription drugs." He chuckled even though it clearly hurt him to do so.

"Whoever beat you up, they weren't after your arthritis medicine," Tag said evenly. He couldn't believe how angry he was at his father for continuing to lie to him. "What were they really looking for, *Dad?*"

His father's expression hardened. "Stay out of this, son. That's why I wanted to see you. I want—"

"That woman who was at your cabin was Mia Duncan, wasn't it?"

Harlan sighed. "I told you. I don't know anyone by that name."

Tag shook his head and tried to still his growing anger. "You just keep lying to me. What business is Uncle Angus away on?"

"Why are you asking me that?"

"Because the two of you are inseparable. You can finish each other's sentences. You have to know where he's gone and why."

"I guess what I should have asked is why is it any of your business?" Harlan said, an edge to his voice.

Tag pulled off his Stetson and raked a hand through his hair as he tried to control his temper. "I know something's going on with the two of you, and it has to do with that woman who was murdered. Angus owns a snowmobile and he knows those old logging roads behind the ranch. You own snowmobiles yourself. I would imagine the two of you have been all over that country behind the ranch. Is it drugs? Is that the business you're in that gets your cabin torn up and you beat up and in the hospital?"

His father let out a sigh. "Do you realize what you're saying?"

"You lied to me. At the bar, I saw you watching the door. You were expecting Mia. You were shocked when I told you she was dead. That's why you didn't ask who was killed. Because you *knew*."

"This conversation is over." He reached for the buzzer to call the nurse.

Tag stepped to the side of the bed and caught his father's arm to stop him. "Tell me it isn't true. Tell me I've got it all wrong." He hated the pleading he heard in his voice.

His father met his gaze. "You have it all wrong."

"Then you don't mind if I keep digging into her death."

"Leave the investigating to the people who are trained for it. Please, son. I don't want to see you get hurt."

His father had already hurt him by not being in his life. But did he really believe Harlan Cardwell was… what? A drug dealer? Worse, a killer?

He met his father's steely gaze. "Then tell the truth."

"Stay out of this, Tag. It isn't what you think."

"I hope you're right—given what I'm thinking."

Harlan closed his eyes. "Tag, I need you to go back to Texas." When he opened them again, Tag saw a deep sadness there. "This isn't a good time for a visit. Please. Go home. Don't wait until after Christmas. If you don't—"

The door opened and the doctor came into the room. Harlan looked away.

"If I don't leave… What are you trying to tell me?"

Tag demanded of his father. "That if I continue digging in your life I'll end up like that woman you don't know?"

"I'm sorry," the doctor said. "Did I interrupt something?"

"No. My son was just leaving," Harlan said. "Please don't tell your mother about this. I'll call you in a few days in Texas."

"Don't bother. I'll see you before then," Tag said, and left.

"YOU HAVE TO tell him the truth," Hud said after the doctor had left.

Harlan looked up at him from the hospital bed. "You know I can't do that." He motioned to the pitcher of water on the bedside table, and the marshal poured him a glass.

"He's your *son*," Hud persisted. "He isn't going to stop. That damned stubbornness seems to run in your family."

Harlan took a drink of water and handed back the empty glass. "I need you to persuade him to go back to Texas."

"I wouldn't count on that happening. He seems to know that you stopped by the ranch earlier today."

"How would he know that?" Harlan shifted in the bed and grimaced in pain.

Hud shook his head. "He knows and he's suspicious as hell of both of us."

"Have you heard anything from Angus?"

"Nothing yet."

"I tried to warn Mia...." Harlan looked away.

"She knew what she was getting into."

"I warned her what could happen if she got too close

to the truth." Harlan turned back to him. "You didn't find anything?"

"Nothing. If she had it, then whoever killed her took it. Tag said she was drunk when he saw her at the bar."

"She had to be pretending to be drunk, maybe so she could leave early and not be stopped. Or maybe they got to her somehow." Harlan gently touched his bruised and swelling jaw. "We still don't know who was waiting for her outside the bar?"

"All Tag could tell us was that it appeared to be a dark-colored pickup and the driver was wearing a cowboy hat. I could take him in to look at mug shots."

Harlan quickly shook his head, then groaned in regret for doing it. "I need my son kept out of this. Do whatever you have to to make that happen."

"I can't very well arrest him without a reason to charge him."

Harlan closed his eyes. "You'll think of something. He seems hell-bent on finding out the truth. You know what's at stake. Stop him."

IT BEGAN TO snow as Tag left the hospital. He felt shaken as he slid behind the wheel of his rented SUV. What were his father and the marshal involved in? A cover-up regarding Mia Duncan's murder? Lily had said that Mia's condo had been ransacked. Clearly, whoever was behind this was looking for something.

He feared he knew what. Worse, that Lily had it.

As he watched large snowflakes drift down through the lights of the parking lot, Tag suddenly realized how late it was. But he couldn't stand the thought that Lily was in danger if that thumb drive was what the killers were looking for.

He started the SUV, still debating what to do because of the late hour and the snowstorm. Was it possible that Lily was right and Mia had put the thumb drive in his pocket? Why would she do that? Why give it to a complete stranger? Unless she knew she had to get rid of it quick?

With a start, he was reminded again of what she'd said.

"You look like him."

Had she known he was Harlan's son?

Tag shook his head. She'd been drunk or high on drugs. She hadn't known what she was saying. He thought of his father. He couldn't believe Harlan and Angus were drug dealers. And yet he didn't really know them. He especially didn't know his father, and the way things were going, he doubted he ever would.

His heart began to beat a little faster as he threw the SUV into Drive. Lily had the computer flash drive. If there was even a chance she was in danger… He drove by his father's cabin and got a pistol from Harlan's gun cabinet. He told himself he was just being paranoid.

As he headed toward Big Sky, he drove as fast as he could. He couldn't help being worried about Lily up in the mountains all by herself. He tried to assure himself that she was safe. No one knew she had the thumb drive.

His mind kept going back to last night in the bar and Mia, though. He remembered the way she'd clutched his jacket. She *could* have put the thumb drive in his pocket. Now she was dead. His father was in the hospital. And the killers were looking for something. It was too much of a coincidence that he'd found the thumb drive in his pocket. And now Lily thought she'd discovered the information on the computer USB was two lists of names in some kind of code?

Ahead, the road to the summit was a series of switchbacks that climbed from the river bottom to nearly the top of twelve-thousand-foot Lone Mountain. The snow fell harder the higher he drove. He had to slow down because of the limited visibility.

His mind was still whirling as he passed Big Sky Resort and left behind any signs of life. Up here, there was nothing but snowy darkness. He still couldn't get his mind around what was happening. His father was involved in whatever was going on, and so was the marshal, and he was betting his uncle Angus was, as well.

Harlan had said it was a bad time for a visit. No kidding. He was determined that Tag return to Texas. Hell, Harlan had almost threatened him, insinuating that if he stayed, it could be dangerous. Would be dangerous.

Heart racing, he reached into his pocket for his cell phone to call Lily. He had to make sure she was all right and to let her know he was almost to her house.

But as he started to place the call, he glanced in his rearview mirror, feeling a little paranoid. *You're not paranoid if someone is really after you,* he thought as he noticed a set of headlights behind him.

He watched them growing closer. The driver behind him was going too fast for the conditions and gaining on him too quickly. Tag looked around for a place to pull over, but there was only a solid snowplowed wall on one side of the road and a drop-off on the other.

Giving the SUV more gas, he sped up as he came out of a curve. Ahead was another curve. He could feel the glare of the headlights on his back, glancing off the rearview mirror and his side mirrors. The vehicle was almost directly behind him.

Tag told himself that the driver must be drunk or not paying attention or blinded by the falling snow. Unless the person behind the wheel was hoping to make him crash.

He tried to shake off even the thought. He wasn't that far from the road up to Lily's house. Suddenly the headlights behind him went out.

Glancing in his mirror again, he was shocked to find the vehicle gone. Had the driver run off the road? Or had he turned off? There had been a turnoff back there....

Ahead, Tag saw the sign. As he turned, he looked back down the main road. No sign of the other vehicle. Breathing a sigh of relief, he drove on up the narrow, snowy road. Wind whipped snow all around the SUV. He had his windshield wipers on high and they still couldn't keep up with the snow.

The road narrowed and rose. He knew he had to be getting close. He thought he caught the golden glow of lights in a house just up the mountain. His fear for Lily amplified at the thought of her alone in such an isolated place.

A dark-colored vehicle came out of the snowstorm on a road to his right. He swerved to miss it and felt the wheels drop over the side of the mountain, the SUV rolling onto its side. His head slammed into the side window. He felt blood run into his eye as the SUV rolled once more before crashing into a tree.

CHAPTER SEVEN

THE SNOWSTORM BLEW in with a fury. Inside the house, Lily could hear the flakes hitting the window. It sounded like the glass was being sandblasted.

She shivered and checked her watch as she went to put more logs on the fire. Tag said he would come as soon as he could. She told herself he'd probably been held up by the storm. She just hoped he would be able to get up the road.

Her house sat by itself on the side of the mountain, far from any others. The road often blew in with snow before the plows made their rounds. Since she didn't usually go to work at her brother's bar until the afternoon, it hadn't ever been a problem.

But tonight, she was anxious to show Tag what she'd come up with so far and she worried since there had already been some good-size drifts across the road when she'd looked out earlier.

She'd worked trying to decode the random letters until her head ached. What if she was wrong? What if this was nothing? But she was convinced that there were two lists of names. She'd gotten at least a start on the code, making her more assured that she was on the right track.

A loud noise from outside made her jump. She stopped stoking the fire to listen for a moment and heard it again. Her pulse spiked before she could determine the sound.

She couldn't help being jumpy. Wasn't it enough that a woman she worked with had been murdered last night and another one was missing? But Lily didn't kid herself. Her nerves were more because of Tag and the thought of the two of them alone in her house.

Another noise, this one a loud thud. She peered out at the porch swing an instant before the wind blew it back into the side of the house again with a loud thump. The shadows had deepened on the porch, running a dark gray before turning black under the pines. The porch light illuminated only a small golden disk of light against the falling snow.

Hugging herself, she assured herself that there was nothing to be afraid of up here. She'd always felt safe. The porch swing thumped against the side of the house, followed by a loud thud closer to her front door. Probably that potted pine she had by the door. She started to turn back to her work when something caught her eye. Fresh footprints in the snow on the steps up to the porch.

A gust of wind blew snow against the glass. For a moment, it stuck, obstructing her view. Tag? Could he have come to the door and she hadn't heard him?

The knock at the door made her jump. She chastised herself as she hurried to the front door, thankful she'd been right and thankful, too, for Tag's company. Even for a short period of time tonight, she would be glad to have him around. Mia's murder must have her more shaken than she'd let herself admit.

As she turned the knob, the wind caught the door and wrenched it from her hand. It blew back on a gale, banging against the wall.

Blinded by the cold bite of the snow and wind, she blinked. Then blinked again in astonishment.

"Gerald?"

LILY HADN'T SEEN Gerald since the day before their wedding that had never happened because he hadn't shown up.

She stared at him now. Nothing could have surprised her more than to find him standing there, caked in snow and huddled into himself to block the wind.

"Would you mind if I came in?" he asked pointedly. "It's freezing out here."

She nodded, still too stunned to speak, and stepped back to let him enter, closing the door swiftly after him.

He brushed snow from his blond hair and slipped out of his wool dress coat, holding it at arm's length to keep the snow off him. He wore dark trousers, dress shoes and a white shirt, including a tie. The knot was a little crooked, which surprised her. Gerald valued preciseness in all things.

As he looked up at her, his blue eyes seemed to soften. She was struck by the memory of the two of them. Just last summer they'd been planning a life together. She remembered the smell of his aftershave, the feel of his fingers on her skin, the taste of his mouth when he kissed her. Like the wind outside, the force of his betrayal scattered those once pleasant memories, leaving her bereft.

She saw with a start that he was still holding his coat out as if waiting for her to take it. She finally found her voice. "Gerald, what are you doing here?"

The one thing she'd told herself she'd loved about this man was that he never wavered. Gerald exuded confidence. While she often felt swept along in his wake, she'd been happy to be part of his life even if it meant accepting that he knew best and always would.·

"I had to see you," he said. He seemed to study her for a moment before he added, "I figured you'd be here. You look…tired."

She bristled at his words. Leave it to Gerald to speak the cold truth. He'd never been good at tempering his observations. "It's been a rough day. One of our servers was murdered."

"*Your* servers? You mean your brother's. You *are* still at the university, aren't you?"

"Yes." It annoyed her that he'd never understood why she spent the past few Christmas and New Year's holidays up here at Big Sky helping her brother. He'd always insinuated that Ace was using her and that serving cocktails was beneath her.

Gerald must have seen that he'd irritated her because he softened his tone and asked, "How *is* James?"

"Fine." There was no reason to pretend any further that Gerald cared about her brother. He had always refused to call him anything but James, saying that Ace was something you might call a dog.

"You said you had to see me," she reminded him.

He was still holding his coat away from him as he looked behind her into the living room. "Is there any chance we could sit down and discuss this like rational evolved human beings?" There was an edge to his words as if he'd expected her to be more gracious.

She thought how he hadn't shown up at the wedding. The pain and hurt had dulled over the past six months, but there was still that breath-stealing reminder when she thought of her humiliation.

She'd hadn't been heartbroken—not the way she

would have been had she and Gerald shared a more passionate relationship.

"We're cerebral," Gerald used to say. "It's a higher level of intimacy than simple passion. Who else could appreciate you the way I do?"

"And who else could love such a math nerd," his sister had said, "but another math nerd?" That, too, Lily had believed was true. So what if they didn't have a passionate relationship? They had math.

She thought of Tag and his comment, *"You counted them?"* He'd thought she was joking. Probably hoped she was joking.

But Gerald had embarrassed and hurt her and left her feeling as if no one would want her if he didn't. Now, though, he was back. What did that mean?

"Yes, please sit down." She took his coat and hung it up, feeling conflicted. She wanted to throw him out and yet she wanted, needed, to hear what he had to say.

Leaning toward throwing him out, she reminded herself that Gerald had understood her in a way no other man had and he had come all this way to talk to her. And while they hadn't been the perfect couple in some aspects, they had a lot in common, since Gerald had been the head of the math department. That was until he took a job in California without telling her.

"Can I get you something to drink? I have a wine you might like," she said, using the manners boarding schools had instilled in her.

He shook his head as he tested the couch with his hand, then sat down. She'd forgotten he did that. He tested things, weighing them as to how worthy they were, she'd always thought. For a long while, she'd thought that was why he hadn't shown up at the wedding. She just hadn't met his high level of quality.

"Please sit," he said, looking up at her still looming over him. "You're giving me a crick in my neck."

She sat across from him and immediately wished she'd gotten herself a glass of wine. Also, her instant response to his command annoyed her. She almost got back up just to show him he couldn't come into her house and start telling her what to do after what he'd done to her.

"I'm sorry," he said, stilling her in her chair.

Those were two words she'd never heard from him before. She waited for more.

"I can't explain my actions."

And still she waited.

"I deeply regret what I did." Gerald had always been a man of few words as if they cost him each time he spoke and he refused to waste a single one.

A gust of wind rattled the window behind her, making her turn. All she could see was blowing snow and darkness beyond the arc of the porch light.

"Are you expecting someone?" Gerald demanded, clearly annoyed that her attention had wavered.

She thought of Tag. He apparently wasn't coming. "No. No one." Lily had barely gotten the words out of her mouth when there was pounding at the door. She jumped up in surprise. So did Gerald.

"I thought you weren't expecting anyone," he said suspiciously.

She said nothing as she hurried to the front door. As she opened it, a gust of wind and snow whipped in, but she hardly noticed.

"What happened to you?" she cried when she saw Tag standing there, his face covered in blood.

"SOMEONE RAN ME off the road," Tag said as she ushered him into the house. "Do you still have the—" The words *thumb drive* died on his lips as he saw the man standing behind her.

"We need to get you to the hospital," she cried.

"No," he said, his gaze still on the man standing in Lily's living room. "I'll be all right."

"Then at least let me clean up that cut over your eye. I'll get the first-aid kit." As she hurried past the man toward the back of the house, she said over her shoulder, "This is Gerald." Lily disappeared into a back room, leaving Tag alone with the man.

A brittle silence fell between them until the man said, "I don't believe I caught your name, but you're bleeding on her floor."

"Here," Lily said, hurrying back into the room with the first-aid kit, a washcloth and a towel. She shot Gerald a warning look as she passed him. "His name is Tag. Tag Cardwell."

"Tag?" The man said it and grimaced. "Charming."

Lily seemed to ignore him. "Sit down here and let me see about that cut. Are you hurt anywhere else?"

Tag grimaced as he lowered himself into the chair she pulled out. "Just beat up and bruised. My ribs hurt, but they don't feel broken. Everything else seems to be working since I was able to walk the rest of the way up here." He grimaced again as the washcloth touched the cut on his temple.

"Sorry," she said, and reached into her pocket. "Here, take two of these. The prescription is a recent one of mine from a sprained ankle I had." She jumped up to hurry to the kitchen for a glass of water.

He took the pills and the glass of water she handed him. He tossed the pills into his mouth and downed them with the water. His gaze met hers as he handed back the empty glass. "Thanks."

"What is this about you being run off the road?" Lily asked.

Now that he was here, Tag was questioning what exactly *had* happened. He'd been so anxious to get to Lily and make sure she was safe... "Just some driver who wasn't used to Montana weather." At least he hoped that was all it had been. The driver had kept going, though, hadn't even stopped to see if he was all right. But if he really was drunk, then he wouldn't want to be involved.

Gerald cleared his throat. "I should probably go since you're obviously busy," he said as he walked over to the table. His fingers ran along the top of the open laptop computer sitting there.

"Please don't touch that," Lily said, and got up to go to the table. She closed the computer and pulled out the thumb drive, dropping it into her sweater pocket before returning to Tag. Picking up the washcloth, she began to bathe his face.

"I can do that," Tag said, and took the cloth from her, smiling at her tenderness. He wiped away the dried and frozen blood he could feel on his face before she took the washcloth back and dabbed at a couple of places he'd apparently missed.

"It seems I'm not the only one anxious to talk to you tonight, although I didn't make as dramatic an entrance as your...friend," Gerald said, plainly irritated. Tag wondered what he had interrupted.

"If you're staying in the area, Gerald, perhaps we could talk tomorrow," she said without looking at the man as she gently dabbed at the area around Tag's cut before reaching for the antiseptic.

"What choice do I have if I hope to get this settled?" Gerald snapped.

"I thought it *was* settled," she said, anger sparking just under the surface. Tag liked the heat he saw in her eyes and thought about the first night they'd met. A woman with attitude, his favorite kind, he thought as he felt the pain pills start to work.

"This is definitely not what I'd hoped for," Gerald said with a sigh. "I will call you tomorrow if you think you can make time for me."

"Fine."

Tag wondered what was unsettled between them, but was smart enough not to ask. Yep, the pills were definitely working. They were strong, which was fine with him. He hurt all over and was thankful when the pain began to numb.

"I'm sorry if I interrupted something," Tag said as the door shut behind Gerald. "It sounded as if he really wanted to talk to you tonight. I didn't mean to run off your boyfriend." Yep, the pills were working. He felt drunk with them. Whatever they were, they were *very* strong.

"He isn't my boyfriend," she said as she put a bandage on over his cut. "He's my former fiancé."

"You were going to marry that jackass?" The words slipped out before he could stop them. "Sorry."

"I'm afraid you witnessed Gerald at his worst," she said as she finished bandaging his wound.

Tag was trying to imagine Gerald at his best. "So, why didn't you marry him?"

"There," she said, and closed the first-aid kit. "He stood me up at the wedding."

"The bastard. If I'd have known that, I would have slugged him for you."

She met his gaze and began to laugh. "That's what my brother always threatened to do."

"Why didn't he?"

"Gerald left town. This is the first time I've seen him since the day before the wedding."

"And you didn't hit him the moment you saw him?"

She shook her head. "I'm a perfectly reasonable woman. I don't hit people."

"I would have hit him."

She rose to put away the first-aid kit, but stopped. "Are you all right?"

He realized he'd been staring at her, wondering how some goofy older guy like Gerald had gotten a beautiful young woman like Lily to even look twice at him. "Fine. What were those pills anyway?"

"I think I'd better drive you to the hospital or at least down to the clinic. Just let me put this away—"

He caught her arm. "I'd rather hear about this code you told me about."

"I think it's a list of names. I'm still decoding them. If Gerald hadn't shown up when he did..." She glanced toward the door and he saw pain in her expression.

The man had hurt her. Tag really wished he'd slugged him. Was it possible he'd been driving the car that had run him off the road? "He didn't give you any indication why he came up here tonight?"

She shook her head.

"Because I interrupted the two of you. I'm sorry."

"Don't be. I'm not sure there is anything he could say under the circumstances." Her smile was filled with sadness.

"Look, he's bound to have realized what a fool he was. He probably came here tonight to beg you to take him back. Maybe you should call him and—"

"Six months ago, he left me at a church filled with our relatives and friends on our wedding day. Apparently he didn't have anything to say that day. I'm sure whatever he plans to say now can wait a day."

If Tag had been up to it, he would have gone after Gerald and kicked his sorry butt. He couldn't believe it had taken the man six months to come back. "I'm sorry he hurt you like that," he said, taking her free hand. She didn't pull away. "Are you sure you want to take him back? You deserve a lot better." He caressed the back of her hand with his thumb pad. Her skin was so warm and smooth.

His gaze went to her mouth. It was a Cupid's bow, as kissable as any mouth he'd ever seen. "Lily—"

"I really should drive you down to the clinic to make sure you don't have any internal injuries," she said.

"You're not driving anywhere in this storm. I hope Gerald is staying on the mountain and not planning to drive all the way to Meadow Village tonight." Lily said nothing. Nor did she draw her hand back. "I'm afraid we're snowed in," he said, lulled by the pain pills she'd given him and this woman.

"I should show you the code I worked out so far on the data from the thumb drive," she said, and started to pull away, but he drew her back. "Or should we call the marshal first? You really should report the accident."

"Do you still love him?" Tag asked as he got to his feet and, taking the first-aid kit, put it aside. He felt a little woozy.

"Gerald?" she asked. "I don't know. You should sit back down. You're hurt."

"Tell me you haven't been waiting around for the past six months for him to come back." He saw the answer in her eyes and swore.

"Tag." His name on her lips was his undoing. Outside, the storm raged. Inside, he threw caution to the wind as he drew Lily to him.

CHAPTER EIGHT

TAG WOKE NAKED and smiling. Without opening his eyes, he felt across the bed for Lily, remembering last night and their lovemaking. Finding the bed empty and cold, he opened one eye. No Lily.

He couldn't help being disappointed. Last night had been amazing. He hadn't expected that kind of passion in her, he thought as he touched his shoulder and felt scratches. He chuckled to himself. She'd been wild, surprising herself as well as him, he thought. But there had also been tenderness. Lily McCabe was all woman, as sexy as any he'd ever known.

"Lily?" No answer. His heart kicked up a beat. She wouldn't have tried to leave this morning on her own? Or worse.

Swinging his legs over the side of the bed, he was reminded of the wreck and the aching parts of his body. He managed to pull on his jeans before hurrying barefoot out to the kitchen. He was met with the welcoming scent of coffee and the sight of Lily standing silhouetted against the bright clear morning.

"Hey," he said, relief in his voice. He'd planned to come up behind her, wrap his arms around her and kiss her on her neck, then do his best to persuade her to come back to bed with him.

But she turned too quickly, separating them with more than the cup of coffee in her hand. He stopped short and felt his heart drop. This was not the wild woman he remembered from bed last night. Her expression warned him to keep his distance.

He blinked, confused. Last night had happened, right? He thought of their lovemaking. Was it possible he'd only dreamed making crazy, passionate love with this woman last night?

Lily's demeanor told him it had only been a figment of his drug-induced imagination and if he wasn't careful, he would make a fool out of himself. It wouldn't be the first time. Or the last, he thought. He had to know.

"Uh, did something happen between us last night?"

"Happen?" She took a sip of her coffee, watching him over the rim of her cup. Her hair was still damp from her shower, smelling of jasmine—just as it had last night in his arms. But she was looking at him as if he was crazy.

He remembered how strong the pain pills had been. Sure, he'd felt groggy, but— "I woke up naked this morning and I thought I remembered you and me…" The look she gave him stopped him from being more specific.

"Do I seem like the kind of woman who would fall into bed with a man I hardly know?"

He studied her, considering her words. She wore a turtleneck sweater and jeans. Buttoned up, that was how he would have described her. Nothing like the woman last night.

"No, you don't. But last night—" Last night he remembered finding a side of Lily that was as unexpected as the way she was acting this morning. "Sorry. It's just that I…" He shook his head and warned himself not to get in any deeper.

"I think you really should see what I found on the

thumb drive," she said, all business, as she moved to the table where she'd left her laptop and the papers she'd been working on.

He was suddenly more aware of the fact that his body hurt all over and his head felt as if it was filled with lint. He stood looking after her, unable to accept that last night had been nothing more than a dream. He remembered every kiss, every touch. Desire stirred in him.

"Tag?" Lily glanced back at him, her gaze taking in his bare chest. "Perhaps you'd like to get dressed first."

"Yeah." He touched his scratched shoulder. Was it possible he'd gotten that in the accident? He met her gaze and for just a moment—

She quickly looked away, busying herself with the calculations she'd made. "We can discuss this when you come back. I'll pour you a cup of coffee. How do you take it?"

"Black and strong." He realized he needed his wits about him. Not only for whatever was going on with his father and this thumb drive, but with this woman.

LILY WATCHED TAG walk to the bedroom and closed her eyes as she fought the images. She couldn't believe what had happened last night. That hadn't been her, she told herself just as she'd told Tag.

All morning, she'd fretted about what they would say to each other once he woke up. She'd never been like that in her life.

But when she'd realized that he hadn't remembered…

"You took the coward's way out," she whispered to herself, and felt her face heat with embarrassment. Better than the desire that had burned through her veins at the sight of him this morning dressed only in jeans.

She was just glad he didn't remember. What had possessed her to fall into the cowboy's arms last night? Lily didn't delude herself. Seeing Gerald again had thrown her into a tailspin. She'd felt all the hurt and betrayal and a part of her had wanted to forget—and possibly even the score.

Lily laid her head on her arms on the table. She knew it had been a lot more than just escape or getting even with Gerald. She'd *wanted* Tag. Wanted him in a way she hadn't even been able to imagine. He was everything Gerald wasn't. She'd known instinctively that their lovemaking would be nothing like what she'd known with her former fiancé.

"Boy howdy," she said, repeating an expression she'd picked up from Tag. As she heard Tag come out of the bedroom, she lifted her head and pushed away those embarrassing thoughts. She hated lying to him. Fortunately Tag had remembered just enough with the pills she'd given him to think he'd dreamed their wanton night of passion. Best leave it that way since it was never happening again.

The thought gave her a dull ache at her center.

What made her angry with herself aside from lying to Tag was that she felt as if she'd cheated on Gerald. She knew that made no sense. She owed him nothing— less than nothing. But she also knew that he wouldn't have come all the way from California and driven up to her house in a blizzard last night if he wasn't planning on asking her to take him back.

She told herself that she and Gerald belonged together. They were perfect for each other. Both math nerds, they had their careers in common. Last night had just been one of those crazy things that never happened to a woman like her.

Lily convinced herself that she would put it behind

her. Gerald was her future. She would forgive him and they would get married—just as it was meant to be.

She quickly straightened as Tag came into the room. But she kept her eyes on the computer screen even though she'd memorized the letters there since she'd looked at them so many times. Remembering she'd said she would pour Tag a cup of coffee, she jumped up and bumped into the edge of the table.

Her coffee sloshed over onto some of the papers. She lunged for them and, off balance, stumbled into Tag—the very last thing she wanted to do.

"EASY," TAG SAID as he caught her.

"I was going to get your coffee," Lily said, more nervous than he'd ever seen her.

"I can get my own coffee. Are you all right?" Holding her like this, he could feel her soft, full curves. He recognized every one of them, he thought with a start. His imagination was great, but not this good. Something had happened last night. But why would she lie?

Because you let her think you couldn't remember, you damned fool.

She pulled away as if realizing he was remembering last night. Or was he still deluding himself? She turned her back to him as she poured his coffee. He could see that her hands were shaking.

Tag wanted to call her on her lie, but when she turned back to him, he saw the glow in her cheeks. Could she be embarrassed about last night? She'd definitely let her hair down, so to speak. How innocent *was* this woman? Surely there were other men besides dull Gerald.

"Thank you," he said as he took the coffee cup she offered him. Lily was clearly rattled. Maybe she regretted last night and really was embarrassed.

What was it she had said? "Do I seem like the kind of woman who would fall into bed with a man I hardly know?"

"So, what's this about a code?" he asked, and took a sip of his coffee. He saw Lily's instant relief as she hurriedly sat back down at the computer. He could see where she had been writing a series of numbers and letters on scratch paper.

"After I came back here, I began to play with the letters. I know they appear to be random, but I don't think they are," she said, eyes bright. She clearly loved this stuff. "They appear to be part of a code. Julius Caesar invented one like it nearly two thousand years ago. He was invading countries to increase the size of the Roman Empire and he needed a way to communicate his battle plans with his generals without the enemy finding out by intercepting his messages."

"How do you know all this?" Tag asked, even more intrigued by this woman.

"It's math. Simple addition or subtraction, actually. Caesar, instead of writing the letter *A,* would write the letter that comes three places further in the alphabet, the letter *D.* When he got to the end of the alphabet, he would go right back to the beginning so instead of an *X,* he would write an *A.* You get the idea."

He did, but he wondered how the devil she'd figured that out and said as much.

"The more I studied the letters, the more they didn't appear random at all. The spaces made me think they were a list of names."

"Written in code?"

She nodded, her eyes bright. She was in her element. He wondered if he would ever see all the different sides of Lily McCabe. "A version of Caesar shift."

"And you can read what it says?"

"Not completely yet. It's a case of trial and error with only twenty-five different possible shifts before you can see a pattern. Caesar shifted the alphabet forward three spaces. This code is tougher, but in the end it will come down to simple mathematics."

He couldn't help smiling at her passion. He had a flash of her in his arms, naked, her skin silken and scented with jasmine, her mouth wet as she dropped it to his. Tag shook himself, the image so real he almost kissed her.

She didn't seem to notice. She was studying the letters on the page and her scribbles again. "Though I would have thought someone who didn't want the code deciphered would have used symbols instead of letters," she said, bending over one of the papers. "That way there could be four-hundred-billion possible combinations instead of only twenty-five. Not that it couldn't be broken by frequency analysis, though. Mary, Queen of Scots, used symbols for her code when plotting against Elizabeth the First. It got her beheaded."

Lily stopped talking and looked up at him, her gaze locking with his. "Your eyes haven't glazed over," she said, sounding surprised.

"This is fascinating. I'm amazed. How did you figure it out?"

"I'm using the frequency analysis method. Since *E, T* and *A* are the most frequently used letters in the English alphabet and there are eighteen *W*s and sixteen *A*s… The *A*s are not really *A*s, you understand. Once you have the most-used letters, it is just a matter of figuring out the rest of them."

He watched her bite her lower lip in thought.

"I can't help thinking whoever made up the code is

a novice at this," she said. "They probably went online, typed in codes and thought 'here's one.' The problem is they must have written this in a hurry because they made mistakes, which is making it harder for me to decode."

Nothing about what she was doing looked simple to him. Just staring at the letters made his headache worse.

"I should be able to break it soon," she assured him.

"Lily, I have a bad feeling that the reason Mia's condo was ransacked and my father's, too, was that they were looking for this thumb drive."

"Then you should take it to the marshal," she said, handing it to him. "I have a copy of the letters on my computer, so I can keep working on the code."

He nodded, although he had no intention of taking it to the marshal. Not until he knew which side of the fence Hud Savage was on.

"Until we know what's really on this," he said, "I wouldn't mention it to anyone, all right?"

She nodded.

"I need to get to the hospital and see my father, but I don't like leaving you here snowed in alone."

She waved him off. "The plows should be along in the next hour or so if you want to take my SUV."

He wasn't about to leave her here without a vehicle even if he thought he could bust through the drifts. "Are those your brother's cross-country skis and boots by the door? If you don't mind me borrowing them, I'll ski down to the road and hitch a ride. My brothers and I used to do that all the time when we were kids."

"If you're sure…." She turned back to the papers on the table. "I'll keep working on the code and let you know when I get it finished."

She sounded as if she would be glad when he left her

at it. He was reminded that she also had plans to talk to her former fiancé today. He felt a hard knot form in his stomach. Jealousy? Hell, yes.

Except he had nothing to be jealous about, right? Last night hadn't happened. At least that was the way Lily wanted it. He fought the urge to touch her hair, remembering the feel of it between his fingers.

"I want you to have this." He held out the pistol he'd taken from his father's. "I need to know that you are safe."

She shook her head and pulled back. "I don't like guns."

"All you have to do is point it and shoot."

Lily held up both hands. "I don't want it. I could never…" She shook her head again.

"Just in case," Tag said as he laid it on the table, telling himself that if someone broke into her house and tried to hurt her, she would get over her fear of guns quickly. At least he hoped that was true.

LILY STOOD AT the window, watching Tag cross-country ski down the snowed-in road until he disappeared from sight. He glided through the new snow with no wasted movement. She could practically see the muscles rippling in his arms and back.

At the memory of the feel of those muscles, she shivered and stepped away from the window, cradling her mug of hot coffee to chase away the chill. Why had she lied to him about last night?

It wasn't a lie. She wasn't the kind of woman to fall into a stranger's arms. Nor did she recognize that woman who'd made such passionate love to Tag last night.

What had she been thinking? She was still shaken.

True, she'd been thrown completely off balance by finding Gerald at her door.

In her heart of hearts, she'd dreamed of him coming back, begging her to forgive him. She'd just expected it to happen a lot sooner. That *was* what he wanted to talk to her about, wasn't it? He wanted her back. He'd realized what a colossal mistake he'd made. That was what it had to be. Gerald was safe, and right now she wanted safe, didn't she?

What would have happened if Tag hadn't shown up when he had? Would she have let Gerald stay? Would they have made love as they'd done in the past? Or would they have had a wild, passionate night as she had with Tag?

Wasn't that what she'd always wanted?

As hard as she tried, she couldn't imagine Gerald ever being like that.

But their relationship was built on intellect and a shared passion for math, she reminded herself.

She closed her eyes, images of her lovemaking with Tag making her go weak in the knees. She quickly opened her eyes. She'd never get the code finished if she kept letting her mind stray.

And yet as she headed for the computer again, she couldn't deny the ache low in her belly. She wanted Tag again.

That was why she had to see Gerald. She needed to put an end to these thoughts. All last night had been was one wild fling before she took Gerald back.

And if Tag had remembered last night?

Lily sighed and glanced toward the open bedroom door and the rumpled sheets. The two of them would be in that bed right now.

She blew out a sigh that lifted her drying bangs from

her forehead. Her skin felt oversensitive as if Tag's touch was branded on it. She hugged herself for a moment, remembering how wonderful he'd been. She worried though that he was in trouble because of the thumb drive.

Determined to figure out the code, she had started back toward the table and her laptop when she saw the gun. Stepping to it, she gingerly picked it up with two fingers, then wasn't sure what to do with it.

One of the drawers in the kitchen was still open from where she'd gotten a clean dish towel out this morning. She walked over to it and dropped the gun into the drawer and closed it. She wouldn't need it. Even if she did, she knew she could never fire it.

She had started back to work on the code when the phone rang not ten minutes later. The sound irritably jerked her out of her calculations. She saw it was Gerald and almost didn't answer.

ONCE TAG REACHED the main road, he easily caught a ride to his father's cabin. The day was bright, sunny and beautiful, so there was a lot of traffic coming and going on the road to the ski hills.

At his father's cabin, he called the rental company about the wrecked SUV. The cabin was still a mess, but the crime-scene tape had been removed. He changed clothes and headed for the two-car log garage next to the cabin, anxious to get to the hospital and see his father.

But when the garage door moaned open, he saw something that stopped him dead. His father's SUV was gone. With a start, he remembered that the SUV had been parked outside yesterday when he'd found his father had been attacked.

He tried to tell himself that a friend must have borrowed it as he climbed into Harlan's old pickup. The key was in the ignition. Harlan always left his keys in his rigs as if daring someone to steal them. Maybe that was what had happened, although he feared there was an even simpler explanation.

When he reached the hospital and walked into his father's room, Tag wasn't surprised to find the bed empty.

"Are you looking for Mr. Cardwell?" a nurse asked as he let the door close with a curse.

"Yes. Has he been moved to another room?" He knew he was only deluding himself.

"I'm sorry, but he checked himself out."

"Against doctor's orders, right?"

The nurse smiled and nodded. "He is a very stubborn man."

"Isn't he?" Stubborn and hiding something. Tag hated to think what.

There were only two other places he could think of to look for his father. He tried his cousin Dana's first.

Tag found her and her two oldest kids putting the finishing touches on the worst-looking Christmas tree he'd ever seen.

"Do. Not. Say. A. Word," she warned him, and grinned. "This tree needed a Christmas."

"It needs limbs and needles," Tag said. "Jingle Bells" played on the radio in the kitchen, and he thought he smelled ginger cookies baking. For a moment, he wanted to help string the paper garland the children had made and curl up in front of the fire. This was the Christmas he'd envisioned. Not one involving lies and murder.

"It's one of Mama's orphan trees," six-year-old Hank said. "It made Daddy laugh."

"But it made Mama cry," the younger Mary said.

"Tears of joy," Dana hurriedly added, and smoothed a hand over Mary's dark hair so like her mother's. "Want to join in the fun?"

"Thanks, but I need to find my father. You haven't seen him, by any chance, have you?"

Dana shook her head. "I did hear that he checked himself out of the hospital. I'm sure he's fine."

Tag wasn't so sure about that. "You haven't heard from Angus, have you?"

"Grandpa is away on business," Hank said, making his mother smile.

"I thought I'd check his favorite bar...." He could see that Dana wasn't going to be of any help. Because she didn't understand her father any better than he did his, she'd taken a "whatever" attitude. He wished he could.

ACE LOOKED UP when Lily walked into the bar. "What's wrong?"

Where did she begin? "Someone ran Tag off the road last night on the way to my place. He could have been killed. He played it down, but I think it has something to do with the thumb drive he found."

"Tag?" Her brother grinned. "On the way to your place? I thought there was a rosy glow to your cheeks."

If he only knew. "That's all you got out of what I just told you?" She shook her head. "Gerald showed up at my place last night."

That got his attention and wiped away Ace's cat-who-ate-the-canary grin—just as she knew it would. "What did that bastard want?"

"I'm pretty sure he wants me back."

"What?" Ace demanded. "I hope you told him where he could stick—"

"Tag interrupted whatever Gerald was going to say. I'm on my way to meet Gerald now."

"You're actually thinking of going back to him."

Her brother had a way of seeing through her that annoyed Lily to no end. "Gerald and I have—"

"So help me, if you take that lily-livered son of a b—"

"It's my life, Ace."

He shook his head. "Exactly. You want to spend it with a stiff shirt like Gerald? Or a man like Tag Cardwell?"

She wanted to point out that neither Tag nor any other man like him had asked, but changed the subject. "Did you hear what I said about someone running Tag off the road last night?"

Ace nodded. "Does he think it was an accident?"

"He pretended it was."

Her brother rubbed his jaw. "Teresa hasn't turned up yet, and with Mia murdered... I just don't understand it. This is usually such a safe place."

She glanced at her watch.

"Don't do it, Lily."

She looked at her brother, confused for a moment.

"I know you. You're going to end up feeling guilty for not taking him back—after *he* deserted you on your wedding day." He shook his head again. "Why aren't you mad? You should be spitting nails. He doesn't deserve you."

She nodded, thinking Tag had pretty much said the same thing. "I have to go. Are you opening the bar tonight?"

"Got to. If Teresa isn't back, I'm going to need you to work."

"Don't worry. I'll be here."

"Lily?"

She had started to leave, but now she turned back to look at her brother. Even frowning, he was drop-dead gorgeous. Why hadn't some woman snatched him up? Or was he like her? Always playing it safe, afraid to really let go and fall for someone who made him see fireworks on a freezing winter night just before Christmas.

Ace shook head as if changing his mind about whatever he had been going to say. "Just be careful, okay?"

She had to smile. Too bad he hadn't been around last night to warn her. It was a little too late now. "Always levelheaded. That's me. And, Ace, don't mention the thumb drive to anyone, okay?"

CHAPTER NINE

IT HAD BEEN weeks in this prison and Camilla was growing all the more impatient. She was wondering what she was going to have to do to make Edna's acquaintance, when one of the woman's minions brought her a note.

She had to think outside the box to decipher the misspelled words, but then again not everyone in prison had a master's degree. Hers was in psychology. Basically, a con man's dream curriculum. No wonder she was so good at reading people.

Except for Hud Savage. You certainly read him wrong, didn't you, Miss Smarty-Pants?

Her mother's voice. She ground her teeth. That "misstep" had cost her dearly. Which was why retribution had such a nice ring to it. *You know retribution, don't you, Mother?*

The note from Edna wasn't a request, but a command appearance, making her think about telling the inmate standing in front of her what she could do with her missive. The woman, a skinny former addict with a tattoo of a rattlesnake around her right wrist, was known as Snakebite. The nickname probably had more to do with her disposition, though, than the tattoo.

Feeling in a generous mood and needing to get her plan moving, she merely smiled and said, "Okay."

"Now, bitch."

Camilla considered kicking the woman's butt, convinced she could take her.

Snakebite had the good sense to take a step back as Camilla got to her feet.

Edna was waiting for them in the craft area of the prison. A kind-looking woman with a huge bosom and small delicate hands, she looked as if she should be in a kitchen baking chocolate-chip cookies for her grandkids. Which could explain her nickname, Grams.

"I heard you've been asking around about me," Grams said, and motioned to the chair across the small table from her. Snakebite took a position next to the wall along with another of Edna's "girls," a large woman called Moose.

"I heard you were the kind of woman who got things done."

Grams lifted an eyebrow.

Camilla leaned in closer. "I didn't get a chance to tidy up before I got sent here."

Grams smiled. "So you're a neat freak?"

She laughed and leaned back. "I guess I am."

"It isn't cheap cleaning up messes."

Camilla smiled. She had money stashed around the country under a dozen different names and she had ways to get to it. "I didn't think it would be."

"How do I know I can trust you?" Grams asked.

"The same way I know I can trust you. Otherwise how would either of us be able to sleep at night?"

The older woman laughed again and slid a pen and paper across the table.

Camilla wrote "Marshal Hud Savage" on the slip of paper and slid it back across along with the pen.

Grams raised a brow again.

"Is there a problem?" Camilla asked.

"Not a problem exactly. I'm just curious. Is this personal or business?"

"I wouldn't think you would care. It's personal," Camilla said, remembering the way Hud had rebuked her. "It's *very* personal."

Grams shrugged and tucked the piece of paper into her bra. "I'll get back to you."

"How long before it's done?"

"Patience," she said as she pushed herself to her feet. "Time is relative in here. But I think you'll be pleased." With that, Grams padded off, her "girls" behind her.

Camilla picked up a lump of clay from a tub left on the table and began twisting it in her hands. First Hud. Then she would take care of the rest of his precious family. As Grams said, she had nothing but time.

WHEN GERALD OPENED his motel room door, Lily took a step back.

"Don't look so surprised to see me," he said irritably. "You act as if you expected me to leave town before you arrived."

When he'd called, he'd sounded…odd. Hurt, no doubt because she hadn't fallen into his arms instantly. Hadn't forgiven him without hesitation. That she'd been more concerned with Tag than him last night.

"Truthfully, Gerald, I don't know what to expect from you," she said as he moved aside so she could step in out of the cold. She took in the room. Gerald had always been excessively neat. The bed was made, his suitcase perfectly packed and open on the luggage rack by the wall.

"I told you I needed to talk to you," he said behind her, a slight whine in his voice.

She turned to look at him. "But you didn't say why."

"I didn't get a chance before your…friend showed up. Lily, I hate to see you get involved with someone like him."

"I beg your pardon?"

"That cowboy. What could you possibly have in common with him?"

If he only knew. "That's none of your business."

Gerald let out a snort. "You can't be falling for a man like that."

She started to deny that she was falling for Tag but stopped herself. "I can fall for anyone I want to."

"Lily," he said impatiently.

"Gerald," she said, matching his tone.

His eyes narrowed.

"Gerald, just tell me what it is you want."

He let out a long sigh. "I had hoped we could sit down and discuss this reasonably like intelligent adults, but if you insist…" He met her gaze. "I shouldn't have done what I did."

"No, you shouldn't have. Is that all?"

"No," he snapped. "I told you about my little sister who lives in California."

Lily frowned. "She works for a bank."

"An investment company," he said, and looked away. "She got into some trouble. I had to…help her." His gaze met hers. "I didn't want to hurt you, but I really had no choice. She's my little sister. That's why I took the job in California, why I've done everything that I have."

"You had a choice, Gerald. You could have told me about your sister, you could have told me you didn't want to get married *before* the wedding. Don't tell me you didn't have a choice."

"You are making this very difficult, Lily."

"Oh, I'm sorry, Gerald." He usually didn't get sarcasm, but she had laid it on so thick, even he got it.

He had the decency to look chastised. "I'm sure it was also difficult for you."

"Difficult, Gerald? You mean when I had to explain to our friends and family why you left me standing at the altar when I didn't have the *slightest* idea?" she demanded, surprised at her anger. Even more surprised that she was letting it out. Gerald had always felt such a show of emotions distasteful at best. In her, he'd seen any emotional display as a sign of immaturity. Since he was eleven years her senior, she'd locked up all her emotions so as not to seem childish.

But now she thought of Tag and her brother, both filled with righteous indignation over what Gerald had done to her and demanding to know why she wasn't furious. Because she had every right. Just as she had every right to let her anger come out now.

"I apologized for that," Gerald said evenly.

"Six months later," she pointed out. "Not that I have any more idea now than I did then why you would do such a rude, disrespectful, embarrassing, ob—"

"I couldn't go through with it right then. My sister needed me and I...I panicked, all right?"

She raised a brow. "*You* panicked?"

"You have to know how hard this is to admit. I found myself in a position where I had to make a decision.... I should have told you."

"You think?" Speaking of childish.

He narrowed his eyes as he studied her. "I knew you'd be upset, but I had hoped you wouldn't be bitter."

She almost laughed.

"You seem so...different."

She *did* laugh. "You know, Gerald, being stood up at the altar changes a person."

He seemed not to know what to say.

Lily hadn't thought she'd changed from the woman who'd agreed to marry the head of the math department at the university, but she realized she had. She was stronger, just as her brother had said. She'd gotten over the initial pain and realized that she'd survived one of the most awful things that could happen to a woman.

Last night when she'd seen Gerald, all those old initial feelings had come back in a rush. Followed quickly by the hurt and betrayal.

Since then, she'd let herself admit that she *was* angry. No, she was furious with him and all the more furious with herself because she'd actually thought about taking him back. She'd actually wanted that ordered life he'd promised.

But standing here with him now, she knew that her night with Tag had changed all that. She'd never loved Gerald the way a woman should love a man she was about to marry. Tag had shown her what she'd been missing. Passion. And now that she'd experienced it, she could never go back to that lukewarm idea of love she'd shared with Gerald.

Nor had Gerald loved her enough to be honest with her. Plus, as Tag had said, Gerald was a coward for not facing her on their wedding day.

"Was there something else?" she asked her former fiancé, feeling the weight of the past lift from her shoulders.

Gerald looked confused. He'd obviously come to her thinking all he had to do was tell her he was sorry and that he wanted her back. He seemed more than a little astonished that that hadn't been the case.

"I guess there is nothing else to say. I made the decision to help my sister. If it matters, you're making that decision easier."

"I'm all about making your life easier, Gerald," she said.

"I didn't mean to make you angry again," he added quickly. "You know I tend to speak sometimes without considering how it affects others."

She started for the door.

"I couldn't help noticing when I was at your house that you were working on something," he said. "Is it something I can help you with?"

Lily turned to look at him. "That's nice of you, but—"

"I would like to help you. I'd feel better about the way I'm leaving things between us," he said.

She felt herself weaken. She'd been interrupted so much she hadn't been able to work on decoding the data she'd taken off the thumb drive. If Tag was right and this information was important in Mia's murder case… "I *could* use your help."

He looked pleased as well as curious as she dug in her bag and pulled out the papers she'd been working on. She set them on the desk, spreading them out as she explained what she'd come up with so far.

"It would be easier if I had the original," he said, glancing at the papers.

"I don't have it with me."

He nodded, pulled up a chair and, taking one of his pens from his pocket protector, began to check her work—just as he had done when he was her teacher.

Lily watched him. She'd known how easily he could

be distracted with a puzzle involving math. The mathematician in her still loved that about him.

"Interesting," he said as he bent over the letters.

GUHA BKOPAR
CAKNCA IKKNA
BNWJG IKKJAU
HSQ SWUJA
YHAPA NWJZ
NWU AIANU

LWQH XNKSJ
IEW ZQJYWJ
YWH BNWJGHEJ
HWNO HWJZANO
DWNHWJ YWNZSAHH
DQZ OWRWCA

She'd decoded enough to see a pattern, but it hadn't held up either because whoever had come up with the code had been in a hurry and made mistakes or because they'd gotten confused and sloppy.

As she watched Gerald work, she saw that she'd been right. There were two lists of names. It amazed her how quickly he filled in the names. She had to give him credit. Gerald really was a master at this sort of thing.

"You were on the right track," he said. "Just off a little." Within minutes, he'd come up with two lists of names. "Is this all?" he asked, sounding disappointed as he handed the sheets to her and rose from the chair. "You're sure there was nothing more on the original data?" He obviously would have much preferred some cryptic message. She would have, as well.

She glanced at the names, one of them taking her breath away.

Gerald didn't seem to notice as he walked over and closed his suitcase with a finality that rang through the room. But when he turned toward her again, he said, "You and I are good together, Lily. You need me, now maybe more than you realize. I should leave you my cell phone number in case you change your—"

"I won't change my mind, Gerald," she said as she shoved the papers into her shoulder bag with trembling fingers.

"I see." He had pulled out his business card as if about to write his new cell phone number on it, but now he stuck it back into his pocket. "I hope you don't live to regret this, Lily. Clearly your behavior has taken a dangerous trajectory—if that cowboy is any indication."

She smiled. She'd never been one to hold grudges, always quick to forgive and forget. But she took some satisfaction in realizing that Gerald was jealous. If he only knew.... "Goodbye, Gerald."

He started to reach for her as if to kiss her cheek as he used to do when they parted, but she stepped back and walked out the door, leaving him standing there.

She had a death grip on her shoulder bag and the papers inside, and couldn't wait to show Tag. As she walked out, she heard Gerald's cell phone ring.

"Yes, I talked to her," he said into the phone. "No, she won't listen to reason."

Gerald had apparently involved one of his sisters, Lily thought as she rushed to her vehicle. *No, she won't listen to reason?* She gritted her teeth, never more glad that she hadn't weakened and gone back to the man.

She was so deep in her thoughts that she didn't even notice the large black SUV parked next to her on the driver's side. Nor did she hear the back door of the SUV open or the man jump out directly behind her.

Lily didn't even have time to scream as something wet and awful smelling was clamped over her mouth and she was dragged into the black pit of darkness in the back of the massive SUV.

CHAPTER TEN

HUD GOT THE call on his way from the hospital. He'd gone by to see Harlan Cardwell only to find that the man had left without anyone having seen him leave.

The marshal listened to the news on the other end of the line with the same sinking feeling he'd had earlier. Another young woman's body had been found.

"I'll be right there," he said, hung up and turned on his flashing lights and siren. If he could have gotten his hands on Harlan Cardwell right now…

Last night at the hospital he'd demanded to know more than the information he'd been given yesterday at the ranch.

"We think it's possible Mia passed information to someone when she knew she was in trouble," Harlan told him. "She and Teresa Evans were apparently friends. Teresa would be the most likely person to give the data to if she was in trouble, which could explain Teresa's disappearance."

Hud had shaken his head in frustration.

"I wish I had an answer for you. They tried to kill me earlier. If Tag hadn't come along when he did…"

"Aren't you getting too old for this?"

Harlan had chuckled even though it must have hurt him. "I only got involved again because of Mia." His voice broke. He cleared his throat. "I just talked to the coroner a few minutes before you came in. Mia had been drugged. We can only assume one of the patrons at the bar stuck her. She must have realized it too late to get the item to me. I'm sure she did everything she could to finish her mission."

"If Mia gave whatever this information is to Teresa Evans, then they have it."

Harlan shook his head. "Apparently Teresa didn't have it. They're still looking for it. At least that's what I'm hearing."

"How many more are they going to kill to get it?" Hud had demanded, and seen the answer in Harlan's eyes.

So the call that a young woman had been found on the ice at the edge of the Gallatin River hadn't come as a surprise—just another blow. Hud felt helpless for the second time in his life. The other time, just months ago, was when he realized a psychopath had his wife and children.

TAG GLANCED AT his watch and then tried Lily's cell phone again. It went straight to voice mail just as it had done the three times he'd tried before. He didn't leave a message.

He'd been trying since he'd gotten her cryptic message.

"Tag, the list is decoded. There's a name on here... you need to see. Call me. It's urgent."

When Lily had mentioned that she thought the thumb drive had two lists of names on it, he'd thought of his father. Was his father's name on it?

Tag thought of the ransacked cabin. His hand went to his pocket. He closed his fingers over the small computer flash drive. He'd thought taking it would protect

Lily. But now she'd decoded it and had found a name. A name that had put her in danger?

Earlier he'd driven down to the Corral Bar, but the bartender said he hadn't seen Angus or Harlan since yesterday. He didn't seem that surprised, which Tag took to mean both men disappeared occasionally.

It baffled him as he drove back toward Big Sky.

Like a lot of Montana winter days, this one was blinding with brilliance. The sun hung in a cloudless robin's-egg-blue sky and now shone on the fresh-fallen snow, turning it into a carpet of prisms.

As he pulled up in front of the Canyon Bar and climbed out, he sucked in a lungful of the freezing air. Nearby pines scented the frosty breeze. He didn't see Lily's car, but he figured her brother would have heard from her by now. The fresh snow creaked beneath his boot soles as he crossed to the bar.

The front door was open even though the bar wasn't scheduled to open for another hour. As the door closed on the bright winter day behind him, Tag stopped just inside to let his eyes adjust to the semidarkness.

"We don't open for another..." Ace's words died off as he looked up from behind the bar. "Tag, come on in. I forgot to relock the door after Lily left."

"So you've seen her today?" Tag asked as he walked over to the bar.

Ace's expression changed into one of mild amusement. "She looked better than I'd seen her looking in a long time."

"Then she told you about Gerald."

"Gerald didn't put those roses in her cheeks," he said with a laugh. "What can I get you to drink?"

"Nothing, but thanks. I was looking for Lily."

"Like I said, she was by earlier. Gerald called her.

She went to see him." Ace stopped in midmotion, a bar glass half-washed in his hand. "You met Gerald, right?"

"Last night."

"Then you know he's all wrong for her."

Tag didn't feel he could weigh in on that.

"I hate it, but she went to hear him out," Ace said with a disgusted shake of his head. "I was hoping we'd seen the last of him. I'm afraid she'll go back to him. Maybe already has."

That would explain why Lily wasn't answering her phone. "Maybe I will have that drink, after all," Tag said, and took a stool. "Just a draft beer."

Ace laughed and reached for a clean glass as the bar door opened again and a large silhouette filled it.

HUD PARKED AT the edge of the fishing access road a few hundred yards from the river and walked. His head ached, his stomach felt oily. It took all his mental strength not to stop and throw up in the fresh snow at the edge of the road.

He could see the flashing lights ahead. The coroner had been called. Second time in two days. Another dead young woman.

The body lay on the edge of the thick aquamarine-blue ice in a bed of snow. At first glance it appeared the woman had lain down in the snow to make a snow angel. Her arms were spread wide, facedown, legs also splayed. He'd guess she'd been thrown there and that was how she'd landed. Which meant she'd been dead before she hit because she hadn't made a snow angel. She hadn't moved.

"What do we have?" Hud asked the coroner after giving a nod to his new deputy, a man by the name of Jake Thorton. He'd come highly recommended but hadn't been tested yet. Nor had Hud made a point of getting to know the man. Jake seemed to keep to himself, which was just fine with his boss.

"Looks like strangulation," the coroner said. "Maybe that combined with hypothermia. Won't know until the autopsy. But she didn't die here."

Hud nodded. "Do we have an ID?"

"Found her purse in the snow over there," Deputy Thorton said. "Her name, according to her Montana driver's license and photo, is Teresa Marie Evans, the missing woman last seen at the Canyon Bar."

Teresa had a winter scarf tied too tightly around her neck—just like Mia. "Tire tracks?" Hud asked Jake.

"The road hadn't been plowed. Didn't look as if any vehicles had been down it. But there were tracks. I saw that she was dropped by snowmobile," he said. "I took photos."

Hud nodded at the young handsome deputy, thankful he was on the case since his own mind was whirling. All his self-doubts seemed to surface in light of another death. Dropped by snowmobile just like the last one.

"I'll let you handle this, notify the family, do what has to be done," he told Jake, and looked at his watch. Police officer Paul Brown's funeral was in two hours. Hud wasn't sure how much more death he could take.

As THE MAN stepped into the Canyon Bar, the door closing behind him, Tag saw that it was Gerald, Lily's former fiancé. Or should he say now current fiancé? Had Lily gone back to him?

He waited almost expectantly for Gerald to approach the bar. The beer he'd downed turned sour in his stomach as he braced himself for the news. Like her brother, Ace, Tag thought this man was all wrong for the woman he'd made love to last night. He reminded himself that Lily had regretted their lovemaking. Had that alone driven her back into this man's arms?

"Lily left this," Gerald said, and dropped a torn sheet of paper on the bar.

Tag's first thought was that she'd left a note for her brother.

"What am I supposed to do with this?" Ace asked after giving it a cursory glance and tossing it back on the bar.

"I wonder why I wasted my time," Gerald said with a shake of his head, and turned to leave.

Tag shifted on the stool to see what was on the sheet of paper. He recognized Lily's neat script. His pulse took off like a rocket when he saw the familiar array of letters from the thumb drive.

He quickly picked up the partial sheet of paper. It had been torn. Only a few of the original letters from the thumb drive were on the sheet. Next to them were other letters that made...*names.*

He didn't recognize any of them and frowned. Lily had been upset on the phone. *"Tag, the list is decoded. There's a name on here...you need to see. Call me. It's urgent."*

She'd wanted him to see a name, but it wasn't on this portion of the original sheet of paper.

"Wait a minute," he called to Gerald's retreating back. "Where's Lily?"

Gerald stopped, impatience in his stance, and then turned with a sigh. "You're asking *me?*"

"*You're* the one she went to see," Ace interjected.

Lily had solved the code. Whatever name had upset her wasn't on this sheet. Tag slid off his stool and moved quickly to Gerald. "*Where's* Lily?"

Gerald gave him a smug, satisfied smile. "The last time I saw her she was leaving my motel room."

"Did you see where she went from there?"

He looked angry. "If you must know, I wasn't paying any attention."

Tag turned back to the bar and Ace. "Lily's message earlier said it was urgent I see these names, but I don't recognize any of them. Where are the rest of them?"

"What does it matter?" Gerald asked sarcastically but he stepped back toward the bar.

"Trust me, it might be a matter of life or death."

"Don't tell me she's in trouble because of what is written on that paper," Ace said as he leaned across the bar to take the scrap of paper in Tag's hand.

"Lily was convinced these letters had something to do with Mia Duncan's murder."

Ace let out a curse.

"That list of names?" Gerald asked. "*Murder?* This was exactly what I feared when Lily insisted on working in a...bar."

"Gerald," Ace said in clear warning. "Don't make me come over this counter and punch you." He turned to Tag. "What do we do?"

"If Lily's right, then I know who I need to talk to," Tag said. "If things go badly, though, can I depend on you to bail me out of jail?"

"I'm going with you," Ace said only seconds before a bunch of skiers came through the door and headed for an empty table. "I'll close the bar and—"

"No. Lily might come back here. Or you might be contacted. Anyway, you can't get me out of jail if you're in there with me." Tag scribbled his cell phone number on a bar napkin. "Call me if you hear anything."

Ace nodded as another group of patrons came

through the bar door. Reggie showed up then in jeans and the Canyon Bar T-shirt, like the one Lily had been wearing the first night Tag met her. The night he'd also met Mia Duncan.

"I suppose you're both going to just assume I would be of no help?" Gerald asked.

"Call the bar if you hear from Lily," Tag told him, thinking Lily might contact Gerald before either him or her brother. "Ace will pass along the message." He started for the door.

"That scrap of paper in your hand. That has only some of the names on the lists Lily showed me," Gerald said. "I can't imagine how it could matter, but I'm the one who helped her decode them. If you have the thumb drive…"

Tag stopped at the door and turned. His hand went to the thumb drive in his pocket. "How do you know about that?"

Gerald rolled his eyes. "How do you think? Lily asked me to help her finish decoding the names."

So it was like that, Tag thought. Lily wouldn't have told him about the thumb drive or asked him unless she trusted him, unless she had gone back to him.

"Ace, can we borrow your computer?" Tag asked, and led the way to Ace's office.

Gerald sat down behind the desk, then held out his hand. Tag dropped the thumb drive into it and sat as Gerald went to work. It didn't take him long. When he finished, he printed out a sheet with the names on them and handed both it and the thumb drive back to him.

Two lists of names, just as Lily had suspected. The names began to jump off the page at him. This was why Lily had wanted him to see them.

Mia Duncan's name was high on the list.

Not far under it was the name Harlan Cardwell. Directly under that was Marshal Hud Savage.

KYLE FOSTER
GEORGE MOORE
FRANK MOONEY
LOU WAYNE
CLETE RAND
RAY EMERY

PAUL BROWN
MIA DUNCAN
CAL FRANKLIN
LARS LANDERS
HARLAN CARDWELL
HUD SAVAGE

What the hell is this? He had no idea, but he was all the more worried about Lily. "You're sure you don't know where Lily went after she left your motel room?" he asked Gerald.

"I thought she must have left with you."

"Why would you think that?"

"Because she left her SUV in the parking lot."

"What parking lot?" Tag demanded, feeling his heart slamming against his rib cage. The names on the list. While he had no idea what they meant, he had a terrible feeling that they had gotten Mia Duncan killed, his father beaten to within an inch of his life and both Mia's and his father's homes ransacked. And now Lily appeared to be missing.

"The Happy Trails Motel down the highway," Gerald said.

Tag headed for the door at a run, praying he was

wrong and that there was an explanation other than the one that had him terrified.

"I'll drive up to her house and check there," Gerald said to his retreating back. "You better not get her killed, Texas cowboy."

Tag didn't have time to go back and slug the suit or he would have.

The drive to the motel, although only half a mile, seemed to take forever.

He was in sight of it when he heard the news report on the radio. He hadn't even realized the radio was on, droning in the background, until he heard the announcement come on.

"A woman's body has been found along the Gallatin River two miles south of Big Sky. The name of the victim is being withheld pending notification of family. If anyone has any information, please call the marshal's office...."

An eighties song came on the radio.

Not Lily. No, it couldn't be Lily.

Ahead, he saw Lily's SUV parked off by itself. His stomach dropped. As he jumped out, he could see where another vehicle had pulled in next to it. And in the snow that the plow had left, he could see that there'd been a struggle.

Lily's boot-heel prints had made a short trail from her SUV driver's-side door to whatever had been parked next to it.

CHAPTER ELEVEN

As Tag drove straight to the marshal's office, he kept remembering the marshal and his father, heads together, arguing about something before his father gave Hud an envelope. Money? A bribe? A payoff?

Whatever it was, it had something to do with Mia Duncan—and if he wasn't wrong, the damned thumb drive in his pocket and the names on it.

He didn't know his cousin Dana's husband. This trip to Montana had been the first time they'd met. Was it possible Hud was crooked?

Tag hoped not for his cousin's sake. But look how she'd turned a blind eye to whatever Harlan and Angus did when they left the canyon. Would she be the same way if her husband were on the take?

All Tag knew was that he didn't trust the marshal. But right now he needed to know who had been found near the river. He glanced at the list again, surprised by the one name that seemed to be missing. Teresa Evans. How did she fit into all this? Or did she? He'd heard that she was missing. Was it her body that was found by the river?

He had to know.

Just as he had to know why both his father's and Hud's names were on the list. He had no idea what to make of that. Or how this list from the thumb drive could have anything to do with what was going on. Why would anyone be ransacking residences at Big Sky, let alone killing people for it?

All he could assume was that the names were important. *Why else had Mia put the thumb drive in his pocket?* he wondered as he stormed into the marshal's department and demanded to see Marshal Hud Savage. How important? He was about to find out since Hud Savage's name was on one of the lists.

"He's gone to a funeral," a pretty, redheaded young woman told him.

That threw him. "Whose funeral?"

"Officer Paul Brown."

The name was like a lightbulb coming on in his face. Paul Brown. He was also on the list.

"I just heard on the radio about a woman's body being found by the river." He held his breath. "Tell me it isn't Lily McCabe."

The woman dispatcher frowned. "Lily? No. But I can't give you—"

Not Lily. He felt his heart rate drop some. Not Lily. Not yet. "Where is the funeral?"

The dispatcher hesitated.

"I wouldn't ask but it's urgent," Tag said. "Another woman has disappeared."

"By now they would be heading for the graveside. Sunset. It's between Bozeman and Belgrade on the old highway. If you hurry—"

But Tag was already out the door.

LILY WOKE TO darkness, dying of thirst. Her mouth felt as if it had been stuffed with cotton balls. She tried to swallow as she sat up and blinked at the blackness around her.

At first she'd thought she was in the bedroom and

Tag was beside her. But in a flash, the earlier events came back with the terror of her abduction.

Panic overtook her like a blizzard. Where was she? Her hand touched something cold and she recoiled. As her eyes became more adjusted to the dark, though, she saw that it was only a water bottle.

She snatched it up and drank half of it before a thought surfaced that made her quickly pull it away from her lips.

What if it was drugged? Or poisoned? Or all the water she had for however long she was going to be trapped here?

She didn't kid herself that she could climb off this mattress and walk out of here. The edges of the room began to take shape as her eyes adjusted to the darkness. Knotty-pine walls, dark with age, a linoleum floor. No apparent windows. One door. She could make out a tiny strip of light around its frame.

A basement, she thought, in some older house or cabin. Probably a cabin, which might mean she was still in Big Sky.

She considered yelling for help only an instant before she heard heavy footfalls coming down what sounded like stairs above her.

Lily thought about getting up, hating to be at such a disadvantage on the bed, but when she tried, she found she was too weak to stand. Sliding on the mattress until her back was against the wall, she stared in the direction of the single door in and out of the room. She told herself that the person wasn't coming to kill her or he would have already done that, but she knew killers probably weren't logical.

Whoever was outside the door put down something on the floor. It made a shadow under the door. Then she heard the key being turned in the lock. The door swung open along with blinding light before a large figure filled the doorway.

STANDING AT THE edge of the graveside service, Marshal Hud Savage tightened his grip on his hat held at his side as he saw Tag Cardwell pull up and get out of his father's old pickup.

Hud was in no mood for trouble and yet one look at the young man's face and Hud knew that was what was heading for him. He stepped a few feet back from the others. "Not here," he said under his breath as Tag reached him.

"Here or you come with me now," Tag said quietly under his breath. "Your choice. Unless you want everyone here to know about you."

Hud gave him a sidelong glance. "I could have you arrested—"

"I have what you've all been looking for. Set up a trade for Lily. *Now.*"

That got Hud's attention. He turned and headed toward the old pickup Tag had arrived in. Once there, he turned on the man. "What the hell are you talking about?"

"Lily McCabe. I know you have her and if you hurt her—"

"Tag, I don't know what you're talking about. Is Lily missing?"

"I'm tired of playing games with you and my father and uncle," Tag said, and swore.

Hud listened as Tag told him about seeing the leather jacket on his father's couch, catching his father in a lie, seeing Hud and Harlan the day Mia Duncan's body turned up.

"You've got it all wrong," Hud said when Tag finished.

"Yeah, that's what my father keeps telling me. Where is he, by the way?"

Behind them, Hud heard the graveside funeral procession breaking up. "We can't talk about this here. What was that that part about a thumb drive?"

Tag smiled. "So you did hear me. Make the call. As soon as I see Lily—"

"I can see how you might think I'm involved in all this—"

"We don't have time to—"

"I'm telling you the truth. Show me what you have. Maybe between the two of us we can—"

"So help me, if you have touched a hair on her head—" Tag swore, and grabbed Hud by the throat. A minute later he was being pulled off the marshal by two other law enforcement officers who'd been at the funeral. A minute after that he was in handcuffs in the back of Marshal Hud Savage's patrol SUV on his way to jail.

"YOU'RE BEING CHEATED."

The raspy words entered Camilla's right ear, the hoarse whisper sending a chill down her spine. She was standing in the prison chow line, not that she was hungry. She ate because food kept her strong. If she ever had a chance of getting out of here, one way or the other, she needed to keep up her strength.

"Don't turn around."

She fought the urge.

"She shouldn't be charging you." She could feel the woman's breath on her neck, hot and damp and putrid.

Camilla waited. Prison was teaching her patience

and she'd become an astute student since she hadn't killed anyone yet.

"Just nod your head if I'm right." The woman moved closer. Camilla had to steel herself not to shudder. "You're paying Grams for a hit on a cowboy cop, right?"

Just like in high school, rumors ran rampant. This one just happened to be true.

She gave a short nod and could no longer contain the shudder.

The woman behind gave a snort. "His name was already on the list."

Camilla turned in her surprise to find Snakebite behind her. Their eyes met, Snakebite's as hard as obsidian. She turned back around as the line moved and felt sick to her stomach. Not because Grams had planned to charge her *and* someone else for the same hit. But that Marshal Hud Savage was about to be killed and it wouldn't be her doing.

She wanted to howl out her pain and yet she couldn't even step out of line. She shuffled forward, the smell of some awful casserole filling her nostrils and making her even more nauseated.

I have to get out of here.

Not just out of the line, but out of the damned prison.

I have to get out of here.

Camilla hadn't realized she'd said the words aloud. Not until she heard the raspy voice answer.

"I thought you might say that."

MARSHAL HUD SAVAGE pulled off onto a narrow snowy road that ended at the river's edge.

"You should take off my handcuffs," Tag said from the back of the patrol SUV. "Might look more believable that I made a run for it when you kill me."

Hud cut the engine and turned to look at him in surprise. "You think I'm going to kill you?" He let out a curse and shook his head. For months he'd been telling himself he'd lost his edge. That he wasn't any good at this anymore. He'd never felt more assured of that than at this moment.

"I'm not a dirty cop," he said, feeling himself hit bottom. "Why would you think—"

Tag snorted. "I saw my father give you an envelope the morning Mia Duncan was found murdered. Tell me that envelope wasn't filled with money."

"It wasn't." He thought of the paperwork Harlan had finally turned over to him. The agency was always holding out on him. With a shock, he had just been told that he had a dead agent on his hands and Harlan had still wanted to keep secrets. They'd argued until Harlan had finally given him some information.

"Look, I don't care, all right?" Tag said. "I just want to find Lily."

"So do I. That's why you have to help me with what you know."

"You expect me to trust you after all the lies you've told me? I know my father was seeing Mia Duncan."

"You have it all wrong."

"So you all keep telling me," Tag snapped.

Hud took off his Stetson and raked a hand through his hair. "I don't know how you managed to get so deep in all this." He met Tag's gaze. "I pleaded with Harlan to tell you the truth, but he didn't want you involved." With a sigh, he said, "Mia was an agent. Your father was working with her."

"An agent?" Tag let out a laugh. "And my father was working with her? What would Harlan—"

"Harlan and Angus are retired, but they often help when needed."

Tag shook his head in obvious disbelief. "You're telling me my father and uncle are…agents?"

Hud nodded. "They've always worked undercover operations because they had such perfect covers with their band. Apparently Mia was getting close to busting a murder ring."

"Murder ring?" he said, sounding disbelieving.

"We're wasting time. You want to find Lily, you have to tell me about these names you said she had." He could tell that Tag didn't believe him. "You have to trust me if want to find Lily."

"Take off my handcuffs. If I can trust you, then trust me."

He hesitated. Tag was a loose cannon. He'd gotten involved and now Lily McCabe was missing. Hud already had two dead women. He hoped he wasn't making another mistake.

"I know you don't trust me, but I have reason not to trust you, either," Hud said as he got out of the patrol SUV and opened the back door. "You show up just before Mia is killed and we only have your word that she left with some Montana cowboy in a pickup."

"You can't be serious. Take off my handcuffs. I think I have what everyone is looking for."

Hud lifted an eyebrow, then unlocked the cuffs and watched Tag rub his wrists. He'd taken a chance with one of Dana's so-called cousins and almost gotten his family killed. And here he was again, taking another chance, one that could get him killed, as well.

TAG'S HEAD WAS whirling. He still wasn't sure he believed Hud, let alone trusted him. But right now he needed all the help he could get finding Lily.

"I have a partial list of some names that came off a thumb drive that I now believe Mia Duncan put in my coat pocket the night she was murdered." He dug out the scrap of paper with only a few of the names and handed it to the marshal.

Hud stared down at it, his eyes widening.

"You recognize the names?"

"Two of them are men who were recently released from prison," the marshal said as he turned the scrap of paper over, no doubt looking for more names. "One of them is dead. The other one, Ray Emery, is from around here. I don't recognize the others. Where is the rest of this sheet?"

Tag felt his heart hammering in his chest. He hoped he wasn't making a mistake that would get Lily killed—not to mention himself. He reached in his pocket and handed Hud the complete list from the thumb drive that Gerald had provided.

KYLE FOSTER
GEORGE MOORE
FRANK MOONEY
LOU WAYNE
CLETE RAND
RAY EMERY

PAUL BROWN
MIA DUNCAN
CAL FRANKLIN
LARS LANDERS
HARLAN CARDWELL
HUD SAVAGE

He heard the air rush from the marshal's lips and watched him swallow.

"This is the murder list," he said. "You say Mia put this in your coat pocket at the bar that night? Those names." He pointed to the ones on the top. "Those are the killers."

"And the names on the bottom?" Tag asked, his heart in his throat.

"Those are the hits."

"My father's name is on that list."

Hud nodded. "So is mine."

"How many of them are already dead?"

"Two that I know of. Paul and Mia. But Cal and Lars could already be dead by now."

"Then my father might be next." He met the marshal's gaze and let out a curse as he had a terrible thought. "You don't think they took Lily, not for the list, but…"

"As bait to flush out your father. Harlan said if you hadn't come by his cabin when you did, he would be dead. They wanted the thumb drive, but they didn't want him dead until they had the list that incriminated every prisoner who'd been released."

"I don't get why it's so important."

"In order to get released prisoners to kill for them, they had to promise their anonymity. If word got out that the feds had gotten hold of one of the lists…"

All Tag could think about was the fact that his father's name was on the list and the ones above might already be dead.

"Where is Harlan now?" When Hud hesitated, Tag said, "It's too late to hold out on me now."

"I honestly don't know. Apparently Mia had been working with a prison snitch. She'd heard that several prisons had started a type of co-op. For a fee, you can have someone on the outside killed. A recently released inmate kills someone he doesn't know, has no connection to. In return he gets either money or a favor. The idea is that the former inmate won't get caught because he has no motive."

Tag got it. His heart pounded as he realized why they were so desperate to get the thumb drive. "This list links the hits with the former inmates." This was incriminating stuff that could shut down the murder ring.

"I know Lily knew Mia and was the one who discovered her condo had been ransacked, but why do you think her disappearing has anything to do with the murder list?" Hud asked.

"Lily was with me when I found the thumb drive in my pocket. Once she took a look at what was on it, she determined it was written in some kind of code."

Hud frowned. "How did they know she had the thumb drive—let alone that she'd decoded it?"

Tag felt his heart drop. "I don't know. I thought she and I were the only ones who knew about it."

As THE MAN entered the room, Lily was blinded by the sudden light for a moment. He carried a tray and she caught the smell of a microwave dinner. Her stomach growled. She was surprised that she was starved. It seemed odd to her to think about food at a time like this.

Her gaze went from the tray to the man. He was big and bulky with hamlike hands and arms covered with tattoos. Over his head, he wore one of those rubber Halloween masks, this one of an ogre.

She didn't miss the irony as she watched him put down the tray on the end of the mattress. She thought about jumping up and making a break for the door. Or grabbing the tray and attempting to hit him with it.

But even if she hadn't felt so weak from whatever they'd knocked her out with, she knew either attempt at escape would be wasted effort. Better to eat the food he'd brought, get her strength back and bide her time.

He didn't say a word as he turned and walked out of the room. Nor did he appear to be worried about a surprise attack from behind.

She thought she probably should have tried to make conversation with him. Hadn't she heard somewhere that in a situation like this you needed to make yourself as human as possible to your abductor?

But Lily was smart enough to know that this wasn't a garden-variety abduction. The fact that they hadn't killed her outright probably meant they were holding her hostage.

Just as she surmised that this had to have something to do with the thumb drive and Mia's murder—as she and Tag had guessed.

The thought of Tag brought tears to her eyes. Why hadn't she admitted that they'd made love? They would have been in her bedroom at the house in each other's arms—instead of her being here.

She'd let fear keep her from him. But she'd never seen herself the way she was with Tag last night. Nor had she ever felt as close to another human being. She ached for Tag Cardwell, and that scared her, too, because she feared Gerald was right and Tag was all wrong for her. A mathematician and a Texas cowboy? Their lives were miles apart in more than distance.

And yet she couldn't get him out of her racing heart. She tried not to let herself think about what would happen if these men didn't get what they wanted as she dragged the tray over to her and dug into the food. It was as wonderful as it was awful. She thought of Gerald and his contempt for any food that wasn't four-star-restaurant quality.

She actually smiled at the absurdity of it all since she practically licked the cardboard container clean. The food made her feel a little stronger. But what boosted her more than anything was the knowledge that Tag would be looking for her.

Lily hugged herself, thinking about last night and their lovemaking. He was the kind of man who would ride in on a big white horse and save her. A sob escaped her lips. What if he hadn't gotten her message? Or worse, what if these men had already found Tag and taken care of him?

She assured herself that the cowboy wouldn't let her die without a fight.

CHAPTER TWELVE

EVERYTHING COULD BE bought for a price. Camilla had learned that at an early age. That price though was often very high—and too often wasn't monetary. So she'd spent her life paying dearly.

Because of that, it didn't come as a surprise that what she now wanted would be very costly. Snakebite had slipped back into the lunch line, returning with a hoarsely whispered cryptic message. "The laundry room. Right after dinner."

Camilla ate as if it were her last meal. It just might be, she thought as she studied the solemn faces around the table. Something was up. She could feel it on the electrified air. Even the guards seemed to sense it. Out of the corner of her eye, she saw them moving restlessly around the perimeter.

The walk down to the laundry room seemed interminable. But her resolve kept her moving. Whatever Snakebite had planned, it would be worth it if she could get the retribution she so desperately needed.

The laundry was busy with worker bees. Most of them didn't look up. Only two guards kept watch. Camilla felt the hair stand up on the back of her neck as first one of the guards stepped out and then the other.

She had one of those panicky moments, pure stomach-dropping, adrenaline-surging, breath-stopping moments before two of the women who'd been folding sheets turned and came toward her.

The first blow knocked the air out of her and smashed her teeth into her lips. The second blow cracked a rib. She tasted blood and began to fight back with everything she had.

Had she been set up from the beginning? Or was this part of the plan?

Right now it didn't matter. She was fighting for her life.

THE SOUND OF a cell phone ringing took both Tag and Hud by surprise. As Tag dug his cell phone out of his pocket and started to answer it, the marshal laid a hand on his arm.

"They could be calling to trade Lily for the thumb drive," Hud said. "Agree to meet them."

The phone rang again. "Hello?"

"It's Ace." Even over the roar of the bar crowd in the background outside his office, Tag could hear fear in Lily's brother's voice. "I just got a call demanding the thumb drive or they are going to kill Lily."

"What did you tell them?"

"To call you."

"Good." He disconnected and looked at the marshal, knowing he'd been listening in. "I'm going to give them the thumb drive."

"You have it on you? Let's take it to the office and make a copy," Hud said as he got out and motioned for Tag to get in the front seat of the patrol SUV. "I need to try to reach your father and let him know what's happening. For all we know, Harlan has already rescued Lily."

Tag wasn't going to hold his breath on that one. He

still couldn't get his head around his father and uncle being agents, even retired ones. His mother had to have known. Was that another reason she'd left Harlan and Montana—or the real one?

As he climbed into the front of the patrol SUV and Hud started the engine, he touched the thumb drive in his pocket and prayed. Whoever had Lily had to believe that no one had been able to break the code. Otherwise, the thumb drive was useless to them and they would have no reason to keep Lily alive.

LILY DIDN'T FEEL so shaky after she ate. She still had a horrible taste in her mouth from whatever had been on the cloth the man had forced over her mouth. And, of course, there was the fear.

She did her best to hold it down, tempering it with the knowledge that someone would be looking for her. Not Gerald. By now he would have flown back home. She realized she probably would never see him again.

Her lack of regret made her feel a little sad. She'd almost married the man, would have if he had shown up that day. Gerald didn't know it but he'd saved them both from a horrible mistake, she thought as she got up from the mattress. Her eyes had adjusted to the dim light enough that she wasn't afraid to move around. She started on the wall next to the mattress on the floor and, moving like a blind woman, felt her way around the room.

She wasn't sure exactly what she hoped to find. Another door other than the one she'd heard the man lock behind him? A window? Anything that would give her a chance of escaping?

The room was larger than she'd thought, cleared of any furniture. The knotty-pine walls made her think it was someone's cabin that was seldom used and that she was in the old, musty basement.

Lily tried to picture where it might be, but she had no idea how long the men had driven to get her here. Nor did she know what time of day it was. Or even what day since she didn't know how long she'd been out. She still felt groggy as she slid her fingers along the wall and took tentative steps.

She no longer wore a watch. She depended on her cell phone for the time. Her phone was in her purse, wherever that was now.

"Ouch." Her fingers connected with a wooden frame. A door frame? No, she realized as she felt around it. A window. She felt cloth and jerked. Dark fabric tore away from a basement window, bringing with it a choking amount of dust. She'd been right. This basement hadn't been used for some time.

With the window uncovered, Lily had hoped for more light. But unfortunately the snow had covered the dirty glass. Still, it was a little brighter inside the room without the dark curtain.

One look at the size of the window and she saw that it wasn't an avenue of escape. She was slim, but not slim enough to get out the window even if snow hadn't been banked up against it.

Taking advantage of the dim light, she quickly moved around the rest of the room, discovering another window and tearing off the cloth that had been tacked up over it. Less snow was banked against this one so it let in a little more light.

She could see the entire room. Definitely a basement. Musty and old and unused. Whose? Did the men who'd brought her here even know? It could be some cabin that no one used anymore.

When she reached the door, she tried the knob but of course found it locked. As she moved back to the bed, she felt her fear increase. She couldn't see how she could possibly escape this room unless she could outsmart her captors.

She had just sat down on the mattress to consider how she might do that when she remembered the sound of the man unlocking the door. No dead bolt. He'd used a key and it had made an odd sound. She stared at the door. It was very old, the wood a dark patina, so old it had a skeleton key.

Quickly she moved to the door and bent down to peer into the keyhole. There were two things about skeleton keys that gave her hope. One was that they fit in a rather loose-locking mechanism. Two was that they were often left in the other side of the door.

She could see the end of the key and the light around where it didn't quite fill the keyhole. At the sound of heavy footfalls, she scrambled toward the bed, stumbling over something. Her purse?

Grabbing it, she quickly searched for her cell phone. Gone, of course.

Hearing someone approaching, she sat down on the mattress and tucked the purse behind her to wait, her mind alive with an idea.

AT THE MARSHAL'S office, Hud copied the thumb drive onto his computer, then made a copy for Tag. "I'm going to have to keep the original."

Tag insisted on checking to make sure it had copied the information before he agreed. Then Hud told him to wait just outside his door while he made a couple of calls.

He'd started to protest, but the marshal cut him off.

"Don't make me lock you up, okay? I'm going to try to reach your father. If you get the call, don't answer it until you let me know."

Tag nodded. He had little choice since all he could do was wait for Lily's abductors to call. Looking for her would be like looking for a needle in a haystack. There were too many places they could have taken her.

All he could think about was that two women had been killed and the killers had Lily. He could feel the clock ticking. He clutched the thumb drive in his pocket and prayed that they wouldn't find out that Lily had decoded what was on it.

He was too nervous to sit still. Getting up, he walked down the short hall until he was just outside the marshal's office. He could see Hud on the phone, his back to him. The door was partially open and as he moved toward it, he heard what Hud was saying.

Tag stopped, frozen in place as he listened.

"Ray Emery, huh? Okay, give me the directions to his ex's house." He repeated them as he wrote them down.

Tag recalled the name Ray Emery had been on the murder list as one of the former inmates. Ray apparently had an ex-wife who lived just outside Big Sky.

Whoever was on the other end of the line must have given him an order because Hud said, "I don't like locking him up, even for his own good...I know. I can't do anything until he gets the call...Don't worry, I won't let him play hero, but I'm doing it my way now...Yeah? So arrest me. This is your mess, Harlan. Your name is on that list next, and mine's after that...Yeah, I'll do that."

Tag had heard enough. His father wanted Hud to lock him up in jail. Once the call came in...

When the marshal hung up, he quickly placed another call. This one to the Bozeman office requesting assistance. He would need two deputies to escort someone to the airport and make sure he made the flight.

Tag didn't have to guess who that would be. He eased down the hall and let himself out the back door. Fortunately someone from the funeral had seen that Harlan's old pickup was returned to Big Sky.

Tag had seen it parked out in back of the marshal's office when they'd driven up. The keys weren't in the ignition or even on the floorboard. But Tag knew where his father kept a spare one. Their mother had learned the trick from Harlan, apparently while the two were married.

He opened the small lid over the gas cap and felt around, smiling as his fingers closed around the key.

Within minutes, he was driving out of Big Sky, headed for Ray Emery's ex-wife's house down the canyon.

WILMA EMERY LIVED in an old cabin off the road in an isolated area on the river. The cabin was pre–Big Sky and the resort, when a lot of people had summer places that were rustic, basic and far from pretentious. This was one of them.

The cabin backed up to the river and was hidden from the road by trees. Tag parked in a wide plowed spot nearby, got out and walked over to look at the river. The land was much higher here than the water.

There was a narrow trail that wound down to the water, one no doubt used by fishermen in the summer. Now it was snow-packed, but there were tracks where some hard-core fisherman had gone down recently and fished in an open area before the surface had frozen over again.

Tag took the trail, half sliding in the snow because

the embankment was a steep wall of rock and snow. He landed feetfirst on a large snowcapped rock at the river's edge.

He felt thankful he hadn't ended up breaking through the ice at the edge. As he glanced to the south where the water curved away, he couldn't see Wilma's cabin. But he knew about where it should be. He made his way across the icy round granite boulders, headed in that direction.

As he reached a point where he guessed the cabin should be just up the steep embankment, he spotted another narrow winding path upward.

The path was full of snow, almost indistinguishable. He kept thinking of Lily, his heart quickening, his stomach dropping. He had to find her. Those words were like a mantra in his ears as he scaled the embankment, slowing toward the top. He'd gotten her into this. He had to get her out.

The cabin was completely surrounded by trees. He stopped behind one large pine, its boughs low and thick, concealing him from view of the windows he'd glimpsed on this side of the cabin.

He listened, not sure what he hoped to hear. Lily screaming? That thought sent ice down his spine. As he moved toward the cabin, he thought of Lily naked in his arms last night. The woman had gotten under his skin as no woman ever had before. He would find her. He just prayed it would be soon enough.

Why hadn't the kidnappers called?

HUD HAD BEEN wondering if he was doing the right thing about Tag Cardwell as he came out from making the calls. "I still couldn't reach your father…" The rest of the lie died on his lips.

Tag was gone.

Hud swore as he hurried out to the dispatcher. "What happened to my prisoner?"

Annie looked up in surprise. "Your prisoner? It wasn't like he was handcuffed or booked…"

Hud didn't wait for the rest. He knew Annie was right. He'd screwed up. Tag had to have known he was going to be either detained in jail or shipped out of state on some other type of security warrant.

He couldn't worry about Tag now. He had to find Lily McCabe before he got the call that another woman had been murdered. He felt a sudden surge of that old feeling of wanting to put the bad guys away, that whole incredibly dangerous and yet amazing need to fight for good over evil, with the belief that he was born to do this.

He'd thought he'd lost it. He'd thought he'd needed to turn in his star because he wasn't up to doing this anymore. It made him furious with himself that he'd had these months of self-doubt. He would go down fighting because in his heart this was who he was. He couldn't escape this any more than he could escape whatever had led him down this path to begin with.

Ray Emery's ex lived down the canyon in a cabin on the river. He was betting she knew where her ex-con husband was. Emery's name was on the list.

Hud's cell phone vibrated. He checked the number. Harlan. Hud hesitated only a moment before he answered the call. "I don't know where your son is," he said into the phone. "He's like his old man. Stubborn and determined."

Harlan swore.

"I'm on my way to see Ray Emery's ex now," Hud said. "If you see Tag again, lock him up."

"Don't worry, I will." He hung up and just hoped Tag Cardwell didn't get himself killed. Assaulting an officer would hold Tag for maybe a few hours, but as determined as Harlan's son was to find Lily, Hud knew he'd be out as soon as he could call a lawyer.

But hopefully all of this would be over by then.

LILY PICKED UP HER PURSE.

Moments ago the man in the mask had come down and taken her tray and brought her another bottle of water. Again, neither of them had spoken. She'd waited until he was gone before she moved to the window with the most light.

She'd just assumed the men who took her would have taken her purse. Digging through it, she saw that other than her cell phone, nothing seemed to be missing—not even the papers Gerald had decoded the names onto.

Her heart began to pound hard. Surely they would have searched her purse for the computer flash drive. They must have ignored the papers with the names. She noticed in the dim light that Gerald had scratched out some of the letters she'd had down, replacing them with others.

She frowned. That was odd. He'd changed all the names but a couple of them. If she'd had the code wrong, wouldn't those have had to be changed, as well?

TAG HAD JUST reached the corner of the cabin when he picked up the sound of an approaching vehicle. Through the trees he watched the marshal's car pull up out front. He waited until he heard Hud pound at the front door before he edged to the back of the cabin.

Through the dust-coated window he could make out

what used to be an old screened-in porch that had been entirely closed in.

He moved to the door and tried it. The knob turned, and the door groaned as he pulled it just open enough to slip in.

The back porch smelled musty. He moved to the rear door, settled his hand on the knob and prayed it, too, would be unlocked. That was what was amazing about most rural places in Montana. People didn't feel the need to lock their doors.

The door opened and he felt his heart soar. The hinges creaked softly as he slipped through. He could hear voices. Hud's deep voice. A woman's higher shrill one.

Tag found himself standing in a short hallway. He moved quickly to the first closed door, opened it. Junk room. Second door, bedroom. Third door, bathroom.

By then he could see the small cluttered living room, off it, a kitchen table and the strong smell of burned coffee.

The marshal and the woman were arguing, the woman's voice rising and falling. He could make out most of what was being said.

"I told you. I don't know where Ray is and I don't care. He won't be coming back here. He knows better than to try."

"I know you're still in contact with him," Hud argued. "You visited him just two weeks ago."

"To make sure he knew he wasn't coming back here," she snapped, voice rising again. "I'm not the criminal here. You don't have the right to come here and threaten me."

"I'm not threatening you, Wilma. Two women

have been murdered. Another is missing. If Ray is involved—"

"It's his business, none of mine. That's all I have to say to you."

Tag heard the creak of the old door as she started to close it.

"If you hear from him—" The door closed.

Tag tiptoed quickly back down the hallway. He realized he wouldn't be able to reach the back door, so he slipped into the junk room.

He could hear the woman muttering under her breath and the moan of the wooden floor under her feet. It sounded as if she'd gone into the living room. To watch from the window to make sure Hud was leaving?

Silence, and then the creak and moan of the floor. She was dialing someone on her cell phone. He could hear that distinctive *beep, beep, beep* with each number she touched, then the sound of ringing.

He realized she must be standing just outside his door in the hallway by her bedroom.

"The marshal was just here," she said by way of introduction when the other end answered. Silence, then, "You *know* what I told him. That I didn't know where you were. He knew I'd come to see you just before you got out." Another beat. "No, he left. I need my money. No, I don't want to come up there. You know how I hate that road."

More silence. He heard her grunt a couple of times, then argue that she was coming to get what was hers.

"Fine. I'll wait until dark, and then I'll drive up… Why do you say that?…Stop being so paranoid. So your name is on some list. What does that prove?…Stop yelling at me. You're the one who got us into this." She sighed and he heard the creak and groan of her footfalls as she moved away.

He held his breath, thinking what the marshal had said to him on their way back into town earlier. "You're not trained for this. You have no idea what you're getting yourself into, just how dangerous it is."

Tag had mentally argued that he did know. But at this moment, he had to admit, he was just starting to realize how out of his league he really was.

CHAPTER THIRTEEN

HUD HAD PLANNED to wait around and see if Wilma Emery made a move. He figured if she knew where her husband was, she might go to him. Or at least contact him.

But as he drove away down the road and pulled over, he got a call from his father-in-law.

"I've got some news," Angus said. "Can you meet me at your house?"

Hud figured if Angus talked to Harlan, he knew about the list, knew that his son-in-law's name was on it. "I'll be right there."

He drove home, ready to pack up his family and send them anywhere that might be safe. He wasn't running because he knew there was no place he would ever feel safe. He felt more alive than he had in months.

When he walked into his house, he saw that Angus hadn't said anything to his daughter about what was going on. No doubt he was waiting for Hud to tell her about the murder list and about his name being on it.

"Dad is back from his business trip," Dana said when he came through the door.

"I can see that. Honey, I need to talk to your dad…."

"I should check on the kids," Dana said, getting to her feet.

Hud was surprised she would leave them alone so quickly. It wasn't like her. He saw her send a curious glance toward them as she climbed the stairs, but she said nothing more. Nor did he and Angus until they heard her close the upstairs bedroom door.

He turned on his father-in-law. "If this is about the list—"

Angus was on his feet, finger to his lips, head cocked toward the kitchen.

Hud followed him. "Lily McCabe is missing. Tag has taken off looking for her only God knows where," he whispered once they were in the kitchen. "I'm sure Harlan told you about the list." He pulled the paper from his pocket and shoved it at his father-in-law. "Lily McCabe was decoding it."

He couldn't help being angry because he'd come into this so late. Until Mia Duncan had died, he thought both Angus and Harlan were out of this business. He'd had no idea that they were still involved in these kinds of things. Like Dana, he didn't pay much attention when either came or went. Until now.

"You should have trusted me," he said as he watched Angus take in the names on the paper. He didn't seem surprised—not even that his son-in-law's name was there.

Paul Brown was dead. Hud hadn't wanted to believe these lists even existed. But now he was staring the truth in the face. Worse, he didn't know who would be coming after him.

After a moment, Angus turned on the water, just letting it run into the sink, before he answered. "Where did you get this list?"

Hud told him what Tag had told him.

"Do you have the thumb drive?"

"Yes, but Tag has a copy. He plans to trade it for Lily."

Angus nodded. "This list," he said, wadding up the paper in his hand and tossing it into the garbage, "isn't the right one."

"What?"

"Lily McCabe must have decoded it wrong or Mia passed the wrong one."

Hud raked a hand through his hair. "Then my name isn't on the list?" He saw the answer in his father-in-law's expression and swore under his breath.

"Harlan's in Billings at the women's prison."

Hud felt his stomach roil. "You're telling me Camilla is the one who put the hit out on me?" He knew that shouldn't have come as a surprise, not after what had happened the day Camilla was sentenced.

As she was being taken from the room, she was led past him. She stopped just inches from him.

"I will get you if it's the last thing I do," she whispered through one of her innocent smiles. "You *and* your family." Then she'd laughed as they'd dragged her away. He'd been hearing that laugh in his sleep for months.

Angus met his gaze. "It's more complicated than that."

There was both compassion and fear in the older man's gaze. Hud didn't even need to hear the rest. He knew. He'd known deep in his soul that this wasn't over. That it wouldn't be over until that crazy woman was dead.

"Camilla Northland has been taken to the hospital," Angus said. "She got into an altercation with two other inmates in the laundry room. Harlan hasn't been able to talk to her yet. But with this hit out on you, we need to get Dana and the kids out of here."

TUGGING OFF HIS Stetson, Hud ran a hand through his hair. The sun had set, and deep shadows had filled in under the pines.

"How do you suggest we get your wife and children away from here two days before Christmas?" Angus asked.

He knew his wife. "We have to tell her the truth. She has a right to know. She's strong. She'll—"

"She won't leave you, you should know that."

"Yes, he should know that," Dana said from the kitchen doorway.

DARKNESS CAME ON quickly in the canyon. From a silky gray as the sun passed behind Lone Mountain, the canyon took on a chill even in the summer.

In the winter once the sun was gone, the canyon became an icebox. Even if the snow on the roads had thawed during a warm December day, the melt now froze solid, the roads suddenly becoming ice-skating rinks.

Tag didn't see the dark coming, but he felt it. Wilma Emery had been moving restlessly around the cabin. He thought he heard her packing, the closet door in the bedroom across the hall opening, the *ting* of metal hangers as clothes were pulled off them, then the sound of dresser drawers being opened and closed.

She dragged something heavy from the bedroom and down the hall toward the front door. He knew he would have to move fast once she left. Not the river route he'd taken to get here. He would have to reach his father's pickup quickly if he hoped to tail her. He couldn't lose her.

He heard the front door open, followed by a series

of grunts and groans and bumps and scrapes; then the door slammed shut.

Tag counted to five and opened the storeroom door. No sound came from the front of the cabin. Hurriedly he moved to the living room and peeked out of a crack in the curtains.

A solid-looking woman was shoving a huge duffel bag into the back of an older dark-colored large Suburban.

He hurried out through the back, the way he'd come in, and worked his way along the side of the cabin in time to see her go back into the cabin. He knew he was taking a chance, but he rushed down the road toward where he'd left his father's truck.

Behind him he heard the sound of an engine kick over. The dual golden beams of headlights shot across the frozen expanse to his left. He rushed into the pines and hurriedly climbed behind the wheel of the old pickup. As he slid down in the seat, the lights of the Suburban washed through the cab.

He held his breath, listening, half expecting the Suburban to slow, and then stop. There was no doubt in his mind that Wilma Emery was armed and dangerous. Or that he was in over his head.

But she didn't slow, didn't stop and a moment later the cab of the pickup went dark again. He sat up, heart pounding. As the Suburban headed out the narrow snowy unpaved road, he noticed that the right taillight had burned out.

Tag doubted that the woman would check her rear-view mirror, but he couldn't take the chance. He waited until Wilma was almost to the highway.

He'd purposely left the key in the ignition, afraid he might lose it on his hike along the river to the cabin.

Now he pressed down on the clutch and brake and

turned the key as he watched the Suburban turn onto the highway. The engine groaned but didn't turn over.

"Don't do this," he said to the truck. "Not now." He tried again. The engine groaned. "No!" He could see Wilma getting away. She was headed to meet her husband—and Ray Emery had Lily. He was sure of it.

He prayed that the pickup would start and tried it again. The engine groaned, but sparked and turned over. It was feeble. The cold engine vibrated the whole pickup as it rumbled.

Tag feared it would die and not start again, but when he put it in gear and let his foot off the clutch, it lurched forward out of the pines. He didn't turn on his headlights, following the darker shadows of the ruts through the snow, until he reached the highway.

He'd seen Wilma turn left onto the highway—away from Big Sky. Tag did the same. He couldn't go too fast. The highway was shiny in his headlights when he turned them on and he could feel the tires slipping on the glaze of ice on the pavement.

The highway was a crooked snake that wriggled through the Gallatin Canyon. This far south of Big Sky, there was little traffic. Skiers would have made their way home by now.

By the second bend in the road and no sign of Wilma Emery, he was starting to panic. Had she turned off? He had been watching, but there were few side roads along here.

Another curve and he saw the one red taillight shining in the distance. His pulse began to drop back to normal. *I'm coming, Lily. Hang on.*

LILY PRAYED FOR darkness, hoping that whoever was upstairs would need sleep. She didn't dare try anything as long as they were moving around up there.

Earlier she'd heard a male voice and figured he must be talking on the phone, but she couldn't make out what he was saying. Her stomach churned at the thought of them talking about her. Talking about what to do with her.

She felt confused. She'd thought they wanted the thumb drive. It was the only thing that made sense. But if that were the case, why hadn't they taken the papers from her purse with the names on them?

And if they didn't want the thumb drive, then why were they still keeping her alive? It didn't make any sense.

She moved to the door again and peered through at the tiny spots of light around the key. She was so tempted to try to get out that if it hadn't been for the sound of footfalls upstairs, she would have tried to get the key.

Hurrying back to the mattress, she curled against the cold pine wall and stared at the door, fearing one or both of them would come down at any moment and kill her.

At the sound of a door slamming upstairs, she froze. Had he left? She waited, praying that he'd left her here alone, because from what she could tell, there was only one man upstairs. She'd seen only one man since she'd been grabbed in the parking lot of the motel.

She heard a door open and close again, then the creak of the floorboards over her head, and knew she wasn't alone. She hugged herself and waited for the darkness outside the window to settle in and hopefully lull her abductor to sleep.

"TELL ME," DANA said as she stepped into the kitchen.

Hud saw her grab the edge of the kitchen table as if she knew she was going to need to hang on to something. He looked at his father-in-law, then at his wife. Dana was strong. She'd weathered many storms on this ranch. She'd single-handedly fought her siblings for the land that was her legacy.

"Someone has put a hit out on me," he said simply.

She nodded, glanced toward the kitchen window. A nervous laugh escaped her lips. She quickly quelled it. "Dee. I mean Camilla." Camilla had come to them pretending to be Dee Ann Justice, a long-lost cousin. "She's the one who put the hit on you, isn't she?"

When Hud didn't answer, she glanced at her father.

"We think it's a possibility," Angus said. His cell phone rang. "I have to take this." He stepped out of the room.

"Do you know who?"

"Apparently some inmates have gotten together and started a co-op type of murder list," Hud said, ignoring the disapproving look Angus gave him from just outside the kitchen. "It will probably be an ex-inmate coming for me. That's why you need to take the kids and leave. Go to my father's. I can call Brick—"

Dana shook her head. "We're safer here, especially if Camilla is involved. She knows everything about us, remember? The first place she would look for us would be Brick's—if she didn't have someone lying in wait for us along the way to West Yellowstone."

Angus stepped back into the room. "I'm sorry, but I have to go."

Hud nodded. Dana studied her father, and then quickly moved to plant a kiss on his cheek.

"Be careful," she whispered.

"Will you two be—"

"We'll manage," Hud snapped, then softened his tone with his father-in-law as he said, "Go. We'll be fine."

"We will be fine," Dana said, and stepped into her husband's arms. Hud held her tight, more afraid than he wanted to admit that they wouldn't be fine. Far from it.

TAG'S PULSE POUNDED in his ears as he stayed back just enough that he would catch sight of the one red taillight every few turns.

At the mouth of the canyon, Wilma slowed, crossed the bridge and turned onto the old river road.

Tag pulled off just before the bridge in a wide spot and waited. He could see her taillight for some distance now. He waited until he couldn't stand it anymore, then crossed the bridge and turned down the narrow old road.

Out of the canyon now, he could see stars in the clear night sky. They glittered from the midnight-blue canopy overhead. As he drove, the moon came up from behind the mountains to the east, a bright white orb that lit the fallen snow.

Ahead, Wilma's taillight blinked as she braked and turned down a road that led toward the river. He lost sight of her in the thick cottonwoods, but he knew she couldn't go far before she ran into the river.

He found a place up the road to pull over, then started to climb out of the pickup. Hud's words came back to him again. He had no idea what he was going to find down that road.

On a hunch, he reached under the pickup's seat. He found an ax handle. All kinds of other junk. No old pistol. He was disappointed in his father. Nor was there a shotgun or even a .22 rifle hanging from the rack behind the seat.

He tried the glove box and was about to give up and see if he could find at least a tire iron, when he noticed something interesting about the passenger-side floorboard.

He lifted a flap in the rubber mat and saw the handle. When he lifted it, he found more than he'd hoped for.

Until that moment, he hadn't really believed his father was an agent of any kind.

But as he pulled out a Glock handgun, then a sawed-off shotgun—both loaded—he became a believer. Sticking the Glock into the back waistband of his jeans, he hoisted the shotgun, grabbed a pocketful of shells and headed down the road.

CHAPTER FOURTEEN

THERE WERE TWO things Tag's father had taught his older sons before they left Montana—to swim and to shoot a gun.

"I'm not having one of my boys drowning in the river because he can't swim," Harlan had told their mother. "And they're going to learn to shoot."

"They're too young," she'd cried as he loaded them into the pickup.

They'd learned to swim in a small deep eddy down in the Gallatin on a warm summer day. Not that the water had been warm. Rivers and lakes in most of Montana never warmed up that much.

But each of them had learned. His father's method hadn't been exactly mother approved. He'd tossed them in one at a time. Sink or swim. They'd learned to swim, kicking and screaming.

With shooting that hadn't been the case. They were boys, after all. Harlan had been strict about safety as well as learning how to load, clean and shoot a gun.

Now as Tag approached the 1940s-looking cabin, he snapped off the safety on the shotgun.

The snow crunched under his feet as he walked. He thought about calling the marshal. Not until he knew for certain that Lily was down here. He still wasn't sure he could trust Hud. The man had been ready to put him on a plane.

Without a cloud in the night sky, the temperature had dropped. His breath came out frosty and white. The moon lit the land, making the snow look like white marble. In the cottonwoods, deep shadows filled the road's ruts. It was hard to see where he was walking. A couple of times he slipped in the icy tracks and almost fell but managed to catch himself.

Tag thought of his brothers. They wouldn't believe it if they saw him, armed and tromping through a dark, snowy night to save a woman. He'd had relationships. He'd just never met a woman who he would have been tromping through a dark and snowy night to save.

Worse, he and Lily didn't even have a relationship. Hell, for all he knew she was planning to go back to her former fiancé. Jealousy dug under his skin at the thought.

Either way, he had to find her.

Ahead, he spotted Wilma's SUV parked in front of the cabin, only this one had a basement. One lone light burned in a window close to the ground at the other end of the building. Inside the house proper, lights blazed.

Tag glanced around. There was no other vehicle. That bothered him. Had someone left but was planning to be back at any time? That seemed more likely than that whoever Wilma had talked to was staying here without transportation.

The thought made him nervous. It was that ticking clock he'd been hearing in his ear since he'd realized Lily was missing. But now it seemed to be ticking even faster.

Move.

He did, through the deep snow, toward the corner of the house that was the darkest. He could smell the river bottom, the scent of decayed leaves that haunted every riverbed.

As he drew nearer to the house, he could hear raised voices, a woman's and a man's. Edging along the side of the house, he got as close to the front window as he could without being seen.

He took a quick peek. Wilma and the man he'd seen help Mia into a pickup that night behind the bar. The two were standing at the edge of the living room arguing. The man had a gun in his hand. He appeared to be threatening Wilma with it.

Tag's cell phone vibrated in his pocket, making him jump.

CAMILLA KNEW IT was just a matter of time before Marshal Hud Savage learned that she had escaped from the hospital.

She would have liked to check into a motel for a few days, get her strength back, heal. But she couldn't chance it. As bad a shape as she was in from her beating, checking into a motel the way she looked would be dangerous. Not only that, but it would give Hud time to get ready for her.

True to her word, Snakebite had seen that everything she needed had been waiting for her on the outside. She had a vehicle, weapons and what tools she might need. She smiled even though it hurt her mouth to do so.

By now the marshal would have heard that she had been taken to the hospital. He was too smart not to know she might be using it to escape. That Hud would be expecting the worst made it all the more delicious. She had to assume the marshal's office would be guarded. So would the ranch house. Fortunately, Hud was a lawman through and through. His one Achilles' heel was that he couldn't resist anyone in trouble.

She'd gotten word that he would soon be headed for a cabin down the canyon where a woman named Lily McCabe was being held captive. Camilla was in awe of the working prison network. Hud being called away from the house would buy her valuable time to take care of a few things in his absence.

That and the fact that she knew the ranch layout— even in the dead of night—would make her plan work. She didn't need to worry about getting away. The worst they could do to her was lock her up again. She was already looking at life in prison. There was no way Hud would ever have let her get paroled, and now that she'd escaped, even more years would be added on to her sentence.

If only Hud had wanted her, she thought. They could have been happy together. He would have gotten over the loss of Dana and the kids. At least that was what she'd told herself last spring. She'd wanted him. Deserved a man like him. She'd thought her life would have been so different if a good man had come into it sooner.

But he hadn't wanted her. He'd wanted Dana. She made a face at the memory of sweet Dana and her children. They were always baking cookies and making a racket. And Hud… A hard knot formed high in her chest at the memory of how he had rejected her. The one man she would have done anything for, and he'd rejected her.

Camilla pushed those thoughts away as she drove toward the Gallatin Canyon. She had a mission. Hud would soon know she was coming. She smiled. He just wouldn't be expecting what she had planned for him.

Tag's phone vibrated again. He felt his heart quicken as he realized that the man and woman inside the house weren't on a phone.

He edged away from the window and into the nearby pines, answering the phone on its third ring.

"Hello." He waited. He could hear someone breathing on the other end of line. "What?" he demanded.

"Don't be so impatient."

He didn't recognize the voice as he moved so he had a view of the living room—and the two people standing nearby in the kitchen doorway. They were both facing each other, still having a serious talk.

Tag had to assume the person on the phone wasn't inside this building.

Who the devil was this on the phone, then?

"What do you want?" he asked, stepping back into the snowy pines out of sight.

"You know what I want."

"Do I?"

A low chuckle.

"What about what I want?" Tag asked, half afraid of saying Lily's name. What if there were more people looking for the thumb drive than he knew?

"Your girlfriend?"

He breathed a sigh of relief even though Lily was far from his girlfriend. Then he had a thought. "What makes you think she's my girlfriend?"

Another chuckle. "I was giving you the benefit of the doubt after what I saw through her bedroom window last night."

His heart dropped at the realization that the man who'd run him off the road had followed him to Lily's. He hadn't seen anyone, but he'd left tracks in the falling snow. He'd led the man right to Lily.

"I want to know that she's all right," Tag said. "Let me talk to her."

"That isn't an option right now even though I can assure you, she is fine."

"Not good enough." He'd seen enough movies to know he needed to have proof that she was still alive. What he really wanted to know was if the man was in the house—and if not, where was he?

"Give me a little time," the man said on the other end of the line. "Ten minutes. Then I'll call you back. You'd better have what I want." The man disconnected.

Tag could still hear the two in the house arguing. He quickly backtracked down the side of the house and around to the back. He heard nothing at any of the windows, but when he reached the basement one with the lone light, he bent down, dug away some of the snow and peered in.

What he saw made his heart beat faster. A tray with a consumed TV dinner on it, an empty bottle of water and a used napkin.

Lily was here. He knew it.

He moved to one of the dark basement windows. As he cleared away the snow, he saw that the glass opening was small. Too small for a person to climb out.

He bent down and tried to peer in. The glass was filthy. He wiped at it with a handful of snow and heard a sound on the other side. Stepping back out of sight, he watched the window out of the corner of his eye. A hand touched the glass. A small, female hand.

Tag quickly bent down again. The basement room was too dark for him to see more than a shadowy figure at first. Then she put her face nearer to the glass and he saw her. His heart almost burst from his chest.

DANA HAD GONE upstairs to check on the kids when Hud's cell phone rang. He took the call even though he didn't recognize the number.

"I know where Lily McCabe is," the woman's voice on the other end of the line said.

"Who is this?" He recognized the voice. Wilma Emery. But he didn't call her on it, fearing she might hang up.

"Never mind that. They're holding her at a cabin." The woman gave him hurried directions. "You better make it fast or they will kill her like they—" There was what sounded like a struggle, and then the line went dead.

Hud swore as he disconnected and looked up as his wife came down the stairs.

"What is it?" she asked.

"Wilma Emery just called. She sounded scared. She told me where they're holding Lily McCabe. I don't like the way the call ended."

Dana's eyes widened in alarm as her hand went to her mouth. "What if this is only a ruse to get you to…" Tears filled her eyes.

"I can't leave you and the kids."

She made quick swipe at her tears and seemed to pull herself together, the way she always did when the going got tough. "You have to go. The kids and I will be fine."

His cell phone rang again. He swore when he saw it was Tag Cardwell calling. "Where are you?" he demanded as he stepped out of the kitchen and earshot of his wife.

"I've found Lily."

Hud listened as Tag gave him the same directions to the cabin on the river that Wilma had given him.

"I'll be right there. Just wait. Don't do anything, do you hear me?"

Tag didn't answer and Hud realized he'd hung up. With a curse, he looked to his wife.

"Go."

He knew he had no choice. He was still the marshal. "Please, Dana, I need you to leave with the kids. Get packed while I'm gone."

"Camilla's in the hospital. They'd let us know if she wasn't." She stepped to him, drawing him into a tight hug. "You just worry about coming back to us safe and sound."

"Always."

CAMILLA FINISHED TAPING her ribs in the filling station bathroom. The antiseptic smell of the recently cleaned restroom made her hold her breath. Not that breathing was all that easy with her cracked ribs.

How long before the hospital realized she was gone? She smiled since her ruse would have bought her time.

As she let her gaze lift to the metal mirror over the sink, she was startled because she didn't recognize herself. Her face was swollen and bruised in shades of grays and yellows. Her right eye was black and almost swollen shut.

There was still dried blood on the cut on her upper lip. She was missing a front tooth.

Camilla let out a small laugh, which she quickly killed because it hurt her chest.

"How do you think you're going to do anything as messed up as you are?" she asked the woman in the mirror.

The clock was ticking since she knew every cop in

the state would be looking for her soon. She'd split right away from the other inmate she'd escaped with.

There wasn't safety in numbers—not with them looking as bad as they did. She'd held her own in the fight and done as much damage as she could. She also knew she would attract less attention on her own.

Her face would heal. So would her cracked ribs. But she couldn't take the time. She had everything she needed: a vehicle, money, weapons. The problem was everyone would know where she was heading.

"You could get out of the country," she told her reflection. "You don't have to do this."

Her eyes narrowed at the thought. "You could go to some warm tropical place and sip tropical drinks with the locals." She smiled at the thought, but knew that wasn't her M.O.

She couldn't live with herself if she didn't finish this. Hud would be expecting her to come for him—especially after he heard about the prison break.

He would whisk Dana and the kids off somewhere, thinking they would be safe. Hud wouldn't run, she thought with a lopsided smile. He would think he could best her at whatever she had planned for him.

She loved nothing better than a challenge. Even beat up and in pain, she felt up to it. Hud would be off saving some other damsel in distress. It would give her plenty of time to take care of things at the ranch before he returned.

She could hardly contain her excitement at seeing Hud Savage again. *Soon, Hud.*

TAG KNELT DOWN by the window. Lily was trying to tell him something, but he couldn't hear her. He motioned for her to move back. He could still hear Wilma and the man he suspected was her ex-husband, Ray Emery, arguing even more loudly from another part of the cabin.

He hoped they were far enough away and the basement deep enough that they wouldn't hear what he was about to do. Wrapping the butt of the shotgun around the tail end of his coat, he leaned down and smashed the glass. The sound felt like a gunshot, it was so loud to him.

He listened, afraid the others had heard it. But with staggering relief, he heard the two inside the house still arguing.

"Are you all right?" he asked the moment Lily appeared at the small broken window. He could see her, but he ached to take her in his arms. It was the only way he could convince himself that she truly was all right.

She nodded, looking scared but definitely relieved to see him.

"How many people are in the house?"

She shook her head. "Someone left earlier. I've only seen one man, but I heard someone come a little while ago. It sounds like a woman."

So there was just the redheaded man and Wilma.

"I think the one just got out of prison."

He could feel the cold seeping in through the knees of his jeans as he knelt on the ground. Time was passing. The man on the phone said he would call back in ten minutes—and let him talk to Lily. He had to move quickly.

"I know how you feel about guns, but I'm afraid you're going to need this," he said as he pulled the Glock from behind him and handed it to her through the window. "It's ready to go. All you have to do is pull the trigger. Aim for the largest part of the body." He saw her cringe. "You can do this."

She nodded, a determined look settling on her features.

He gave her a smile, then pulled off his glove and reached through the broken window to touch her face with his fingertips. She closed her eyes, leaning into his warm palm. Tears beaded her lashes when he pulled his hand away.

"I'll be down to get you in a few minutes. If anyone else comes through the door, shoot them."

With that, he stood. From inside the house came the loud report of a gunshot followed by a scream and another gunshot. Tag grabbed the shotgun and ran toward the front of the house.

LILY LISTENED. She heard nothing overhead following the two gunshots and the scream. Her heart was beating like a war drum. Tag had come for her. She'd known he would. He was that kind of cowboy. Wasn't that why she'd made love with him last night? She'd known the kind of man he was. Otherwise, she would never have—

Another gunshot and the pounding of footfalls. She held her breath as she looked toward the door, then down at the gun in her hand. Her heart was in her throat now. Was Tag all right? He'd come to save her, but what if—

She couldn't bear to let herself even think it.

She had to get out of here. She couldn't just stand here waiting for that door to open. Dropping the gun onto the mattress, she moved to the door, willing her trembling to stop.

When she'd heard someone at the window, she'd been just about to push the piece of paper she'd written the codes on under the door. In a perfect world, once she pushed the key through from her side, it would fall on the sheet of paper and she would pull it through. Once she had the key, she could open the door.

This wasn't like any mathematical problem she'd ever come across. This was her life. She didn't know why they had kept her alive. But she feared all of that had now changed. They would kill her and Tag if they got the chance.

She'd held her breath, waiting and praying that the next sound she heard was Tag's voice on the other side of the door.

But there had been nothing.

Lily didn't know how long she'd waited. Until she couldn't take it any longer.

Finally she pushed the sheet of paper slowly under the door, her heart in her throat. She half expected the paper to be jerked away, the door to fly open…

But nothing happened.

Now, willing her fingers not to tremble, she used the piece of plastic fork she'd kept to carefully poke gently into the keyhole.

She felt the key move. If she pushed too hard, the key would fall out—away from the door and the paper she'd pushed under the door.

Too slowly and she chanced that someone would come downstairs—someone other than Tag.

She pushed and prayed and a moment later she heard the key fall and land with a *clink*.

Her heart dropped. It sounded as if the key had missed the sheet of paper. Now it would be out of her reach.

She could barely stand even the thought as she knelt down to see where the key had gone. To her shock, she saw it lying half on, half off the paper.

Her fingers were trembling too hard for her to touch the sheet of paper and try to pull it back inside the room.

She took deep breaths. She had one chance. She stilled her trembling as she knelt farther down and at a snail's pace, she began to pull the corner of the paper with the key hanging off it toward her.

The light caught on the key. It flashed, so close now that she could almost feel it in her hand when she opened the door.

A huge foot suddenly stomped down on the key and sheet of paper. She let out a scream before she could catch herself and fell back on her butt.

As the man put the key in the lock and threw open the door, she scuttled backward, unable to get her feet under her quickly enough to stand.

The large man loomed over her, sans his mask. The light caught on the gun in his hand as he raised it, the barrel pointed at her chest.

"You're too smart for your own good," the man said.

The gunshot was deafening in the basement room. Lily didn't realize that she'd closed her eyes until she opened them to find the man still standing over her.

He had an odd expression on his face.

Lily looked down expecting to see blood, expecting to feel life leaking from her. When she saw nothing, she looked back up in time to see him falling toward her.

She rolled away at the last instant. As he fell face-first within inches of her, she saw the hole in the back of his shirt and the blood seeping out.

As a shadow filled the doorway, her gaze swung to it. The next moment she was in Tag's arms and he was holding her. "We have to get out of here," Tag whispered next to her ear, but he moved as if he couldn't bear letting her go.

She nodded against his chest, then drew back to look at the man lying on the basement floor. "Is he…?"

Tag didn't answer. He picked up the Glock from the mattress, took her hand and led her up the stairs. As they neared the top, he motioned for her to stay back.

She caught only a glimpse of a woman's body lying on the floor near the kitchen as Tag hurriedly drew her toward the outside door. "Was that—"

"Ray Emery's wife. The two of them were arguing. He killed her before I came in."

They stepped out into the cold, wintery night. The sky was ebony and adorned with tiny white jewels. A moon washed over the snow, turning it to alabaster. The freezing air stole her breath. That and the sound of a vehicle roaring toward the cabin, the lights bobbing on the rough snow-packed road.

TAG DREW LILY toward a barn on the back of the property. As they slipped into the pitch-black, he held her to him for a moment until his eyes adjusted to the light.

Now if he could just get Lily out of here. He could hear the sound of the vehicle's engine growing louder. Not the marshal. Not the way the rig was roaring down the road without flashing lights or a siren. No, it was probably whoever he'd spoken to earlier on the phone.

His eyes finally adjusted to the darkness. They fell on the large snowmobile at the door. He stepped away from Lily for a moment to feel if the key was in it. It was.

"When I start the snowmobile's engine, open the barn door the rest of the way and hop on," he told Lily as they heard two car doors slam, followed by shouts from the house moments later.

He started the snowmobile and threw it into gear, as

Lily swung the door wide. He pulled her on as he hit the gas and burst out into the freezing night.

The headlight of the snowmobile bobbed as they took off, racing through the deep snow of the field. Tag headed for a stand of pines, knowing that as long as they were in the open field, they were too perfect a target.

A bullet whizzed past.

Lily wrapped her arms around his waist as they sped across the field, the snowmobile busting through drifts and sending up a cloud of fresh snow. The air filled with ice crystals as it blew past. Moonbeams played over the surface of the fresh-fallen snow. The winter night seemed to be holding its breath.

When Tag dared look back, he saw the light of another snowmobile coming after them.

CHAPTER FIFTEEN

As HUD RACED toward the cabin where Tag had said Lily McCabe was being held, the urgent call came in from Harlan.

"Camilla Northland has escaped from prison."

The words hit like a sledgehammer. He tried to breathe, to keep his heart from banging out of his chest. Ahead, he could see the turnoff into the cabin. All he managed to say was, "How long ago?"

"Four hours ago."

"Four hours! Wasn't there a guard outside her door?"

"She got the jump on him. Unfortunately there was a bus accident and the doctors and nurses were busy...."

Four hours would give Camilla plenty of time to get to where she was headed. For all he knew, Camilla was in Big Sky. Even on the ranch. There was no doubt in his mind that she would be coming after him and his family.

Hud fought to take a breath. Fear paralyzed him for a moment. Fear, and the memory of just how far that crazy psychopath of a woman would go to get what she wanted.

He touched his brakes at the turnoff and swung down the old river road. "How?"

"She'd gotten into an altercation with two other women. They were all taken to the hospital because of their injuries. Two of them escaped. Camilla was one of them."

All these months when Dana had been afraid that Camilla would find a way to come after them again, he'd told her not to worry. That Camilla was never getting out of prison. That she could never get to them again.

"She's on her way to the ranch if she isn't already there," he said, hoping Harlan could tell him otherwise.

Instead, the former agent said, "I just talked to Angus. He's headed back there now. I'm on my way, but I can send a deputy—"

"Does Dana know?"

"Angus hasn't told her yet."

"Tell him to call and tell her. I'll be there as soon as I can." He hung up. It took everything in him not to turn around and race toward the ranch. But Tag Cardwell and Lily McCabe were in the cabin ahead. He couldn't let them die even to save his own family.

Ahead he saw two snowmobiles racing toward him.

CAMILLA MOVED THROUGH the dark toward the house. Her ribs hurt. She stopped and had to shift the gun stuck in her waistband. The snow was deeper than she'd thought it would be and had worn her out quickly. Either that or she was in worse shape from the fight than she thought.

In the distance she could see the lights on at the ranch house. Had Dana heard yet that her "cousin" was on the way? Had Hud?

She'd checked before she began her hike. The marshal was still involved in the showdown by the river. Subterfuge at its best.

Camilla pushed on through the fallen snow until she reached the backside of the house. When she'd stayed here last April, she'd come and gone in the middle of the night several times. She'd learned the darkest parts of the yard and the best way to enter so as not to be seen.

Nearing the house, she slowed to catch her breath. Hud's patrol rig wasn't parked out front. She had to believe her information was correct and Hud was still involved down the canyon.

She tried the door. Locked. She smiled, realizing she would have been disappointed if Dana had left the door open for her.

She glanced at her watch. Dana was a creature of habit. She would be upstairs putting the kids to bed right now.

It took only a few moments to pick the lock and, easing the door open, slip inside.

THE WHINE OF the snowmobile behind them grew louder. Tag ventured a look back. He'd gotten Lily into this. He had to get her out. Another bullet zinged past, this one so close it took his breath away. The pines were ahead. Just a little farther and they would be in the trees.

He didn't see the dip in the snow until it was too late. The snowmobile roared down into it, but the skis caught in the deep snow and then hit the ground underneath.

Tag flung the two of them to the side as the snowmobile nose-dived. He rolled. He felt Lily slam into him as they hit the ground and were instantly covered with snow.

He came up only to be blinded by the lights of the other snowmobile. The light suddenly shut off as the sound of the snowmobile motor died and a large dark figure loomed over them.

Tag pulled her closer so his body shielded hers. He could see the shotgun lying just feet away. The snowmobile, its engine still running, its lights dim, buried in the deep snow, idled just feet away.

The moonlight caught the glint of metal as the man

pulled a gun from his coat. "The two of you have caused nothing but problems," he said between gritted teeth. "All you had to do was give us the damned flash drive." He aimed the gun at Tag's chest. "Hand it over now or I'll take it off your body. Which is it going to be?"

Tag dug in his pocket and pulled out the computer thumb drive. He tossed it to the man, knowing the man would miss it. The small device fell into the deep snow, making the man swear.

Behind Tag, he felt Lily loosen her hold on him, felt her take the pistol from his pocket. She raised the gun. He could feel her trembling, the hand holding the gun shaking. The killer saw it, too. She couldn't pull the trigger.

Tag lunged for the shotgun lying next to the snow-mobile in the snow. The sound of the gunshot made him flinch. He heard Lily cry out. For a moment, he thought she'd pulled the trigger. But the shot had come from farther away.

The man standing over them appeared surprised as he looked down at his chest. The gun in his hand wavered, then fell from his fingers into the deep snow. The second shot dropped the man.

Marshal Hud Savage waded toward them through the snow. Behind Tag, Lily was crying and saying, "I just couldn't pull the trigger. I just couldn't."

Tag took her in his arms, assuring her that it didn't matter, but he could tell that it did matter much more than it should have to her.

As Camilla came around the corner from the kitchen, Dana came face-to-face with the woman she'd thought was her cousin only months before.

"Dee—" She caught herself. "I'm sorry, it's Camilla, isn't it?"

"Actually I go by Spark now." She smiled but didn't raise the gun she clutched at her side.

"Cute," Dana said, still surprised how much the two of them resembled each other even though they shared no blood. It had made it so easy for Camilla to pretend to be her cousin. Dana hated how vulnerable she'd been just months ago.

"What now?" Camilla asked, still smiling.

"I guess that's up to you. I always wondered what I would do if I ever saw you again."

"Really?" Her gaze went to the shotgun in Dana's hands, the barrel aimed at her heart. "And now here we are. You know, we would have made great cousins. We're so much alike."

"We're nothing alike," Dana snapped.

Camilla's smile wasn't quite as self-assured as it had been. "Are you sure about that?" She looked past Dana. "I thought you would be putting your children to bed." She cocked her head. "I don't hear the patter of their little feet."

"They aren't here. They're with Hilde."

"Hilde, your good and loyal friend," Camilla scoffed. "You tried to destroy that friendship, but you failed."

"I'm surprised your *good* friend would leave you, knowing what you were up to."

"I talked her into taking the children so I could get packed to leave since you'd put a hit out on my husband."

Camilla raised an eyebrow. "I don't see you packing."

"No, I've just been waiting for you. You wouldn't just want Hud. You'd come after me and my children again. I decided to get it over with."

"You were that sure I'd come here?"

Dana smiled. "I knew you couldn't let anyone else do your dirty work. You enjoy it too much."

"You might have more backbone than I thought." She glanced toward the front window. "Or you're expecting your husband to come save you."

Dana laughed softly. "You think I'm weak, certainly no match for you, since you were able to fool me so easily, isn't that right?"

Camilla didn't bother to answer, the truth in her smirk. "I bet that shotgun isn't even loaded."

Dana laughed. "Wanna bet?"

"Have you ever killed anyone?" Camilla sighed. "It's not easy. You'll have to live with what you've done."

Dana laughed again. "How would you know anything about living with what you've done? You have no conscience."

"You're wrong. I never wanted to do the things I've done. If I could do it over—"

"That won't work with me anymore," Dana interrupted. "I know you. I can see into the darkness where your soul should be."

Camilla smiled and took a step toward Dana.

"I wouldn't do that if I were you."

"You don't have what it takes. I can see it in your eyes. I'm betting I can raise my gun and fire before you have the guts to pull that trigger."

"That will be the bet of a dead woman."

Camilla stopped moving. Her fingers holding the pistol at her side twitched. "I'm beginning to see what Hud sees in you. Where is he, by the way?"

"Right behind you," Dana said.

"You expect me to fall for that? I turn around and

you jump me?" Camilla shook her head. "What we have here is a standoff. I shoot you. You shoot me."

"Except I have a shotgun which means after I shoot you, you won't be going back to prison so you can escape again and hurt someone else. Nor will I live in fear anymore. This ends here."

HUD HEARD THE shots as he raced toward the front door of his ranch house. He burst in, gun in hand, to find his wife on the floor in a pool of blood. A few feet away, Camilla Northland was struggling to get to her feet. Her left side was a mass of torn bloody fabric. But one look at her and he knew she would survive this—just as she had survived everything else in her life.

The marshal stepped to her quickly and smashed his boot heel into the hand holding the pistol. She didn't even make a sound as he kicked the gun out of the way and rushed to his wife.

"Call 911," he yelled as Tag Cardwell appeared in the open doorway. Hud had told Tag and Lily to stay in the patrol vehicle. He wasn't surprised that Tag hadn't.

"Dana," Hud cried. "Dana, can you hear me?" Leaning down, he placed his head to her chest and with a groan of relief, felt it rise and fall. She was still alive.

Tag was on the phone with the 911 operator. In the distance, Hud could hear the sound of sirens. He saw the crease along his wife's skull where the bullet had grazed her. She was losing blood fast. He quickly yanked off his jacket and shirt and pressed the shirt to her wound as a shadow fell over him.

"Look out!" Tag cried.

As Hud spun around, he instinctively picked up the shotgun lying beside his wife. Camilla loomed over him, a knife raised high. But it was the expression on her face that froze his breath in his throat. She was smiling broadly, her eyes as bright as the moonlight on the snow outside.

She drove down with the blade, aiming for his heart. He rocked back, raised the barrel and fired. As he rolled to the side at the last minute, the knife plunged past him so close he thought he'd felt the whisper of the blade, which stuck in the floor as Camilla fell on top of him. With disgust, he shoved her body aside.

Outside the ambulance's lights flashed as it swung into the yard and two EMTs jumped and ran toward the open door.

"Dana," Hud whispered next to her ear. "Don't leave me. Please don't leave me."

CHAPTER SIXTEEN

WHILE HUD WENT to the hospital with his wife, a deputy marshal by the name of Jake Thorton took Tag's and Lily's statements. By now it was almost daylight.

Tag felt numb. Tomorrow was Christmas Eve. So much had happened that he couldn't imagine celebrating the holiday now. Camilla Northland was dead. His cousin Dana was in the hospital in a coma. Both Angus and Harlan were tying up the loose ends of the murder list case.

"I almost got you killed," Lily had said on the way to the marshal's office. She looked and sounded exhausted. There was a haunted look in her eyes that Tag had desperately wanted to exorcise, but nothing he'd said or done had.

"No," he said, and touched her arm. She flinched and tears welled up in her eyes.

"I couldn't pull the trigger. I just…couldn't."

"It's all right. We're all right. It's over."

She shook her head. "It was all so…senseless."

He knew that she came from an ordered life, one where things always added up and made sense. One and one were always two. She was shaken and remorseful and he would have done anything to change that. But just the sight of him was a reminder that she'd failed herself, and no matter what he said…

He recounted everything that had happened for the

second time to the deputy marshal, and then signed the paper that was put in front of him. Lily was being questioned in a separate room. He could see her through the window. She was crying.

His heart ached and he wanted desperately to go to her. But when she happened to look up, her gaze met his and she quickly looked away.

As he left the room, he saw that Ace was waiting for his sister.

"You saved her," Ace said, and shook Tag's hand.

"It wasn't like that."

"Yeah, it was. You found her and got her out of there."

"I almost got her killed because of a stupid flash drive with useless names on it." Lily was right. It had all been for nothing. "Take good care of her."

"Where are you going?"

"Back to Texas. I'm the last person your sister wants to see right now."

Ace looked sad about that. Not half as sad as Tag. He told himself it would never have worked out anyway. He lived in Texas. She lived in Montana. Even if she wasn't going back to her ex… And yet he kept thinking of her hand against that dirty pane of glass and her face in the faint moonlight.

The ache was like a hard knot inside him. He and Lily had never stood a chance. That was all it had been. A chance encounter doomed from the start. So why did it feel as if he was losing something he would yearn for for the rest of his life?

As he looked out into the faint light of daybreak, he heard Christmas music playing somewhere in the distance. Colorful lights glittered across the village of Big

Sky. He hoped he could get the first flight out. He'd had all he could take of Christmas in Montana.

"YOU'VE BEEN THROUGH a lot," Ace told Lily on the way back to his place. The sun was just starting to come up; the sky behind the mountains to the east was silvery with sunrise.

The day was cold and frosty, a misty fog hanging low in the snowcapped pines. Lily watched the landscape slide past and hugged herself even though it was warm in her brother's Jeep.

"I always thought I could take care of myself." She felt her brother glance over at her. "I've never thought of myself as helpless or weak."

"You are neither. I'm not sure I could have pulled that trigger, either."

She shot him a disappointed look. "We both know better than that."

"Come on, Lily. It's over. Cut yourself some slack. You were abducted. You could have been killed. You survived."

She nodded and looked out at the passing wild country. She'd survived but at what cost?

Ace reached over and squeezed her arm. "I'm so sorry. If I hadn't hired Mia in the first place—"

"You sound like Tag. He blames himself for finding the thumb drive when I was there. It's nobody's fault. It's just that it was all for nothing. The names were of no use. Everyone was killing each other for *nothing*. The list was of no use because half the names were wrong on it, I heard at the marshal's office. Apparently, Mia either messed up or they were onto her and gave her a fraudulent one."

Ace drove in silence the rest of the way to his apartment over the bar.

"I'm going to my own house," she said when she looked up and saw that her SUV was parked in the lot behind the bar.

He started to argue, but she cut him off. "All the bad guys are locked up. It's over. I want to go home. Need to go home."

"I don't like the idea of you being alone," her brother said.

She smiled at him. "I need to be alone. I'll drive down tomorrow. We can talk then. Right now—"

"I know, you just need to be alone," he finished for her, and smiled. "You've always been like that. I need people when I'm upset. You need solitude."

"Thank you for understanding."

"The marshal had your car picked up at Gerald's motel and brought here," he said. "Gerald stopped by earlier to say he was flying back to California. Does that mean you didn't take him back? You aren't reconsidering, are you?"

"Would that be so bad?" She held up a hand as her brother started to tell her again what he thought of Gerald. He didn't understand. Gerald offered her a quiet, safe life. Right now that sounded like just what she needed. She opened the passenger-side door of the Jeep and climbed out. "Tomorrow. We'll talk about it tomorrow."

With that she walked to her SUV, beeped open the driver's-side door and climbed in. She needed familiar right now, her own things around her. She turned the key in the ignition. The engine roared to life.

Her brother stood at the front door of the bar, waving as she left. She could tell he didn't like letting her go—letting her even consider going back to Gerald.

The past twenty-four hours were like a bad dream. Gerald showing up, making love with Tag, being kidnapped and held hostage and then Tag's rescue and, ultimately, her own part in it.

She could still remember the feel of the gun in her hand, the weight of it, the touch of the trigger. She'd let herself down. Let Tag down and almost gotten them both killed.

Her phone rang. She glanced at the caller ID. Tag. She couldn't bear to pick up. He would be flying home to his life in Texas. She'd heard him telling the deputy marshal of his plans.

"I need to go back to Houston," he'd said in response to the marshal's question about where he could be reached. "My brothers and I own a barbecue business."

"You're not staying for Christmas?"

Tag had glanced in her direction, and then said, "No, I don't think so."

He'd come over to her then and tried to talk to her, but she'd already put that cold, unemotional wall back up—the one Gerald had always admired about her. She could tell that Tag had been hurt and confused. He'd wanted to help her through this.

She shook her head at the thought as she pulled into her drive. There were tracks in the snow. But she didn't think too much about them. Everyone had been looking for her. Someone must have checked her house after the snow quit falling.

Lily pressed the garage-door opener and watched

the door slowly rise in the cold mountain air before she pulled in. She'd just cut the engine, the door dropping behind her, and gotten out when she realized she wasn't alone.

As Tag was getting ready to leave the marshal's office, his father walked in. Tag wasn't up to seeing anyone right now, still stung from the rebuke Lily had given him. She'd acted the same way the morning after their lovemaking. In those moments earlier, she'd made it clear that there was nothing between the two of them.

So it wasn't surprising that he felt a lethal mixture of emotions at just the sight of Harlan Cardwell right then.

"Well, if it isn't my father the agent."

"Retired CIA agent," Harlan said.

"Whatever." He started to walk past him, but his father caught his arm. "We need to talk."

"Really? I flew all the way up here hoping that you might have five minutes for me. *Now* you want to talk? Let me guess. You want to talk about this case—not about you and me. You really don't know how to be a father, do you?"

"No, I don't," Harlan said. "I still need to talk to you."

Tag shook his head. He couldn't help the well of anger that boiled up in his belly. When he'd flown up here for Christmas, he'd told himself he'd had no expectations. That had been a lie. He'd come hoping to find the father he'd never had.

"Why don't we step into Hud's office?" his father said.

"Are you ordering me?"

"I'm asking."

They stood with their gazes locked for a few moments, before Tag relented and stepped into the office. "Okay, let's get this debriefing over with," he said as Harlan closed the door behind them and motioned his son into one of the two chairs in front of Hud's desk.

"I'm sorry," his father said as he sat down. "You're right. I know nothing about being a father."

"And you never tried to learn."

"I did at first, but I let my job get in the way. It seemed more important."

Tag saw how hard that was for Harlan to admit. "It still is."

Harlan shook his head. "I only got involved because I used to work with Mia's father. I've known her since she was a baby. I could see that she was in over her head and yet..." He raked a hand through his hair. Tag noticed the streaks of gray he hadn't before. He saw the lines around his father's eyes. Saw how much he'd aged as if it had all been in the past twenty-four hours.

He'd seen his father as a guitar-playing, beer-drinking good ol' boy who just wanted to have fun. Now he saw the man behind that facade.

"Stay for Christmas," Harlan said.

"Was the computer thumb drive really worthless?" Tag asked. "Or is that just another lie?"

His father looked sad and disappointed for a moment that Tag had turned their conversation back to business, but finally said, "The original drive was corrupted."

Tag frowned. "Corrupted? Well, at least you have the list that Lily provided you."

"The names Lily McCabe decoded were incorrect. Useless, since there was no way to match up those ex-cons with the deaths of the law officers on the list."

Tag let out a curse. "Lily was so sure—"

"Some of them were right. I don't know why she

wasn't able to get the rest of them. But whatever the reason, it probably saved her life," Harlan said.

Tag felt his heart bump in his chest. He and Lily had tried so hard, but ultimately, they'd both failed. "So now what?"

"I'm retired again. That's why I'd like you to stay for Christmas."

A cheer came up from another part of the office. The dispatcher gave a thumbs-up and mouthed that Dana was going to make it.

"I'll think about it," Tag said, and rose to his feet. His father did the same and held out his hand. Tag shook it, feeling his father's strength in that big hand. "Did Mother know?"

Harlan nodded. "She couldn't live with never being sure if I was going to make it home for dinner."

Tag nodded.

"I hope you stay for Christmas, but I'll understand if you don't."

At the cabin, he packed up his things, realizing he couldn't leave without seeing Lily one more time and saying goodbye. He swung by the bar to find it closed. After a few minutes of pounding on the door, Ace appeared.

"Is Lily here?"

"She was determined to go to her place. I tried to talk her into staying with me, but my sister is one stubborn woman."

Tag smiled. "Determined and strong."

"Well, she's not feeling all that strong right now. She feels she let herself down and almost got you killed. I'm not sure she can ever forgive herself."

"It wasn't like that."

"Tell her that."

"I've tried."

Ace glanced toward the old pickup Tag was driving. "You're leaving."

"I am, but I don't want to go without seeing her again."

"She says she needs to be alone. Sorry."

"Okay." Tag turned to leave.

"I suppose you won't be back."

"Not likely," he said as he walked to his father's pickup and climbed in. The sun had come up behind the mountains and now washed the countryside with cold winter sunlight.

As he drove out of Big Sky, Tag found himself mentally kicking himself. If he hadn't gone to the bar that night and Mia hadn't stumbled into him... If he hadn't found that stupid thumb drive in his coat pocket and let Lily see it. If...

His heart began to pound as he remembered something. He turned around to head back toward Lone Mountain and called his father. "About those names. You said the thumb drive was corrupted and so was the copy Hud made, right? Lily told me that she had decoded some of them, but hadn't had a chance to finish. It was her former fiancé who gave us the list." Tag swore. "I let him use the original flash drive."

Harlan instantly was on alert. "What's his name?"

"Gerald Humphrey."

"What do you know about him?"

"Nothing. Nothing except that it took him six months to show up after he'd stood Lily up at the altar. He supposedly already left on a flight from Bozeman to Los Angeles, California, today."

He heard his father clicking on a computer keyboard. "I'm showing that he was on the flight."

"Is there any way to verify that?" Tag turned onto Lone Mountain Road and headed toward Lily's while he waited.

"I can try to contact the airport."

"But why would Gerald corrupt the thumb drive or give Lily the wrong names?" He could hear his father clacking away at the computer keyboard.

"He recently left his job in Montana to take a lesser one in California at a small private school," Harlan said. "Wait a minute. Next of kin. Gerald Humphrey has a younger sister who was recently sentenced for embezzlement. She got fifteen years and is serving time in a prison in California near the private school where he is now teaching."

Tag's mind raced. Was it possible Gerald was up to his neck in this? He hadn't come back to sweet-talk Lily into taking him back. He'd come back because Mia worked at the Canyon Bar—and she had managed to get the list. Tag cringed. He'd given the thumb drive to Gerald to decode and now it was corrupted.

"Lily mentioned something about Gerald taking a job in California," Tag said to his father. "This co-op killing group isn't just in Montana, is it? It's nationwide?"

"Tag—"

He floored the old pickup as he headed for Lily, praying he wasn't too late.

LILY FROZE AT the sight of a large dark figure standing in the doorway to the house. Her breath rushed from her as her heart took off on a downhill run.

"Lily, I knew you'd come alone."

"*Gerald?*" He moved then into the dim light so she could see his face. The familiarity of it let her suck in a couple of calming breaths before she asked, "What are you doing here? I thought you flew back to California."

"I couldn't leave just yet," he said. "Are you going to just stand in the garage all day or come inside?"

She bristled at his tone, but quickly quelled her irritation. There was a reason Gerald treated her like a child. Around him she felt like one.

He was still blocking the door as she approached, but he moved aside at the last minute to let her into her own house. She glanced around. Everything looked just as it had yesterday before she'd left to meet him. Yesterday she'd been so sure of herself. So sure she wanted something different. *Someone* more exciting.

"I'm glad you didn't leave," she said as she took off her coat.

"Really?" Gerald took the coat and hung it up.

She noticed his was also on the coatrack by the front door—in the same place it had been just two nights before. He'd certainly made himself at home, she thought, noticing that he had a small fire going in her fireplace. She'd picked up the hint of smoke as she'd come in, but hadn't registered why until this moment.

Lily resisted the part of her that resented Gerald thinking he could just come in and do as he pleased in her house.

"How did you get into the house?" she asked suddenly, and glanced toward the front door, recalling locking it before she left.

"Through the garage. You do realize I am smarter than your garage-door opener, don't you?"

She studied him, faintly aware that he seemed different. That alone threw her since Gerald had always been so solidly…Gerald.

"I've never questioned how smart you are."

"Really?" he said as he moved around the dining room table, his thick fingers dragging along the smooth edge of the wood.

She saw him slow as he reached her computer and realized that all the paperwork she'd left on the table was gone. She shot a look toward the fire. One of the papers hadn't completely burned.

Her heart began to pound so hard she thought for sure he would hear it. She glanced toward the computer screen but couldn't read what was on it.

"I'm surprised that you never asked me why I decided to move to a small private school in California," Gerald said, drawing her attention back to him.

"I didn't really get a chance to ask before…" She let the rest of what she would have said yesterday die in her throat. She wasn't up to a fight with Gerald. His standing her up at the wedding no longer mattered. It seemed a lot more than six months ago.

"Yes, the wedding," he said, and stopped moving to look at her.

"I don't want to argue about—"

"I didn't come here to try to change your mind."

That surprised her. "Then I guess I don't understand."

"Don't you? I would have thought you of all people would have put it together by now. You were my best student. You disappoint me, Lily."

She frowned. "I don't know what you're talking about."

"The code."

With a sigh, her body heavy with exhaustion, weary from the events of the past twenty-four hours, she said, "None of that matters. The names were wrong anyway. I almost died for nothing. I almost got Tag—" She stopped herself.

"*Tag.* What kind of name is that anyway? Like Ace? Another name you might call your dog?"

Lily studied Gerald then, feeling the weight of the world settling on her shoulders, and said, "I'm sorry if I hurt you, Gerald. Is that what you need me to say? Is that what you're doing here? Because I just don't know what you want from me."

He took a step toward her. "There was a time you would have known." He shook his head as he stopped within inches of her and reached out to touch her cheek with his fingers.

She closed her eyes, trying not to think of Tag's touch, of Tag's embrace, of Tag.

"But that time has long passed."

She opened her eyes, hearing the thinly veiled anger in his voice. "That's why you missed your flight? You just wanted to tell me you don't love me anymore?" A stab of anger made her heart beat a little faster. "Fine. Give it your best shot. I've disappointed you. I'm not good enough for you. Whatever it is, let's hear it. Then leave." She had started to step past him when he grabbed her arm.

"You can't possibly think that I have gone to all this trouble just to have the last word. Don't you know me any better than that?" he demanded. "Are you so besotted with that cowboy that he's turned your brain to mush?"

She tried to jerk free of his hold, but he only tightened it. "So this is about jealousy? You didn't want me but you don't want anyone else to have me, either?"

"So he has had you." He swore, something she'd

never heard him do before. He'd always said that cursing was a lazy, uneducated waste of the vernacular.

She shot him a withering look.

"Stupid cow," Gerald snapped. "Didn't you even question once why your code and mine were so different?"

Lily blinked, thrown off for a moment from the lightning-fast change of topic. "You said mine was off—"

"And you believed me." He laughed. "I guess I will always be the teacher and you will always be the pupil."

She stared at him as if seeing a stranger. She had wondered why she'd gotten some of the names right and yet others Gerald had said were wrong. If her original decoding had been accurate, then...

"I just assumed you were right and I was wrong," she said more to herself than to him. She saw how foolish that had been, not only with the code but also with her entire relationship with this man.

"Come on, my little pupil. *Think.* Don't you remember me telling you about my younger sister who lives in California?" His fingers clutching her arm tightened painfully.

"You're hurting me, Gerald."

"I told you how proud I was of her, that she was even smarter than me," he said as if he hadn't heard her or was ignoring her. "Well, guess what? All that money she was making hand over fist? It was one big lie. Embezzlement. She used that magnificent brain of hers to steal, and worse, she got caught!"

"I don't understand what that—"

"They sent her to prison! *Prison!* They put her with common thieves and killers. My precious baby sister."

His throat worked, his last words coming out in a croak. Tears welled up in his eyes.

Her mind tried to make sense of what he was saying, but she was so emotionally and physically wrung out... She jerked free of his hold and took a step back, banging into the edge of the kitchen counter.

Looming over her, he glared at her as if she were the one who'd sent his sister to prison. "Do you know anything about prison, Lily? No, of course you wouldn't know what a woman like my sister has to do to survive there."

Lily felt a chill run the length of her spine. The murder list. Her mind leapt from that thought to the most obvious one. "You didn't come here after six months to try to get me back."

Gerald gave a laugh, but it came out sounding like a sob. *"Finally."* He met her gaze, his challenging. "I did what I had to do to keep my sister safe. Just as I am going to do what I have to now."

Lily gripped the kitchen counter behind her. She was so exhausted she was having trouble understanding what he was talking about. "Gerald, it doesn't matter anymore. They say the thumb drive was corrupted—"

"I destroyed the information on the thumb drive when your boyfriend let me use it to decode the names," he said with his usual arrogance. "The information is worthless. I also destroyed the paper copies you left at the motel. The one you left was worthless. The original is gone."

Her gaze went to her computer and he laughed.

"While I was waiting for you, I put a virus in your computer that by now has destroyed everything— including the hard drive. I figured you might have used your brother's computer at some point, so when I used it to give your boyfriend the names, I also made sure a virus will destroy all his data."

He was enjoying showing how superior he was to her and the rest of the world. She'd seen that trait in him but never quite like this. What scared her was the feeling that he'd come here to do more than gloat.

A bubble of fear rose in her throat until she thought she would choke on it. "So you took care of everything."

"Not quite," he said as he closed the narrow space between them. "There is only one more copy I need to destroy." He tapped her temple. "I used to be so jealous of the way you could remember the most random things. You could remember entire lists of numbers and letters." He smiled and nodded. "You do remember the original thumb drive lists, don't you? I knew it. You've never been able to hide anything from me."

CHAPTER SEVENTEEN

TAG LEFT THE truck at the bottom of the last hill and ran the rest of the way up the road to Lily's house. He'd brought one of the guns from his father's hidden stash, but he was praying he wasn't going to have to use it.

Maybe Gerald really had gotten on the flight to California. Maybe the fact that he had a sister in prison had nothing to do with anything that had been going on.

Tag knew he was clutching at straws. There were two many coincidences. Gerald was up to his eyeballs in this. Worse, Tag had handed over the thumb drive to him. He'd trusted Gerald because he'd been so desperate to find Lily and get her out of this mess. He'd only gotten her in deeper.

Unfortunately there would be no way to prove Gerald had corrupted the thumb drive. Even the fact that he'd given the feds the wrong names could be swept under the rug as a simple mistake.

So why would Gerald do anything stupid right now when he could walk away free?

Because Lily still had a copy of the information on her computer, Tag thought with a sinking heart.

As he neared the house, he prayed he would find Lily alone, Gerald long gone.

But when he climbed up onto the deck and moved to the front window, he saw Lily and Gerald in the kitchen. He didn't need to hear what they were saying to each other. He could tell by their body language and their expressions that they were arguing.

His stomach roiled at the sight. Lily was backed up against the kitchen counter. Gerald was looming over her.

Tag tried the door, not surprised to find it locked. He was afraid to knock. He needed the element of surprise, and even with it he feared what would happen next.

He picked up a large flowerpot from the deck and, stepping back, hurled it through the window. Glass rained down in a shower onto the deck as the huge window shattered.

Pulling his gun, Tag quickly jumped through the opening into Lily's living room.

Gerald had turned in surprise at the sound of the breaking glass. His eyes widened at the gun in Tag's hands.

"Get away from him!" Tag yelled as he strode toward them, the gun aimed at Gerald's chest.

Lily seemed nailed to the floor. Her eyes widened in alarm, her mouth opened as if to scream, but nothing came out.

In that instant, Gerald took advantage of her inability to move and grabbed her, locking his arm around her throat as he backed the two of them against the kitchen counter.

"That's far enough," Gerald said as Tag advanced. "Come any closer and I'll break her neck."

Tag stopped at the edge of the dining room. Out of the corner of his eye, he saw Lily's laptop still open on the table, but the papers she'd been doing her decoding on were gone and there was the faint smell of smoke from the fireplace in the room.

"Drop your gun. Slowly," Gerald ordered.

Tag could see the painful hold Gerald had on Lily and knew he couldn't get a shot off without risking her life. Gerald was using her like a shield. Tag slowly lowered his gun, but didn't drop it.

"What's going on, Gerald?" he asked as he carefully bent down and placed his weapon on the floor, never taking his eyes off Lily's.

"Now kick the gun over here."

Tag did as he was told. The gun skittered across the floor. Gerald slowly reached down, dragging Lily with him, and picked up the gun with his free hand, never releasing his hold on her.

"You really should have gone back to Texas and left Lily alone."

LILY HAD FELT too tired to fight Gerald earlier. Now things had changed. She found a reserved strength she hadn't known she possessed. Gerald had the gun pointed at Tag. For the second time in two days, she was faced with a life-or-death situation after more than thirty-two years of an ordered, overly structured life. The only time she'd felt she wasn't in control was when she came up here to the Canyon to work for her brother.

Until this.

"Let him go," Lily said hoarsely from the choke hold on her throat. "This is between you and me."

Gerald's laugh held no humor. "That might have been the case yesterday when I pleaded with you to come back to me. Maybe we could have worked something out then...."

"You sold out your own fiancée," Tag said as he took a step toward the dining room, forcing Gerald to turn a little in order to keep her in front of him.

"Ex-fiancée," Gerald snapped, and motioned the gun

at him. "Didn't she mention that to you? I'm surprised. I thought the two of you…"

"That's what I planned to tell you," Lily said. She shifted so she was closer to the kitchen counter. Her hand snaked behind her as she sought out the drawer where she'd dropped the gun earlier. "I was hoping it wasn't too late for us, Gerald. I wanted the life you offered where I knew who I was." There was a ring of truth to her words since that was exactly what she'd been thinking on her way home.

Tag's gaze widened a little, his expression saddening.

"It's not too late, Gerald," she continued as she eased the drawer open. "As you said, there's no proof you've done anything wrong. You've destroyed everything, all that you need to worry about anyway. If you kill this man, then that all changes."

She eased the drawer open, feeling Gerald loosen the hold on her a little. Her fingers curled around the handle of the gun.

"You had second thoughts?" Gerald said quietly next to her ear.

She nodded. His hold loosened even a little more. She could breathe, and for a moment that was all she did. Then she slowly lifted out the gun, holding it at her side out of his range of sight. "I was going to come back to you."

As if he felt the truth in her words, his surprise moved through his body. He seemed to slump against her.

"I don't understand," he whispered.

Tag was looking at her as if he didn't understand, either.

"I wanted safe," she said.

"Safe?" Gerald repeated, and let out a hoarse laugh, the irony not lost on him.

Tag's gaze went to her side. He gave a small shake of his head at the sight of the gun clutched in her hand.

"Nothing has changed," Gerald said, his tone almost pleading. "We can get past this. Our lives can be exactly like we planned. Even better after this."

Lily had to bite her tongue. Did he really think they could pick up where they'd left off? All forgiven and forgotten?

He was crazier than she'd thought.

In the distance, she heard sirens and realized how badly this could go if she didn't move quickly. "Tag, you should go," she said.

Gerald shook his head and tightened his hold on her. "Lily. We can't let him just walk away. Not now."

"We have to, Gerald. It's the only way."

But even as she said it, she felt Gerald tense the arm holding the gun. He leveled it at Tag's heart. "I'm sorry, Lily, but I think it's too late for us."

TAG KNEW WHEN he came through the door that Gerald was dangerous. The man had come too far and knew there was no turning back. Gerald Humphrey had crossed a line that a man like him couldn't come back from.

For just an instant, Tag felt sorry for him. He could understand wanting to protect someone you loved.

He looked down the barrel of the gun Gerald had pointed at him, saw the man steady it and knew all the talking was done.

At the same time, Tag saw Lily make the decision. "No!" he yelled as he dived to the side. The first gunshot was followed only an instant later by a second.

The scream that filled the air made the hair rise on the back of his neck. He hit the floor and rolled, coming up to find Gerald Humphrey on the floor holding the thigh of his right leg and writhing in pain.

Lily stood over him, the gun still in her hand, her face as white as the snow outside. Gerald had gotten off one shot before dropping his weapon and grabbing his wounded leg.

Tag quickly stepped to him to kick his gun away before reaching to take the pistol from Lily. She had a death grip on the gun. He eased it from her fingers.

She gave him a barely perceptible nod.

He smiled as he cupped a hand behind her neck and drew her to him, wrapping her in his arms. She hugged him tightly as he breathed the words into the soft, sweet scent of her hair. "You saved my life."

On the floor, Gerald began to curse. "Are the two of you just going to let me lie here and bleed to death? Call a doctor!"

In the distance, Tag could hear the sirens. He pulled out his cell phone, hit 911 and asked for an ambulance as flashing lights flickered across the fallen snow outside the window. Tag watched his father and Deputy Marshal Jake Thorton come racing up to the house, weapons drawn, and pulled Lily closer.

CHAPTER EIGHTEEN

CHRISTMAS EVE IT began to snow and became one of those winter nights when the flakes are as large as goose feathers. They drifted down in a wall of white so thick they obliterated everything out the window at Cardwell Ranch.

"Merry Christmas," Tag said as he came up behind Lily.

She leaned back into him and watched the falling snow to the sound of Christmas music and children's laughter. In the kitchen, Stacy and the kids were finishing up baking gingerbread men. Dana had been relegated to sitting at the kitchen table and helping ice the cookies. The smell of ginger wafted through the old ranch house, mingling with the even sweeter scent of evergreen.

Lily could hear her brother in the kitchen. He'd volunteered to help with the cookie decorating, as well. She'd never seen Ace with kids before. He was a natural.

"I always dreamed of a Christmas like this," Lily said, turning in Tag's arms to look up into his face. "I would come home from boarding school to find the house was already decorated by some designer my mother had hired. We always had a white-flocked tree with different-colored lights on it depending on what was in that year. Everything was very…tasteful."

"Compared to an amazing tree like this one?" Tag joked, nodding toward Dana's "orphan" tree.

Lily laughed. The tree wasn't what most would consider a Christmas tree, but she loved that it was decorated with ornaments the children had made. Her mother would never have allowed a tree like that in her house.

How different her life and Ace's would have been if her mother had adopted an orphan tree and let her children decorate it. Would Lily have ever agreed to marry a man like Gerald Humphrey?

She thought of Gerald. He'd confessed to everything but refused to name names to protect himself in prison—as well as his sister. Lily had been able to supply the letters from the original thumb drive from memory. After they were decoded, the FBI had the names and was now rounding up the former inmates who had done the killings. For the time being at least, the co-op murder group had been shut down.

"That is the most beautiful Christmas tree I have ever seen," she said, feeling tears sting her eyes as she turned to look at him. They'd been through so much together in such a short time and yet she felt as if she had always known him.

Tag cocked an eyebrow at her, then smiled and pulled her in for a kiss.

"You're only supposed to kiss under the misseytoe," said a small voice behind them. Lily turned to find Dana's daughter, Mary, pointing at the mistletoe hanging near the door. "That's where Mommy and Daddy kiss."

Mary's older brother, Hank, came into the room in time to make a grimacing face. "They are always kissing. Gross."

Tag and Lily laughed. A moment later Ace came

into the room carrying a tray of gingerbread men. The twins, Angus and Brick, now fourteen months old and their cousin, Ella, now almost two, came toddling into the room following the cookies. They had icing smeared across their faces. They were followed by their aunt Stacy with a washcloth.

"I decorated those," Ace said with obvious pride as he pointed to the perfectly decorated cookies.

"I did those," Mary said, pointing to some cookies that were unrecognizable under all the different colors of icing.

"I can't tell the difference." Lily grinned at her brother.

Hud and Dana joined them, Dana in the wheelchair her husband had insisted she stay in until she was stronger. She was plenty strong, Lily thought. She recalled her own moments over the past few days when she'd been stronger than she'd ever believed she could be. So much had changed, she thought, glancing over at Tag. Or maybe she'd just changed. She would never admit it to her brother, but she had been afraid to live life. She'd thought she'd wanted safe and sedate, just as she and Ace had been raised.

But Tag had changed all that. No matter what happened in the future, she knew she could never go back to being the woman who'd been willing to settle for what Gerald Humphrey had offered her.

At the sound of sleigh bells, everyone in the room went quiet. Christmas music played faintly from the kitchen as heavy boots stomped across the porch. An instant later the door flew open and a Santa Claus suspiciously resembling Tag's father filled the doorway.

Mary and Hank let out cheers and ran to him. Santa

was followed into the house by Angus dragging a huge bag loaded with gifts. Tag looked at Lily and saw the delight in her face. He wished he could see that look on her face always.

Jordan and his very pregnant wife, Deputy Marshal Liza Cardwell, arrived moments later with presents. Not long after that, Dana's brother, Clay, landed by helicopter out by the barn in a shower of snow. He came in singing Christmas carols and got them all singing around the fireplace and the orphan tree.

As Tag felt Harlan's aka Santa's arm drop over his shoulders, a lump formed in his throat. He'd wanted a Montana Christmas, and he couldn't have asked for a more perfect one than this.

He wished this night would never end, he thought as he watched his family opening presents around the tree. But the holidays were almost over and Texas and the rest of his family and their business loomed large on the horizon.

LILY WOKE JUST as the sun was peeking over the mountains. She hadn't wanted to open her eyes. Lying under the down comforter, she was warm and cozy, still feeling the effects of her lovemaking with Tag not that many hours ago.

It had been the best Christmas Eve of her life and she thought it funny she could think that, given that she'd almost been killed in the days before. Last night, Tag had been so gentle. She shivered at the thought. He'd brought her back to her house after midnight, swept her up into his arms and carried her to the bed.

He'd kissed her so gently, so sweetly. She'd thought she'd only imagined the passion from their first lovemaking. But then the kisses had become more amorous.

She'd felt heat race through her veins, making her skin sensitive to the touch. He'd peeled away her clothing, kissing each patch of skin he revealed, finding places on her body to caress as if memorizing every inch of her.

She'd reciprocated, loving the feel of his skin and the way he shuddered with delight as she moved over him. They kissed and touched until, both naked and barely able to contain themselves, they'd finally coupled. Locked in each other's arms, they'd let their passion run wild like the storm outside.

Just the thought of their lovemaking made Lily reach over to the other side of her bed, expecting to find Tag's warm body. Earlier they'd been spooned together.

Her eyes flew open. The bed was empty. Loss raced through her on the heels of fear. Would Tag just leave? Last night he'd said he didn't know how he would be able to tell her goodbye when the holidays were over. Had he gone back to Texas?

Grabbing her silk robe, she moved toward the living room, terrified she would find a scribbled note and Tag Cardwell gone.

But as she rounded the corner, she did a double take. With everything that had been going on, she hadn't had time to do the little decorating she normally did for Christmas.

That was why she was shocked to see a large beautiful Christmas tree standing in the front window. It shone with an array of colored lights and ornaments. Tag stood in front of it wearing nothing but a pair of jeans.

She looked at him in surprise.

He grinned. "You like it? I got Hank and Mary to make ornaments for it, and my father gave me some of the ones from when I was a child."

Tears welled up in her eyes. "I *love* it."

"I wanted you to have that old-fashioned Christmas you always dreamed of—not just the one at Cardwell Ranch."

She rushed to him and threw her arms around his neck. "Oh, Tag."

He held her to him, the lights of the tree flickering in the early-morning light. "I can't leave you, Lily. And I can't ask you to quit your job to move to Texas," he said finally, holding her at arm's length.

She tried to swallow past the lump in her throat.

TAG LOOKED INTO Lily's beautiful face and felt so much love for her that it nearly knocked him to his knees.

"There is only one thing I can do," he said. "It was actually my father's idea."

Last night, Harlan had stopped him as Tag and Lily were leaving Cardwell Ranch. "Are you really headed back to Texas?"

"Christmas is over," Tag had said as Lily walked on out to her SUV they had arrived in. "I have a business to run with my brothers."

"I just wish we'd had some time to get to know each other better."

Tag had laughed at that. "Oh, I think we got to know each other quite well."

"I'm serious. I wish you would stay longer. You know Big Sky could really use a good Texas barbecue joint."

"Your father gave you the idea?" Lily said now.

He nodded, smiling. "He thinks I should open a Texas Boys Barbecue joint in Big Sky. What do you think?"

She laughed and leaned up to kiss him. "That is the best Christmas present I could have asked for."

"Really?" he asked with a grin. "Then I guess I'll have to take this back." He drew a small dark velvet box out of his pocket. "I was going to wait until later under the Christmas tree, but I can't wait another moment."

Her heart began to pound.

"I know it probably seems fast—"

She shook her head and he laughed.

"Yeah, that's kind of the way I feel," he said, and he opened the box. The winter light caught the diamond, sending a prism of brilliant light ricocheting around the room.

"I love you, Lily McCabe. Marry me someday? Someday soon?"

Lily laughed and nodded through her tears as he slipped the ring on her finger.

* * * * *

KEEPING CHRISTMAS

This one is for my Uncle Jack Johnson, whom we lost this year. Jack will be greatly missed, especially his big heart, his laugh and his Texas barbecue.

PROLOGUE

THE RAIN HAD stopped, but the parking garage seemed unusually cold and dark as Dixie Bonner started to step from the elevator.

One booted foot poised on the edge of the concrete, she hesitated, sensing something was wrong. She stood listening for whatever sound had alerted her, only now aware of how late it was. The library had closed for the night as had all the other businesses around it except the coffee shop back up the street where she'd been the past few hours.

She hadn't realized the time or noticed how dark and empty the streets were. All the holiday shoppers had gone home for the night. She'd foolishly paid no attention because she'd had other things on her mind.

Now she felt vulnerable. Not that she wasn't used to taking chances. It went with her job. But taking chances was one thing. Just being plain dumb was another.

She let one hand drop to her shoulder bag as she eased back, but kept her free hand holding the elevator doors open as she scanned the parking garage.

Her fingers found the purse's zipper and began to slowly glide it open, speeding up as she heard the scrape of a shoe sole on the concrete floor of the garage.

She was in danger, but then she'd suspected that the moment the elevator doors had opened. She'd been on edge all night, at one point almost certain someone had been watching her beyond the rain-streaked window of the coffee shop.

There were two vehicles left in the unattended garage. A tan cargo van and her fire-engine-red Mustang. The van was parked right next to the Mustang.

Her hand closed over the can of pepper spray in her purse as she debated making a run for her car or returning to the upper level of the parking garage. Neither seemed prudent.

The decision was made for her as a man wearing a black stocking mask suddenly appeared in the open elevator doorway. A gun glinted in his right hand. She hit the door close button at the same time she brought up the can of pepper spray and pointed it at the man's face.

He let out a howl and stumbled back as the full force of the pepper spray hit him in the eyes and soaked into the mask.

She shoved past him through the closing elevator doors, her eyes tearing from being in close quarters with the spray. Running, near blind, tears streaming down her face, she sprinted toward the red blur of her car.

Too late she sensed movement out of the corner of her eye. A second masked man tackled her and took her down hard, knocking the air from her lungs. She landed on her stomach, gasping for breath even before he jammed his knee into her back to hold her down.

She still had the pepper spray can in one hand, a tight grip on her purse in the other. But she had a bad feeling that these men weren't after her purse.

She tried to yell for help, knowing it was senseless. There was no one around. No one would hear her cries even if she had enough breath to scream.

Strong fingers twisted the pepper spray from her hand. She heard the can land where the man threw it, the can rolling away into the silence of the vacuous parking garage.

With her face pushed into the gritty cold-damp concrete, she could see nothing but the tires of her car next to her. She'd almost made it to safety.

She heard the first man come running up.

"Bitch." He cursed. "My face is friggin' on fire."

She heard the anger in his voice and knew things were about to get a whole lot worse. The kick caught her in the ribs. The pain was excruciating, her cry pitiful, as the air was knocked out of her again.

She gasped for breath, fighting the terror that now had a death grip on her. She didn't stand a chance against two men. Not alone in this garage. With a sabbatical from work and her lousy relationship with her family, it could be weeks before anyone even realized she was missing.

"Stop!" the second man ordered. "For hell's sake don't kill her yet. We have to find out where she put the damned journal and the disks before you—"

The second blow was to her head. Pain glittered behind her eyes just before the darkness.

DIXIE WOKE IN blackness, her head throbbing, her body cramped. She shifted position, bumped an elbow and a knee, and started to panic, gasping for breath as she realized she was in a cramped dark space.

She fought not to panic, not to let her mind tell her that her small prison was slowly closing in on her.

Breathe. You're alive. Temporarily. *Breathe.*

"Just bring the damned computer and all the disks you can find." It was the voice of the second man from the parking garage.

"I thought it was supposed to look like a robbery," the first demanded.

"You let me take care of that. What about her journal? Have you found it yet?"

"It's not in here."

She heard the sound of footfalls heavy nearby as if someone was treading up stairs. She held her breath, trying to calm her breathing, her panic.

Her fingers moved slowly, cautiously, along the inside of the space around her. She frowned, feeling cool metal, rough carpet. She could hear the sound of things breaking, larger things being knocked over. She sniffed and caught a familiar scent. Laundry detergent. She'd bought a box at the market earlier and put it—

She was in the trunk of her car!

The realization sent a shot of hope racing through her. Hurriedly, she oriented herself, scrunching her body to get her feet against the rear seat, the one with the broken latch. She could hear voices. The two men arguing.

Bracing her body against the opposite side of the trunk, her feet against the rear seat, she pushed with all her strength.

At the sound of a loud crash, she kicked the seat hard. The latch gave, the seat flopped down.

Through the hole came light. She wiggled around until she could peer out. The car was parked in her garage. The two men were inside her house, the adjoining door open.

She listened, afraid they would come back now. No sound. Had they heard her?

She moved fast, half afraid they would be standing outside her car amused at the futility of what she thought was her great escape. But she had *no* chance cramped in the trunk. She didn't have much chance in the back seat. But even a little edge was better than nothing.

Slithering through the space with the seat down, she ducked behind the front seats and looked out. No sign of the men in the garage. The door to the house was still open, but she couldn't see anything but light coming from the kitchen. Where were the men?

She heard the sounds of more objects breaking, things being knocked over and destroyed. She grabbed the back door handle and, as quietly as possible, popped it open.

Inside the house she heard another crash, then voices. She slipped out of the car, making the decision just as quickly. The keys were in the ignition. She opened the driver's side door, slid behind the wheel and locked all four doors as she reached for the garage door opener and said a silent prayer.

The garage door began to lift slowly and noisily as she fired up the car's engine, her eyes on the door leading into the house.

The overhead garage door was too slow. Hurry! She had the car in Reverse, engine revved, ready, her gaze flicking nervously from the slowly rising garage door to the open door to the house. The garage door was a third of the way up. Just a little higher.

The two men came flying out of the house, stumbling down the steps that dropped into the garage. One of them slammed into the side of her car and groped for the door handle.

The garage door was almost up enough. The second man shoved past him, a gun in his hand. The man with the gun started to raise the weapon as she tromped down on the gas. The car shot backward under the rising garage door, the antenna snapping off.

She thought she heard a shot as she swung the car around in the driveway, slammed it into first and took off, tearing across the lawn, jumping the curb, tires squealing as they met pavement, engine screaming.

She hadn't realized she'd been holding her breath until it came out on a sob. She was shaking so hard, she could hardly hold on to the steering wheel. But she kept going. They would be coming after her. She'd seen the van parked just down the street from her house.

Worse, she'd seen their faces.

She'd known in the parking garage that they'd planned to kill her. But now they had no choice.

She'd recognized one of them—and he knew it.

CHAPTER ONE

ALL CHANCE WALKER wanted was to get to the cabin before the snowstorm and the holiday traffic got any worse.

He'd only stopped in for a minute, but now he couldn't wait to get home. He glanced around his office, ignoring the dust that had accumulated while he'd been gone. The light was flashing on his antiquated answering machine. For a moment he thought about checking his calls.

But it was only days until Christmas and he told himself he wasn't in the mood for anything to do with work. Anyone he wanted to talk to knew he hadn't been in his office for weeks and wouldn't be for a while longer. The only reason he'd stopped by this evening was to gather up any bills from the floor where the mailman had dropped them through the old-fashioned door slot.

Chance nudged his dog awake with the toe of his boot. From in front of the old radiator, Beauregard lifted his head and blinked at him, the dog not looking any more anxious to go out in the cold than Chance was.

"Come on, boy. Once we get to the cabin I'll build us a fire and make us both big fat steaks. It's the holidays. I think we deserve a treat."

The dog keyed on the word "treat" and jumped to his feet, padding to the door, tail wagging.

Chance glanced around the office one last time to

make sure he hadn't missed anything, not sure when he'd be back. The private investigator business was slow this time of year in Montana and he knew he hadn't completely recuperated from the bullet Doc had taken out of his shoulder.

While the physical wound had healed, Chance's heart wasn't into work yet. He wasn't sure when he would be again. Certainly not until the holidays were long gone. This time of year was always the toughest for him.

He saw Beauregard's ears perk up as they both heard the outside door open. Chance didn't give it a thought since he shared the building with a beauty salon, an insurance firm, investment office and a knitting shop.

With Christmas just days away, he knew the beauty shop and knitting store had been busy. That would explain the small, slowly melting snowdrift that had formed just inside his door. With the main entrance door opening and closing all the time, gusts of snow blew up the hallway and under his office door. He'd turned down the heat in his absence, planning to hide out until after the holidays and things slowed down again in his building.

He picked up his old black Stetson from his desk and snugged it down on his head, then moved to open the door, turning out his office lights as he and Beauregard stepped into the long hallway.

At the other end, a bundled-up figure had just come in. Snowflakes, light as feathers, skittered along the wood floor as the man shut the front door behind him, closing out the snowy December evening and the sound of a bell jingler nearby.

Chance slammed his office door, checking to make sure it was locked, and started down the hallway.

The man hadn't moved. Probably waiting for his wife in the beauty salon or the knitting shop.

But as Chance drew closer, he felt a familiar prickle of unease. The man was good-size, huddled in a sheepskin coat, fine boots and slacks, his face in shadow under a pale gray Stetson. A wealthy Montana rancher or— Chance felt a start and swore under his breath.

Or a rich Texas oilman.

"Chance Walker," the man drawled in a familiar, gravely voice.

Next to Chance the dog let out a low growl as the hair stood up on the back of the canine's neck.

"Easy, Beauregard," Chance said as he reached down to pet the mutt, surprised his dog had the same reaction Chance did to the man.

"You named your dog Beauregard?"

"Couldn't think of a better name for a stray, mean-spirited mongrel."

Beauregard Bonner let out of howl of laughter and thrust out his hand, grabbing Chance's and pulling him into a quick back-slapping hug. "Damn, boy, I've missed you." Beauregard, the dog, growled louder in warning. "Call off your dog and tell me where we can get a stiff drink in this town. You and I need to talk."

Chance couldn't imagine what he and Beauregard Bonner might have to talk about. The last time Chance had seen Bonner it had been in the man's Texas mansion outside of Houston. Bonner had been gripping a shotgun and threatening to blast a hole the size of Texas in him.

"Damn, this is a cold country," Bonner said, rubbing his gloved hands together and grinning good-naturedly, but there was a nervous edge to the man that Chance didn't miss. "I don't know about you, but I really could use that drink."

Chance had a feeling he would need one himself. He pointed to the Stockman Bar across the street, his curiosity getting the better of him. What would bring a man like Bonner all the way to Montana in the middle of winter?

Nothing good, of that Chance was certain as they crossed the street in the near blizzard, the dog trotting along beside them.

"They let dogs in bars up here?" Bonner asked in surprise as the dog followed them through the door and down the long bar to sprawl on the floor under Chance's stool.

"Actually, they prefer dogs over Texans," Chance said.

Bonner looked over at him with a Don't Mess With Texas scowl. "I don't care how long you've lived here, you're still a Texan, born and raised."

Chance said nothing as Bonner ordered them both a drink. Bonner still drank expensive Scotch neat. Chance had a beer, nursing it since he had the drive ahead of him to the cabin—and he knew to keep his wits about him as he studied the man sitting on the stool next to him with growing dread.

Beauregard Bonner had aged since Chance had last seen him. His blond hair had grayed and the lines around his eyes had deepened. But the booming drawl was that of the filthy rich oilman Chance remembered only too well.

"Guess you're wondering what I'm doing here," Bonner said after downing half of his drink.

Chance stared down into his beer, waiting. A Christmas song was playing on the jukebox and the back bar glittered with multicolored lights. There was a Christmas tree decorated with beer cans at the other end of the bar and a large Santa doll with a beer bottle tucked in his sack.

"It's my daughter," Bonner said.

Chance's head shot up. "Rebecca?" Last he'd heard, Rebecca had married some hotshot lawyer from back east who'd gone to work for her father. They lived in a big house near Houston and had three kids.

"Not Rebecca." Bonner made a face. "*Dixie.*"

"Dixie?" Rebecca's little sister? Chance recalled freckles, lots of them, braces and pigtails, an impish little kid who'd been a real pain in the neck the whole time he'd been dating Rebecca.

"Dixie might be in some trouble," Bonner said as he scowled down at his drink.

Chance could not for the life of him imagine what that had to do with him and said as much.

"I want to hire you to find her."

Chance pulled back, even more surprised. "They don't have private investigators in Texas?"

"She's not in Texas. She's in Montana. At least, it's where the last kidnapper's call came from."

Chance swore. "*Kidnapper?*"

"I need you to find her. I'm worried this time because the ransom demand is a million dollars."

"This time? What was it *last* time?" Chance asked, half joking.

"When Dixie was three, it was a hundred dollars. Then a hundred thousand in high school. Five hundred grand in college. I figured Dixie was too smart to ever ask for a million, but damned if she didn't."

Chance couldn't believe this. "Have you contacted the police? The FBI? Shouldn't someone be looking for her?"

"There's something you have to understand about

Dixie. The last time she had herself kidnapped in college, I had cut off her money over a little dispute between us. The FBI got involved. It was ugly. She was dating some loser…" He drained his drink and signaled the bartender for another.

Chance motioned that he was fine. "Loser?" he repeated, remembering when Bonner had called him the same thing. It was about the time he'd started dating Dixie's older sister Rebecca. Chance supposed Bonner would still consider him just that, a loser. So why come all this way to hire *him?*

Rubbing a hand over his face, Chance asked, "So you're saying that Dixie hasn't really been kidnapped. You're sure about that?"

"I can't be sure of anything with Dixie." Bonner tipped up his glass and swallowed. "That's why I want you to find her. I trust you more than I do the police or the FBI, and you can do it with more discretion."

Chance shook his head. "For starters, I don't have the resources of either of those agencies and I'm not working right now. I'm taking the holidays off."

Bonner nodded. "Heard about you getting shot." He smiled at Chance's reaction. "I've kept my eye on you over the years."

Nothing could have surprised Chance more, but he did his best to hide it. "Then you know that I'm not taking any cases right now."

"I know you almost got killed, but that the guy who shot you is dead and won't be hurting anyone else thanks to you," Bonner said.

"Don't try to make killing a man a virtue, all right?"

"You had no other choice," Bonner said. "I saw the police report. Also, I know that your shoulder is as good as new." He smiled again, a twinkle in his eye. "Money talks…"

Chance swore under his breath. Bonner hadn't changed a bit. He believed he could buy anything—and most of the time he could. Bonner's was a famous Texas story. Raised on a chicken-scratch farm, poor as a church mouse, Beauregard Bonner had become filthy rich overnight when oil had been discovered on the place his old man had left him.

Ever since, Bonner had used his money to control as many people as possible. And vice versa if what he was saying about his youngest daughter was true.

"Go to the authorities," Chance said irritably. "You've come to the wrong man for this one."

"I can't," Bonner said, looking down into his drink again. "They wouldn't take it seriously. Why should they, given that she's pulled this stunt before and there is no evidence that she's been abducted?"

"What about the ransom demand and the fact that she's missing? There was a ransom demand, right?"

"Just a male voice over the phone demanding a million dollars before I even knew she *was* missing," Bonner said. "I thought it was a joke. The call came from a pay phone in Billings, Montana."

Chance studied the older man for a long moment. "What is it you aren't telling me?"

Bonner sighed. "Just that I need her found as quietly as possible. I'm involved in some deals right now that are sensitive, which I'm sure is why she's doing this now."

Chance stared at the man. "You're telling me your business deal is more important than your daughter?"

"Don't be an ass, of course not," Bonner snapped. "Don't you think I pulled a few strings to find out what

I could? All the recent charges on Dixie's credit cards have what they say is her signature. From the pattern of use it would appear that she's up to her old tricks."

Chance groaned. "She's *kidnapped* herself?" Again. Why did she have to pick Montana this time, though? "Why don't you just give her the million? Hell, she's going to inherit a lot more than that someday anyway, right?"

Bonner looked over at him and shook his head. "She'd just give it all away. To save some small country somewhere. Or a bunch of damned whales. Or maybe free some political prisoners. She's like my brother Carl. I swear it's almost as if they feel guilty that we have money and want to give it all away."

"Generosity, yeah, that's a real bad trait. No wonder you're so worried."

Bonner ignored the jab. "You don't know Dixie."

No, he didn't. Or at least he hadn't since she was twelve. Nor was he planning to get to know the grown-up version.

He pushed away his beer and stood, Beauregard the dog getting quickly to his feet—no doubt remembering the promise of a treat once they got to the cabin. "Sorry, but you'll have to get someone else. When you came in, I was just closing up my office for the rest of the holidays and going to my cabin."

"The one on the lake," Bonner said without looking at him.

Chance tried to tamp down his annoyance. Clearly Bonner had been doing more than just keeping track of him all these years. Just how much had he dug up on him? Chance hated to think.

"I know about the cabin you built there," Bonner said, his gaze on his drink, his voice calm, but a muscle flexed in his jaw belying his composure. "I also know you need money." He turned then to look at Chance. "For your medical bills. And your daughter's."

Chance felt all the air rush out of him. He picked up the beer he'd pushed away and took a drink to give himself time to get his temper under control.

It didn't work. "You wouldn't really consider using my daughter to get me to do what you want, would you?" he asked through gritted teeth.

Bonner met his gaze, but something softened in his expression. "Dixie is a hellion and probably payback for what a bastard I've been all of my life, but she's my *daughter,* Chance. My flesh and blood, and I'm scared that this time she really *is* in trouble."

CHAPTER TWO

CHANCE DROVE TO his cabin, Beauregard sitting next to him on the pickup's bench seat, panting and drooling as he stared expectantly out at the blizzard.

On the seat between him and the dog was the manila envelope Beauregard Bonner had forced on him. Chance hadn't opened it, had barely touched it—still didn't want to.

Snow whirled through the air, blinding and hypnotic, the flakes growing larger and thicker as the storm settled in. He drove the road along the edge of the lake, getting only glimpses of the row of summer cabins boarded up for the season until he came to the narrow private road that led to his cabin.

His cabin was at the end of the road. He shifted into four-wheel drive, bucking the snow that had already filled the narrow road. Although mostly sheltered in pines, his cabin had one hell of a view of the lake. That's why he'd picked the lot. For the view. And the isolation. There were no other cabins nearby. Just him and the lake and the pines stuck back into the mountainside.

He was still mentally kicking himself as he pulled up behind the cabin and cut the engine. He wasn't sure who he was angrier at, himself or Beauregard Bonner. He couldn't believe he'd taken the job. The last person on earth he wanted to work for was Bonner—not for *any* amount of money.

But Bonner, true to form, had found Chance's weakness. And Chance had been forced to swallow his pride and his anger, and think only of how the outrageous amount of money Bonner was offering him would help take care of the medical bills.

Not that the whole thing hadn't put him in a foul mood. And it being so close to Christmas, too.

He sat in the pickup, listening to the ticking of the engine as it cooled, taking a moment to just stare out at his cabin, the storm and what little he could see of the frozen white expanse of lake that stretched for miles.

Nothing settled him like this place. He'd built the cabin with his own hands, every log, every stone. His daughter had been born here on a night much like this one.

Beauregard pawed at his arm, no doubt wondering what the hold up was on that treat. "Sorry, boy." Chance smiled as he reached over and rubbed the dog's big furry head. Beauregard really was the ugliest dog Chance had ever seen. A big gangly thing, the dog was covered with a mottled mass of fur in every shade of brown. But those big brown eyes broke your heart. Two pleading big brown eyes that were now focused on him.

Chance had found him beside the road, starving and half dead. He'd seen himself in the dog—the mutt was the most pathetic thing Chance had ever laid eyes on. He'd worn no collar, had apparently been on his own for a long time, and hadn't had the best disposition. Clearly they were two of a kind and meant to be together.

"I know," Chance said, opening his pickup door. "I promised a treat." The moment he'd said the word treat, Chance knew it had been a mistake.

Beauregard bounded over the top of him, knocking the beat-up black Stetson off Chance's head as the dog bolted out the door and along the walkway to the deck at the front of the cabin.

Laughing, Chance got out, as well, retrieving his Stetson and slapping the snow from it as he followed the dog. On his way, he grabbed an armful of firewood and took a moment to pause as he always did to say a prayer for his daughter.

REBECCA BONNER LANCASTER pressed her slim body against the wall in the dark hallway, feeling nothing like the Southern belle she pretended to be.

She could hear her husband on the phone, but was having trouble making out what he was saying.

It was hard for her to believe that she had stooped this low. Spying on her husband. What would her friends at the country club think? Most of the time, she couldn't have cared less what Oliver was up to.

Everyone in Houston knew he'd had his share of affairs since they'd been married. She suspected that most wives pretended not to know because it came as relief. As long as he left her alone, it was just fine with her.

As the daughter of Beauregard Bonner, she had her friends, her charity work, her whirlwind schedule of social obligations. That kept her plenty busy. Not to mention overseeing the nanny, the housekeepers and the household.

Rebecca couldn't say she was happy, but she was content. She doubted most women could even say that. No, she told herself, no matter what her husband was up to, she'd made the right decision marrying Oliver Lancaster.

Oliver came from a family with a good name but no money, and while the Bonners had money, they didn't have the pedigree. Because of that, it had been a perfect match. Oliver had opened doors that had been closed to her and her family. He was good-looking, charming and tolerant of her family and her own indiscretions.

Of course, her money helped. That, and his prestigious job working for her father. She knew Oliver didn't really "do" anything as legal consultant at Bonner Unlimited. The truth was he'd barely passed the bar and provided little consulting to her father. Beauregard had a team of high-paid lawyers, the best money could buy, when he really needed a lawyer.

But Oliver didn't seem to mind being paid to do nothing. And the title didn't hurt in social circles either.

"What?" she heard her husband demand to someone on the phone.

Rebecca held her breath. For days now she'd noticed something was bothering Oliver. She'd hinted, asked, even had sex with him, but whatever it was, he was keeping it to himself.

So, she'd gone from snooping through his suit pockets to eavesdropping on his phone conversations.

Oliver swore. She could hear him pacing, something he only did when he was upset with her or her father.

"What the hell did he do that for?" Oliver demanded into the phone, then lowered his voice to ask, "Where is he now?"

Rebecca frowned, wondering who Oliver was talking about.

"That son of a bitch," Oliver swore again.

There was only one person Oliver referred to in that tone and in those exact words. Her father. What had Daddy done now? She closed her eyes, relieved there was nothing more to it than Oliver finding fault with her father.

"Montana?" Oliver said.

Rebecca's eyes flew open.

"What the hell is he doing in Montana?"

Daddy was in Montana?

"You've got to be kidding me. That damned Dixie."

Dixie?

Her husband had moved to the other end of the room now, his voice muffled. She slipped along the wall silent as a cat, knowing it would be ugly if she got caught. And Oliver hated ugly scenes.

She could hear him talking, but still couldn't make out most of the words. Then she heard a name that stopped her cold.

Chance Walker.

Daddy was in Montana and it had something to do with her sister Dixie and Chance Walker?

All the breath rushed out of her. She hadn't heard Chance's name in years. She'd completely forgotten about him. Well, maybe not completely. But she had been sure her father had.

What possible reason would Daddy and Dixie have for going to Montana—let alone that it involved Chance Walker?

"Don't worry, I will. As long as nothing holds up the deal. I told you, you can count on me. No, no, I believe you. As long as you say it isn't going to be a problem. All right. If you're sure."

Rebecca was shaking so hard she could barely catch a breath. Chance Walker. She'd thought she'd never hear that name again. But now that she had, she felt sick as it brought back the memory of the choice she'd made so many years ago—and why.

As Oliver hung up the phone, Rebecca retreated down the hall as quickly and quietly as possible. He was the last person she wanted to see right now.

AFTER CHANCE HAD a big roaring fire going in the stone fireplace, he spotted the manila envelope where he'd tossed it on the table. It wasn't too late to call Bonner to tell him he'd changed his mind.

Every instinct told him that Bonner was holding out on him. He hadn't been telling him the truth. Or at the very least, the whole truth.

Cursing himself and Bonner, he picked up the envelope and pulled out Dixie Bonner's most recent credit card records. It amazed him what money could buy. Confidential records being probably the least of it.

Shoving away thoughts of Beauregard Bonner, he concentrated on the records. If Dixie wanted her kidnapping to appear real, why would she use and sign her own credit cards?

Unless someone was forcing her to use them.

He focused on the charges for a moment. They made no sense. No car needed gas as often as she'd used her cards. Unless she was crazy—or stupid—she had to know she was leaving a trail any fool could follow.

According to this, Dixie had bought gas at the most southeastern part of the state, then begun what appeared to be a zigzag path across Montana.

Beauregard let out a bark, startling him. He looked up from the report to see the dog staring at him, recrimination in those big brown eyes now.

"Sorry." He tossed the credit card report aside and headed for the kitchen where he melted half a stick of butter in a large cast-iron skillet until it was lightly browned, then dropped in two large rib-eye steaks.

As they began to sizzle, he stabbed a big white potato a couple of times with a fork and tossed it into the microwave to cook. He considered a second vegetable but instead pulled out a Montana map and spread it out on the table. Retrieving Dixie Bonner's credit card reports, he traced a line from town to town across the state.

Alzada. Glendive. Wolf Point. Jordan. Roundup. Lewistown. Big Sandy. Fort Benton. Belt.

Chance heard the steaks sizzling and turned to see that Beauregard was keeping watch over them from his spot in front of the stove. Chance stepped to the stove to flip the steaks, opened the microwave to turn the potato, dug out sour cream, chopped up some green onions and found the bottle of steak sauce in the back of the fridge—all the time wondering what the hell Dixie Bonner's kidnappers were doing.

If there even were kidnappers.

Either way, zigzagging across Montana made no sense. Why not light somewhere? Any small Montana town would do. Or any spot in between where there was a motel or a cabin in the woods—if a person wanted to hide.

But if a person wanted to be found...

He pulled the skillet with the steaks from the burner and turned off the gas. He could hear his potato popping and hissing in the microwave.

Beauregard was licking his chops and wagging his tail. The dog watched intently as Chance cut up one of the steaks, picked up Beauregard's dish from the floor and scrapped the steak pieces into it.

"Gotta give it a minute to cool," he told the dog as he considered his latest theory.

He slapped his steak on a plate, quickly grabbed the finger-burning potato from the microwave and lobbed it onto a spot next to his steak on the plate.

Beauregard barked and raced around the cabin's

small kitchen. Chance checked the dog's steak. It was cool enough.

"Merry Christmas," he said to the pooch as he set the dish on the floor. Beauregard made light work of the steak, then licked the dish clean, sliding it around the kitchen floor until he trapped it in a corner.

Chance cut a deep slit in his potato and filled it with butter, sour cream and a handful of chopped green onions as he mentally traced Dixie Bonner's path across Montana and told himself one of them was certifiable.

He took his plate to the table and ate a bite of the steak and potato, studying the map again.

Dixie wasn't trying to hide.

He'd guess she wanted to be found and she was leaving someone a message.

He frowned as he ate his dinner, trying to imagine a mind that had come up with zigzagging across the state as a way to send a message.

Then again, Dixie was a Bonner.

And unless he missed his guess, she was headed his way. He checked the map, convinced he would be seeing her soon.

Why though? He doubted she even remembered him. But he might be the only person she knew in Montana and if she was desperate enough... More than likely something else had brought her to Montana. He wondered what. Was the answer on his answering machine at his office? He swore at the thought but realized there was no getting around it. He could speculate all night or go back into town in a damned blizzard and check the machine.

As OLIVER LANCASTER hung up the phone, he saw a shadow move along the wall from the hallway. Quietly he stepped to the den doorway and watched his wife tiptoe at a run back up the hall.

It was comical to see, but he was in no laughing mood. Rebecca eavesdropping? He couldn't have been more shocked. Not the woman who strove to be the epitome of Southern decorum.

How much had she overheard?

He tried to remember what he'd said as he watched her disappear around the corner. Nothing he had to fear. At least, he didn't think so.

She would just think it was business. Not that she took an interest in anything he did. He put her out of his mind. It was easy to do. Rebecca looked good and played the role of wife of the successful legal consultant for Bonner Unlimited well, but the woman was a milquetoast and banal. Too much money and too much time on her hands. She bored him to tears.

He closed the door to the study, wishing he had earlier. She'd probably heard him on the phone and decided not to disturb him. Long ago, he'd told her not to bother him with dinner party seating charts or menus. That was *her* job. He hardly saw her and that was fine with him. Fine with her, too, apparently.

Oliver cursed under his breath as he moved to the window to stare out at the darkness. Even though he knew the security system was on, the estate safe from intruders, he felt strangely vulnerable tonight. And it didn't take much to figure out why.

He prized this lifestyle, which at the center was his marriage over all else. Without Beauregard Bonner's good grace—and daughter—Oliver would be nothing but a blue blood with family name only, and he knew it.

Rebecca had all the money and that damned Beauregard, for all his country-boy, aw-shucks hick behavior, was sharp when it came to hanging on to it. Oliver had been forced to sign a prenuptial agreement. If he ever left the marriage, he'd be lucky to leave with the clothes on his back and his good name.

That meant he had to keep Rebecca happy at all costs.

Which had been easy thus far. She seemed as content as he was in their "arrangement." He left her alone and she did the same. The perfect marriage.

Nothing had changed, right?

As he started to turn from the window, he caught his reflection in the glass. He stared at himself, surprised sometimes to realize that he was aging.

He always thought of himself as he had been in his twenties. Blond, blue-eyed, handsome by any standard. A catch. Wasn't that how Rebecca had seen him? He didn't kid himself why she'd dumped Chance Walker to marry him.

Now he studied himself in the glass, frowning, noticing the fine lines around his eyes, the first strands of gray mixed in with the blond, the slightly rounded line of his jaw.

He turned away from the glass and swore. So he was aging. And yet that, too, made him feel vulnerable tonight.

He glanced around the expensively furnished room almost angrily. He wasn't giving up any of this. He'd come too far and had paid too high a price. He wouldn't go down without a fight. Especially because of Rebecca's damned dysfunctional family. Or some cowboy in Montana.

Weary at the thought, he headed upstairs hoping Rebecca was already asleep. Or at least pretending to be like she was normally. He couldn't play the loving husband. Not tonight.

THE BLIZZARD WAS a total whiteout by the time Chance drove back into town to his office. He'd been forced to creep along in the truck, often unable to tell where the shoulder and center line was on the highway, the falling and blowing snow obliterating everything in a blur of dense suffocating white.

His office building, when he finally reached the nearly deserted town of Townsend, Montana, was dark, all the shops closed.

He let himself in, surprised when Beauregard took off running down the hall to bark anxiously at the door to the detective agency.

Chance thought about going back to his pickup for the shotgun he carried. He hadn't carried his pistol since the last time he'd used it to kill a man, but he was almost wishing he had it as he headed down the hall.

He reminded himself that Beauregard wasn't very discriminating when it came to being protective. There could be another mouse in the office, something that had gotten the old dog worked up on more than one occasion.

Moving quickly down the hall, Chance quieted the dog and listened at the door before he unlocked his office.

Beauregard pushed open the door and streaked in the moment he heard the lock click. As Chance flipped on the light, he tensed. Beauregard Bonner's visit had him anxious. So did the dog's behavior.

He could hear the dog snuffling around his desk.

Edging into the room, Chance scanned the desktop. He could see at a glance that the papers he'd left there had been gone through.

Dixie Bonner. Was it possible she was already in town? But what could she have been looking for on his desk?

It made no sense.

Then again, little about the Bonners ever had.

Unfortunately there was no doubt that someone had been here. Just the thought made him angry.

He stepped behind the desk and checked the drawers. He didn't keep anything worth stealing, which could have been why nothing appeared to be missing.

He had a safe but it was empty. He checked to see if the intruder had found it hidden behind the print of the lower falls of the Yellowstone River he kept on the wall—the only art in the office. Moving the framed print aside, he tried to remember the safe's combination. It had been a while.

His birthday. He had to think for a moment, then turned the dial and opened the safe. Empty and untouched as far as he could tell.

Turning, he looked around the office, trying to understand why anyone would care enough to break in. He had no ongoing cases, had nothing to steal and kept any old files on CD hidden at the cabin. He didn't even leave a computer in the office, but brought his laptop back and forth from the cabin.

And maybe more to the point, anyone who knew him, knew all of this.

But Dixie Bonner didn't know him.

That's when Chance noticed the dog. Beauregard stood next to the desk, the hair standing up on the back of his neck and a low growl emitting from his throat.

Chance moved around the desk to see why the dog was acting so strangely. The desk was old. He'd picked it up at a garage sale for cheap. Because of that one of the legs was splintered. He'd had to drill a couple of screws into the oak. One screw had hit a knot and refused to go all the way in.

He stared at the head of the screw that stood out a good inch. A scrap of dark cloth clung to the screw head—a scrap of clothing that hadn't been there earlier. Just like the blood hadn't been there.

Chance took perverse satisfaction in the fact that his old desk had gotten a little bit of the intruder since, with a curse, he realized what *was* missing.

The light on the antiquated answering machine was no longer flashing and he could tell even before he opened it that the tape would be gone.

It was.

CHAPTER THREE

CHANCE WOKE TO Christmas music on the radio and sunshine. Through the window, he could see that it was one of those incredible Montana winter days when the sky is so blue it's blinding.

He could also see that it had snowed most of the night, leaving a good foot on the level. He dug out early, knowing it was going to be a long day as he cleared off the deck, then started shoveling his way to his pickup.

The moment Chance had opened the door, Beauregard bounded outside to race around in the powder. Half the time the dog had his head stuck down in it, coming up covered with snow, making Chance smile. All he could think as he shoveled was that his daughter would have loved this.

Once he had a path to the pickup, he loaded Beauregard in the front seat—against his better judgment. Sure enough, the first thing the darned dog did was shake. Snow and chunks of ice and water droplets flew everywhere.

Chance swore, brushed off his seat and climbed in after the dog. The pickup already smelled like wet dog and he knew it wasn't going to get better as he started the engine, shifted into four-wheel drive for the ride out and turned on the heater.

Beauregard, worn out by all the fun he'd been having, curled up in the corner of the seat and fell asleep instantly.

Chance turned his attention to navigating the road out of the cabin—and thinking about Dixie Bonner. Last night, after finding his office had been broken into, he'd checked his Caller ID. He recognized all but one of the calls that had come in—a long-distance number with an area code he didn't recognize. There had been eight calls from that number.

Dixie?

When he checked with the operator, she informed him that the area code was from a cell phone out of Texas. He was betting it was Dixie Bonner. But if she had a cell phone number, why hadn't her father given it to him?

He'd tried the number and got an automated voice mail. He hadn't left a message.

This morning he drove up the road far enough away from the shadow of the mountain that he figured he might be able to get cell phone service and tried the number again. Same automated voice mail.

He hung up without leaving a message and drove on up the lake to his favorite place to eat breakfast. Lake Café was at the crossroads. Anyone headed his way would have to stop at the four-way.

According to Beauregard Bonner, Dixie Bonner drove a bright red Mustang with Texas plates. Add to that a Southern accent and, no doubt, the Bonner family arrogant genes. All total, Dixie would be a woman who would stand out in a crowd. Especially a Montana one.

Chance took a booth by the window, figuring he wouldn't miss a red Mustang with Texas plates when it came by this way because he was betting he would see her before the day was out.

A radio was playing back in the kitchen. Country and western Christmas music. Another reminder that he should be at home in front of the fire, feet up, dozing on a day like this with Beauregard sprawled at his feet.

Instead he was chasing a damned Bonner.

To lighten his mood, he thought about what he would do when he had her. Christmas or no Christmas, he wasn't in a joyous let alone forgiving frame of mind. If Bonner was right about this kidnapping being bogus, then it was high time someone taught Dixie Bonner a lesson she wouldn't soon forget.

And this morning, Chance Walker felt like the man who could do it.

OLIVER WAS NOWHERE around the next morning when Rebecca woke up. She just assumed he'd gone to work already but as she came down the stairs she saw her uncle Carl heading down the hallway toward Oliver's den.

"Good morning, Rebecca." Carl was older than his brother Beauregard, about the same size but nothing like her father in nature. Carl was quiet and less driven. A whole lot less driven.

"Is Daddy here?" She couldn't help being confused. It wasn't like Carl to stop by unless there was a family dinner of some kind going on.

"I just stopped in to see Oliver," Carl said as she descended the stairs.

"Oh." Rebecca couldn't imagine what Carl would want to see her husband about. Both were employed by Bonner Unlimited, but it was no secret that neither had anything to do there.

And she knew that Carl had never approved of Oliver. She remembered when she'd announced her engagement to Oliver. Carl had taken her aside and asked her if she was sure this was what she wanted.

She'd been angry with her uncle that day and had brought up the fact that he wasn't one to give advice on relationships given that he'd never married.

"The woman I wanted was in love with someone else," was all he'd said. "I couldn't bring myself to settle for anyone else."

"Oliver is the man I want," she'd snapped.

"I just want you to be happy." He'd kissed her on the cheek and left her feeling terrible because she'd been unkind to her favorite uncle. But also, she realized now, because he'd been right to question her choice.

"Rebecca?"

She blinked.

Carl had stopped in the hallway and was studying her. "Is everything all right?"

She forced herself to smile. "Fine."

He nodded. "You have a good day, okay?" he said pleasantly as he smiled, then continued down the hall to the den.

She watched him open the den door without knocking and step in, closing it behind him. He wasn't smiling, she noticed, when he closed the door. Did this have something to do with Daddy going to Montana? Was Uncle Carl who her husband had been talking to last night on the phone?

No, she thought. More than likely he'd been on the phone with the one person who resented Daddy even more than Oliver—her father's cousin, Ace Bonner. Ace, who was Daddy's age, had recently gotten out of prison.

Daddy being Daddy, he had given Ace a job at Bonner Unlimited. She got so sick of her father feeling guilty for having so much money. He wore it like a chip on his shoulder. No matter how arrogant he came off, Beauregard Bonner didn't feel he measured up, and she hated that about him.

As she reached the bottom of the stairs, she heard raised voices, startling her. Carl never raised his voice. What had Oliver done now? Something that Carl was upset about. Let it have something to do with Bonner Unlimited, she thought. Just like Dixie being in Montana. *Just don't let it have anything to do with me.*

Rebecca had enough problems. But as she headed for the kitchen, desperately needing coffee, she couldn't shake the feeling that her world was on the verge of crumbling around her.

She found the nanny in the kitchen with the children. Amy was pounding on the high-chair tray, splashing milk everywhere. Tanya was yelling for the nanny, Ingrid, to do something about Amy. And Linsey was on her cell phone talking to her best friend Miranda.

"I'm going out," Rebecca called to Ingrid, trying to escape before the nanny took the spoon away from Amy. As Rebecca hustled back upstairs, she shut off Amy's shrieks only after reaching her bedroom and closing the door. When the house was built, she'd had extra insulation put around their bedroom for privacy. At least that's what she told the builders.

She hadn't wanted her sleep disturbed by the children waking up in the middle of the night. That's what she had a nanny for. A light sleeper, she had to have the room a certain temperature and complete darkness. And she had the money to get exactly what she wanted.

As she climbed into the shower, she thought about her lunch date with her best friend Samantha "Pookie" Westbrook. Pookie was everything Rebecca had always wanted to be. The daughter of a well-known Houston old-money family with an impeccable reputation and the grace and charm of Texas royalty.

Imagining as she often did what her life would have been like if she'd been the Westbrooks' daughter instead of Pookie, kept Rebecca from worrying about what Oliver and Uncle Carl had been arguing about in the den.

AFTER ORDERING HIS breakfast, Chance stepped outside to see if he could get cell phone service. It was always iffy in the mountains. He'd never been able to get a signal at the cabin, which was just fine with him.

He dug his cell out, cursing the damned thing, and on impulse, first tried the cell phone number again that had been on the Caller ID at his office. He got voice mail again and again didn't leave a message. Then he dialed the number Bonner had left for him.

"Hello?" Beauregard Bonner boomed.

"It's Chance. Any word from Dixie?" He'd been holding his breath, hoping Dixie had found her way home. Or at least there'd been some contact.

"Nothing," Bonner said. "I just flew into Houston and was going to find my other daughter."

Chance thought about telling Bonner to say hello to Rebecca, but instantly came to his senses. "Do you have a cell phone number for Dixie?"

"No. I'm sure she has one. I tried to get the number, but couldn't."

Chance smiled to himself, hearing the frustration in Bonner's voice. Even Beauregard Bonner didn't get everything he wanted.

"I'll let you know when I come up with something," Chance said and snapped the phone shut.

Back in the café, he kept an eye on the four-way stop,

hoping he was right about Dixie. Of course, that brought up the question of why she was zigzagging across the state, why she was headed his way in the first place. If she even was.

All he could guess was that Dixie Bonner liked to play games—just like her father.

As Chance waited for his breakfast, he dumped the contents of the manila envelope Beauregard Bonner had given him out onto the table. Last night he'd looked at the credit card report, convinced like the police and FBI that Dixie was anything but the victim of a kidnapping.

Disgusted, he hadn't even bothered to see what else Bonner had provided him. But this morning, as the contents of the envelope spilled onto the table, a photograph fell out and he recalled that Bonner had said all he had was an older photo of Dixie.

It was a three-by-five, shot by a professional in a studio, and appeared to be Dixie Bonner's high school graduation photo.

Strange, Bonner didn't have a more recent photo of his youngest daughter. Not a snapshot taken at some birthday party, Christmas or family get-together. Chance wondered if that didn't say a lot about the Bonners and what had been going on with that family since he'd left Texas.

He stared at the young woman in the photo. Pixielike, her hair was cropped short and dyed a glaring hot pink. At the center of thick black eyeliner were two twinkling blue eyes that radiated a mischief he remembered only too well. Dixie had always been cute. The cheekbones were high and maybe her best feature. Her lips were full and turned up in a devilish grin. A hellion. Just as her father had described her.

Chance chuckled to himself thinking Dixie probably

was Beauregard Bonner's comeuppance. Maybe there was justice on earth after all.

"REBECCA? *REBECCA*."

Rebecca Bonner blinked.

"You haven't heard a word I've said," Pookie snapped irritably. They were having lunch at Rebecca's favorite restaurant. She'd hoped that lunch with her friend would improve her mood. So far it had been having the opposite effect.

"What is going on with you today?" Pookie demanded.

Rebecca shook her head, realizing this had been a mistake. She should have gone shopping instead, bought something outrageously expensive and skipped lunch. "I think I might be coming down with something."

Pookie did an eye-roll. "What is really bothering you? Is it the kids?"

It wasn't the kids. Not that Rebecca had really wanted children in the first place. It was just something you did. Like the big house, the expensive car, the clothes and the husband.

She'd had a nanny from even before she brought Linsey home from the hospital. She gave the kids little thought except when they were screaming like this morning and she had so much on her mind.

"It's not the kids."

Pookie lifted one perfectly shaped brow. "What's the bastard done now?"

"It's not Oliver, either." She sipped her strawberry daiquiri.

"Of course it is."

"Have you heard *something?*" Rebecca asked, her heart starting to pound. Pookie often knew things almost before they happened. That was one reason Rebecca had called her for lunch today. If there was a rumor going around, Rebecca wanted to be the first to hear about it and make sure it got nipped in the bud quickly.

"I haven't heard a thing." Pookie held up three fingers. As if she was ever a Girl Scout. "And I can't believe I wouldn't have heard."

Rebecca was counting on that. "You'd tell me at once if you did."

"Of course." Pookie looked worried. "Why, have you heard something about Adam?" Adam was her friend's husband. A balding, pot-bellied, thirtysomething attorney at a top agency in the city who kept Pookie in a style even better than she'd been accustomed to—which said a lot given that Pookie was born to Houston society.

"Come on, what's going on with you?" Pookie asked, leaning toward her, grinning. "Give. Who is he?"

Rebecca shook her head and tried to wave away Pookie's protests. Pookie would be surprised if Rebecca told her that she hadn't been with a man other than her husband in months. Her friend went through a lot of men and thought everyone else did, too.

"Come on. You and I have never kept secrets."

Rebecca thought how naive Pookie was. *Everyone* kept secrets. Even from their best friends if they were smart.

"I told you about my pilates instructor." Pookie pretended to pout.

"There isn't *anyone*," she said, feeling even worse. Not even Oliver. Except for that one night. He'd acted so strangely that night. She brushed the memory away, hating to remember his attempts at lovemaking. They'd never made love that she could recall. Intimacy at their house was more like a corporate takeover.

"Oliver's been acting…strange," Rebecca confided, seeing no harm in the obvious.

Pookie lifted a brow as if to ask how she could tell. "Well, if it isn't another woman…"

"He's involved in some kind of deal at work. I'm sure that's all it is. He has this thing about winning." That, she knew, was his form of orgasmic release. He had never seemed that interested in sex. Or maybe it was just her he wasn't interested in.

Pookie narrowed her eyes, studying her. "There isn't a man? Come on, I saw that look in your eye."

Rebecca groaned, knowing her friend would keep after her until she gave her something. "I was thinking about Chance Walker," she said, and braced herself for her friend's reaction.

WHEN HIS FOOD arrived—his usual—a slab of bone-in ham, two eggs over easy, hash browns and whole-wheat toast with blackberry jam, Chance placed the picture next to his plate, studying it periodically as he ate.

If he was right and the photograph was taken eleven years ago, who knew how much Dixie Bonner had changed. She was probably more outrageous than ever.

He shook his head as he thought about the kid he'd known. Would he even recognize her now?

"Girlfriend?" the waitress asked, moving for a better look at the photo.

"Not hardly. Actually, it's a case I'm working on. Any chance you've seen her? She'd be eleven years older than when this was taken."

Lydia, an older, stocky woman, shook her head.

"Sorry. And believe me I would have remembered the hair if it was still that color."

"I have a feeling this one has tried it all," he said, looking at Dixie's photo.

"You sound like you know her."

"Used to, when she was twelve," he said with an amused shake of his head. "She was hell on wheels back then. I just assumed she would grow up and be more like her sister."

Lydia raised a brow.

"I dated her older sister." It surprised him the regret he heard in his voice. Not that he hadn't married Rebecca. Just that things had ended so badly.

"First love?"

"I guess it was. She went away to college back east and met someone…" Someone more appropriate. "I hear she has three kids now and her husband is a hot-shot attorney in Houston."

Lydia put a hand on his shoulder. "Honey, something tells me you are better off without her."

Chance laughed. "I have no doubt about that."

"Want the rest of that ham wrapped up for Beauregard?" she asked as she cleared his table.

"Please." He put everything back in the manila envelope, including Dixie's picture, finished his coffee and took the envelope and foil-wrapped ham out to the pickup.

Beauregard devoured the ham in one bite and waited for more as Chance started the pickup. "Sorry, bud, that's it until dinner."

Taking out the map of Montana, he stared at the jagged line he'd drawn on it last night as he'd traced Dixie Bonner's route.

Dixie hadn't come to him, so that meant he'd have

to go to her. If he was right, there was a definite pattern to her movements. She was headed his way. All he could figure was that she didn't want anyone to know it.

Chance found that pretty humorous since someone obviously knew and had gone to some trouble to break into his office to take his answering machine tape. He wondered what message she'd left and why it was important to whoever was apparently looking for her.

He planned to ask her when he saw her.

There was also the remote possibility that she really had been kidnapped, that the kidnapper had foolishly left eight messages on his machine. But that brought up the question of why call him? Also, what kidnapper would leave eight messages on his machine?

He figured no matter what was going on, Dixie wouldn't have left her location or where she was headed on his answering machine. And neither would her kidnappers.

Chance swore and headed down the lake and eventually into town, figuring she should be here today if she continued her traveling pattern. The day was brilliant, the sky a deep blue, the mountains glistening white, the sun blinding overhead.

He glanced in his rearview mirror and saw a light-colored panel van pull out behind him.

"You were thinking about Chance *Walker?*" Pookie cried, then ducked her head as several of the nearby diners frowned over at her. *"Why?"* she asked in a hushed whisper. "It wasn't like you were ever serious about him. Marrying him would have been social suicide."

Rebecca nodded. All true. She hadn't even considered *marrying* Chance. But what she hadn't told Pookie was that she'd thought he would stay around Houston. She would have had an affair with him in a heartbeat.

She'd never dreamed Chance would go to Montana to work for the summer and not return to Texas. One of the secrets she'd never told Pookie was about the breakup. Pookie had always assumed that Rebecca had broken it off with Chance because she'd met Oliver and he was the better catch hands down.

What Pookie didn't know and never would was that Chance had been the one to break off their relationship. He'd figured out that she'd never planned to marry him. Oliver knew she'd been dumped and had never let her forget it. The bastard.

So even if Chance had stayed around Houston, she doubted he would have been up for an affair. Just the thought made her angry and upset.

And now her sister was in Montana.

With Chance?

The thought killed her appetite.

"Why are you even thinking about Chance at this late date?" Pookie demanded quietly.

"I wasn't. It's just that I think Daddy is in Montana and it made me think of Chance." At least she assumed that was the "son of a bitch" Oliver had been referring to, and Oliver had said something about Dixie.

Pookie started to say something, then stopped as she looked past Rebecca and smiled. "Well, he's not in Montana anymore," she said under her breath as Rebecca heard someone approach the table from behind her.

IN HIS REARVIEW mirror Chance watched the van coming up the road behind him. The two-lane highway ran along the lake, over the dam, then headed south to Townsend where his office was located. This time of year, the road got little traffic with most of the places on the lake closed up for the winter.

Chance slowed to give the driver of the van the opportunity to pass. The van slowed, as well, staying right with him, and confirming his suspicions.

As the road began to snake around the north end of the lake, Chance sped up. The van sped up, too, the driver doing his best to stay with him, even taking some dangerous curves too fast, leaving little doubt that the driver was determined not to lose him.

Fortunately this morning there was no other traffic on the road. As Chance came around a corner with a nice wide deep ditch on each side, he braked, coming to a stop, blocking both lanes.

The van came flying around the corner. The driver hit his brakes but clearly realized there was no way he could stop on the snow-packed road and aimed the van for the ditch.

Chance pulled his pickup over to the side of the road and, taking the shotgun from the rack behind the pickup seat, jumped out to bound down into the snowy ditch to jerk open the driver's side door.

He shoved the shotgun in the man's face. "Why the hell are you following me?"

"Easy," the man cried, throwing his hands up. "I'm a private eye. Just like you."

Chance swore at the man's thick Texas drawl. "Who the hell are you?"

"Let me reach into my jacket…"

"No way." Chance reached in and withdrew the man's wallet—and a 9 mm pistol. He chucked the pistol over the top of the van where it disappeared in the deep snow. The wallet he flipped open to the man's ID. J. B. Jamison, Private Investigator, Houston Texas.

"Who hired you?" Chance asked as he tossed the wallet into the back of the empty van. Not that he didn't already know the answer.

"Bonner. Beauregard Bonner."

"What the hell did he hire you to do?" Chance demanded. "Follow *me?*"

"Find his daughter and take her back to Texas."

Chance was still pointing the shotgun at the man. "And that has what to do with me?"

"Bonner told us she might contact you."

So that was it. Beauregard was covering his bets. Setting Chance up because he thought Dixie would come to him. But lacking faith that Chance could get Dixie back to Texas. Now why was that?

"So you broke into my office and stole my answering machine tape," Chance accused.

The man looked genuinely surprised. "No. I was just tailing you, hoping you'd lead me to Ms. Bonner. That's all."

"Roll up your pant legs," Chance ordered. "Whoever broke into my office scraped his leg on my desk."

Jamison didn't look happy about it, but he pulled up one pant leg, then the other. No sign he'd been the one to get hung up on the desk.

"Get out."

Jamison looked out at the deep snow, then at Chance and the shotgun. "I didn't break into your office. There is no reason to—"

"Out." Chance stepped back so the Texas P.I. could get out of the van. The man stepped gingerly into the deep snow. He wore loafers and slacks, although he'd been smart enough to get himself a down coat.

Chance quickly frisked the man, found no other

weapon and ordered Jamison to walk out a dozen yards, through the snow and trees, from the van.

While the man's back was turned, Chance threw the van's keys into the snow and searched the van.

No answering machine tape. But what Chance did find shocked him. In the back of the van was everything a man would need to hog-tie and bind a woman to transport her back to Texas.

He felt sick as he left J. B. Jamison cursing him to hell beside the road and drove off. That bastard Bonner hadn't mentioned he put another P.I. on the case let alone that he'd sent the man to bring Dixie back to Texas.

Chance's job was to find Dixie. Period.

Under most circumstances, Chance would have quit right there. But after what he'd seen in the back of Jamison's van, he was afraid for Dixie Bonner and even more anxious to find her.

CHAPTER FOUR

REBECCA FROZE AS she felt her father come up to her table from behind her.

"Well, look who it is," Pookie gushed. "My favorite man. I hope you're planning to join us." Pookie had the irritating habit of flirting with older men. Especially the ones with money and few had more money than Daddy. Her friend rose demurely to plant a kiss on Beauregard's check.

"You are a sinful woman," Daddy said to Pookie, but clearly enjoyed the attention. "Rebecca," he said with a nod as he stepped around to face her. She hadn't moved, hadn't said a word.

She and her father rarely spoke. He never seemed to know what to say to her. He could talk for hours with Dixie. But then, Dixie was his favorite, no matter what he said. Oh, he tried to make Rebecca feel loved. That was the problem. He tried too hard, as if it didn't come naturally the way it did with Dixie.

"What brings you into town?" Rebecca asked as sweetly as she could while pasting a smile on her face. "Are you meeting someone?" she added, looking around the restaurant expectantly, all the time hoping he was.

"Samantha, honey, could you excuse us for a moment?"

Pookie gave Rebecca a curious look. "Of course. I'll just go powder my nose."

Beauregard Bonner took a seat across from his daughter and she saw that he was upset. She braced herself, afraid suddenly of what he was going to tell her.

"Have you seen your sister?" he asked.

She blinked, so taken off guard that she wasn't even sure she'd heard him correctly. "I beg your pardon?"

"Your sister. Dixie. You might remember her from last Christmas? No, that's right, you went back east for Christmas."

She didn't like his tone. "I remember my sister," she said coldly. He always blamed her that she and Dixie weren't closer. She was the oldest, he'd say, as if that made a difference.

"I believe you missed Christmas, as well," she shot back. "Jamaica, wasn't it? What was her name? Carmella? Lupita? I lose track."

Her father didn't seem to hear. He was trying to get the waiter's attention, no doubt for a drink.

She couldn't care less about last Christmas. Or the one before it. They'd never been that kind of family. They might have been, if her mother had lived. But she hadn't.

"What has Dixie done now?" She tried to sound bored by this conversation, but her heart was pounding. What *had* Dixie done?

"Have you talked to her lately?" he asked.

She frowned. "No, Daddy, I haven't. How about you?"

"She's…missing."

Rebecca laughed, politely of course, since they were in one of Houston's most elite restaurants. Another reason she really didn't want to have a discussion about her sister here, now.

"She's *always*…missing. I really don't see what that

has to do with me." Rebecca picked up her bag from the chair next to her and started to rise. "I'm sorry, Daddy, but I really must get going. Please give my apologies to Pookie."

"Sit down." He hadn't raised his voice, fortunately. But she knew by his tone that he could at any moment. He had no compunction against making scenes. In fact, he seemed to enjoy them as if he never wanted to forget his poor white-trash roots. As he was fond of saying, "If Houston society don't like it, they can kiss my cherry-red ass."

She sat back down.

"I think she might have been kidnapped," he said quietly, and picked up her water glass and downed it. "How do you get a drink in this place?"

Rebecca caught the waiter's eye and mouthed Scotch neat. She didn't have to tell the waiter to make it the best they carried. That was a given.

"What makes you think she's been kidnapped?" she asked carefully. Bringing up Dixie's other shenanigans would only set her father off, although she would have loved to have listed them chapter and verse.

"I got a call." The waiter set down the drink and Beauregard snatched it up, downing it in two gulps before motioning for the waiter to bring him another. "You don't seem all that upset about it," he said a little too loudly.

"Because I don't believe it," she said, keeping her voice low by example. She could always depend on her father to embarrass her. Oh, why couldn't she have come from old money like Pookie and her other friends?

"The ransom demand is a million dollars."

She stared at him. "You can't be serious?"

He gave her a deadpan look.

"How silly of me. It's *Dixie*. It is only a matter of time before she'll want it all for some foolish cause of hers." And Daddy will give it to her, Rebecca thought angrily. Oliver had warned her that Dixie would get everything in the end, hadn't he? "So you paid it. What's the problem?"

"Hell no, I didn't pay it."

The waiter set down another drink and looked nervously at Beauregard as if, like Rebecca, afraid he might be a problem.

Rebecca watched her father take one gulp. "You haven't paid it yet?" This did surprise her.

"I'm *not* paying it."

He would. Eventually. He always caved when it came to Dixie. "So what *are* you doing?"

"Obviously trying to find her."

Rebecca glanced around the restaurant. "If you'd called, I could have told you she wasn't here, Daddy."

His eyes narrowed. "Why do you have to be such a bitch?"

His words stung more than she thought they would. She knew he was only striking out because he was worried about his *other* daughter. "Why do you have to be such an ass?" she hissed back at him.

He gripped his glass, anger in every movement as he downed the last of it, and carefully put it down.

She knew she'd gone too far. But she was sick of being the other daughter. The one her father never gave a concern to. "I heard you went to Montana." She waited, hoping he would deny it.

"Who told you I went to Montana?"

She stared at her father. "You really *did* go?" She hadn't meant to sound so shocked. But she was. So she'd been right about the "son of a bitch" Oliver had been referring to.

"Isn't that what you just— Never mind," he said, and motioned to the waiter for another drink. "That's where I guess she is."

This was all too surreal, especially on top of the two strawberry daiquiris she'd consumed—and what little she'd gleaned from Oliver's phone conversation she'd overhead last night.

"I hired your old boyfriend to find her."

There it was. She hadn't been mistaken. She felt light-headed. For an instant she thought about pretending ignorance and saying, "What boyfriend would that be, Daddy?"

Instead she said, "You hired Chance Walker to find Dixie?" saying his name carefully as if the words were expensive crystal that were so fragile they might break otherwise.

"He's a private detective. Damned good."

Was that supposed to make her feel better?

Daddy was looking at her, studying her, his eyes glazed from the alcohol, but he wasn't drunk. Nor was he stupid. "You were a fool not to marry him."

"I beg your pardon?"

He picked up the fresh drink the waiter left on the table and stared down into it as if it were more fascinating than her by far.

"I beg your pardon?" she said again, leaning toward him over the table, working to keep her voice down. After all, she was part of this family and no stranger to loud, ugly scenes. Just not in public.

"You, of all people, *know* why I married Oliver," she said, her voice low and crackling with fury. "To give this family respectability because even with all your money, Daddy, you couldn't buy it, could you?"

He didn't look at her, but what she saw on his face shocked her. Shame.

She felt sick. He'd known what she'd done and why. He'd never believed that she married Oliver for love. He'd known that she had sacrificed her own happiness for the family and he hadn't even tried to stop her.

She rose from the table, picking up her purse, glaring down at him. "As I said, I have things to do." She turned on her heel.

Just as he hadn't stopped her from marrying Oliver, he didn't stop her from leaving the restaurant.

CHANCE DROVE DOWN the road to where a wide spot had been plowed at the edge of the lake and pulled over. He tried to calm down before he called Bonner again.

"Hello?" Bonner sounded asleep. Or half-drunk. Because of the hour and the bar sounds in the background, Chance surmised it was the latter.

"What the hell are you trying to pull?" He'd planned to be calm, not to tell Bonner what he thought of him. But just the sound of the oilman's voice set Chance off.

"Chance?"

"I just met the private eye you hired from Texas. J. B. Jamison. Want to tell me what the hell that was about?"

"I don't know what you're talking about."

"A Texas private investigator named J. B. Jamison."

"He said *I* hired him? Well, he's mistaken. You're the only private investigator I hired."

Chance swore. "Mistaken? How could he mistake that?"

"Maybe someone hired him using my name, but it wasn't me," Bonner snapped. "I give you my word."

For what that was worth. It was all he could do not
to tell Bonner what he thought of that. Instead, Chance
thought of his own daughter.

"Someone broke into my office last night," Chance
said. "From what I can tell, it wasn't Jamison. That
means there is someone else looking for Dixie."

"Well, I didn't hire them," Bonner said, sounding
angry. "How many times do I have to say it?"

Chance shook his head, fighting to rein in his temper. If not Jamison, then who had broken into the office
and taken the answering machine tape?

"Let's be clear on this," Chance said. "I'll find your
daughter. That's what you're paying me to do. I'll even
give her a ride to the airport so she can return to Houston, if that's what she wants. But I won't let anyone use
the kinds of methods Jamison does and hog-tie her and
haul her across state lines all the way back to Texas.
That's kidnapping and I won't be a part of it no matter
what's going on between you and Dixie."

He heard Bonner take a long drink. Glasses tinkled
in the background, the clatter of dishes, the murmur of
people talking. The bastard was having lunch.

"Just find my daughter as quickly as possible. I got
another ransom demand. A million and a half. There
was also a package waiting for me at the airport when
I landed. Dixie's locket was inside it. It's the one I gave
her on her sixteenth birthday. She wore it all the time."

Chance groaned. "Damn it, Beauregard. Call the
FBI. They can start tracing the calls."

Beauregard the dog lifted his head, coming awake
at the sound of his name—and Chance's angry tone.

"We've already had this discussion," Bonner said,
sounding tired. "She used her credit card again. Some
place called Neihart, Montana? Call me the minute you

have her. But I warn you, finding her and hanging on to her are two entirely different things. By the time you're done, you'll understand why this Jamison uses the methods he does." Bonner hung up.

Chance snapped off the phone with a curse. What the hell? Bonner sounded as if he still didn't believe his daughter had been kidnapped. But he was worried about her. What was going on?

Beauregard the dog barked, letting him know he didn't appreciate being awakened by Chance's raised voice when he'd done nothing wrong.

"Go back to sleep. I'll wake you for lunch." Chance patted the dog's big head and Beauregard curled back up, dropping off to sleep again instantly. Dogs. They really did have the life.

Every instinct told Chance to call the oilman back and quit the case. Unfortunately it had gone beyond the money. Chance couldn't let Jamison find Dixie first. No matter what a hellion the woman was. Someone had damned sure hired Jamison to haul her back to Texas. But why?

Bonner wasn't going to the feds because whatever was really going on, he didn't want them involved. What the hell had Dixie done? Whatever it was, Bonner just wanted her quietly returned to the longhorn state. Illegally returned, since Dixie was twenty-nine.

Why wasn't Bonner worried that his daughter would press charges against him once he got her back to Texas?

Another good question.

He dragged out his map again. If he was reading her traveling pattern right, she was headed for White Sulphur Springs.

He couldn't wait any longer. It was time to cut her off at the pass.

Ace Bonner was leaning against Oliver's Porsche, grinning as Oliver came out of the Bonner Unlimited building. Ace was a big fifty-something man with thick gray hair. He'd probably been fairly good-looking, like most of the Bonners, when he was younger. But prison and an indulgent lifestyle since hadn't done much for him.

"What are you doing here?" Oliver snapped as he glanced back at the Bonner Unlimited building, afraid Carl or Mason might be watching them from the window.

"Cool your jets," Ace said, putting his arm around Oliver's shoulder. "Hell, we're family. Nothing wrong with the two of us being seen together."

"There is when we have a deal going down," Oliver said under his breath as he shrugged off Ace's arm and walked around to the driver's side, hoping to make a fast exit. "And stay off my car."

"We need to talk," Ace said, the grin gone.

Oliver looked at him. "What? Something to do with the deal?"

"I need to grease another wheel." He raised his hands before Oliver could protest. "It's almost a done deal. Just this one guy who could hold things up. No reason to get cheap now."

"Except that I don't have it," Oliver snapped.

Ace cocked his head at him. "Don't give me that crap, Lancaster." His gaze went to the car. "What's another twenty-five grand to you?"

"Twenty-five grand." He choked on the words.

"I promise that will be the last of it. Hell, we're in a position to make six mil. You're going to bitch about twenty-five lousy grand?"

Oliver glared at Ace, too angry to speak. "If this

deal doesn't go through and I find out that it was all a scam—"

"Please. I'm going to blow three million dollars for the measly hundred grand you've given me for the deal?"

"Two."

"Two what?"

"Two hundred thousand dollars," Oliver said, elongating each word.

"You want me to swing by your house and pick up the money?" Ace asked.

"No." He hadn't meant the word to come out so sharply. "I'll contact you when I get it."

"Right," Ace said, grinning, but there was a sour look in his eyes that Oliver didn't like. Once this deal went through Oliver was going to put as much distance as he could between himself and Ace Bonner.

As Chance drove into White Sulphur Springs, he watched for Dixie's red Mustang. He couldn't imagine the kidnapper driving it. Or Dixie, for that matter. If she didn't want to be found, she would have ditched it for something less noticeable. Even if the kidnapping was bogus, by now she had to have realized that people were looking for her.

Chance told himself that this could be nothing more sinister than a power struggle between father and daughter. Bonner was definitely stubborn enough. And probably Dixie, too, from the sounds of it. Maybe Chance was overreacting. Maybe she wasn't in any kind of trouble. Her father, either.

But still, Chance couldn't shake the feeling that Bonner sincerely was afraid for his daughter. And with good reason.

Chance drove down the main drag, then started down side streets, wondering if he wasn't nuts. This felt like a wild-goose chase. Maybe there was no rhyme or reason for Dixie to zigzag across the state. No message. No game plan.

But as he was driving past a house known in these parts as the Castle, he saw something that made him pull up short.

When the Castle had been built in 1892, it was a stone mansion constructed out of local carved granite. The story was that the house had been built for the owner's soon-to-be wife, with no expense spared, including a bathtub.

As Chance remembered the story, the marriage didn't work out, bathtub and all. The Castle was now a museum. The story of past disappointments seemed to fit given that parked behind it was a bright red Mustang with Texas plates.

Chance pulled his pickup over across the street from the Castle and stared at the woman standing out front. No one else was around, the museum apparently closed.

He'd thought he wouldn't recognize her. Not after this many years. Dixie had looked nothing like her sister Rebecca. Rebecca had been petite and dainty, her blond hair a sleek cap that framed her perfect face.

This woman standing in front of the museum was as long-legged as a colt, and she was wearing a pair of form-fitting jeans that hugged her derriere. She had a slim waist that tapered up to nice broad shoulders that were only partially hidden by a wild dark mane of long curly hair.

The last time he'd seen Dixie Bonner she'd been twelve. Not even filled out. But she'd been tall for her age, slim and had this wild, dark, curly long hair...

He opened his pickup door and stepped out. She didn't turn as he started across the street, but he had the distinct impression that she knew he was here although she still seemed intent on studying the museum hours. Definitely not acting like a woman who'd been kidnapped or who feared for her life. More like a woman who had nothing more on her mind than a vacation.

The squeal of tires and the growl of an engine startled him. He turned in time to see a large black sedan come roaring up the street. For an instant he thought it might be teenagers acting up. But teens in these parts drove old pickups or clunker cars with primer paint and missing fenders—not what looked a whole lot like a full-size rental car.

The car came to a skidding stop in front of the museum between him and Dixie. The passenger side door flew open and a large man launched himself at Dixie.

No doubt she'd heard the car approach. She swung around almost as if she'd been expecting them. She caught the big man in the face with her shoulder bag and then kneed him in the groin. He dropped like a sack of Idaho potatoes, fell off the museum steps and into the snowbank where he floundered in pain.

The driver started to get out, but saw Chance come running across the street, gun drawn.

Horn blaring, the driver hit the gas, almost leaving his passenger who, covered with snow, limped hurriedly after the car. The big man barely managed to get in before the driver gunned the engine, the tires squealing as the car took the first corner and disappeared.

"Are you all right?" Chance asked, running up to her. If he'd doubted before that she was Dixie Bonner, he didn't now. Only a Bonner attracted trouble the way magnets attract tacks.

She glanced at his gun but other than that had no reaction, as if this was a daily occurrence, men trying to grab her off the street and others running up with loaded guns in their hands.

Her gaze skimmed over him. He saw he'd been wrong about her best feature. From her high school senior portrait he'd thought it was her high cheekbones. Now he couldn't decide if it was her big blue eyes fringed in dark lashes or her mouth, the full lips turned up at the corners in a perfect bow.

He was about to go with the mouth when she drawled, "You certainly took your sweet time getting here, Chance Walker."

CHAPTER FIVE

"EXCUSE ME?"

Dixie took Chance Walker in as if he were a cool drink of water. What she'd loved about him when she was twelve were the same things that Rebecca had tried to change about him. Chance had always been rough around edges.

Montana, it seemed, had made him more so. She saw that he'd aged, but wonderfully, like a good leather couch. There were fine lines around his eyes, but his brown eyes were softer somehow as if life had humbled him over the years and yet at the same time made him stronger.

"Excuse me?" he repeated with a shake of his head. "I believe 'thank you' would be the appropriate response since I just saved your scrawny behind."

"My behind is definitely *not* scrawny," she said. "And it's debatable just how much help you were."

His grin brought it all back. Chance Walker was just as Dixie had remembered him. Obstinate, arrogant and positively the best-looking man she'd ever seen at the age of twelve.

She'd had *the* worst crush on him and could still recall the horrible ache she'd felt whenever he was around. He'd treated her like the kid she was at the time. That hadn't made it hurt any less.

"Right. That was genius the way you waited in front of a castle for them," he snapped.

She wanted to tell him how good it was to see him. Because it was. She wanted to throw herself into his arms. But at the same time she didn't want him to see how scared she was and had been for days.

She flashed him a grin that was more cocky than she felt. "I was waitin' on *you*. Nice you finally got one of my messages and figured out where I would be."

"Me, and everyone else apparently. Why didn't you just send up a flare?"

She glared at him. "I figured if I waited for you in front of a castle on the edge of town you couldn't really miss me."

He shook his head and looked down the street. "Well, unless you want to wait for those guys to come back, I suggest we hightail it out of here."

She nodded, irritated with him. She tried to relax, telling herself she had nothing to worry about now. Hadn't she known that Chance would find her? He'd been her hero when she was twelve. She'd always known that if there was one person she could trust it was Chance Walker if she ever got into any real trouble. And she was in a world of trouble.

"I thought I'd be seeing you *before* this, given the number of messages I left," she said as they started across the street. She slowed, looking over at him when he didn't answer right away.

He glanced down the street, frowning, then settled his gaze on her. "I didn't get the messages. Someone broke into my office and took the answering machine tape before I could get them. I haven't been working for a while."

She stopped dead in the middle of the street. "Then how did you know where…"

He stopped, too, looking at her as if she'd lost her mind. "We really need to get out of here. Unless I miss my guess, we'll be seeing those guys again."

"How did you find me?" She couldn't move because even before he said the words, she knew.

He sighed as he pulled off his cowboy hat and raked a hand through his thick hair. "Your father told me you were in Montana. I figured out where you were headed by tracking the credit card charges he gave me."

She stared at him, her heart sinking like the *Titanic*. "My *father?* Why would my father…" She couldn't believe this. Fear shot through her, mixed with equal amounts of anger and disappointment. "No. You wouldn't."

He rocked back, seemingly surprised by her reaction. "Could we talk about this somewhere else besides the middle of the street?"

She felt her car keys in her coat pocket and glanced toward the back of the museum, gauging whether or not she could reach her car before he caught her.

It wasn't her anger that brought the hot stinging tears to her eyes but the betrayal. She would have trusted Chance with her life. *Had.* She'd stupidly contacted him believing he was the one person who couldn't be bought by her father.

"What is my father paying you to do?" she asked, trying to keep her voice steady.

He was looking at her closely now, a wariness in his gaze. She knew he'd seen her anger—as well as her tears. He didn't even try to deny that her father had hired him. "Look, clearly you're in trouble. I just want to help you."

She laughed and looked away, biting at her lower lip, still considering making a run for it. "If you're working for my father then you aren't here to help me." She met his gaze. "What did he pay you to do? Stop me?"

"He just wants you to come back to Texas. He's afraid for you. But I would imagine you know more about that than I do."

She stared at the man she'd measured all men by since she was twelve. "You bastard." She turned and took off at a dead run for her car.

Chance couldn't believe it. He tore off after her. She was fast, all legs, but he caught her before she reached the curb. Grabbing her arm, he spun her around to face him.

"What the hell is wrong with you?" he demanded, holding her shoulders in his palms.

"What the hell is wrong with *you?*" she snapped instantly, anger flashing like lightning in all that blue. Her voice was deeper than her sister's. This was no mealy-mouthed, soft-spoken Southern belle. This woman had attitude, as well as backbone. She was a firecracker, hotheaded and sharp-tongued. A real handful—just as her father had warned him.

He should have known that the unmanageable, stubborn, too-smart-for-her-britches girl he'd known at twelve would grow into this fiery to-be-reckoned-with woman.

In answer, she swung that shoulder bag, to cuff him the way she had the other poor sucker, but he'd been expecting it. He caught the bag and blocked her next move, not interested in being kneed in the groin or ending up in a snowbank.

"Damn it, I'm trying to help you. Why can't you believe that?" he said, holding on to both of her arms and keeping her at a safe distance from his groin.

"Because you were bought by my father, just like the rest of them." She spit the words at him, her eyes narrowed to slits. He could feel the anger coursing through her body and feared if he let go of her, she would launch herself at him again. They were wasting valuable time arguing on the street like this.

"I wasn't bought by *anyone*. Especially Beauregard Bonner. Don't you know me better than that?"

"I *thought* I did."

"Look, whatever this is between you and your father, I don't care, okay? I want to help, starting with getting us both out of here." He gave her arms a little tug. "Come on." He thought she'd fight him. But somewhere in the distance came the roar of an engine.

He watched her face, trying to read her expression. Fear? Or something else?

She didn't look happy about it but she let him hustle her across the street to his pickup.

Fortunately with the holidays so close, this part of town was pretty deserted with people either at work or shopping. They reached the truck without incidence, but Chance had a bad feeling it wasn't going to last.

"Where are you taking me?" She sounded suspicious and worried as she walked around to the passenger side of the truck.

"Somewhere safe." He waited for her to open her door and get in, half expecting her to try to take off again. He remembered what Bonner had said about "keeping" Dixie once he found her.

"What about my car?" she asked, looking back toward the museum.

"We'll come back for it." What he really meant was

that he'd see that it got back to Texas. "Get in." He planned to get this job done and enjoy Christmas, come hell or Dixie Bonner.

She opened the pickup door and he did the same on his side. They looked at each other across the bench seat over Beauregard the dog who was sprawled like a lumpy blanket on the floor under the steering wheel out of Dixie's sight.

Her gaze, a mind-blowing blue, locked with his and he thought he glimpsed an instant of vulnerability. She still had a light sprinkling of freckles across those high cheekbones that she'd had at twelve, but on her they were now nothing short of sexy.

Any man looking into that face would have melted on the spot.

Unless that man had known the twelve-year-old Dixie Bonner and had an inkling of what she was capable of.

Or unless that man was Chance Walker and incredibly suspicious of everything—and everyone—by nature. Especially Dixie Bonner.

"You have to believe me, Chance," she said, her eyes locked with his, but still not getting into the pickup. Waiting for him to say he believed whatever she was going to say? Or stalling for time so that car with the two guys would have a chance to come back?

He couldn't help but think that the scene he'd just witnessed had been set up just for him. If Dixie wanted him to believe she was in danger, why not set it up so two big guys try to abduct you at the same time dumb ol' Chance Walker shows up?

It was that damned suspicious nature of his.

But added to what Bonner had told him about his

youngest daughter—and what Chance himself already knew, he wouldn't put anything past her.

"We can talk about this in the truck," he said.

"Someone's trying to kill me." Those big baby blues misted over. She bit her lower lip, then looked away as if embarrassed by her moment of weakness.

He felt a strong tug at his heartstrings, then had to remind himself again who he was dealing with. But until he had her in the pickup... "Who's trying to kill you? The guys in the car?"

She said nothing as she looked down the street and blinked back tears.

"How *many* people are after you?" He hadn't meant it to sound so flip. "Come on, get in the truck. We need to get going. You can tell me all about it."

He saw her hesitate, then finally acquiesce. Swearing under his breath, he started to climb behind the wheel. Was she serious? Crazy? Lying? All of the above?

Dixie stepped up on the running board to climb in and let out a surprised sound when she finally saw the dog come up off the floor. "What is it?"

"A *dog*."

She mugged a face at Chance. "I can see that. What kind?"

"Heinz 57 varieties. Just like me."

She eyed him. "Just like a lot of people. Does he bite?"

"Only people who piss me off."

She smiled faintly. "Then I guess I've been warned."

"Scoot over, Beauregard, and let her in," Chance said, dragging the dog over to give her more room.

"You named your dog *Beauregard*?"

It was Chance's turn to smile. "That's exactly what your daddy said."

"I bet he did." Beauregard grudgingly curled in the middle of the bench seat and Dixie climbed in, her nose wrinkling at the smell of damp dog. Beauregard sniffed her hand then settled himself and went back to sleep.

"Damp dog your normal cologne? Bet you don't date much," Dixie said as she slammed the pickup door and he started the engine, muttering under his breath.

At least they were on a familiar level. She'd been a smart-mouthed kid at twelve, always giving him a hard time. And vice versa.

Out of the corner of his eye, he watched her relax a little as she leaned back in the seat and gazed out at the mountains. It surprised him, but he realized that he'd missed her smart mouth. He shook his head at the thought. He hadn't missed her older sister Rebecca and that seemed a terrible thing given that she really had been his first love.

He turned his thoughts back to the problem at hand as he skirted town, debating where to take her. The obvious thing to do was to head back the way he'd come. But that would no doubt involve running into J. B. Jamison. And there was also whoever had broken into his office.

Clearly, someone after her knew about him and would expect him to return to his office in Townsend. But why take the answering machine tape? Just to find Dixie? Or to keep her from telling him something?

That last thought struck a chord.

He warned himself not to get any more involved. He'd found Dixie. All he had to do was to give Bonner a call. His job would be over and he could get back to enjoying the holidays like he'd planned.

"I'm serious, Chance. I left Texas because someone is trying to kill me," she said, not looking at him.

"What did you do in Texas to make someone want to kill you?" he asked, only half joking.

She glanced over at him, a thin smile curling that amazing mouth of hers. Who would have ever thought that Rebecca's kid sister would grow into such a stunning woman? It was that combination of big blue eyes, wide, bow-shaped mouth and high cheekbones. Not to mention that it was framed by wild dark hair that shone in the sunlight streaming in the pickup windows. She had the kind of face you couldn't help staring at.

"What did my father tell you about me?" she asked.

He could feel those blue eyes on him. "Not much. Just that you're a hellion. That you've kidnapped yourself a few times. That the ransom demand has been going up steadily since you were three."

"That's *all?*" she asked.

"There's *more?*" Of course there was more or they wouldn't be here now.

"Aren't you curious why my father is so intent on getting me back to Texas?"

Hell yes, he was. He pulled up to a stop sign and looked over at her. "I don't get paid to be curious." Which just happened to be true. But he also knew that getting curious about Dixie Bonner would lead to nothing but trouble.

"Look, if you'll just take me back to my car—"

"I can't do that."

"I beg your pardon?"

He met her gaze. "Your father hired me to make sure you were safe. Clearly you wouldn't be safe back at your car."

Her face reddened with anger. "I'm twenty-nine years old. If you try to take me back to Texas, I will have you arrested for kidnapping."

He laughed. "You can't have it both ways. Do you really believe the cops or the feds are going to believe that you've been kidnapped? They've already written off your latest attempt to extort money from your father as just that."

She stared at him. "What are you talking about?"

"The million dollars you were demanding for ransom. Excuse me, I guess it's gone up to a mil and a half now."

"I don't have any idea what you're talking about."

He stared into that face. He wanted to believe her. He really did. But then he wanted to believe anything that came out of that mouth.

"I'm talking about those guys back there," he said, getting angry. "You set up that whole show, the Castle in the background, two guys driving up just when I did, you managing to fight them off. Come on, admit it. This is just some game you and your father are playing."

She looked away. "I heard you were a pretty good private investigator."

The "pretty good" rankled even though that was pretty much how he would have described himself.

She swung around to face him, eyes piercing him like laser beams. "If you think this is a game, then you're a lousy P.I. and an even worse judge of character. But then again, you *are* working for my father, aren't you?"

Chance swore. Hadn't he known that getting involved with the Bonners was like sticking his hand into a wasps' nest hoping he wouldn't get stung?

She reached for the pickup's door handle but he reached faster, his hand clamping down on her arm as he leaned over the dog.

"I don't know what you're trying to pull, but it

isn't going to work on me. So why don't you try being straight with me?"

Even if her blue eyes hadn't been snapping with anger, he could feel her rage under his fingertips where they gripped her arm.

"I didn't kidnap myself. I never made a ransom demand. Whether you believe it or not, my life is in danger."

He didn't believe it and it must have shown because she jerked free of his grip. But she didn't try to get out of the pickup as he drove on through the intersection and headed north out of town.

He was going the wrong way to get back to Townsend.

But he didn't care because whether he liked it or not, he needed to know what he was dealing with before he went any further.

Dixie was frowning, chewing on her lower lip, eyes angry slits. But there was also a hurt in her expression that bothered him like a sliver just under his skin.

What if she was telling the truth?

He reminded himself that lying ran in some families like freckles or high cheekbones. Dixie Bonner came by her lying genes honestly enough. And Bonner had gotten proof from the kidnappers. "The kidnappers mailed your father your locket."

Her hand went to her throat. She seemed surprised to find her locket gone. Or was that, too, part of the act?

"You telling me someone took it from around your neck without you knowing about it?" he asked, unable to keep the sarcasm out of his voice.

"I would imagine they took it while I was knocked out after they abducted me in Texas. I've been a little too distracted to have noticed since then."

He turned to stare at her. "You were abducted in Texas and brought to Montana?"

"Not exactly."

He groaned inwardly, still debating the best place to take her as she told him a story of being attacked in a parking garage in Houston, knocked out, waking up in the trunk of her car in her garage to hear the men ransacking her house, and then miraculously getting away.

"Wow, that's some story," was all he could say when she finished. He felt her gaze on him and looked over to see her big baby blues brimming in tears.

She made an angry swipe at them. "Damn you, what about that don't you believe?"

He didn't know where to start. Surely Bonner had gone to check his daughter's house. Wouldn't he have mentioned if the house had been ransacked? "So how exactly did you get away?"

She eyed him as if she thought he was just humoring her. And when he thought she wasn't going to tell him, she changed her mind and did.

He listened as she told a harrowing tale of how she had narrowly escaped from the trunk, leaving him torn between disbelief and distress at the thought that this really could have happened to her.

"I didn't know what to do. I just knew I had to get out of Texas. I needed help, but mostly I needed someone I could trust." She let out a sarcastic laugh.

He shot her a look, thinking that was pretty sad if true. Was there really no one in Texas she felt she could trust to help her? At the same time, he was touched that she'd come to him. Just as it made him suspicious of her motives.

She glanced out the side window, turning quickly back his way and sliding down a little in her seat.

Past her, he caught sight of a dark gray SUV at a side street. Had she thought it was the black car for a minute? Is that why she'd reacted the way she had?

He took the road out of town and saw her glance back then sit up a little straighter. In his rearview mirror, he saw that there was no one behind them as they left White Sulphur Springs. No dark gray SUV.

He glanced at Dixie, unable to shake the feeling there was more she was keeping from him. "Wouldn't most women have gone to the police the moment they escaped?"

"I don't know what most women would have done," Dixie said, an edge to her voice. "I'm not *most* women. I'm the daughter of Beauregard Bonner, remember? That comes with its own rule book. I just know what *I* did under those circumstances."

He said nothing.

"Obviously you have no idea how much power my father now wields in Texas," she said. "And it seems his power extends all the way to Montana, given how easily he bought you."

Chance ground his teeth, checked his rearview mirror—and let out a curse as he spotted a car coming up way too fast behind them. The dark gray SUV.

CHAPTER SIX

MASON ROBERTS WAS waiting for Beau in his office. As Beau stepped in and closed the door, Mason turned from where he stood at the window looking out.

"You have the best view in the entire building," he said in answer to Beau's unasked question as to what he was doing in the boss's office. Mason knew him too well, anticipating that he would come back here rather than go to that huge empty house alone.

"It's not a bad view," Bonner agreed, even though he knew the view had nothing to do with why Mason was waiting for him.

"Is everything all right?" Mason asked as he moved to the bar to make them both a drink as he always did.

Beau took a seat behind his desk. Mason had lived down the road and been like family since they were kids, both going their own ways for a while, but ending up back in Texas. Beau had offered his old friend a job and Mason, who was as smart as anyone when it came to money, had taken it.

"Why wouldn't everything be all right?" Beau asked, wondering what Mason had heard.

"Dixie?" Mason asked, turning from the bar with a glass in each hand.

Bonner took the Scotch Mason offered him. He didn't need any more to drink today but he never turned down Scotch—especially the good stuff he kept stocked in his office.

He was tired, worn out and discouraged. This wasn't the way it should have been. He was rich, damn it. He'd always thought that once he had enough money all his troubles would just fade away. Even those from the past.

"Dixie?" he repeated, pretending he didn't know what Mason was getting at.

"She up to her usual?" Mason asked.

So Mason had heard. "I'm afraid so, but I have it covered." He downed the drink, avoiding his friend's gaze as he let the alcohol warm him to his toes.

"If there's anything I can do…."

Mason had been running interference for him since they were kids. His friend seemed to be waiting for Beau to tell him what was really going on.

Not this time. "It's a family matter."

Mason winced as if Beau had hit him and Beau realized belatedly that he'd hurt his feelings. "You know what I mean. Just my daughter being Dixie." Beau put down his glass and rubbed his temples, feeling a headache coming on.

Chance would find Dixie and, with any luck, she would be flying home in time for Christmas. He would talk to her. Explain everything. Dixie was smart. She could be made to understand.

Then they would have a nice Christmas like a normal family. But even as he thought it, Beauregard Bonner knew the chance of having a normal Christmas was out of his grasp. Dixie had made certain of that.

CHANCE WATCHED THE CAR behind him coming up fast. Out of the corner of his eye, he caught Dixie's expression as she turned in her seat to look back again.

"How many people did you say were after you?" he asked as the dark gray SUV bore down on them.

Not surprisingly, she didn't answer, but he noticed that she'd slid down again in the seat as if she didn't want to be seen.

He swore, determined to get her somewhere and to get the truth out of her. More and more he was convinced the earlier scene at the museum had been staged, that the guys in the black car were in on whatever was going on and that he was a pawn in all this. So who was in the dark gray SUV?

The driver closed the distance and Chance saw what appeared to be a single occupant in the car.

He still held out hope that the driver might not even be someone interested in them at all. Maybe even someone who didn't want to run them off the road or shoot at them. Could be just some kid driving his parents' SUV too fast.

Unfortunately he'd seen the way Dixie acted after spotting the vehicle the first time. The SUV filled his rearview mirror just an instant before he heard the blare of the horn and the driver roared around him, pulling alongside as if to pass on the two-lane. But, of course, didn't.

"Get down!" Chance yelled to Dixie as he braced himself for some defensive driving if not some defensive ducking in anticipation of the barrel end of a weapon pointed in his direction.

Instead the driver was waving frantically for him to pull over.

Was the guy nuts?

The driver laid on his horn again, waving wildly and pointing—not at Chance. But at what little could be seen of Chance's passenger.

Chance shot a look at Dixie. She had slid down some more, one hand on her forehead, the other resting on Beauregard, her face turned away as if pretending this wasn't happening.

"You know this guy?" Chance demanded.

OLIVER LANCASTER WAS having a bad day. He'd gone to lunch after running into Ace and come back into the office hoping to find a way to get another twenty-five thousand together.

He'd cleaned out every reserve he had, including his children's college funds. Not that he wasn't going to replace the money. He had to before Rebecca found out and went postal over it. Or worse, went to her father.

This deal was taking too long. He'd gone from nervous to scared. Everything was riding on it paying off the debts he'd incurred before anyone knew about them.

But Ace needed another twenty-five thousand.

And Oliver not only didn't have it, he wasn't sure he could even scrape that much together. He'd borrowed money on everything he owned, including the house that Beau had purchased for them as a wedding present.

Oliver was starting to sweat just thinking about it. He couldn't go to Beau for the twenty-five grand. Or Carl, not after that impromptu visit from his wife's uncle this morning. Carl had come by to give him some speech about being a better husband to Rebecca. What the hell had that been about?

Like any of this was Carl's business.

But it had still scared Oliver because it must mean that even her uncle Carl had noticed that Rebecca hadn't been happy lately. Great. Oliver did not need this on top of everything else.

He'd promised Carl he'd make every effort to be a

better husband. So going to Carl now for money was definitely out.

Even if Beau hadn't been in Montana, Oliver couldn't ask him for the money. As Carl had said, Beau had a lot on his mind. He was under enough stress without having to worry about Rebecca.

Carl had made him promise also not to let any problems between Oliver and his wife become something else that Beau had to worry about.

What an ass the man was.

The only reason Oliver had made the stupid promises was to get rid of the man. He'd been expecting a call from Ace and the last thing he needed was Uncle Carl getting wind of the deal he had going with Ace. Ace Bonner was the family outcast. For sure Carl wouldn't have approved of that association even if Beau was helping Ace get back on his feet.

It was odd, though. Carl had mentioned the stress Beau was under and Mason had said something about how Beau seemed to be making bad decisions, losing some of his edge, and had hinted that maybe it was time for Beau to retire as president of Bonner Unlimited and let someone…younger take over.

Since Oliver was the youngest of the bunch, he'd assumed Mason was trying to tell him something. With Beau out of the way… Well, the possibilities were unlimited.

But until then…

"I can't take this any longer," Oliver said to his empty office. He needed to get out of here, go to the club for a few drinks and try to win the twenty-five thousand. Maybe his luck would change. Hell, maybe he could win a bundle.

He touched his intercom and informed his secretary

he'd be leaving for the day. But as he started around his desk he heard his private office door open.

"Oliver?"

Damn.

"Beau," Oliver said, forcing himself to sound glad to see his father-in-law. Just his luck.

"I ASKED YOU if you knew this guy?" Chance repeated as the SUV stayed right with them and the man behind the wheel continued to motion for Chance to pull over.

Dixie leaned forward to do a quick glance across the dog and him to the driver of the SUV. "He doesn't look familiar."

Chance looked over at the driver of the SUV again. The guy appeared really upset now, having seen Dixie look over at him. He was mouthing something Chance couldn't make out. But it wasn't as if the guy was trying to tell him that he had a taillight out or a tire going flat.

No, this guy was angry. And he seemed to be spewing all that venom in Dixie's direction. He hadn't tried to kill her, though. Apparently he just wanted to talk to her.

As they came around a curve, Chance looked up and swore. A semi-truck was approaching in the SUV's lane and a rancher on an old tractor was puttering along dead ahead in Chance's lane.

In a split second of insanity, Chance tromped on the gas pedal, zooming ahead of the SUV and forcing the driver to drop back behind him. With the speedometer climbing, Chance swerved between the farmer on the slow-moving tractor and the semi barreling toward him in the opposite lane.

The semi blew by with a half dozen cars backed up behind it on the two-lane an instant later.

Chance heard Dixie let out a held breath. He checked his rearview mirror. Just as he'd hoped, the SUV driver had been forced to come to a crawl behind the tractor as the semi and the line of cars passed.

Chance had bought himself a little time.

He glanced over at Dixie. She looked pale but relieved. He caught her glancing in her side mirror and chewing at her lower lip. What the hell was going on with her? He hated to venture a guess, but one thing was certain. There were definitely people after her.

But to kill her?

Or to drag her back to Houston?

Something had Dixie Bonner on the run.

What were the chances it was because of something she'd done?

"HAVE A MINUTE?" It wasn't really a question as Beau closed the office door and motioned for Oliver to sit back down. Beau went straight to the bar. He made sure that even Oliver's office was stocked with his own favorite Scotch.

But to Oliver's surprise, his father-in-law poured himself a cup of coffee from the carafe left by the secretary.

Fortunately, Beau seldom came to the office and didn't seem to have any interest in the way Oliver spent his days as long as there were no problems with what little Beau let him handle. Or on the home front.

He motioned that he didn't want any coffee or a drink but Beau apparently had poured him a drink anyway. Hell, was he going to need one? Had Rebecca found out about the children's college funds? Or the other things Oliver had to mortgage?

"What's up?" Oliver asked, still standing.

"Dixie's taken off," Beau said as if this were news. He handed Oliver his usual vodka tonic and, with the coffee in hand, dropped into the deep leather chair across from Oliver's desk. Another addition Beau had made to the office for his rare visits.

"What do you mean 'taken off'?" Oliver asked as he lowered himself back into his chair, pretending this was news. And hoping it had nothing to do with him.

Beau looked him in the eye and for a moment Oliver felt as if the man was two steps ahead of him—maybe even more. "Rebecca didn't tell you?"

"I haven't spoken with her today," Oliver said. True, but an obvious mistake to tell the father-in-law just how little contact he had with the man's daughter. "We've been playing telephone tag all day."

Beau sent him a look that was equal parts disgust and disbelief. He didn't have to tell Oliver that he'd better keep Rebecca happy. But, of course, Beau did.

"I just saw my daughter having lunch with a friend. She didn't seem happy. There's no problem with you and my daughter, is there?" he asked, his tone making it clear that if there was, then it was Oliver's fault.

"No. Why would you think it had something to do with me?" Oliver had the bad feeling that his father-in-law knew more about Rebecca's state of mind than her own husband did. Had Rebecca said something to her father? Had she told him about the conversation she'd overhead last night on the phone?

He felt himself begin to sweat as Beau didn't answer the question—instead just studied him thoughtfully before taking a sip of his coffee.

"You said Dixie has taken off?" Anything to get the conversation off him and Rebecca. Even talking about his *least* favorite subject, Dixie.

Beau sighed and took a sip of his coffee. Oliver tried to remember the last time he'd seen his father-in-law drink coffee instead of Scotch this time of the day and couldn't.

"Did Dixie say anything to you?" Beau asked, settling his gaze on Oliver.

"No," he said, unable to hide his surprise. He spoke with Dixie even less than he did with his own wife. "Why would she tell *me* anything?"

"You *are* her brother-in-law, or don't you see her, either?"

Oliver didn't like the edge to Beau's voice. He plunged in, figuring it might be easier if they just got it out of the way right now. "Is there something I've done to upset you, Beau?"

The older man seemed to give that some thought. "I'm just worried about my daughters." His expression didn't change though. Oliver told himself he'd better watch his step. Something more had set Beau off and since he and Beau had never been close and now Chance Walker was in the picture…

He tried to assure himself this was just about Dixie. Beau's youngest had kept him upset more often than not over the years. What had she done this time? Oliver wondered.

"I've hired someone to find Dixie," Beau was saying. "Once she's back in Texas…" Beau rose awkwardly from the chair and Oliver realized with satisfaction that the oilman was getting old. Beau looked embarrassed to be seen at all feeble in front of him. "If you hear from Dixie…" He seemed to realize how unlikely that would be.

Like Oliver, he must have been wondering why he'd come in here to begin with. Or maybe he'd just been testing him, waiting for his son-in-law to hang himself. But then, Oliver had been feeling more than a little paranoid lately.

"I'll let you know if I hear anything," Oliver lied.

Right now, his only thought was Rebecca. Had she gone to her father about him? Her timing couldn't be any worse with him under so much strain. This deal had to go through and in a hurry. His life depended on it.

In his rearview mirror, Chance watched the tractor get smaller and smaller until they went around a bend and it disappeared. No sign of the SUV.

He looked over at Dixie, not surprised to see one arm around Beauregard's neck, the other hanging on to the door handle. Her face was still pale and for the first time, she looked scared.

"Is it my driving?" he joked.

She glanced over at him as if her mind had been a thousand miles away. "It's fine."

"Fine?" He snorted. "That was an amazing example of my driving ability and you say it was *fine?*"

He finally had her attention.

She smiled. She had a gorgeous smile. "I'd forgotten how full of yourself you are."

He smiled back at her, worried as hell. Based on the number of people after her, Dixie Bonner was in a world of trouble.

The problem was that while she'd said she'd come all the way to Montana because he was the only person she could trust, she no longer trusted him. So getting her to tell him what was going on could pose a problem.

Well, all that was about to change, Chance told himself as he saw a sign for a mountain lodge just ahead.

He didn't slow down until he reached the turnoff and pulled off onto the snow-packed gravel road.

Still no sign of the SUV.

But he had a bad feeling it wasn't the last they'd see of the people after Dixie Bonner.

And soon he would know why.

Dixie glanced back, more relieved than Chance could know that he'd lost the SUV. She watched him shift the pickup into four-wheel drive as he headed up the snowy road, wondering where he was taking her.

It hadn't slipped her mind that Chance was working for her father. Who knew what kind of deal they'd made?

Just the thought made her sick to her stomach. She'd thought Chance was the one person who couldn't be bought by her father. If she'd been wrong about Chance, then what hope was there?

"Where are we going?" she asked, worried. Ahead, all she could see was a mountain, the road disappearing into the snowcapped pines and what appeared to be a wide expanse of roofline.

"Somewhere safe," was all he said as he drove up the winding road, but she could feel his gaze on her every few minutes, as if he had a lot of questions.

She was sure he did.

She had a lot herself. She'd been so sure that once she had found him, all she had to do was to pour her heart out to him and he would be there for her.

Now she wasn't sure what to do next. Trusting Chance could be her worse—and last—mistake. So far he hadn't believed anything she'd told him.

She hated to even think what he would say when she told him the rest.

"I'm going to help you," he said quietly, as if sensing her wrestling with the problem.

She could only nod. Whatever he had planned for her, she would figure out a way to keep one step ahead of him. Hadn't she gotten this far all by herself? She didn't kid herself that a lot of it had been luck. Her would-be killers hadn't expected her to go to Montana.

No, she decided. Trusting Chance now would be a mistake. Better to keep her options open and try to get away from him the first opportunity that presented itself.

"Montana is so beautiful," she said, trying to hide the affect her decision had on her. She turned to look out the side window, secretly brushing away her tears. She'd been such a fool. All these years of comparing every man she met with Chance. He had been her hero. The man of her dreams.

"Well, you've apparently seen a lot of the state, I'll give you that," Chance said.

She turned to look at him, almost as angry with him as she was disappointed in him. "I wondered why you stayed here. I guess you weren't just hiding out from my father and Rebecca."

"I'm not the one who has the whole state of Texas after her."

She ignored that and saw him check his rearview mirror. "Did my father tell you about his heart attack?"

"Is this just chitchat or are you leading up to something?" he asked, cutting his eyes to her. "Like maybe the truth about what's really going on."

The truth? She had to smile. Even if he hadn't been hired by her father, there was another reason she was reluctant to tell him. There wasn't a chance in hell that he was going to believe her.

"I just thought you'd want to know the score. The doctor said the heart attack was minor but that he had to slow down," she continued. "Unfortunately he's too controlling to turn over the reins, not even to Mason. Forget Uncle Carl, he wants nothing to do with running an empire, and Ace would steal every dime. I think Daddy isn't so naive he doesn't know that. Nor would he ever give Oliver control. Oliver is Rebecca's husband." She glanced over at him. "Daddy can't stand him. Uncle Carl says if Daddy keeps giving Oliver enough rope, he'll hang himself and Rebecca will be the best-dressed widow at the funeral."

"I see you're still getting along well with your family," he said.

"You have no idea."

Chance could feel her gaze on him but he kept his eyes on the road and his mouth shut. She was just trying to get a rise out of him. And damned if it wasn't working.

"I guess *Daddy* didn't tell you that he's also getting into politics?" she said.

He noticed the contemptuous way she said "Daddy." He wondered if she was making fun of her father and her relationship with him. Or if this was about Rebecca since, as he recalled now, she'd always called Beau "Daddy."

Either way, it made him all the more convinced that this drama was just some power struggle between Dixie and her *daddy*. And it made him mad as hell that he'd gotten involved. Especially for *money*.

"Beauregard and I didn't do a lot of talking," Chance said after a few moments, curious, though, where she was headed with all this. She'd seemed vulnerable a few moments ago and he'd made the mistake of being nice to her. She didn't react well to sympathy.

"I'm not surprised he's going into politics, though," Chance admitted. Money and politics seemed to go together and Beauregard Bonner had his fingers in anything that would benefit him. Given his money and his need for power, it had been just a matter of time before he got into politics. "But if your father is so powerful in Texas, then why didn't you let him help you out of whatever mess you're in?"

"You wouldn't believe me if I told you," Dixie said, looking away. "After all, you still don't believe that someone is trying to kill me."

"Now why wouldn't I believe you? Let's see. One, you haven't given me one reason why anyone would want you dead. Two, you don't seem to have been kidnapped, but someone is trying to get a million and a half out of your rich old man—and they just happened to have your locket. Three, your father doesn't want to go to the feds or the police any more than you do. Four, he's hired not one, but a bunch of guys just to haul you back to Texas as if he has some reason to believe it might be difficult and a necessity. Five, you seem pretty damn relaxed for someone who supposedly has killers after her."

"You have no idea how scared I am," she snapped. "Would it make you feel better if I were hysterical, crying and wringing my hands and begging you to tell me what to do?"

For a few moments there was only the crunch of the tires on the cold snow, the dog's soft snores and the steady throb of the pickup's engine.

Chance kept his mouth shut, knowing that anything he said would be wrong.

"Look," Dixie finally said. "I've been taking care of myself for quite a few years now. Because of who my father is, I've always had to be careful. Most of the men I meet just want my father's money. Even some women try to befriend me for the same reason. From the time I could walk I was told I had to watch out for kidnappers." She cocked her head at him. "Is it any wonder I kidnapped myself to get what I wanted a few times when I was younger?"

He said nothing, unable to imagine her life. He'd come from middle-class parents, an adequate house but no pool. As a kid, he'd gotten a paper route to make extra money, then lawn-mowing jobs later. After high school, to help save for college, he'd gone to work in one of Beauregard Bonner's oil fields for the summer. That was until he'd inadvertently caught the attention of Bonner himself, who'd hired him as security for his daughters even though Chance was only a few years older than Rebecca.

Bonner had liked him, noticed how hard he worked in the field, and come up with the job. Maybe Bonner had hoped all along that Chance would marry his oldest daughter. Or maybe that was the last thing he'd ever wanted.

"I told you why I was waiting for you at the museum."

"Right. You were just making my life easier along with making it easier for the guys in the black car."

"You really have become incredibly cynical and not very trusting."

He laughed. "You're a *Bonner*. And I haven't forgotten what you were like as a kid."

"Those were just childish pranks," she said with a wave of her hand.

"Like kidnapping yourself."

She looked away. "I'll admit I've made a few mistakes in the past. But whether you believe it or not, I've changed."

He nodded, not believing it. "Your father doesn't believe you've changed."

She glared over at him. "Since when have you started trusting my father? I thought you were smart enough that you would remember my father *always* has ulterior motives for everything he does."

"He says he's trying to protect you."

She laughed. "And you believe that?"

He thought about Jamison, the duct tape in the back of the van.

"I can't go back to Texas or they'll kill me."

"You already said that. But what I'd like to know is why you didn't just come straight to my office instead of zigzagging your way across Montana."

She gave him a how-ignorant-are-you look. "That would have been pretty stupid, don't you think? Obviously someone knew where I was headed. My father, for instance. And how do you suppose someone knew to break into your office and steal the answering machine tape with my messages?"

He wished he knew.

"What is wrong with you?" she demanded angrily. "Don't you see? My father *had* to get to you first. He had to make you distrust me. I'm sure he offered you some outrageous amount of money. He knew I'd come to you. He had to make sure you wouldn't believe me when I told you why they want me dead. And he had to make sure you didn't get my messages."

"Are you trying to tell me your father is in on this? He's the one who gave me the record of your credit card charges. Why would he do that if he didn't want me to find you?"

"He wanted to make sure you didn't believe anything I told you," she said with a quirk of her brow. "Worked, didn't it?"

Chance wanted to argue the point but knew she was right at least about his preconceived notions about her—and where he'd gotten most of them.

He watched her rub one of Beauregard's big ears. The dog moaned softly and snuggled against her.

Don't get used to that, Beauregard. Dixie Bonner is on her way back to Texas just as soon as I can get her butt on a plane.

CHAPTER SEVEN

DIXIE LOOKED UP as Chance slowed the pickup. A building appeared from out of the snowy pines draped in red and green lights. Hot Springs Lodge. The log structure was set against a backdrop of rocky cliffs and snow-capped trees. It was as picturesque as anything she'd ever seen, even with the Santa Claus and sleigh with the silhouettes of reindeers out front.

"Is that where we're going?" After Chance moved to Montana, she'd read everything she could get her hands on about the state. This is exactly how she'd pictured a Montana mountain lodge.

She tensed as she heard a buzzing sound off to her right and looked in her side mirror to see a snowmobile racing along beside the pickup just a few yards off the road. Behind it was a half dozen more snowmobiles.

Chance parked in front of what appeared to be a full-fledged Montana resort complete with log hotel, store-front café, gift shop and hot springs.

"You approve?" he asked, sounding amused.

"I love it. They have food and a *pool*."

He chuckled. "I forgot how much you liked to eat—and swim—as a kid. I guess some things don't change."

She met his gaze. He was smiling at her, the look in his eyes so familiar. Who knew what Chance had promised her father when Beauregard had hired him? But at that moment, Dixie weakened. She would have bet everything that she hadn't been wrong about Chance Walker, that he was still her hero, that ultimately he would save her.

She told herself it had nothing to do with the fact that he looked so darned good. Or that she'd missed him. She'd once thought that Chance would always be around. She'd been more devastated than Rebecca when Chance hadn't come back to Texas.

But was she willing to stake her life on him?

The driver of the lead snowmobile stopped in front of the lodge.

"I'll be right back," Chance said, apparently recognizing the man. "I'll get us a couple of rooms, some food and then we're going to have a talk."

Her stomach somersaulted. "Great. But what's the point if you aren't going to believe me?"

"You're going to *convince* me," he said with a grin, and opened his pickup door.

She watched him go over to the large man still straddling the snowmobile, the motor rumbling, the exhaust puffing out gray clouds into the cold late afternoon.

The other riders took off in a beehive of noise and activity. Dixie couldn't hear what was being said, but she saw Chance tell the man on the snowmobile something that made him glance in her direction. Then the man started up the snowmobile again and followed after the others.

Chance opened her side door. "We're all set."

She wondered what that meant. Dixie realized that neither of them had any luggage. She'd left what little she'd purchased in her car. She hadn't even thought to retrieve it, but then, she hadn't been thinking clearly for days now. And it wasn't as though Chance had given her much of an opportunity.

Her stomach growled.

Chance grinned, clearly hearing it.

She climbed out of the truck, the dog jumping out after her. Beauregard trotted along beside them as they entered the lodge, and Chance went behind the front desk to get a key.

Only one key?

Every daydream she'd ever had about Chance suddenly blossomed. She felt her face heat as her heart did a little Texas two-step. Around them Christmas music played softly. A white Christmas in Montana. It was more than she could have dreamed possible.

"There a problem?" he asked, cutting his eyes to her and grinning.

She really had to quit being so transparent.

"It's the family lodge unit," he explained. "*Two* bedrooms. One key. After all, someone is trying to kill you. I can't let that happen."

She made a face at him and looked around the lodge as she and the dog followed him up the stairs. The walls were log with a rich patina that had built up over the years. There was a huge stone fireplace, comfortable chairs and couches spread around it and a massive stuffed moose head on the wall. The moose was wearing a red and white Santa hat.

She couldn't believe she was in Montana, in a place like this and with Chance Walker. Too bad that's where the fantasy part ended.

"This way," Chance said.

She nodded and followed him down a rustic hallway, still looking around, taking it all in. Hadn't she imagined Chance Walker in just such a place? Only she'd always thought of him as the cowboy in the white hat who lived by the Code of the West. Which meant he would be on *her* side. Not her father's.

She'd truly believed he was the one person Beauregard Bonner couldn't manipulate. She realized now how naive that had been. Her father was the master manipulator. And what he couldn't manipulate he could afford to buy.

But then, she was pretty good at getting what she wanted, she reminded herself. After all, she'd learned from the best.

What would it take, though, to get Chance to believe her? she wondered as he unlocked their room and pushed open the door. The dog trotted in and Dixie followed.

The family lodge unit was spacious, much like a two-bedroom apartment. The walls were knotty pine and everything was decorated with prints of cute bears and even cuter moose.

She walked through the place, noting the only other exit was the second-floor deck. Something told her he'd picked this room because there would be little way for her to escape without him knowing it.

"I think I'll take a hot shower," she said, and smiled at him.

He glanced into the bathroom and smiled at her. There was no window. No way out. "I'll order us something to eat."

Once in the bathroom, she turned on the shower and let it run as she thought about her options. Try to get Chance to believe her? Or plan how she'd get away when he didn't?

THE MOMENT BEAU left his office, Oliver called Rebecca's cell phone number. He had to know what she'd told her father without letting her know he'd seen her last night and that he knew she'd been eavesdropping on his phone conversations.

Her cell rang four times and just when he was starting to worry, she picked up.

"Dixie?" she asked, sounding out of breath. She hadn't had time to check the caller ID apparently.

"No, it's me." Why was she out of breath?

"Oh. Oliver." She sounded so disappointed he was instantly angry.

"Is everything all right?" he asked, masking his anger. "You sound out of breath."

"Fine."

"You were hoping it was Dixie," he said.

"Yes."

He gritted his teeth. Last night, after she'd overheard him on the phone, he'd gone up to their bedroom. He'd heard her breathing, had said her name. She hadn't answered and he couldn't see her in the dark. She kept their bedroom so damned dark he'd become adept at getting around it without stumbling over anything. And she often used earplugs even though the room was soundproofed. She didn't even want to hear him breathing at night.

He'd known she wasn't asleep—just pretending as usual. And that had been fine with him.

"I spoke with your dad," he said now and waited.

No response.

"I know Dixie's in Montana and that you're worried about her," he said.

"Is that what he told you?"

Had it always been this hard to talk to her?

"He told me he hired Chance Walker to find her."

Silence. She wasn't taking the bait.

"What are you doing for dinner?" He hated that he was forced to resort to a romantic dinner and probably making love to her.

"I have plans."

It had been months since they'd dined together. The nanny always fed the children early unless Beau was coming over. He had the feeling that they both avoided sitting across a table from each other and that's why they often had separate plans.

"It was just a thought," he said, relieved. At least he'd made the effort. He'd make sure Beau knew that he'd tried and it had been Rebecca who had *plans*.

"I might work late then," he said. "I have a ton of work to do."

Still nothing on her end. More than likely she knew it was a lie. Another reason he resented her.

Just like now. She was forcing him to fill the silence. "Have a nice evening then." He hung up, cutting off anything she might have said. Not wanting to know that all she'd done was hang up, as well.

He went to the bar and washed down antacids with alcohol, liking the way the alcohol burned all the way down. Damn the bitch. She was killing him.

WHILE DIXIE WAS IN the shower, Chance made the call to Bonner. "Dixie is with me," he said when the older man answered.

He heard relief and when Bonner spoke, he sounded choked up, making Chance feel guilty for questioning the oilman's motives. Maybe he really had just been worried about his daughter and believed he could keep her safe back in Texas.

That would explain why he was so insistent about getting her back there. Not to mention it was Christmas.

Of course, he'd want her near him for the holidays. It wasn't as though Bonner had a reason he didn't want her in Montana.

"With the holiday, there won't be any flights out of here," Chance told him.

"I'll send my jet. Let me see when I can arrange it." Bonner put him on hold to check with his pilot.

The sooner the better, Chance thought, glancing toward the other room. He could hear the shower running, the bathroom door closed, and felt a strange stab of guilt. He'd purposely waited to call Bonner until Dixie was out of earshot.

Not that he hadn't been up-front about his plans. She knew he was working for her father. He was just doing what he'd been paid to do.

So why did he feel like hell?

"The soonest, apparently, is the day after tomorrow about this time," Bonner said, coming back on the line. "You found her a lot quicker than I expected."

Chance swore under his breath. He'd hoped to be done with this assignment tomorrow. Forty-eight hours? Still, he should be finished with it and at his cabin by Christmas Eve.

"Okay, I'll bring her to the airport, but if she doesn't want to go with you, I won't help you force her," Chance said.

"Is Dixie *there?*"

"Yes. If you want to talk to her…"

Chance started to tell Bonner that she was in the shower in the adjacent room, but before he could, the old man said, "No. I'm just glad she's all right."

"Have you gotten any more calls from the kidnapper?" Chance asked, a little surprised Bonner wasn't asking the kinds of questions a father might ask when there was even a possibility that his daughter had been kidnapped.

"No. No more calls. Obviously, it was just a prank."

Chance frowned. "You think Dixie sent her locket to you?"

"Has she said anything?"

Anything? "Like what?"

"I don't know," Bonner said. "Dixie's always had a very active imagination. Who knows what story she'll make up to sway your opinion of her?"

"Well, she didn't imagine all the men you hired to bring her back to Texas."

Bonner either didn't hear what Chance said or ignored it. "Dixie can be very persuasive. Believe me, she'll try to con you in some way before this is over."

"Yeah? And what exactly is *this?*"

"Just a little family disagreement," Bonner said.

"Right."

"I'm just glad that Dixie is all right."

Whatever was going on, Dixie didn't seem all right. And Bonner seemed worried about what Dixie might tell him.

"By the way, have you gone over to her house?" Chance asked. "She says it was ransacked."

"Really? I can send someone over to check."

"Why don't you go yourself?" Chance suggested. "Maybe it will clear some things up."

"Things are clear enough," Bonner said. "Your job is to just make sure she's at the plane. There's a bonus in it for you if you get her there without any problems."

"I can't imagine why I'd have any problems, can you?" Chance asked facetiously.

"She's my daughter. That should tell you something." Bonner hung up before Chance could respond to that.

When he turned, he saw Dixie standing in the middle of the room. If looks could kill, he would have been dead as a doornail before he hit the floor.

"You called my father while I was in the shower," she said, her voice low and furious. But what cut him to the quick was her betrayed expression.

"It didn't really matter what I was going to tell you, did it?" she said, advancing on him. "You'd already made up your mind that you were going to help ship me back to Texas one way or the other because that's what Daddy's paying you to do."

"Dixie, I wanted to let your father know you were all right."

She shook her head, smiling ruefully. "I heard you make arrangements for a jet."

"The plane isn't coming for forty-eight hours."

"How much is he paying you?" She raised a brow. "Knowing *Daddy,* he's even promised you a bonus, right?" She smiled as she must have seen the answer in his face. "How much?" she asked as she stepped to him, her body brushing against his in a way that told him what was coming next.

She smelled good. Her skin was flushed from her shower, her hair pulled up to expose her long slender neck. "Dixie—"

"I don't have as much money as my father, but now that we both know you can be bought, let's decide exactly what your price is," she said as she shoved him backward. He stumbled and dropped into one of the overstuffed chairs.

She bent over him.

"Don't." The word didn't come out with as much force as he'd hoped. "You don't want to do this."

She raised a brow. "You think this is worse than

selling out to Beauregard Bonner?" She laughed and shook her head. "This is child's play compared to that."

"Dixie." A single lock of her hair brushed across his cheek as she bent closer, the movement emitting the sweet scent of her. Eyes locked with his, she brushed her lips over his. Just a promise of a kiss. It had been so long and his pain so deep, he'd thought no woman could ever arouse desire in him again.

He was wrong.

"Come on, Chance. What's it going to be?" she asked in a soft whisper near his ear, her warm breath caressing his neck.

It would have been so easy to let her seduce him. So easy. He grabbed her shoulders a little harder than he meant to and held her away as he pushed up from the chair, driving her back until they both stumbled into the living room wall.

He was breathing hard and one look in her eyes told him that she knew the effect she'd had on him. There was triumph in all that blue and yet he could feel her body trembling under his palms.

His gaze traveled over her face, lighting on her lips. How easy it would have been to kiss her. Not a light, teasing kiss like the one she'd just given him but a real honest-to-goodness kiss.

The thought shocked him because he wanted to kiss her senseless. He wanted to bury his fingers in her hair and to pull her to him until his body…

He let go of her, turning away, trying to hide the conflicted emotions that boiled up inside him. She wasn't just a job, she was Rebecca's little sister.

"I'm not my sister, Chance," she said, as if she knew what he was thinking, what he was feeling. "I *know* you," she said, stepping in front of him to block his escape.

He shook his head. "I'm not the man you think I am."

She cocked a brow at him. "You think putting me in a private jet and sending me back to Texas is any different from what the other men my father hired would do to me?"

"Dixie—"

"No, if that's what you want to do, then you're right. You aren't the man I knew. Or one I want to know."

"Your father believes that the only place you're going to be safe is Texas."

"Then you should listen to my father," she said, eyes blazing with anger before she spun around and headed out the deck door, slamming it behind her.

He swore as he watched her walk to the edge of the railing, her back to him. The light breeze stirred her hair. He could see her breath coming out in small white puffs. Forty-eight hours. Hadn't Bonner warned him not to let Dixie get to him? Just find her and take her to the plane. Period. Bonner had said it was a family matter. Let them work it out. It had nothing to do with him. Hell, what were the chances that anyone was really trying to kill her anyway?

He shook his head. He couldn't let himself get caught up in this little rich girl's fantasies. She was running a scam on her father. Upping the stakes to a million and a half. No wonder Bonner wanted Dixie stopped. He'd been through this with her before.

Not that any of that rationale helped the situation right now because Chance was caught in the middle, feeling guilty when it wasn't his fault that Dixie had purposely involved him by coming to Montana.

He groaned. Come to Montana because she'd said

she thought he was the one person she could trust to help her.

He looked out on the deck. The sun had dipped behind the Big Belt Mountains. He swore and opened the deck door. Cold darkness had settled in the pines, the shadows growing long and black beneath them in the snow.

Quietly opening the deck door, he stepped out, joining her at the railing. He knew she had to be cold. She stood, her arms wrapped around her. As he looked over, he saw that her eyes were closed and she seemed to be breathing in the cold evening air as if gasping for breath. As he watched, two tears rolled down her cheek.

She seemed to sense him standing there. Her blue eyes came open. She turned away, brushed at the tears and took a moment before she looked at him.

He saw that she was embarrassed that he'd caught her with her defenses down. The men chasing her were enough to scare anyone. He leaned against the railing next to her and looked out at the snowy land. Ice crystals danced in the air like glitter.

"I should have told you I was going to call your father," he said quietly.

She made an angry sound. "Is it true you haven't married because you never got over Rebecca?"

His gaze flew to her. "Where did that come from?"

"Is it?"

"No." He looked back out at the valley. "I just haven't found anyone I wanted to marry. Do you always ask such personal questions?"

"Yes."

He realized she preferred seeing *him* off balance than the other way around. "What about you?"

"What *about* me?"

"Why aren't you married?"

"I'm too young." She grinned, her cocky attitude back.

"You're what? Thirty?"

"Twenty-nine and you know it." She shivered, wrapping her arms tighter around her. "It's cold out here." She started to turn to go back inside.

On impulse he grabbed her arm to stop her. "It's okay to be scared. It would help if I knew what you had to be afraid of, though."

She met his gaze and held it. "Yes, it would help, wouldn't it? But then you said you weren't interested. Your job was just to get me to that jet back to Texas." She pulled free and strode into the lodge, hips swinging, head high, the door slamming behind her.

Chance watched her go, cursing under his breath. Bonner had warned him that Dixie would play him. So what if she told him her side of the story? That didn't mean she'd tell him the truth.

But even as he thought it, he knew he'd let her get to him.

CHAPTER EIGHT

As Dixie heard Chance come in from the deck, there was a knock at the door. She'd told herself she wasn't hungry, but the smell of food made her stomach rumble as a young man from the lodge served what they called the Montana Special.

"Food," Chance said, as if offering an olive branch after the young man left.

She was still furious with him, but the food smelled too good and she caught sight of what looked like pie. She did love pie. And he knew it.

They consumed buffalo burgers, cattleman fries and moose-tracks chocolate milkshakes in silence.

"I thought you might like this," Chance said, handing her a piece of the pie. "It's huckleberry. A local favorite."

She took a bite. The food had taken the edge off her anger. That and the fact that Chance seemed to be trying to placate her.

"Bring your pie in here," he said, and got up to go into the living room area to sit in one of the plush recliners. His dog plopped down at Chance's feet to sleep off the two burgers he'd devoured. "So tell me what's going on, really," Chance said when she joined him.

She forked a bite of pie and ate it.

He leaned back, all his attention on her. "Dixie, talk to me. Why is someone trying to kill you?"

She told herself, why bother telling him? Even if he believed her, he was getting paid to take her to a jet in forty-eight hours because her father apparently was bound and determined to get her back to Texas—one way or another.

She looked into Chance's handsome face and feared she was about to make the biggest mistake of her life.

But at least it would be her last mistake.

CHANCE WAITED, REMEMBERING how stubborn she'd been as a kid. She hadn't changed that much, he realized. She was furious with him. Not that he could blame her.

"Let me make it easy for you," he said. "Who was the guy chasing us on the highway?"

She bit at her lower lip for a moment. "Roy Bob Jackson. He works for my father."

"And? Come on, I know there's more to it. He seemed to want to talk to you about something."

She glanced away and sighed. "He probably just wants his engagement ring back."

Chance let out an oath. "He's your *fiancé?* And you didn't think to mention that while the guy was chasing us?"

"It's a long story."

"I bet it is," Chance said with a shake of his head. "So much so that you forgot to mention you were getting married."

"I'm not *marrying* the bastard."

"He gave you a ring!"

"No, he put it in my Christmas stocking."

Chance frowned. "You already looked in your stocking?"

Dixie mugged a face at him. "You know I could never wait until Christmas Day."

He'd forgotten how she was always snooping around the tree, shaking packages. "So the guy left a ring and a note asking you to marry him? Romantic."

"He couldn't look me in the eye and do it."

"So you never told him your answer?"

"My life got a little complicated right after that."

He shook his head in disbelief. "Now you won't even *talk* to him?"

"He works for my father. He lied to me. I'm sure *Daddy* set him on me, deciding I needed a husband," she said, looking away as if embarrassed that she'd been played the fool.

Bonner just never learned. Is this what was going on between father and daughter?

"Where is the engagement ring now?"

"In my purse."

He raised a brow. "You just happen to have it? You must have been at least thinking about accepting it."

"I'd planned to throw it in his face."

"If you'd have told me, I could have stopped the pickup."

"For all I know my father sent Roy Bob to try to convince me to forget all this."

"This?" Chance said. "The two men who jumped you in the parking garage?"

She nodded. "I was at the library doing research."

"Research? You mean, like for a *job?*"

She sighed. "You know it really ticks me off that you think I'm just a younger version of my sister. I work for a newspaper."

"I didn't know Beauregard owned a paper." He quickly laughed and held up his hands. "Just joking."

She looked over at him with murder in her eye. "It so

happens that I majored in journalism and I'm one hell of an investigative reporter. I've won awards, damn you."

Her outburst seemed to amuse him.

"You just assume that I couldn't get a job unless my father got it for me?"

"I'm sorry, okay? Tell me about your research. Was it for something you were working on at the paper? Maybe that's why you were attacked."

"No. It was personal research."

He raised a brow and she could already see the doubt in his eyes. She hesitated. But wasn't there the remote chance that she could convince him she was telling the truth? Otherwise, Chance Walker, her hero since she was twelve, would just be another man who'd let her down.

And she couldn't bear that.

Chance had tried to hide his surprise at hearing that Dixie had a real job. But from what Bonner had told him about his youngest daughter, who could blame him?

Why hadn't Bonner mentioned that Dixie was an investigative reporter? Obviously there was more to Dixie Bonner than he'd been led to believe. She'd been a mouthy, tough kid. Now she was a woman with one hell of a fiery temper and a lot more grit than he would have expected given the family money and social status.

"I recently found out that I had family I knew nothing about," she said.

He nodded. "And?"

"And it's going to get me killed unless I can convince you to help me."

He shook his head to clear it. "Wait a minute." He scratched his head. He'd been hoping it would be the kind of investigative reporting that would explain her story about the abduction in the parking garage. "Okay, let me get this straight. This has something to do with *genealogy?*"

"I should have known you wouldn't understand," she snapped, and got up to go to the window.

"I'm sorry. I'm *trying* to understand."

She turned from the window. "The men who attacked me were after my research and the photographs."

"Photographs?"

"They're what started it," Dixie said with an impatient sigh. "I found three old photographs in a jewelry box that Uncle Carl gave me when I turned sixteen. He said he found it, but I knew it had belonged to my mother from the way my father reacted when he saw it." She sounded close to tears. "It's the only thing I had of my mother's."

Chance held his breath as Dixie went to her purse, opened it and took out a small envelope. From it, she withdrew three black-and-white snapshots.

"The men who abducted you didn't get the photographs?" He couldn't help sounding skeptical.

"They left my purse in the car when they went into the house for the rest of my research materials," she said and, with obvious reluctance, held out the photographs to him.

He took them, treating them as she had, as if they might disintegrate.

"The photographs were hidden beneath the velvet liner of the jewelry box. I would never have found them if I hadn't bumped against the box and seen a corner of a photo sticking out."

He felt the hair rise on the back of his neck as he looked down at the first photograph. It was of a woman and a baby. He turned it over. On the back in a small delicate script were the words "Glendora and nephew Junior."

He set the photo on the coffee table. The next was of the woman Glendora and another older woman who resembled her. Both were standing at graveside. It was raining, the day dark. Both women wore black veils, their faces in shadow, but he recognized the Glendora woman by her shape. He turned the photo over. "Junior's funeral."

The third photograph was of a baby being held by the woman identified as Glendora. On the back, it read "Rebecca and Aunt Glendora."

He felt his heart do a little dip and flipped the snapshot back over to stare down at the baby, then at Dixie.

She nodded. "It seems Rebecca and I have an Aunt Glendora."

"You showed these to your father?" he guessed.

She nodded. "He said the jewelry box wasn't my mother's, he'd never seen the people in the photographs before and that it was just a coincidence that the baby's name was Rebecca."

"Quite the coincidence," Chance agreed.

Dixie took a breath and let it out slowly. "My father swears there never was a Beauregard Junior. Nor did my mother have a sister."

"Maybe that's the case."

Dixie shook her head. "I believed that, too, until he insisted on getting rid of the photographs for me. When I refused to give them to him, he became upset. I knew then that he was lying."

Or at least had something to hide, Chance thought as he looked at the snapshots again, then at Dixie. "So that's when you decided to dig into your family history."

She nodded. "You know me so well."

Didn't he, though. He'd thought this woman would be a stranger to him, that she would have changed so much he wouldn't know her. He'd been wrong about that. He wondered what else he might be wrong about.

"So you've been trying to find evidence of the people in the photographs."

She nodded and sat across from him.

"And you believe the two men who attacked you were after your genealogy research," he said carefully, trying not to make her mad again but hoping to point out how foolish that sounded.

"When the men were ransacking my house, they were looking for my research materials—and my journal."

He recalled that she'd always kept a journal from the time she was little. Rebecca had teased her about it.

It's a journal about my life—not a diary about which boy said I was cute, Dixie snapped.

Oh, please, Rebecca said. What does a twelve-year-old have to write about?

"Did they find your journal?" he asked.

"I would assume so. I always kept the original photographs with me in my purse. But I also made copies."

Smart woman. "Did your journal have information about this in it?"

She nodded, her gaze almost pleading for him to believe her. "Nearly everything I'd found out was in the journal."

"*Nearly* everything?" he repeated.

She didn't seem to hear him. "How much do you know about my mother, Sarah Worth Bonner?"

"Not much. She died when you were a baby."

"Thirteen months old. Rebecca was five. I think I

remember Mother, but I'm not sure it isn't just something I made up, you know?"

He did. His parents had died when he was nineteen and he still wasn't sure a lot of the memories weren't ones he wished had happened.

"Over the years I've asked my father, but he always said he didn't like talking about her because it was too painful. For that reason supposedly, he kept no photographs of her."

Chance thought of his own daughter and the few cherished photographs he had of her. He wouldn't have parted with them for anything in this world.

"I started by trying to find out what I could about my mother through the usual sources, birth and death certificates, marriage licenses, social security," Dixie said, as if warming to her subject. "I found a marriage license and a death certificate, but no birth certificate. Social security had no record of her."

"Maybe she never worked," he suggested.

"Everyone has a social security card, but even if for some reason she didn't, she would definitely have had a birth certificate. That's not all. My father had told me my mother was an orphan with no siblings."

"You think this woman in the photograph is her sister."

Dixie nodded. "I know this doesn't seem like anything anyone but me would care about, except I found a record of a Glendora Worth. She would have been older than my mother. I remember Uncle Carl once telling me that my mother had been born up north. Glendora Worth was born in Ashton, Idaho."

He nodded. "Okay."

"There's more."

"I suspected there was."

"When the two men attacked me in the parking garage they were wearing masks, like I told you before. But when they came running out of the house and into the garage as I was getting away, they'd removed their masks and hadn't bothered to put them back on in their haste to stop me. I recognized one of the men. He works for my father."

Chance sat up abruptly. "You just mention this now?"

"You didn't believe that anyone was even trying to kill me. I knew what your reaction would be if I told you my father was behind it."

"Well, if you think I believe that your father paid two hired guns to kill you so you wouldn't find out your mother had a sister—"

"See what I mean?" She let out a small bitter laugh and leaped to her feet. He grabbed her arm as she started past him, but she wrestled free and stalked over to the glass doors to the deck. "Don't you think it breaks my heart to think that my own father might be involved? But, Chance, I went to him when I found the photographs. I showed him what I'd found. He's the only person who knew."

He watched her place her forehead against the window, her breath condensing on the glass.

"Dixie, you have to admit, this sounds crazy," he said with a frustrated sigh. "It's just hard to believe that even if there was some deep, dark secret in your family, that *anyone* would have you killed to keep it quiet."

She didn't turn around, her voice was muffled. "You know how my father is. He does whatever he has to. I thought you would believe me since you know him. You know what he's capable of."

"Your father isn't responsible for breaking me and Rebecca up," he said.

"No," she said, turning from the window. "But he was responsible for getting you to Montana, wasn't he? You think that first job on the ranch just happened to open when you needed it? Or that scholarship to Montana State University?"

He stared at her. He'd always suspected Bonner was behind it. Things had worked out a little too well. "If you're insinuating that he got rid of me—"

"I'm telling you that he sold you down the river," she said, stepping toward him, settling those big blue eyes on him. "Daddy was all for Rebecca marrying Oliver and we all know why."

"It doesn't matter. Rebecca and I would never have gotten married even if I'd stayed in Texas," he said, knowing in his heart it was true.

She nodded. "I agree. But it shows how low my father will stoop to get what he wants. He sold off Rebecca to further the Bonner name. You think he'd let anyone sully that name after everything he's done to get where he is today? Especially since he's about to throw his hat into the political ring."

Chance shook his head, not wanting to believe it. Hadn't Bonner warned him not to believe anything Dixie told him?

Dixie nodded and smiled as if sensing that even against his will he was starting to believe her. "I start digging into my family's background and now someone is trying to kill me. So, you still believe the two aren't connected and that my father isn't involved?"

CHAPTER NINE

"HELLO, MR. LANCASTER."

Oliver was feeling better by the time he reached the club. He'd managed to put off thinking about the future. At least for tonight.

Rebecca had plans. What did it matter who they were with? He just needed to concentrate on the problem at hand—winning twenty-five thousand dollars.

"Your coat, Mr. Lancaster?"

He let the man help him out of his coat and get him a drink, thankful that men's clubs still existed, albeit underground. Otherwise some woman would protest and the next thing you knew, the place would be full of them and everything would be ruined.

"Any interesting games going on?" he asked as he took the drink. He didn't even have to tell the man what he drank. So much better than home where Rebecca was often out of his favorite.

No, he thought, looking around at the exquisite furnishings, this was his true home.

"I believe there is a game in the Ashbury Room that you might enjoy, sir."

Oliver smiled and asked for an advance, giving the man a hundred dollar bill before heading to the Ashbury Room.

He felt lucky tonight. At least he hoped so. If his luck

didn't change soon, he would have no recourse but to do something desperate.

DIXIE COULD SEE that Chance was having the same trouble she was, trying to understand what she'd found—and why it had put her life in jeopardy.

"Before you tell me I'm crazy, you should know. Glendora Worth is still alive. From what I've been able to find out, her name is Glendora Ferris now." Dixie hesitated, bracing herself for his reaction to the rest of the news. "She's widowed and living in an apartment for elderly people in Livingston."

"Montana?"

She nodded. "Don't give me that look. I came to Montana to hire you just like I said. It's not my fault Glendora Worth Ferris just happens to live here."

"So what did she say when you saw her?"

Dixie shook her head. "I haven't yet. I wanted you to go with me. To keep me safe." She glanced at him. "Okay, I didn't want to go alone. Are you happy?"

He smiled. "You were smart to wait. If you're right…" He stopped as if catching himself. "I'm not saying I'm buying any of this—especially the part about your father trying to have you killed, okay? And you can't be certain this Glendora Worth is your mother's sister, right?"

"No. But what if she is?"

"Then you would have an aunt you knew nothing about," he said. "But it wouldn't give anyone a motive to want you dead. This isn't much of a secret, Dix. So you have an aunt."

"And a brother who died."

"Did you find any record of a Beauregard Bonner Junior?"

"No," she had to admit.

Chance raised a brow as if that proved something.

"That's why I have to see this woman. If she really is my aunt, maybe she can provide the answers I need."

His gaze locked with hers. "What if your father is trying to protect you?"

"By having me killed?"

"I'm serious, Dixie. Maybe there's a reason he doesn't want you to know about this." He waved a hand through the air. "Maybe it's painful. Or dangerous."

She laughed. "Apparently it is. You still don't believe I was abducted in Texas, do you? You think I made it all up? Why would I do that?"

"To involve me in this."

Her heart was beating too hard, her pulse loud in her ears. "I can't believe you. I knew my father would try to find a way to stop me from getting to Glendora. I just never dreamed it would be you." She picked up the photographs and put them back in her purse. "I think I'll turn in early. I haven't had much sleep the last few days."

"Dixie."

She started toward her room, but turned to look back at him. "By the way, you didn't use the lodge phone to call my father, did you?"

He looked surprised.

"Because if you did, then he knows where we are." She nodded. "You just signed my death warrant."

CARL BONNER STOOD behind the two-way mirror that allowed him to look into the Ashbury Room and watch the poker game—and Oliver Lancaster.

Carl had kept an eye on Oliver from the first. Not that

he'd told Beau. He watched Oliver dig himself a hole the arrogant bastard would never be able to climb out of.

"How much has he lost?" Carl asked the man who'd let him into this room.

"Tonight? Over a hundred thousand."

Carl said nothing as he mentally totaled just how deep Oliver was down. And the fool kept playing, like all gamblers, believing eventually he would win.

He'd never liked Oliver and over the years had grown to despise him. Oliver was a lousy husband and father. Carl was tired of seeing the man hurt Rebecca.

Carl watched Oliver sweat. Beauregard paid Oliver well, but not well enough to lose this kind of money almost every night of the week. Oliver had to be getting desperate to cover his compulsive gambling—and his debts. He couldn't go to Beauregard. Nor Rebecca.

So who did that leave poor Oliver?

Ace, Carl thought, with a smile. Only Oliver would be stupid enough to go to a known criminal for help.

"Put more pressure on him," Carl told the man waiting next to him. "Let him play, though. Don't worry, I'll see that he meets his obligations."

"As you say, sir."

Yes, Carl thought as he left. *As I say.* Carl turned and saw another window, this one into the Bradbury Room. Like other nights he'd come here to check on Oliver, Carl saw Mason sitting at one of the poker tables.

"What about Mr. Roberts?" Carl asked.

The man hesitated and Carl had to look hard at him for a moment before the man said, "He enjoys a good game. He wins some, loses some. He always quits before he loses too much."

Yes, that sounded just like Mason. Careful. But still a gambler at heart.

"You can tell a lot about a man by the way he plays cards, don't you think?" Carl said.

"Yes, sir. I assume that's why you don't play."

Carl laughed. Life was enough of a gamble, he thought as he followed the man out. Not that a man didn't have to take chances. Otherwise, he was doomed to live a truly mediocre existence. No one knew that better than Carl Bonner. He remembered the day that he'd changed his luck and his life so many years before—with just one roll of the dice.

CHANCE STARED AT Dixie's closed bedroom door and told himself that she was just being dramatic. While the family photographs were intriguing, he still didn't believe Bonner was behind any threat to his daughter over some old snapshots.

So why couldn't he quit mentally kicking himself for calling Bonner on the lodge phone? Beauregard Bonner was a lot of things. But a killer?

Chance swore, the cold December night pressing against the windows as he saw a few lights glitter in the distance.

Hell, he was a professional and right now he felt like a damned amateur. What if Dixie was right and he'd put her life in jeopardy?

Worse, he was starting to believe her.

What bothered him was how easily he'd bought into what Bonner had told him about Dixie. That and the fact that she *was* his daughter. That's why Chance had given Dixie the room with a window, but no way out other than the door she'd just closed.

"Hell, what if she's right?" he asked himself again as he checked to make sure the doors were locked be-

fore going to his room. He left the bedroom door open.
It was that darned suspicious nature of his.

It was going to be a long night. He hadn't gotten that
much sleep last night after seeing Bonner and taking
this job against his better judgment. He would have
loved nothing better than a hot shower, but he opted
for a bath, leaving the bathroom door open so he could
hear Dixie if she tried to leave.

The hot water felt good. He tried to relax. Less than
forty-eight hours and Bonner would send a jet for his
daughter.

Chance had always prided himself on the fact that
he could read people pretty well. But he had to admit
there was too much water under the bridge to do that
with Beauregard Bonner. Because he didn't trust him,
he tended to go the other way and cut him more slack
than he probably should have.

As for Dixie… Just the thought of her stirred emotions he didn't want to acknowledge, let alone deal with.
He remembered earlier, her leaning over him, that light
kiss on his mouth—

Standing up in the bath water, he turned the water
to cold and stood under it. Although painful, the cold
shower did the trick. He turned it off and got out.

Toweling dry he smiled at his own foolishness. The
woman knew the affect she had on him. Had on a lot
of men. Like her almost-fiancé, who had also followed
her to Montana.

Or been sent by Beauregard Bonner?

Chance hated to think how Bonner had set him up
all those years ago. The job in Montana. The scholarship. It was hard to be angry. Chance was thankful for
the life he enjoyed now. But it did remind him how
Bonner operated.

He pulled on his jeans and sprawled on the bed. He

knew he wasn't going to be able to sleep now even if he
wanted to. He couldn't get Dixie off his mind. Wasn't
there a song like that in Texas?

He got up, too restless to even lie on the bed. Keeping his eye on Dixie's closed bedroom door, he pulled
on his coat and went out on the deck. He made a couple of calls, using his usual sources to get confidential
information that the average person couldn't access.

There was a Glendora Ferris living in Livingston, just
as Dixie had said. A couple more inquiries and he had
her maiden name: Worth. The same as Dixie's mother's
maiden name. The same information Dixie had gotten.

Was it possible Glendora really was Sarah's sister?
More to the point, was there some deep, dark family
secret that Dixie had stumbled across that someone was
determined she would take to her grave?

He swore again as he stepped back in from the cold,
closed the deck door and walked over to tap on Dixie's
bedroom door. He figured she wouldn't be asleep yet.

"Yes?"

"If you want, we could go to Livingston first thing
in the morning and talk to Glendora Ferris." He didn't
have to add that the woman could have moved, might
be senile, might not even be the right Worth. Nor did
he have to tell Dixie that he wasn't anxious to get involved any further in this.

He heard a surprised sound on the other side of the
door, could almost hear her smile. He started to step
away from the door.

"Chance?"

"Yeah?" he said, moving back to the door again.

"Thank you."

He touched the door with the tips of his fingers.
"Yeah."

NOT LONG AFTER midnight, Chance heard the lodge room

door open and close quietly. He glanced at the clock, gave her a few seconds, then picked up his gun.

He had stayed dressed in his jeans expecting something like this. And yet, he couldn't help being surprised. And disappointed. He'd started to buy into her story. He'd even agreed to take her to talk to Glendora Ferris. So had it all been just a ruse?

He pulled on his coat and boots. Opening the door quietly, he peered out. Dixie tiptoed down the hallway dressed in jeans and a T-shirt, no shoes.

He frowned. No shoes? Where was she going barefoot in December in Montana?

She had something tucked under her arm.

He waited until she turned the corner before he went after her. At the L in the hallway, he stopped to peer around the corner. She stood at the door to the hot springs outdoor pool. Even from where he was he could see that the pool was clearly marked closed for the night.

He watched her with interest since he suspected the door to the pool was kept locked at night.

She pulled the barrette from her hair she'd used to tie it back earlier. It took her a few minutes but to his amazement, she picked the lock and slipped in.

She was going *swimming?*

He hurried down the hallway only to find the door locked again. He'd never been great at lock picking, but he was hell on wheels when it came to fence climbing. Backtracking he circled around the rear of the lodge to come out at the fence along the dark side of the pool.

Steam rose off the surface, dissipating into the cold darkness. For a moment he didn't see her and thought she'd given him the slip. But then he spotted her discarded clothing piled on one of the chairs near the deep end, a towel lying on top.

At the sound of a splash, he saw her surface halfway

down the pool in a cloud of steam and was surprised how relieved he was. She hadn't tried to get away. She'd just wanted to go for a swim. He smiled, shaking his head. Would this woman ever quit surprising him?

She dove back under the water and he quickly climbed the wooden fence, moving to the edge of the pool as she surfaced.

He remembered that she'd been part fish back in Texas, always in her family pool. Always calling, "Hey, Chance, watch this." Even back then she'd loved attention. And had known no fear, diving off the highest thing she could find if it would shock him. He realized she hadn't changed.

He'd expected to surprise her, but if he did, she hid it well.

"Hello, Chance," she said with a grin.

"The pool is closed, Dixie. Also, I believe swimsuits are required."

Her grin broadened. "Why would anyone swim in a suit if she didn't have to? And close a pool on a night like this?" She looked up, her face softening. "Look at those stars. I had no idea there were so many." Her breath came out on a puff of frosty December air.

He saw that her hair was starting to freeze. Frost glistened on her eyelashes. A snow angel. Her beauty took his breath away.

She must have seen his expression because her gaze heated as it met his. Her smile widened. Oh, that mouth. Incredible full lips that arched up in a perfect bow that any man would have been a fool not to want to kiss.

She laughed and ducked under the water, disappearing beneath the steam—but not before he'd glimpsed her sleek naked body moving through the water.

Chance swore and glanced toward the lodge and the rooms that faced in this direction. Several of the blinds were open, lights out, but he'd bet Dixie had an audience and unless he missed his guess, she knew it and was enjoying it. "Damn it, Dixie."

As she surfaced, her laugh filled the air. "You should see your expression."

"You like shocking people."

She turned serious. "You're wrong. I just like swimming naked on a night like this."

Clouds scudded across the stars and with a suddenness that pretty much summed up Montana weather, it began to snow. The flakes were huge and, like delicate white feathers, drifted lazily down. Dixie laughed, the delight of a child, and leaned back to catch one in her mouth.

"You don't know what you're missing," she said, looking at him again through the steam rising up off the surface of the pool. He got the feeling she wasn't talking about swimming.

She cocked her head at him. "Sure you don't want to join me?"

"Positive." His voice sounded odd to him and he knew she'd heard it.

"I won't look if you're shy." She chuckled then turned her back, daring him to strip and join her.

He'd been tempted plenty times in his life, but this one topped the list.

"Scared?" she asked in that Texas drawl of hers.

"Aren't you worried your killers will find you? You are rather…exposed."

She turned back to give him a disappointed look. "You aren't going to spoil this for me, Chance Walker."

Her words hit him like stones. He hated that he'd even tried. But damn it, his job was to keep her safe. And he hadn't wanted this job. He should have been at his cabin with his dog and a roaring fire, not standing out here in the cold watching the damned woman swim naked in a closed pool.

Hell, if there had been a sign that said, No Diving, she would have been doing a jackknife off the side right now.

He reminded himself who she was. Not just a Bonner, which was bad enough, but Rebecca's little sister. Unfortunately that didn't help. Rebecca had been a lifetime ago.

He turned his back and listened to her swim, fighting the ache inside him. There'd been something about Dixie Bonner at twelve that had been likeable even though a lot of the time she was an impossible noisy little brat.

But the grown-up version was everything that had made Dixie unique at twelve—and a whole hell of a lot more.

After a while, he heard her climb out, listened to her pull on the jeans and T-shirt.

"You can turn around now."

He did.

She stood, her head cocked to one side, looking at him through a wet wall of dark hair. She brushed her hair back from her face and grinned, no doubt at his expression. She'd dried with the towel she'd carried under her arm from the room, and had put her clothing on over her damp body. The T-shirt clung to her breasts, leaving little to his imagination. There was no way she wasn't aware of that, as well.

"Your hair is starting to freeze," he said, mad at himself, mad at her. It was all he could do to keep from tossing her into the pool, clothes and all—and jumping in after her.

And that, he realized, is what really had him upset. He wished now that he'd gone in the pool with her, for he feared that when he was a very old man this would be his one regret in life.

"Let's get you back to the room," he said, taking off his jacket to put it around her.

She let out an amused laugh. "I never knew you were such a prude. You should have come into the pool," she said as she wrapped her long hair in the towel, her back to him. "You have no idea what you missed."

He cursed softly, just imagining.

She turned to grin at him. "You know I'm starting to understand why my sister didn't marry you."

"I was the one who broke it off with her," he snapped, instantly regretting it.

Her brow shot up. "Very gallant of you to admit that."

He swore under his breath. "I didn't mean it to come out like that. Hell, why am I apologizing? Your sister was already practically engaged to some blue-blooded lawyer student by then."

"You could have come back to Texas and put up a fight for her," she said over her shoulder as she walked toward the door to the lodge.

"Oh, yeah, that would have done a lot of good."

She grinned back at him. "You should have heard what she said about you. She said—"

"Don't even." He thought about some of the things Rebecca could have told her little sister and wished this subject had never come up.

Dixie laughed as they reached the door back into the lodge. Apparently it didn't lock from this side. "Didn't you ever wonder what your life would have been like if you'd stayed in Texas?"

"No," he lied. He stepped past her and into the lodge, planning to end this conversation by doing the only thing he could—run away from it.

"Did you know she kept a diary?" Dixie asked in a whisper as she caught up to him.

Rebecca kept a diary? He continued walking. The last thing he wanted to talk about was her sister. Especially after he'd just seen her little sister swim naked. Nor did it seem the right topic for a walk in the lodge hallway in the wee hours of the morning.

Dixie was probably bluffing anyway about the diary. But now that he thought about it, Rebecca was the type who would have kept a diary. One of those little pink ones with a lock and key. And Dixie was just the type to break into it and read it.

"Would you like me to quote you chapter and verse?" She didn't give him time to say no. "'Oh, today was just the most awful day,'" Dixie mimicked in a voice that was eerily like Rebecca's. "'Daddy forbade me to go out with that Chance Walker boy. My heart just ached and I cried throughout all of dinner but to no avail. Daddy was just impossible.'"

Chance groaned, the words sounding too much like Rebecca's for this not to be true. He stopped, turning to glare at her. "I'm surprised your sister didn't throttle you for reading her diary," he whispered back.

Dixie let out a snort. "She had no idea I ever read it. Rebecca, being Rebecca, wore the key around her neck and always kept the diary locked. Have you ever seen the flimsy locks on a diary?" Dixie chuckled. "I could pick locks a lot harder than that when I was seven."

All he could do was shake his head.

"Stop looking so shocked. I'm willing to bet you're no slouch when it comes to lock picking," she said as they reached their suite and she waited for him to open the door.

As he started to use the room key, he realized she'd expected him to follow her to the pool. That's why she hadn't even bothered to take the key. Or maybe she'd planned to pick the room lock, too.

"Only private detectives on TV pick locks," he snapped. "It's considered breaking and entering." He opened the door and, following her inside, closed it after them.

"Don't disillusion me with that legal mumbo jumbo. I've heard it all. Anyway, I wouldn't believe it." She grinned. "After reading Rebecca's diary, I know everything about you. And I do mean *everything*."

"Everything." He grumbled under his breath. "Just like your father." He saw the change in her expression.

"If you want to get along with me, don't compare me to him." She turned toward her room, her back stubborn-straight, her hips swaying from side to side in a way that could blind a man.

"Who says I want to get along with you?" he called after her. "You're the one who came to Montana. I didn't want this damned job to start with. I wanted nothing to do with your family."

"That's right," she called back over her shoulder. "I came to Montana. Looking for you. Because I had this crazy idea that you were one of the good guys. Instead, you go to work for my father. You didn't just sell out, Chance Walker. You broke my heart."

He saw her hesitate at her doorway as if she hadn't meant to add that last part. He wasn't sure why it touched him. He didn't even believe there were killers after her, right? Let alone that his going to work for her father had broken her heart.

"Do you still love her?"

He wasn't sure he'd known what love was until his daughter was born. "Rebecca? *No*."

"Did *she* break your heart?"

"No." He hated to admit it. She'd been his first love.

First loves were supposed to be ones you never got over, right?

"You were both so wrong for each other," Dixie said, shaking her head.

He couldn't argue that.

"You needed a woman who cared about more than what she was going to wear or whether her hair was just right or what her friends were going to say about her—and you."

He laughed since that was Rebecca to a T. She cared more about outward appearances than anything else. He hoped she was happy with…what was his name? Oliver?

"Like you know what kind of woman I needed," he said with a laugh, wanting to draw the subject away from Rebecca.

"Someone like…me," Dixie said, and disappeared into her bedroom, closing the door behind her.

He laughed, thinking she had to be joking.

In his room, he stripped down to his shorts and sprawled again on the bed. He couldn't help but think about some of the things Dixie had said. He'd let her down and that bothered him more than he wanted to admit.

He tried to push her out of his mind, but the minute he closed his eyes all he could see was Dixie Bonner swimming through fog-cloaked water like a ghost mermaid, a million stars glittering overhead on a cold December night in Montana.

CHAPTER TEN

CHANCE BOLTED UPRIGHT out of a deathlike sleep. He looked around, at first not sure where he was. As he came fully awake, he remembered it all—including the sound that had awakened him. The closing of a door.

Only he was pretty sure it was a neighboring door he'd heard from another unit.

Still, he jumped up and rushed into the living area. Dixie's door to her bedroom was standing open, her bed made. Had she even gone to bed last night?

In a panic, he checked her room, not sure what he thought he'd find. She'd had no luggage—just the clothing on her back, which he was pretty sure she'd taken with her. The room was empty. Dixie was gone.

Cursing, he stormed to the door and looked down the hallway. Empty. He glanced at his watch, then through a crack in the blinds on the deck doors. It was barely light out.

He felt foggy. He'd obviously drifted off at some point in the night, but didn't feel as if he'd gotten any rest. Who could blame him, knowing that Dixie Bonner was in the next room?

Or at least had been.

Where had she gone? He couldn't believe this. The woman was driving him crazy. Maybe that had been the plan all along.

Unless everything she'd told him had been a lie…

Or maybe she hadn't trusted him. Maybe she thought him no better than the others her father had hired to find her.

That thought grounded him like a crashed plane.

He rushed back into his room, threw on the rest of his clothing and hurried down to the lodge lobby, hoping she'd just gotten hungry and gone to breakfast.

"Have you seen the woman I had with me?" he asked the young man behind the desk who'd brought up their food. From the man's expression, he had. "Where did she go?"

"Said she wanted to take a walk." He pointed toward the window.

A walk? Chance turned to look out. The day was bright, the sky clear blue, the rising sun blinding on the snow, the temperature hovering around freezing. Was she crazy? Of course she was. She was a Bonner.

He could see a packed snowmobile trail that led out into the trees. "Is that the way she went?"

The young man nodded.

It hadn't been daylight long. She couldn't be that far ahead of him.

"It's an easy trail," the male clerk called after him as Chance ran for the door. "I'm sure she's fine."

Chance wished he could be sure of that. What had Dixie been thinking? Outside, he saw his friend who'd given them the suite for the night. "I need to borrow a snowmobile."

Two minutes later, Chance was roaring up the trail as it wound through the darkness of the trees, then rose up over a hill and into the faint morning sunlight. No sign of Dixie.

He should have caught up to her by now. What if the clerk was wrong? What if she'd taken another trail? Or what if she'd been right and his calling her father had the killers waiting outside—

He slowed and spotted her tracks in some soft snow that had fallen from a pine bough into the packed trail. She was running. From what?

Gunning the snowmobile, he raced up the trail as it curved and dipped in and out of the snowcapped pines. The cold winter morning air burned his face and lungs.

As he came around a curve in the trail, suddenly there she was. She'd heard the snowmobile coming and had stepped off the track.

"What's wrong?" he demanded as he shut off his machine and grabbed her, pulling her close as he drew his weapon. Hurriedly he searched the cold, dark shadows. The trees were dense here in the creek bottom, visibility poor.

"Nothing," she said, pulling free. "I just came out for a run."

He glanced over at her. "A *run?*"

"I like to run. It clears my head."

He stared at her as he slowly holstered his weapon and tried to still his thundering pulse. "Did you ever think that going for a run when there are so many people after you might be a bad idea?"

"No one knows we're here, right?"

Her reasoning was pushing him over the edge. "You're the one who said my call yesterday would have your father and his men breaking down our doors last night."

"I guess the lodge is harder to find than I thought," she shot back with a grin.

"What's so damned funny?"

"You. As you recently said to me, you can't have it both ways. Either you believe my life is in danger. Or you don't. Obviously, you do."

"You scared the hell out of me." It was out before he could call it back.

She cocked her head at him. "Admit it. You believe that someone wants me dead."

"Anyone who's ever met you probably wants to kill you," he said, his pulse finally dropping back to normal. Ice crystals glistened in the morning sunlight. The air smelled of pine and snow. And Dixie looked great.

"Whatever," she said with a little shake of her head just as she'd done when she was a kid and he'd wanted to turn her over his knee.

Some things just didn't change.

Beauregard Bonner had known where they were, but no hit men had shown up to take her out. That had to be one hell of a relief for her. She'd been wrong about her father.

"Ever been on a snowmobile?" he asked.

She shook her head, eyes wide and bright, her face suddenly alive with excitement.

He grinned. "Hop on."

The gunshot came out of nowhere. A tree just past Dixie's head splintered, the sound a loud crack that echoed across the mountainside. As he lunged for her, he heard the second shot. It whistled past his head as he tackled Dixie and took her down hard behind the snowmobile.

"You believe me now?" There were tears in her eyes. "I knew it. I knew it."

He cursed himself, his own stupidity. He shouldn't have made the call yesterday from the lodge phone. But he'd been so convinced that her father only had her best interests at heart. What the hell had he been thinking?

"Stay here and stay down," he ordered, pulling his weapon as he crouched behind the snowmobile, then made a run for it, dodging in and out of the trees, shielding himself as he moved quickly in the direction of the gunfire.

He could only estimate where the shot had come from, given where the first bullet had struck the tree. But as he moved, he came across the tracks in the fresh snow. They crisscrossed the mountainside, moving first in one direction, then back the other way.

Chance took off at a run following the tracks, keeping to the trees just as the shooter had. He hadn't gone far when he heard the sound of a vehicle engine turning over, then the spinning of tires in the snow.

It was hard to run fast enough through the snow. He reached the clearing just in time to see the sun catch on a rig's rooftop as it dropped over the side of the mountain. He couldn't tell what the vehicle had been, let alone the color with the sun glinting off it.

DIXIE WAS LYING in the snow on her back, staring up at the blue sky overhead. She didn't look in Chance's direction as she heard him approach, but she recognized the sound of his footfalls.

She'd been lying there, more frightened than she'd ever been before—even waking up in the trunk of her own car. Her fear had been not for herself but for Chance. She'd involved him in this and now she regretted it.

His shadow fell over her and she hurriedly wiped at her tears, not wanting him to see just how scared she was, how upset.

"I'm sorry," he said, and offered her a hand up.

She took it. "I'm the one who's sorry. I should never have gotten you into this," she said, brushing off what snow she could, her jeans caked with snow. But she didn't feel it. Felt nothing but an unbearable pain in her heart.

"Don't be ridiculous. This is what I get paid to do," he said.

"Then it's a stupid job." Her gaze met his, anger sparking between them mixing with the fear in an explosive combination. "As far as I'm concerned, you're fired."

"Sorry, but I don't work for you."

"That's right. You work for my father." She turned to run back to the lodge but he grabbed her arm and spun her into him. Her body slammed against his, knocking the breath out of her even before his mouth dropped to hers and his arms wrapped around her.

The kiss was all passion and fire, fear and regret. She'd seen the way he'd looked at her last night at the pool. The kiss took the rest of her breath. She leaned into him, letting him take her weight as she lost herself in his lips. His arms bound her to him as if he never wanted to let her go.

The sound of an approaching snowmobile droned loudly, bringing them both back from that amazing place the kiss had taken them.

His arms loosened but his mouth stayed on hers until the last possible moment. They parted just an instant before a snowmobile came roaring up over the rise in the trail.

She saw Chance's hand slip inside his coat to where she knew he'd holstered his weapon only minutes before. The snowmobile slowed, the rider's features ghostly behind the smoked glass of his helmet. He gave a nod and throttled the machine up as he zoomed past in a clatter of engine and cloud of gray smoke.

Dixie felt weak, as if it had taken all her energy to stand after what had just happened between her and Chance. Hadn't she always dreamed of this day? Not that it had happened as she'd hoped. No, nothing about this was how she'd imagined it.

Like the way he was looking at her now. As if he was mentally kicking himself for what he'd just done.

"Don't," she said, shaking her head. "Don't try to take that back. You messed up big-time not coming in the pool with me last night and we both know it. Don't make it worse by telling yourself you're sorry about that kiss."

He chuckled, his lips turning up in a grin. "You think you know what I'm feeling right now?" He shook his head. "I shouldn't have kissed you, but believe me I have no regrets."

She smiled. "Then I guess we're making progress."

"It's not going to happen again," he said, taking a step back as if he feared being too close to her.

She laughed. "We'll see."

"We need to talk about what just happened."

"I thought we were."

"Someone just *shot* at you," he said, way too serious.

"It isn't the first time. I told you, they shot at me in Texas as I was getting away."

He sighed as he raked a hand through his hair, his gaze locked with hers. "You're taking this awfully well."

She shook her head. "Don't you know me well enough by now to understand that I'm not one of those women who falls apart? When this is over..." She grinned. "Well, that will be another story. Right now, I just need to get to my aunt's before whoever took a shot at me does."

"You're right."

Her smile widened as she looked at him. "You should say that more often. I really like the sound of it."

"You know this doesn't necessarily mean that your father is behind this. It could be someone close to him.

Someone he confides in. Or even someone who's put a tap on his phone line."

She cut her eyes to him. "Why are you defending him?"

"I just don't like jumping to conclusions," he said.

"No, you can't imagine a father wanting his daughter dead." She saw that she'd struck more than a nerve. "Will you tell me about your daughter some time?"

He reared back in surprise, shaking his head, his gaze warning her not to push this.

She took a breath, still trembling inside from her encounter both with a near bullet wound—and her even more intimate encounter with Chance Walker. At this point, she would have been hard-pressed to say which had the most affect on her.

"That offer of a ride still open? Because my not-so-scrawny behind is freezing."

Chance looked relieved and maybe a little surprised that she'd dropped the subject so easily. Clearly he'd hoped she didn't know. He'd underestimated her. But then, he had from the start. Since the day Chance Walker had left Texas, she'd made a point of keeping up with his life in Montana. She was her father's daughter, after all.

CHANCE SAID NOTHING on the ride back to the lodge. On entering their suite, he picked up the phone, then put it back down again.

"You aren't going to call the police?" she asked, relieved.

He looked at her and she could tell he was struggling with this. "It isn't because I'm worried that your father's money has corrupted the local sheriff."

"So let me get this straight," she said. "There are times that it's a *bad* idea to call the cops?"

He scowled at her. "The sheriff would have to drive out for our statements. It would take hours. He'd check the tracks in the snow and find what I did. Man-size boot prints, nothing distinguishing about them. He would find the slug in the tree and figure out that it came from a rifle. He would trail the footprints to tire tracks."

She nodded.

Chance sighed. "In the end, he'd make the report and conclude it was probably a stray bullet from a late hunt."

"A hunter? You believe that?"

"No." He met her gaze and shook his head. "I still don't know what to believe."

She nodded, knowing the feeling only too well. "I meant what I said earlier. Call my father and quit. I don't want your death on my conscience."

"You have a conscience?"

"I'm serious, Chance."

He shook his head. "Sorry, but you didn't hire me, so you can't fire me. I'm in this to the end now."

"If it's the money—"

"It's not the money," he said, eyes snapping. "I finish what I start."

She cocked her head at him and grinned. "Really? That's good to hear." She hoped that also applied to what he'd started on the trail earlier.

"I mean it, Dixie. We're going to Livingston to talk to Glendora Ferris. I'm not finished until we find out who's trying to kill you and why."

She looked into his eyes and saw that he did mean it. "I just don't want you to be sorry."

He laughed. "Hell, I was sorry the minute I laid eyes on your father again. The way I see it, things can only get worse."

She wasn't sure how to take that since his gaze went to her lips as if he was remembering the kiss.

Unconsciously she touched the tip of her tongue to her upper lip. He groaned and turned away, leaving her smiling.

"Strip out of those wet clothes," he ordered, his back to her. "While you get a hot shower, I'll get your clothing dried. We'll stop by your car on the way to Livingston and get the rest of your clothes."

She stripped down and tossed her wet, cold clothing on the floor right behind him. He didn't move until she went into the bathroom and started to close the door. What was he so afraid of? But she knew the answer to that.

She turned on the shower and stepped under the spray, her skin red and chilled. She wrapped her arms around herself and stood under the hot water, thinking about Chance Walker, thinking about his daughter, and finally thinking about what had happened in the woods.

For a while, flirting with Chance, she'd been able to put it out of her mind. Hadn't she known that Chance had alerted the killers where she was by calling her father from the lodge phone?

Tears stung her eyes. What was it she'd stumbled across digging in her family's past that could make her own father want her dead?

CHAPTER ELEVEN

WHILE DIXIE WAS in the shower, Chance put in a call to Bonner in Texas and wasn't surprised when his call was answered by an abrupt, "Don't tell me you no longer have Dixie."

"Call off your thugs," Chance ordered.

"I told you I didn't hire anyone else."

"Bull."

"Chance, if there is anyone else after Dixie…well, I don't know anything about it. Have you asked *her?*"

"Listen, Bonner, someone just took a potshot at your daughter. I want to know what the hell is going on."

Bonner swore. "She's all right?"

"For the moment."

"You sure she isn't behind it? I wouldn't put anything past her—even setting up getting shot at to get you on her side."

"Her side? What the hell does that mean?"

"Just that Dixie gets things into her head—"

"Like trying to find her mother's relatives?" Chance asked.

Silence. "So she told you."

"Why don't you want her finding out about her mother's family? What are you afraid she's going to uncover?"

"I didn't even know Sarah *had* any relatives that

were still alive and that's the truth. I just don't want Dixie digging into things that should stay in the past."

"Too late for that. Wanna tell me what in the past you're afraid is going to come out?"

"I told you there isn't any—"

Chance swore. "Did you go over to her house?"

"Just because the place was messed up doesn't mean Dixie didn't do it herself."

"For hell's sake, get your head out of the sand. Dixie's in trouble. If I find out you have anything to do with someone shooting—"

"She's my *daughter*. If anyone should know how a man feels about his daughter, it should be you."

"I mean it," Chance said, ignoring Bonner's last remark. "I won't rest until I see you behind bars if I find out you are in any way involved with trying to harm her."

GLENDORA FERRIS LIVED in a four-story white clapboard apartment house a few blocks from downtown Livingston.

The drive hadn't taken long from White Sulphur Springs. Chance had put country-western music on the radio and Dixie had dozed, too nervous to let herself think about what they might find once they reached Livingston.

Now, in the shadow of a massive peak, Dixie climbed out of the pickup to look up at the apartment house. Wind buffeted her hair and whirled snow around her. Christmas lights strung across the front slapped the side of the apartment house to the rhythm of the gusts.

The house was old and in poor shape, paint peeling, the boards of the porch sagging and cracked. Faded curtains hung in what windows she could see from the front. She wondered if Glendora Ferris was watching them from behind one of those curtains.

As they started up the steps, clouds hung low over the town, the light flat, the wind icy-cold, as if another snowstorm was moving in. In the lobby, Dixie glanced at the decrepit elevator. It was small and dark and smelled of cooked cabbage.

She headed for the stairs. Chance didn't argue. As she recalled, he didn't like small, tight spaces any more than she did. The cab of the pickup had been intimate enough. She secretly suspected he liked having Beauregard the dog between them.

Because of Montana's higher altitude and the climb up four floors, Dixie felt winded by the time they reached Glendora Ferris's apartment. Dixie waited a few seconds to catch her breath, knowing part of her hesitancy was fear. She was depending on this woman being her aunt. On finding answers behind this door.

At her knock came the sound of an older female voice on the other side. "Just a minute."

Dixie wiped her palms down the sides of her jeans, jittery with nerves, and glanced at Chance. He gave her an encouraging nod. He was the one person who knew how much was riding on this. Finally, she might get the answers she so desperately needed.

She warned herself not to get her hopes up, but it was too late for that. She couldn't help her excitement as the door opened a crack and a weathered face peered out between the door and chain.

Dixie looked into a pair of watery-blue eyes. "Glendora?"

The woman blinked. "Yes?"

"My name is Dixie Bonner. My mother was Sarah Worth?"

"Elizabeth?" The door closed.

Dixie looked over at Chance. *Elizabeth?* The chain grated in the latch. The door opened again.

The woman standing in front of them was anywhere from her seventies to late eighties. She wore a faded housecoat. Her hands were boney-thin and flecked with age spots. But it was the expression she wore that made Dixie's heart take a nosedive.

The woman looked totally lost, her gray hair poking up at all angles, her eyes blank. "Elizabeth?" She was looking around as if she'd expected someone else.

"I'm the daughter of Sarah Worth," Dixie said, bringing the woman's attention back to her. "I'm looking for her sister Glendora?"

"Elizabeth?" The woman didn't move, but her body began to quiver and she reached for the doorjamb as if needing it for support. Dixie moved quickly to her, putting an arm around the frail shoulders and leading her back inside to the couch.

"I'm sorry. I didn't mean to upset you," Dixie said, patting the woman's boney hand as she lowered her to the couch.

Behind them, Chance stepped in and closed the door.

The poor woman had no idea who Dixie was.

"Can I get you some water?" Dixie offered, glancing toward the kitchenette.

The woman shook her head, never taking her eyes off Dixie. "I thought you were a ghost." She reached out to take Dixie's hand, pulling her down beside her on the couch. "You look so much like her. Elizabeth isn't with you?"

"Elizabeth?" Dixie asked, fighting her disappointment. This woman wasn't going to be of any help.

"Elizabeth." She seemed unaware of the tears on her

translucent cheeks. "That was her real name. Sarah was her *middle* name."

Dixie stared at the woman in shock. "Then, you're her sister Glendora?"

The woman smiled. "What did you say your name was?"

"Dixie."

"Dixie." She looked confused again. "I thought her daughter's name was Rebecca?"

Relief washed over Dixie. She laughed. "My older sister's name is Rebecca."

"Elizabeth had more children?" Glendora sounded surprised by that. Almost disapproving. She still hadn't seemed to notice Chance waiting by the door.

"I lost track of Elizabeth after she had her little girl," Glendora said, then lowered her voice as if the walls had ears. "I couldn't understand how she could have two babies with that man. I guess things must have gotten better since she had you. You did say your name was Bonner, right?"

Dixie nodded. "You didn't like her husband?"

"Husband?" Glendora huffed. "He didn't want anything to do with marriage. I never saw him shed a tear for his *own* son when he died." She wagged her head. "Elizabeth was so young, so innocent. She didn't know that some men are scoundrels. I tried to warn her about him. I was six years older, more like a mother to her since we'd lost our parents and lived with a maiden aunt."

Dixie listened, trying to imagine her mother, young and naive, falling for a scoundrel.

"She was so heartbroken when she lost her son. I suppose that's why she wanted another baby. That, and to try to hang on to that man." Glendora's expression softened as she reached out to touch Dixie's face. "You look just like her. Is she still…"

Dixie shook her head. "She died when I was thirteen months old."

Glendora's watery eyes filled with tears. "I guess I always knew that she wasn't long for this world. She was too good." She met Dixie's gaze. "She was still with him?"

"Yes," Dixie said.

"I heard he moved her to Texas to work some farm."

The Bonner farm. Was it possible oil hadn't been discovered on the land yet? "So she had the baby boy in…?"

"Idaho, where we lived." She scowled. "Only lived a few weeks."

"Then my brother is buried in Idaho?"

"Ashton." She was staring at Dixie again, her eyes brimming with tears.

"What did she name him?" Dixie asked.

"Beauregard Bonner Junior Worth," Glendora said.

No wonder Dixie hadn't found him. She'd never dreamed her mother hadn't been married yet.

"I never knew what happened to my sister once she went to Texas. He didn't like her having anyone but him." She glanced toward the door and seemed to see Chance for the first time. "You have a handsome husband."

Dixie didn't correct her. "I never knew my father was ever in Idaho." She'd heard her uncle Carl and Mason and Ace all talk about their adventures. Her father hadn't always stayed in Texas, but he'd never said where he'd been. She thought she now knew why.

Strange, though, that he'd never mentioned that was where he'd met her mother. Or that they'd had a son

who died up there and then had Rebecca before moving back to Texas.

All to hide the fact that he hadn't married her yet?

Is that why he'd flatly denied knowing the people
in the photographs? She'd known he was lying, but she
couldn't understand how or why he would lie about his
own son and daughter, no matter the situation.

"There must have been something about my father
that made her fall in love with him," Dixie said.

"Oh, he was smooth. Cocky and full of himself.
Swept Elizabeth off her feet with all his grandiose plans.
Did he ever make anything of himself?"

"Not really," Dixie said, and heard Chance chuckle
where he leaned against the wall by the door.

She glanced around the small apartment. "Is there
any chance you have a photograph of my mother?"

Glendora looked toward the back of the apartment,
her expression vague. "I had some. Let me see if I can
find them." She pushed herself up from the couch and
disappeared into the bedroom.

Dixie looked over at Chance. She knew what he must
be thinking. Why would anyone want to kill her over
any of this? It made no sense. There was no mystery
here. No deep, dark secret unless it was the fact that
Rebecca had been born out of wedlock. Wouldn't Rebecca have a fit if she knew.

"Sounds like your father has a few secrets," Chance
said.

She nodded, thinking this would explain why she'd
had trouble finding out anything about her mother given
that her mother's real name apparently wasn't Sarah,
but Elizabeth Sarah Worth and she was born in Idaho—
not Texas.

Glendora returned with a rubber-banded shoe box.

She set it on the coffee table in front of the couch. "There might be something in here. I've moved so much, a lot of things have been lost over the years."

Dixie slipped off the rubber band and lifted the lid on the shoe box as Glendora joined her on the couch again.

The box was filled with black-and-white photos, the edges rough, the paper yellowed and curled.

She looked up at Chance, then with trembling fingers reached into the box and began to go through the photos.

Glendora couldn't remember most of the names of the people in the snapshots. "It's been too long," she said.

Dixie looked for a face that resembled her own, given that she'd been told she looked like her mother. The deeper she dug in the box, though, the more disappointed she became. Most of the photographs, it turned out, were from Glendora's first husband's family.

"You're so lucky to have a sister," Glendora said. "I wished my sister and I could have stayed together."

Dixie nodded, feeling guilty since she and Rebecca had never been close even though they now lived only a few miles from each other. "Would you like me to send you some photographs? Rebecca has three children."

Glendora smiled, her eyes misty. "I would love that."

Dixie picked up a photograph of a cute little girl with long blond hair making a face at the camera.

"That's Amelia," Glendora said, and reached for the photograph, smiling as she studied the girl's face.

"Amelia?"

"Amelia Hardaway. She married the oldest McCarthy boy." Glendora fell silent and Dixie could see that all this was tiring her. She quickly dug through the rest of the photographs, holding out little hope any of her mother had survived.

Glendora was still clutching the photo of the little girl. "Amelia was your mother's best friend. Those two…" she said, as if lost in the past. "They were inseparable."

Dixie could feel Chance's gaze on her. "Is Amelia still around?"

"I got a Christmas card. Was it this year or last?" She frowned as if trying to remember. "She didn't get far from home. Still lives on the farm outside of Ashton. Or she did. I think she said her husband died."

Dixie turned one of the last photographs over and froze. It was of two young girls, one about eleven, the other in her late teens.

Her heart took off in a gallop as she stared into the face of the younger girl. She felt Chance's palm on her back and looked up, and realized she must have made a sound that brought him to the end of the couch next to her.

She showed the snapshot to Glendora, not wanting to let go of it. "Is that you and my mother?"

Glendora smiled and nodded, eyes misting over. "My baby sister."

Dixie quickly looked through the few remaining photographs, finding only one other one of her mother. In it, both girls were older. Glendora was standing next to a bus, a suitcase at her feet. Beside Glendora was her younger sister holding a baby and next to Dixie's mother was a man wearing a fedora, his face in shadow and turned away from the camera as if he didn't want his photo taken.

"That was the day I left home," Glendora said, leaning in to look at the snapshot. "My aunt took the photo of all of us. It was the last time I saw Elizabeth and Rebecca. Our aunt died a few years later, but Elizabeth didn't come back for the funeral."

Dixie stared at the photo, running her finger over her mother's face. There was definitely a resemblance between her and her mother at this age. She could understand now why sometimes she caught her father looking at her with such a sad expression.

"Who is the man standing next to my mother?" Dixie asked.

Glendora looked up at her in surprise. "Why that's your father. He was a lot younger then, but that's him, all right. Beauregard Bonner. Like I could ever forget that name."

Dixie stared at the man in the photo. It was definitely not Beauregard Bonner.

CHAPTER TWELVE

CHANCE FELT AS shaken as Dixie looked as they left Glendora's apartment. "You all right?" he asked once they were outside.

Dixie nodded, seemingly afraid to trust her voice. He watched her breathe in the cold air, taking huge gulps.

He knew that everything was finally starting to catch up with her. Saying nothing, he put his arm around her and pulled her close as they walked to the pickup. Beauregard was fogging up the window watching them. Tiny snowflakes glittered suspended in the air. Across the street, a gust of wind whirled snow across a yard, knocking over a huge plastic Santa Claus.

Dixie had the two photographs gripped in her fingers. She protectively stuck them in her purse as he rushed to open her door and shoo Beauregard over.

Chance saw her glance up at the fourth-floor window before she climbed in. He shut her door and ran around to his side, still trying to make sense of what Glendora had told them.

As he slid behind the wheel, Dixie took the photographs from her purse and looked at them again. He started the truck, pretty sure he knew where they were headed next, but first he wanted something hot to drink and food wasn't a bad idea, either.

He found a café next to the old train depot. The lunch

crowd had already cleared out so the place was practically empty. They took a booth at the back.

"Food," Dixie said as she sat.

Chance laughed. "I should have known that would be the first word out of your mouth."

They ordered the lunch special. Dixie laid the photographs on the table as gently as if they were made of glass.

"Who is he?" she asked, looking up at Chance, her eyes blank as if in shock.

"Glendora could be wrong."

Clearly, Dixie didn't believe that any more than he did. "That man, whoever he is, fathered a son who died, then Rebecca. That means that Rebecca is my *half* sister. We didn't have the same father." Dixie seemed blown away by that thought. "It would explain why we are so different."

He still didn't know what to make of any of this. "The obvious answer would be that Glendora is wrong about the man in the photograph. He could have just been a friend of the family."

"I might believe that if my father hadn't tried so hard to talk me out of searching for the people in the photographs I found."

"Okay," he said. "But then, where does your father fit in all of this?"

"I don't know and that's what worries me," she said, and glanced out at the darkening sky over Sheep Mountain. She reached into her bag and took out her cell phone. "There is only one way to find out."

"Are you sure that's a good idea?" Chance asked as she pulled on her coat and rose from the booth.

"Are you kidding? At this point, I'm not sure anything is a good idea." She waited as if needing his encouragement.

"Maybe he'll clear everything up."

She shook her head at him in wonder. "You slay me. Maybe he'll call off whoever he's hired to kill me and tell me the truth. Right." She turned on her heel and headed for the door as she keyed in the number and put the phone to her ear.

Chance watched her go, wishing he could spare her this conversation because no matter what Beauregard Bonner told his daughter, he had a bad feeling she wasn't going to like it.

DIXIE STEPPED JUST outside the café, leaning against the building out of the wind. A banner flapped loudly nearby. Snow blew past in swirling white gusts. She stared down the train tracks as the phone rang.

"Hello?"

Just the sound of her father's voice stopped her cold. She felt tears burn her eyes. She flashed on Christmas mornings when she was a child and saw her father excitedly handing out presents.

They always got way too much, but it was his delight at being able to give them everything they wanted that she thought about now. She couldn't remember the last time they'd all had Christmas together and the thought filled her with sadness. Had she changed? Or her father?

"Hello?" He sounded ready to hang up.

She swallowed hard, the wind whistling past her. "It's Dixie."

Silence. Then, "Are you all right?"

"That's hard to answer."

"Isn't Chance there?"

She smiled at that. "I haven't given him the slip, if

that's what you're asking. I need to ask you about my mother and this time I need you to be honest with me."

He made a sound, a groan, then she heard a chair creak as he sat down. "Dixie…"

"I found my aunt Glendora. My mother's sister. Aren't you going to say anything?"

"Your mother told me she was an only child," he said, his voice soft, almost sad. "Her parents were deceased."

"I know about Rebecca."

"Dixie…" The sadness of that one word told her he wasn't going to deny that Rebecca wasn't his. "Dixie, come home so we can talk about this."

"We could have talked about it when I showed you the photographs I found in my mother's jewelry box," she snapped. "Instead you lied and said they didn't even belong to our family and that you would get rid of them for me."

"I should have told you then, but I was so shocked to see that she'd kept photographs…" His voice broke. "I knew your mother had been in love with another man. The man abandoned her. She had a baby girl with him."

"She had two children with him. The first one, a boy, died when he was a few weeks old."

A strangled sound. "I didn't know. She never told me." He sounded heartbroken. Was it possible he was telling the truth?

"If you had just been honest with me…"

"I never wanted your sister to know. She was *my* daughter. I raised her from the time she was just a child. I *loved* her just as I loved you." He sounded as if he was crying. "You're my girls."

She felt the tug on her heartstrings so strong it made her legs weak. How could she believe he was trying to have her killed? He was her *father.* "Who was the man?"

He blew his nose, cleared his throat. "I don't know. Honestly. She never told me."

"You never asked about my sister's father?"

"I didn't want to know. He'd abandoned Sarah when she'd needed him the most. What kind of man does that?"

What kind of man does *anything* to keep the past from surfacing? "Dad—" her voice broke "—how far would you go to keep me from finding out the truth?"

"Dixie, what are you talking about?"

"Someone is trying to kill me and now that you're trying to get into politics…"

"Dixie, you can't believe that I—"

"I saw the men who grabbed me. One of them works for you."

Beauregard Bonner let out a curse. "Dixie, if that's true, tell me who he is. I'll get to the bottom of this—"

"I don't know his name. But I've seen him at Bonner Unlimited. He might have been one of the security guards at the main desk."

"And you decided because of that, he was working for me?" her father demanded, sounding angry and hurt. "Damn it, Dixie, he might have been fired and just wanted to get even with me. I don't personally hire any of those men and you know it."

"What matters is that the men were after my research on the family. I heard them when they were ransacking my house looking for my journal."

"Dixie, I don't know what's going on, but you're scaring me. Please. Come home so I can keep you safe here. The jet will be there tomorrow. Meet me there. Please."

She made a swipe at her tears as she glanced back

into the café. The waitress was putting her order on the table. "I have to go."

"Tell me you'll be at the plane. You know I'd move heaven and earth to keep you safe, don't you?"

"That why you hired Chance?" she asked.

"I knew I could trust him. He won't let anything happen to you."

She closed her eyes. "This other man that my mother was in love with…he called himself Beauregard Bonner."

"*What?* It wasn't me. You have to believe me."

"I do believe you. It might be the only thing I believe that you've told me. I saw an old photograph of the man. It wasn't you. I have to go." She snapped off the phone, her hand trembling. Tears burned her eyes. She stood, huddled against the wind, afraid to let herself believe her father. Afraid he'd do more than disappoint her.

BEAUREGARD HAD JUST HUNG up when he realized he wasn't alone. He spun around, half expecting it would be his worthless son-in-law. He was only partially relieved to see that it was Mason.

"What? First I find you in my office when I'm not here and now you just walk in without knocking," Beau snapped.

Mason held up both hands. "The door was open. Since when do I have to knock anyway?" He stepped in, closing the door behind him. "Tell me what's happened that has you biting my head off?"

Beau leaned back in his chair, feeling more exhausted than he'd ever been before. "I'm sorry. I just got a call from Dixie. She found some photographs in her mother's jewelry box and has been trying to find the people in the snapshots."

Mason took a chair. "Snapshots?"

"Sarah had a sister, apparently."

Mason looked surprised. "I thought you said she was an only child."

"Apparently not."

"Is Dixie sure about this? I mean, why wouldn't Sarah have told you?"

Beau shook his head. "There is a lot Sarah didn't tell me. She had another child with the man. A son who died."

"This is what Dixie's been doing? Why would she drag all this up knowing how much it hurts you?" Mason was on his feet, pacing the floor.

"I should have told her when I saw the photographs from Sarah's jewelry box. If I had been honest with her—"

"Like that would have stopped Dixie." Mason shook his head irritably. "This is all Carl's fault. He had to give her that damned jewelry box…"

"Carl couldn't have known the photographs were in it. They were hidden under the velvet lining, Dixie said. They'd been there for years."

Mason swung around. "Didn't Carl know? Damn it, Beau, he resents the hell out of you. He's not even your real brother."

Beauregard felt as if he'd been touched with a live wire. The shock ricocheted through him, taking his breath. "I never want to hear you say that again. Do you hear me?" He was on his feet. "Carl *is* my brother. I don't give a damn if the old man denied it. He's my *brother*. Just as Rebecca and Dixie are sisters."

Mason raised a brow. "That's what you're really afraid Dixie's going to find out, isn't it? You feel guilty because the old man left everything to you. Didn't leave a cent to his first son. You got rich. And Carl...well, Carl gets a free ride. Not quite the same as being the son his father loved though, is it?"

Beau could feel his blood pressure soaring. "I won't hear another word about this. Especially from a man who doesn't even know who his father was."

Mason looked stunned and Beau instantly regretted his words. "I'm sorry."

Mason waved the apology away. "You're upset. I understand that. I just hate to see you get hurt any worse, Beau." He stepped to the bar and poured them both a drink. Mason had a knack for calming him down. "I didn't mean to set you off, but damn it, Beau, you have to know what's at stake here."

Oh hell, yes, he knew. He'd known since the day his father died and left him what Earle Bonner thought was nothing but a worthless Texas farm with a dirty flea-ridden shack on it.

"Don't you think Carl suspects you knew about the oil before the old man died?" Mason asked quietly as he handed him a drink and took his own to a chair. "Hell, I've always had the feeling he's been waiting for the day he could even the score with not just you, but me, as well."

"Carl has nothing to do with this," Beau said as he cradled the drink in his hands without taking a sip. He'd been drinking too much lately. He had to slow down, get his head clear.

"You remember the story of Cain and Abel from that summer at Bible school?" Mason asked. "Carl has always been jealous of you. You think that doesn't eat away at a man over the years. Your old man denied Carl's parentage and treated him like the bastard he was while you could do nothing wrong. If Carl saw a chance to even the score, you telling me he wouldn't take advantage of it?"

"Mason, please," Beau said, too tired to argue.

Mason downed his drink, sighed and took his glass to the sink at the bar. As he started to leave, he stopped to place a hand on Beau's shoulder. "I'm your oldest friend. If I step over the line sometimes, I'm sorry, but you know I have your best interests at heart and always have. I told you not to hire Carl or that no-good cousin of yours."

"What has Ace done now?" Beau asked, although he didn't really want to know.

"Didn't show for work all week, but apparently got an advance on his wages," Mason said. "Beau, you can't throw money at people to placate them. It only makes them more bitter. Ask my ex-wife if you don't believe me." He paused. "I'll call you when I get back in a few days."

Beau looked at him in surprise.

"You do remember that I'll be out of town on business?" Mason was frowning. "You told me to take the small jet? Beau, don't tell me—"

"Sure, sure," Beau said. "It just slipped my mind." He didn't remember but he'd had a lot on his mind lately. He wondered what business, but didn't ask, not wanting Mason to know just how forgetful he'd been lately.

"Are you sure you're all right?" Mason asked. "Maybe I should put this off—"

"No, you go ahead. I'm fine. Please. Dixie will be flying home tomorrow. I can handle things here."

Mason hesitated, but had the good sense to leave without another word.

The moment he was gone, Beau put down his drink and rubbed his forehead. He was getting another headache. He'd had a lot of them lately. That was probably another reason he was having trouble remembering things. He'd also been misplacing things. It was the strain of running a company this size.

But in truth he knew what was bothering him. He closed his eyes, thinking about what Mason had said.

He thought about his brother Carl. Mason didn't understand their relationship. Carl didn't care about his birthright as the oldest son. He'd hated the farm. And hated their father.

Beau felt a chill as he recalled the day their father died. Both of their mothers had been gone for years. Beau had come back to the farm to help. Carl had, too, after years of kicking around the country.

That day, Beau had come into the house to see Carl coming out of the old man's room. Carl had a funny expression on his face. "He's gone," Carl had said to Beau. "The devil has him now." And Beau had thought Carl had been fighting tears as he'd come out of the room. But the truth was, Carl had been smiling.

CHANCE NOTICED THAT Dixie hadn't come right back into the café after her phone call with her father. He'd watched her through the window, reading her body language, knowing how upset she was. He was just getting ready to go out to see if she was all right when she opened the door and came toward him.

Now as he saw her face, he knew it had gone better than maybe she'd hoped. She seemed stronger. Or, at least, she was giving it her best show. With Dixie, he never knew.

"He says he doesn't know who the man was," she said, sliding into the booth and picking up her fork.

"He swears my mother told him she was an orphan with no siblings."

Chance nodded. "Maybe he didn't know the people in the photographs, then. Your mother probably didn't tell him about her sister because it was all tied to that other man and the past."

She shrugged and took a bite of the lunch special. He suspected she wouldn't even be able to taste it in the mood she was in.

Chance checked his cell phone, not surprised to find a message from Bonner. He listened to it, a command to call. He looked at Dixie, then put the cell phone away.

"You aren't going to call him?" she asked.

"I'll call him when I know what's going on," he said. He knew Bonner would want details, as well as a promise that Dixie would be at the plane tomorrow. Chance couldn't make that promise right now and he figured telling Bonner wasn't going to help matters.

"He says he's not hiding anything and denies he would ever hurt me."

"And if he's telling the truth?"

She looked at him, her eyes misting over. "I was thinking about that. Who else has something to lose besides my father? Who else wouldn't want the truth coming out?"

He saw where she was headed. "The man in the photograph."

She nodded. "He could have his own reasons for not wanting me to find out who he is. Look at the way he has his face turned away from the camera, as if he didn't want his picture taken."

Chance nodded. "You're saying he somehow found out that you were trying to find your mother's relatives and he's the one who's been trying to stop you?"

She nodded as she cupped her hands around her coffee mug, clearly needing the warmth.

"You do know what that would mean," he said.

"Since one of the men who tried to kill me works for my father—or at least, used to—that would mean that the man is connected to Bonner Unlimited. Maybe even close to my father."

"Given the fact that the man used your father's name more than thirty years ago, I'd say he not only knows your father but has known him for a long time," Chance said.

"You think he might have been blackmailing my father so the truth didn't come out about Rebecca?"

Chance shook his head. "Your father would never have bowed to blackmail."

"Even if he knew that the news would kill my sister? You know how Rebecca is. She cares more about what those snob friends of hers think about her than anything in this world. Even her money and possessions. All that is just to impress them, to get them to accept her. Imagine if it came out that she's not even a Bonner?"

He could imagine that. He could imagine even worse. "This man sounds pretty unsavory."

Dixie nodded, tears in her eyes. "I'm sorry I ever opened this Pandora's box. Rebecca will be devastated when she finds out."

"That would have given the man motive for blackmail," Chance agreed. "Maybe that's why your father is so desperate to get you back to Montana where he can protect you from this person because he does know how dangerous the man is."

Dixie looked thoughtful. "That's why we need to find out who—" A freight train roared past within feet of where they sat. The café windows rattled loudly, making being heard impossible. It wasn't until the train was long past that she could finish "—who the man is in the photograph."

Dixie picked up the snapshot again, studying it in the light. "It's too bad it's not a better photograph. With his face in shadow…" She handed it over to him and watched as he inspected it.

"Add to that the fact that this was taken at least thirty years ago," Chance said, thinking out loud. The man was tall and lanky, young, maybe late teens or early twenties. It was hard to tell. "Who knows what he looks like now."

"It still doesn't explain why someone wants me dead," Dixie said as they ate, and made an attempt to lighten the conversation. "Unless Rebecca took out a contract on me so I wouldn't tell her friends in Houston society."

"There's nothing quite like sibling rivalry."

Dixie laughed.

He was glad to see her smile. She really did have a great smile.

"If Rebecca is behind it, though, I don't know why she wasted her money on hit men," Dixie continued. "She should have tried to bribe me first."

"Like she has anything *you* want," he said, joining in.

When she didn't say anything, he looked up from his plate to see her staring at him, her face deadly serious.

"She had you," Dixie said.

Joking or not, he wasn't going there. He was having trouble thinking of her as Rebecca's little sister. Dixie was a beautiful woman and he would have been a fool to pretend he hadn't noticed. And he wasn't that big of a fool.

Or maybe he was, he thought, remembering kissing

her. Not that he regretted the kiss. What he couldn't do
was get distracted. Too much was at stake. Someone
had shot at Dixie this morning. He couldn't keep kidding himself that her life wasn't in danger. He'd been
hired to find her and to keep her safe, and he always
did what he was hired to do.

That is, he always had. Unfortunately, he was starting to realize that he might break that rule tomorrow
when Bonner sent a private jet to pick up his daughter
in Helena.

Unless Chance could be sure Dixie would be safe
returning to Texas, then there was no way he was letting her near that plane.

DIXIE WATCHED CHANCE out of the corner of her eye as
he ordered them pie for dessert. Banana cream, her favorite.

"You realize this is the first thing we had in common," she said.

He glanced up, his fork loaded with pie partway to
his mouth. "What?"

"You and me," she said. "We both loved to eat. Remember those nights when you would bring Rebecca
home from a date and the cook would have just baked
cookies or a pie or one of those chocolate-covered
cherry cakes with the really thick fudge icing?"

He laughed and nodded as he took a bite of his pie.

"You and I would sit in the kitchen and talk and eat
while Rebecca searched the fridge for celery or tofu
or carrot sticks." She made a face remembering how
Rebecca was always on a diet even though she'd never
been even close to fat.

"I think my favorite was your cook's buttermilk pie.
Remember it?" he asked.

She rolled her eyes as if in ecstasy. "Oh, I'd forgotten all about that pie."

They talked of food and laughed about some of the late-night conversations they'd had discussing everything from religion to space aliens and crop circles.

When they'd finished their desserts, they walked out to the pickup in a companionable silence. Chance tensed, though, his hand staying close to the weapon strapped under his coat and his gaze taking in everything around them as they left the café.

It wasn't until they were safe in the pickup that he said, "I used to really enjoy those talks with you. You were pretty smart for twelve."

"Thanks. I think." Dixie spotted a bell ringer in front of one of the shops. He was dressed as Santa. On impulse, she reached into her purse, dug around and pulled out the diamond ring Roy Bob Jackson had left in her Christmas stocking. She ran across the street to drop the ring in the man's pot, then ran back to the pickup.

She climbed in, giving Beauregard the treat she'd brought him, most of her Salisbury steak from her lunch special. He gobbled it down and curled up against her leg. She put her hand on his big soft furry head and waited for Chance to start the engine. She could feel his gaze on her.

"Ol' Roy Bob won't be happy about that," Chance said.

"No, he won't," she said, and grinned. "That ring was worth about fifty grand. So we're going to Ashton?"

"Was there ever any doubt?"

"Thank you, but could I ask one favor? Could we stop back by Glendora's? I want to ask her more about the man in the photograph. I was so shocked before, I didn't know what to say."

Chance agreed it was a good idea. Maybe Glendora might remember something about the man that would help.

Where did her father fit into all this? Or did he? Maybe he was telling the truth and he hadn't known anything about her mother's past. But then, why was he so afraid for Dixie? What was it he still feared she would find out? The name of her mother's lover?

Dixie took in the small western town, her own fears gripping her as Chance drove down the main drag. Livingston sat in a hole, hemmed in by the Yellowstone River and the mountains. Wind whipped an American flag, the edge frayed, and sent snow skittering across the pavement.

She could feel the cold just outside the pickup window. She snuggled against Chance's warm, big dog, telling herself it was too late to quit. Even if she decided to stop looking for answers now, she doubted it would stop whoever was after her.

A chill rippled through her as they neared Glendora's apartment house that had nothing to do with the cold winter day. She heard sirens.

CHAPTER THIRTEEN

Chance heard the sirens just an instant before he saw the flashing lights. A cop car stopped next to an ambulance in front of Glendora's apartment house.

Dixie's face mirrored his own thoughts as he parked at the curb up the block from the house. A crowd had gathered on the sidewalk. Another police officer was directing traffic around the ambulance parked at the curb.

"It might not be Glendora," he said as they approached the scene, hoping to hell that was the case.

"Right," Dixie said, her voice breaking as she quickened her pace.

At the edge of the small crowd, Chance took her arm to hold her back. "Let me find out."

"What happened?" he asked an elderly woman in the crowd.

"One of the tenants. They say she fell down the stairs," the woman said.

"Who was it?" he asked.

The woman looked to a younger woman standing next to her. "An elderly woman who lived on the fourth floor. They said the elevator wasn't working and she must have tried to take the stairs."

Chance still had his hand on Dixie's arm and could feel her trembling. The wind whipped at their clothing and sent snow showering down on them as the ambulance attendants came out of the front door of the apartment house with the stretcher, the body in a black bag.

Chance let go of Dixie, stepped over to one of the policemen and flashed his credentials before asking the name of the deceased.

"Name's Glendora Ferris. A neighbor heard her fall down the stairs and called 9-1-1," the cop told him.

Beau stood at his office window, waiting. He really did have one hell of a view.

"You wanted to see me?"

He turned to look at his brother standing in the office doorway. Carl was wearing a Western shirt, jeans, boots. His gray hair needed to be cut and his white Stetson cleaned. Carl Bonner looked nothing like the multimillionaire he was.

Beau instantly regretted calling his brother into the office. Mason was wrong. Carl had more money than he would ever use. Nor was he apt to dream up some lame kidnapping plot that had failed to get a million and a half out of Beau anymore than he would give Dixie the jewelry box hoping she would find the photographs inside.

Because that would mean that Carl knew about the photos. Knew about Sarah's past. And how was that possible?

"Thought you might like to join me in a drink," Beau said, and motioned his brother in.

"Little early for me," Carl said, but closed the door and entered the office. "What's up?"

Beau poured himself a Scotch, figuring he was going to need it. "I wanted to ask you about Dixie."

"Dixie?" Carl said, frowning.

"Have you seen her?"

"Not for a while. Is something wrong?"

Beau took his drink back to his desk and sat, motioning for Carl to do the same. "She's in Montana."

Carl's brows lifted as he took a seat. "What's she doing up there?"

"Trying to find out more about her mother's family," Beau said, sorry to hear his words edged with criticism.

Carl nodded. "Bound to happen."

Beau opened his mouth to argue the point and closed it. He didn't want to fight about this. "She found some photographs in that jewelry box you gave her."

Carl frowned. "Photographs?"

"Apparently from Sarah's life before me," Beau said.

"You didn't know she kept them?"

"No. Did you?"

"What are you asking?" Carl said quietly.

What was he asking? What possible reason would Carl have for purposely giving Dixie her mother's jewelry box if he knew there were old photos hidden inside? None. Carl wouldn't want to hurt the girls. Not only that, Dixie'd had the jewelry box for years and had only just now found the photographs.

Beau rubbed his temples feeling a headache coming on. "Never mind me. I'm just in a foul mood." He'd made the mistake of not telling Dixie the truth straightaway. Instead all he'd done was whet her curiosity and when Dixie got on the scent of what she thought was a secret, she was like a hound dog after a buried bone.

"Sarah had a sister," Beau said. "She never mentioned it to me, but Dixie found out somehow."

Carl shook his head and said nothing.

"What?" Beau demanded.

"Nothing, it's just that you knew Sarah had a life before you."

"I didn't care about her past," Beau snapped, not wanting to admit that Sarah had lied to him. Maybe that's what hurt the most.

"I remember the night the two of you met," Carl said.

Beau felt all the air rush from him. He swallowed hard, picked up his drink and downed it. He'd forgotten about the first time he'd seen her.

CHANCE STARED UP at Glendora's apartment building windows as the body was loaded into the ambulance. Christmas lights strung across the front entry slapped the side of the house in the wind. A piece of newspaper blew by. Somewhere in the distance a horn honked, brakes squealed.

"Come on, let's get out of here," Chance said, steering Dixie toward the pickup, all the time watching the street and residences around them. For all he knew, the killer might be watching them at this very moment.

"You know she didn't fall down the stairs."

He could hear the anguish in her voice. The woman had been her aunt. Dixie had promised to send pictures of Rebecca's children to her. He put his arm around her as they neared the pickup.

"I'm so sorry, but it could have been an accident. You heard them say the elevator wasn't working," he said.

Dixie shook off his arm and climbed into the pickup. As he slid behind the wheel, she snapped, "Do me a favor. Stop trying to protect me from the truth."

"I don't know what the truth is and neither do you," he said as he watched the crowd disassemble and the cops leave. "We probably will never know what really happened to her."

"I led a killer straight to her. I just as good as murdered her," Dixie said.

He looked over at her, seeing how hurt and angry and scared she was. "Dixie, this isn't your fault."

"If I hadn't found those photographs in my mother's jewelry box…"

"Your mother kept them obviously because she couldn't part with them and had no idea that someday you would find them and this would happen," he said. "What you're not considering is that the man in the photograph has known about Glendora for years."

"Maybe he didn't know where she was, though, until I led him to her."

Chance shook his head. "It doesn't make any sense. Why kill Glendora? What did she really know? That Rebecca was another man's child? She didn't even know the man's real name. The photos were gone. So why kill her? We'd already been there. She'd already told us everything she knew."

Dixie knew what he was saying was true. It didn't make any sense. She took the photographs from her purse and studied them again. "He's tying up all the loose ends, probably wishing he'd done it years ago. But now maybe he *has* to." She looked over at Chance. "For whatever reason, he is more desperate to keep that life a secret."

"To protect himself?" Chance asked. "Or someone else?"

She shook her head. "Rebecca's his illegitimate daughter. What if he doesn't want her to know who he is?"

"Maybe."

"And why did my mother change her name from Elizabeth Worth to Sarah Worth when she went to Texas?"

They had more questions than answers as Chance

headed out of town, all the time watching his rearview mirror. They hadn't been followed to Livingston. He was sure of that. Just as they hadn't been followed to Glendora Ferris's apartment.

"I know you're going to think this is crazy," she said as she glanced behind them. "But I feel as if the man has more to lose now than ever before. He's determined to bury the past and me with it."

THE FIRST TIME Beau had seen Sarah Worth she'd been in the small café not far from the Bonner farm, sitting with Carl and Mason, talking.

He recalled how she'd looked up, their gazes meeting. Carl or Mason had introduced him.

"Beauregard Bonner?" She'd smiled as if she'd liked his name. Liked him.

Hell, he'd always told himself it was love at first sight. But now he knew that she was more than familiar with the name. Because her lover had been using it. Rebecca's real father.

"So did Sarah tell you anything about her baby's father that first night before I came in?" Beau asked his brother now, trying to keep the emotion out of his voice.

Carl shook his head.

"Damn it, Carl, if you know who he is…"

"Did you ask Mason?"

Beau stared at his brother. "You think she told Mason?"

Carl shrugged. "Mason's the one who bought her a cup of coffee and invited her over to our table."

"Mason has always been a womanizer." Sarah was a beautiful woman. What man wouldn't have been interested? He remembered how surprised he'd been when he'd seen the baby sleeping peacefully in the carrier on the chair next to her. He'd fallen in love with both of them. "I'm sure Mason lost interest the moment he realized she had a baby."

Carl shrugged again. "I saw Mason talking to Sarah quite a few times in town. Looked like pretty heated conversations."

"Come on, you were always talking to Sarah. Looked pretty serious at times." Beau regretted his words instantly. But he was sick to death of Mason and Carl constantly backbiting. They were more like brothers than Beau and Carl, jealous and convinced Beau liked one more than the other.

Carl was smiling now. "Sarah and I liked to talk about books. You were always busy trying to make more money. If you think I envied you because you had Sarah…" His smile broadened. "You're damn right I did. She was a fine woman and you were damned lucky that she loved you."

Beau felt even more like a heel. "I'm sorry."

"Look," Carl said reasonably, "Sarah's dead. What difference does any of this make now?"

"Because Dixie is determined to find out," Beau snapped. "I'm afraid for her. She's convinced that I hired someone to…kill her to keep her from learning the truth."

Carl raised a brow.

"You don't really think I would do that, do you?" Beau demanded. "All I can figure is that the man Sarah was with before me got wind of what Dixie was doing and doesn't want her digging in the past."

"Why do you think that?" Carl asked.

"Who else? I guess he doesn't want any of this coming out especially considering that when he was with Sarah he called himself Beauregard Bonner."

Carl laughed and shook his head. "Everyone always wanted to be Beauregard Bonner."

"Even you?" Beau asked.

Carl laughed harder. "Not a chance. I like being in the background, out of the line of fire. But it would explain how Sarah came to this part of Texas. Otherwise it is one hell of a coincidence to just happen to meet the real Beauregard Bonner, wouldn't you say?"

"You think she came here looking for him?"

"Or his family. After all, he'd abandoned her and her daughter, right?"

Beau nodded. Carl was right. It would explain the way she'd looked at him the first night he'd met her. By then, she must have realized the other man had been an imposter. And worse.

"You'll have to tell Rebecca. You don't want her to find out from someone else."

Beau rubbed his hand over his face, his head aching. This was the last thing he'd ever wanted to tell his oldest daughter. There was already bad blood between them. And now this.

"I know how I felt when the old man used to swear I wasn't his son," Carl said thoughtfully. "Was all right by me. I always hoped I wasn't related to the son of a bitch. He used to say he had more bastards around than a female barn cat."

Beau had always heard rumors that Earle Bonner had children all over Texas. He hadn't married Carl's mother, so Beau could definitely understand why Carl would want anyone for a father other than the one he'd had.

Beau cursed their father's soul to hell for the way he'd treated Carl. Beau had tried to make up for it, but all the money in the world couldn't take away the hurt from a father who hadn't wanted his child. Just as Mason had said.

"I would give anything if none of this came to light," Beau said as his brother fell silent. "I tried to convince Dixie not to do this but—"

"She's Dixie and definitely *your* daughter."

Beau lifted his head, hearing something in his brother's voice he'd never heard before. "Do you hold a grudge about the old man's will?"

Carl leaned back in his chair. "I wondered when you'd get around to that." He laughed and shook his head. "Hell, Beau, I don't know what to do with half the money I have thanks to you. You've been more than generous when the fact is, you didn't have to give me a cent. Our old man is rolling over in his grave right now because of what you've done for me."

Beau didn't know what to say. The old man had always shown favoritism, making it no secret to anyone, especially Carl, that he preferred Beau. But when Earle Bonner had left Beau the farm, he hadn't thought he was doing him a favor. In fact, he'd talked about leaving the farm to Carl, saying Carl deserved to be stuck on the farm the rest of his life. The old man died before the first oil well came in a gusher.

"It was a crappy deal, the way things turned out."

Carl grinned. "Are you kiddin'? Things turned out great. Stop beating yourself up." He rose to his feet. "Just for the record, I didn't know there were any photos hidden in that jewelry box. I retrieved it from where you'd thrown it in the trash because I thought Dixie should have something of her mother's one day."

Beau nodded. "I wasn't thinking clearly back then. I couldn't bear to see anything of hers. You did right."

"I try," Carl said. "Tell Rebecca before she finds out

from someone else." He paused. "You don't look good, Beau. You've got to start taking care of yourself." He tapped his fingers over his heart. "Life is short, Beau. Enjoy it a little. Hell, it could all end tomorrow."

Carl left, leaving Beau staring after him. He couldn't help feeling there was still a whole hell of a lot unsaid between them, no matter what Carl professed.

Hadn't he known there were secrets from the past? Secrets that, when they came to light, were going to blow his life to hell.

DIXIE LOOKED OUT at the Montana landscape of towering mountain peaks, snow and endless sky, all her fears coming together in a rush. "What if Glendora was murdered and before she died, she told her killer about Amelia? We have to warn her," she said, digging out her cell phone.

"What are you going to tell her?"

"I don't know. Maybe to go to a neighbor's and stay put until we get there. Or not to answer the door." She reached Information and asked for Amelia McCarthy. No listing. Dixie asked about any other McCarthys in the Ashton area. Only one. Buzz and Rita McCarthy.

Dixie dialed the number on her cell.

It was answered by a woman on the third ring. She sounded breathless. "Hello?"

"I'm trying to locate an Amelia McCarthy. Amelia Hardaway McCarthy?"

"Yes, she was my sister-in-law," the woman said.

Dixie couldn't help the disappointed sound that escaped her. "She's *deceased*?"

Chance looked away from his driving in surprise.

"Yes, six months ago. Can you tell me what this is about?"

Dixie told her as briefly as possible that her mother had been friends with Amelia and she was hoping to talk to her since her mother had died when she was very young.

"I'm so sorry. What was your mother's name?"

Dixie caught herself before she said Sarah. "Elizabeth Sarah Worth."

"Oh, my gosh. My sister-in-law used to talk about her all the time."

Dixie tried not to get her hopes up. "I don't know much about my mother. I was wondering if Amelia and my mother remained friends after my mother moved to Texas."

"They sure did," Rita McCarthy said. "Your mother wrote my sister-in-law nearly every week. Amelia was so worried about her. Elizabeth was calling herself Sarah and was so unhappy. Then she wrote that she'd found a wonderful man who loved her daughter as his own. She said she had to keep her past a secret, and that bothered her. She really struggled with that. I suppose you know all that, though."

"About the man my mother had two children with before moving to Texas," Dixie said. "Did you ever meet him?"

"No. I wasn't living here then." She seemed to hesitate. "Maybe I shouldn't say this..."

"Please. I'm trying to find out who he was. The man used the name Beauregard Bonner, but that wasn't who he was."

"Oh, my goodness. Well, I can tell you this. My sister-in-law didn't like him. She didn't trust him. He wasn't very nice, I guess."

So Dixie kept hearing. "You said my mother wrote Amelia?"

"That's right. Sarah, that's what she was calling herself then, was worried that he'd find out that Amelia was writing her so she got a post office box outside Houston. That's how my sister-in-law knew something had happened to her. When a bunch of her unopened letters were returned, she contacted the post office and was told that the box holder hadn't paid her rent for some time and the mail had been returned to the sender."

Dixie felt sick. Her mother had lived a lie all those years.

"It was so wonderful that your mother had finally found happiness. Well, as much as that horrible man would let her. Not her husband, the other man," Rita said. "Amelia told me about how your mother didn't find out that he'd been lying to her until she got to Texas and met the real Beauregard Bonner and was forced to play up to him for money."

Dixie couldn't breathe. She could feel Chance's gaze on her. "What is it?" he whispered.

She shook her head, sucked in a breath and said into the phone, "So it was all about money?"

"Honey, she had no choice. She had her baby girl to take care of and…" Rita seemed to hesitate. "Amelia said that your mother feared for her life if she didn't do what he wanted."

Dixie felt sick. This woman had been her mother. A weak woman who'd fallen for the wrong man, had two children out of wedlock, lied and cheated for money. Was this why her father had no photographs of her? Why he never wanted to talk about her? Because he'd found out the truth?

Dixie didn't know what to say. No wonder her father hadn't wanted her digging into the past, finding out the truth about her own mother.

She realized that Rita was saying something and tried to focus on the woman's words.

"...the last letter she got from your mother. Sarah wanted to tell your father the truth about her past. She loved him and couldn't go on deceiving him, she said. She said she was going to tell him and asked my sister-in-law to pray for her."

Her mother had fallen for the real Beau Bonner? "Did she tell my father?" Dixie asked.

"Amelia assumed she did. But then the letters stopped and she later found out that your mother had died. I probably shouldn't say this, but Amelia always believed that he killed her."

"My father?" Dixie asked, unable to keep the shock out of her voice.

"No, no, the other one. The one masquerading as Beauregard Bonner. The one who used the past against her to keep getting money out of her."

"Are you saying he *blackmailed* her?"

"He threatened to tell her husband that she'd only married him for his money and once your father knew about her past... It would give a man pause if he knew that she hadn't truly loved him at first. That it had been about the money. What man would believe she'd really fallen in love with him?"

Dixie looked over at Chance. Had her mother told Beauregard the truth about her past? Or had she died before she could? Dixie felt cold inside.

"Amelia finally contacted the newspaper down there and found out about the car accident."

"Her car went into the lake," Dixie said, her voice breaking.

"How horrible for her," Rita said.

Had she also planned to tell the other man? Maybe refused to be blackmailed anymore?

The thought sent a spear of ice down her spine. "Did Amelia keep the letters from my mother? Or any photographs?"

"I'm sorry. Amelia destroyed the letters and all the photos just as Sarah made her promise to do. I think she was afraid for my sister-in-law."

Dixie could understand that. "Is there anything about the man, anything Amelia might have mentioned, that would help me identify him?" The cell phone connection was growing dim as the highway cut through the mountains.

"None I can think of. He was nice-looking enough, I gather. Quite the charmer. But it was so long ago, you know."

Yes, she knew. "Well, thank you. I'm so sorry to hear about Amelia's passing. I wish I could have met her."

"I hope you find what you're looking for, dear."

Dixie glanced over at Chance. She already had.

"AMELIA McCARTHY IS DEAD," Chance said as Dixie snapped off the phone and leaned back in her seat.

She nodded, devastated. She'd been so sure that Amelia might be able to help them find the man. "I talked to her sister-in-law, Rita McCarthy." She told him what she'd learned about the letters and what her mother had planned to do just before her death.

Dixie sighed. "Apparently, my father made her happy." She had to admit knowing that made her feel a little better. Maybe they had loved each other. Wasn't that what every child wanted? For her parents to have loved each other. Even if it ended badly.

But she couldn't shake the feeling that her mother

had been murdered—and by a man she had once loved. "He killed her so she couldn't tell my father the truth."

"The police ruled it was an accident, right?"

Dixie rolled her eyes. "Just like Glendora's. My mother decides to tell my father the truth and ends up at the bottom of a lake. Don't tell me the timing doesn't make you suspicious."

"Everything makes me suspicious. What if it does turn out that he's a killer, that he not only killed your mother, but is the one who hired the men to come after you? He's Rebecca's *father*."

His words chilled her. She was looking for a man who was contemptuous, probably capable of anything. She hadn't focused on the fact that this man, whoever he was, was Rebecca's father.

Dixie shook her head, fighting emotions she wasn't used to. Normally she was in control. But she'd set something in motion and there seemed to be no stopping it. She wished she'd never begun digging into the past.

"Can you imagine how this will hurt Rebecca?" Chance said. "This will devastate her."

She nodded, fighting tears, as he reached over to squeeze her hand. "There's no reason to go to Idaho."

"No."

"What do we do, Chance?"

"We meet your father's plane tomorrow. We tell him what we know. Maybe with the information you've gathered and his help, we can figure out what the hell is going on."

She studied his handsome face. "You think my father knows the man, don't you?"

"I think it's a real possibility," he said as the land stretched ahead of them in rolling wheat fields. "Otherwise, why was your mother so afraid to tell him the truth? She saw that other man as a threat. I think he stayed around to get money, to make sure she never told."

"This man has gotten away with it all these years," Dixie said, aching at the thought of what her mother had gone through. "Who could he be?"

"That's the million-dollar question, isn't it?"

"Million and a *half*," Dixie said, remembering what Chance had told her about the ransom demand. "He tried to make it look like a kidnapping to cover up the real reason I was going to be killed."

She felt Chance look over at her, then back at his driving. "Looks that way." She watched him glance into her rearview mirror, saw his expression.

She turned, afraid of what she would see. Her fear ratcheted up another notch as she saw a van that looked exactly like the one she'd seen in the parking garage the night this had all begun.

CHAPTER FOURTEEN

CHANCE HAD EXPECTED trouble once they left the interstate and got on the two-lane Highway 287 headed north toward Townsend. There had been enough traffic that he hadn't been able to spot a tail, but he now suspected they'd been followed since Livingston.

Traffic was horrendous around Bozeman, but once they left there and drove west, it began to thin out.

Most of the cars had ski racks on top. Some out-of-state plates, people up here for the Christmas vacation. With Big Sky Ski Resort only forty miles to the south and Bridger Bowl about twenty to the north, Bozeman had become a winter destination along with being the home of Montana State University and ten-thousand-plus college students.

Chance swore under his breath as the van closed the distance between them, but didn't even attempt to pass even when he slowed down.

The road narrowed along the Missouri River, dropping away on each side. There was no guardrail on either side and little traffic. This was the stretch of highway where the van driver would make his move.

Chance sped up. The van sped up, as well, keeping the same distance between them. The road curved as it wound by the slow-moving, dark, ice-rimmed river.

The van closed some of the distance between them.

"That's the two men who attacked me in the parking garage," Dixie said, looking back.

He heard the tremor in her voice. "Put the dog on the floor," he ordered. "And brace yourself."

They were almost to the bridge. The van filled the rearview mirror just an instant before the bumper slammed into the back of the pickup.

Chance swore as he fought to keep the truck under control. Out of the corner of his eye, he saw Dixie's face. It was leeched of all color, her blue eyes wide with fear. He met her eyes and saw something flicker in her gaze.

"Give me your gun," she said, her voice breaking.

"What?"

The van slammed into the back of them again. The pickup fishtailed, one tire going off the edge of the road and kicking up snow that blew over the van's windshield, forcing the driver to hit his wipers and back off a little.

Dixie unhooked her seat belt and got on her knees to face the back window. The pickup was made for a camper in the bed so it had a small sliding window that she now unlatched. Cold air rushed in.

"Get back in your seat!" Chance yelled as the van came at them again. He sped up, but ahead was another tight curve, the drop-off much steeper on each side of the road.

"Give me your gun," she said over the roar of the van's engine as it came at them again.

The van slammed into the bumper. Chance gripped the wheel, fighting to keep the truck on the road as Dixie held on to the back of the seat with one hand and reached under his coat, unsnapped the holster and withdrew the gun.

"You don't even know how to shoot a gun," he said, swearing as he heard her snap off the safety.

"Slow down," she said, sounding almost too calm.

He shot her a look. She was braced on the back of the seat, the weapon gripped in both hands and pointing out through the small window opening, the cold wind whipping her hair, her eyes narrowed in concentration.

A sharp turn was just ahead with steep drop-offs on each side of the pavement. The van driver started to make another run at them.

"Hang on," Chance said, and hit his brakes.

The move took the driver of the van by surprise. In his rearview mirror, Chance saw the driver literally stand on his brakes. The van fishtailed wildly just before it struck the back of the pickup with a force that sent the pickup rocketing forward.

The shot was deafening as it echoed through the cab of the pickup. Chance managed to just barely keep the truck on the pavement, the right back tire dropping dangerously over the edge of the highway before he got it back.

In his side-view mirror he saw the van's windshield shatter into a web of white an instant before it blew out, showering the driver and the man next to him with tiny cubes of glass. The driver of the van was also fighting to regain control of his vehicle.

Chance swore as he saw the passenger level his own weapon at the pickup. At Dixie. "Get down!" he yelled.

Dixie got off another shot that boomed in the cab. In that same instant, Chance saw the front tire blow on the van, saw the driver fight to get the vehicle under control. It was the next sound that took his breath away.

A shot fired from the van. It thundered just behind

him, metal chips flying from where it had struck the cab and ricocheted.

Dixie fell over in the seat as Chance took the curve.

"Dixie!" He reached for her, glancing in the rear-view mirror as his hand found her shoulder, fear spiking. "Dixie!"

"I'm all right," Dixie said in a small voice.

"Are you hit?"

"I'm all right."

He stole a look at her and saw the tiny cuts from the flying metal on her face oozing blood, and swore.

Behind him he watched as the van driver lost control, the blown tire flapping and throwing up chunks of debris. The van skidded sideways, the blown tire rim digging into the asphalt. The van rolled twice before it left the highway and tumbled down the embankment and disappeared.

Chance hit the brakes, coming to a stop at the edge of the road. He was shaking as he looked over at Dixie. Tears welled in her eyes and she chewed at her lower lip.

"Who taught you to shoot?" he said.

"I'm from Texas," she said. "Do you think they're—"

The explosion drowned out her words as behind them the sky filled with a ball of fire.

Chance did a highway patrol turn and drove back toward the smoke and flames, pulling to a stop at the edge of the highway. The van was consumed in flames. In stunned silence they watched it burn, clouds of smoke billowing up into the winter evening.

There were no footprints in the snow around the van. No bodies. The men hadn't gotten out.

Dixie stared at the smoke pouring up from the van, shaking so hard her teeth chattered. She fought tears as she stared at the van, imagining the charred remains of the men inside.

"Are you all right?" Chance asked as he took the gun from her hands and closed the back window.

She nodded, telling herself that they would have killed her and Chance, remembering the one who'd kicked her in the head, reliving the night in the parking garage in Houston. But it did little to take away the appalling shock that she'd killed two men just as certainly as if she'd shot them to death.

"I know how you feel right now, if that helps."

She looked over at him and nodded. It did help. She didn't know what she would have done if he hadn't been with her.

"You saved our lives," he said softly, and brushed his fingers over her cheek.

She nodded, tears blurring her eyes as he dragged her into his arms. Behind them several cars had pulled up. One of the drivers jumped out and ran up to the side of the pickup.

Dixie pulled back from Chance's embrace as the man tapped on the window.

"Have you already called in the accident?" the man asked, looking from Dixie's tearful face to Chance's.

"Our cell phone isn't working," Chance said. "Can you call it in?"

"Any survivors?" the man asked.

Dixie watched Chance shake his head. "Saw it happen in the rearview mirror."

"Looks like the driver lost control and missed the curve," the man said. "I'll call it in."

"Thanks," Chance said, and waited until the man got back into his vehicle to place the call before he shifted the pickup into first and pulled away. Up the road he turned around and headed north again.

Dixie felt numb, everything surreal. She wanted to believe it was over. The men who'd tried to kill her were dead. But whoever had hired them wasn't.

Beauregard jumped up on the seat next to her again. She wrapped her arms around the dog's neck as she buried her face in his soft fur. This was far from over.

BEAU PICKED UP THE PHONE and held it for a long moment as he thought about how he was going to tell Rebecca.

Hell, he had no idea. How did you tell a woman like Rebecca that her whole life had been a lie?

He put down the phone, then picked it up again and hurriedly dialed Rebecca's number before he lost his nerve.

Rebecca answered after four rings. He could hear soft music in the background, the soft clink of expensive crystal, hushed voices. A party?

"Rebecca?"

Silence.

"Is this about Dixie?"

"No. I need to see you."

"What's happened?" She sounded scared.

"Honey, where are you? Could I come over?"

"What? Tonight? Now? Can't it wait?"

"No. Rebecca. There's something I should have told you a long time ago. Now that Dixie's... Well, there's just things about your mother that..." He stopped himself. "Anyway, I don't want to do this on the phone."

"Something Dixie told you?" Rebecca said. "Daddy, I have company. I'm sure whatever it is can wait until morning. Why don't I come over to your house in the morning first thing? I hope you don't take anything Dixie says too seriously. You know how she is."

"Yes." He wished that were the case this time. Beau hated the relief he felt. "In the morning then." And yet he didn't want to break the connection. "Rebecca, I love you." He waited and realized after a moment that she'd already hung up.

BY THE TIME Chance reached Townsend, it had begun to snow. He drove through town as snowflakes spiraled down. At a stop sign, he watched a young couple pick through the last of the Christmas trees in an empty lot. The falling snow blurred the red-and-green strands of lights strung around the lot. There was something hypnotizing about watching the snowflakes drift down through the lights.

"Where are we going?" Dixie asked dully.

"Home." It was Christmas Eve and the only place he wanted to be was the cabin. He felt a need to go home. He wanted to believe that the death of the two hit men in the van would be the end of it. But whoever had hired them was still alive and if he knew anything about secrets and the people who tried to keep them, that person wouldn't let it end here. But that was another reason he wanted to go home. Let it end on his turf rather than along some lonesome two-lane.

As he drove down the main drag, he heard a Christmas carol being piped out from one of the bars. He looked over at Dixie. She appeared shell-shocked. From the night she was attacked in the parking garage, she'd been running on adrenaline and bravado, but clearly she'd run out of both.

He knew she hadn't had time to assimilate everything, let alone the impact of what had happened and what she'd learned. She needed some down time.

"I'm taking you to my cabin."

She looked over at him, her gaze softening as she nodded, her smile small. She'd been through so much.

He pulled into a gas station with a convenience store and filled up while she went inside. He found her sitting in a small plastic booth, her hands wrapped around a foam cup of hot coffee, her eyes hollow.

He got himself a cup of coffee. They still had a long drive out to the lake and he had no idea what they would find. For all he knew there might be someone out there waiting for them.

"Have you talked to my father?" she asked.

His eyes locked with hers. "No."

She nodded and put down her cup. Not even caffeine could keep her system revved up anymore. "I'm so tired," she said in a voice he'd never heard before. She met his gaze, hers filling with tears. "I'm tired of running. Tired of being scared. I'm just…tired."

He nodded, smiling his sympathy as he reached across the table and touched her fingers. They were ice-cold. "It's going to be over soon." That he did believe. The outcome he couldn't promise, though. "I will protect you to my last dying breath."

She smiled, a tired teary smile. "I knew you would."

"Come on, Dix," he said, rising to pull her to her feet. He scooped up the box of groceries he'd bought and, with his free arm around her, walked her to the pickup. She cuddled next to Beauregard and was asleep before Chance even had the engine started.

As CHANCE TURNED onto the road into the cabin, he stopped to study the tracks. The new snow had filled the only tracks in or out—his tracks from over thirty-six hours before.

No one else had been down the road. He shifted into four-wheel drive, the pickup bucking the deep snow, headlights bobbing through snowcapped pines. The only sound was the roar of the engine as he drove, his headlights finally flashing on the cabin ahead, filling him with such a sense of relief that it made him weak.

He pulled up beside the house. Beauregard lifted his head and began to wag his tail. Chance wasn't the only one glad to finally be home.

He opened his door and Beauregard bounded over the top of him and out into the snow.

Dixie had awakened and was looking out through the snowy darkness at the cabin. Some of her color had returned and she looked less beaten down. It buoyed his spirits to see her strength.

"Home," he said, feeling almost shy.

"You built it," she said.

He nodded, studying her. In some ways, she was so like her father. Stubborn. Self-confident. Determined. And at the top of the list: inquisitive to a fault.

"Is there anything you don't know about me?" he asked, only half joking.

She turned then to look at him. The falling snow cast a silky light into the cab of the pickup. "No, I don't think so. But if there is time, I wouldn't mind learning more."

He laughed. "Nice to have you back, Dixie," he said, and got out.

As Dixie stepped into the cabin, he tried to see his home through her eyes. He'd always been proud of the place since he'd built it himself. But now it seemed too functional. It lacked warmth, what some might have called a woman's touch. Strange that he'd never noticed that before.

"It's not much, but it's home," he said.

She said nothing as she seemed to take it all in. Finally she turned to look at him. "It's wonderful. I love it." She smiled and her smile alone warmed the whole place and made it seem better instantly.

He smiled his thanks and let out the breath he hadn't realized he'd been holding. "I'll get a fire going. You must be freezing." As he made the fire, he watched her out of the corner of his eye. She moved through the place touching the stones he'd laid, running her fingers along the logs he'd peeled by hand, stopping to study a photograph he'd taken of the lake one summer evening at sunset.

That life seemed a million years ago now. He felt as if he could barely remember it. That's what only a couple of days with Dixie Bonner did to a man. When she left, the cabin would seem vacuous and empty. He found himself dreading that inevitable day.

As he got the logs crackling in the firebox, she came to stand next to it, her eyes shiny as she looked into the flames. He knew she was thinking about the two men who'd lost their lives today. He knew what it was like to take another life. To look into a person's eyes that instant before he pulled the trigger and saw them die.

He hoped never to have to pull that trigger again. But unless he quit the P.I. business and took up a job as a ranch hand again....

"What is today?" Dixie asked.

"Christmas Eve."

She nodded and held her hands out to the fire.

He glanced past her at the cabin. There was no sign anywhere that it was Christmas. Not that he would have decorated even if he hadn't taken this latest job. He didn't do Christmas. Hadn't since his daughter's last one three years ago.

"Hungry?" he asked.

To his surprise, Dixie shook her head.

In the kitchen, he put away the groceries and saw that Dixie had moved to the front window.

Through the falling snow, the lake appeared endless. Nothing but white into the darkness. The snow blanketed the cabin and lake in cold silence.

"Can I help?" she asked, as if sensing him watching her.

"You cook?" He hadn't meant to sound so skeptical.

She cocked her head at him, a warning look in her eye.

He raised his hands in surrender and laughed. "Go ahead, tell me you're a gourmet cook, you've won prizes and that I'm the worst chauvinist you've ever met."

She shook her head, started to say something, but seemed to lose the words. She turned away but not before he'd seen her face crumple.

He dropped the groceries on the counter and rushed to her. "Dixie?" He put his hands on her shoulders and turned her to him. She was crying, huge shuddering sobs. He thumbed away her tears, cupping her face in both hands. "Dixie." Her name was a whisper on his lips as he pulled her into his arms. "Oh, Dixie."

He let her cry as he held her and stroked her hair, her back, all the time trying to soothe her with soft words and gentle caresses.

The sobs subsided, her trembling body stilled, softening as it fit to his. She felt so right in his arms. He had the thought that he never wanted to let her go.

He pulled back, realizing the foolishness of that. Her lower lip trembled as she looked up at him.

He bent toward her as if he didn't have a mind of his own. His lips brushed over hers, her mouth sweet and supple with just the hint of salty tears.

He knew he should stop, but her lips parted as he deepened the kiss, opening to him as her body melded again into his.

He breathed her in, all his senses acutely in tune with her. Desire rippled through him in waves each stronger than the next. He'd never wanted anyone the way he wanted this woman. This damned woman had more than gotten to him.

To his surprise it was Dixie who pulled back this time. The look in her eyes surprised him. He'd thought this was what she'd wanted.

"What?" he asked, half-afraid.

"I have to know something first."

"I'm sorry, I thought…"

"That I wanted you?" She smiled up at him. "Oh, I do, Chance. I *always* have."

He caught his breath as he sensed exactly where this was going.

"But I have to know if it's me you're kissing. Or my sister."

"Rebecca? Dixie, she's married with three kids."

"You were in love with her."

"A lifetime ago. Dixie, that kiss was about you. No one else." He reached for her. "Oh, Dixie," he said as he brushed a lock of her wild hair back from her beautiful face. "There is no one like you. No one who's ever made me feel like this."

She looked into Chance Walker's eyes and saw the answer she needed, had wanted since the first day she'd set eyes on him when she was twelve. It had been love at first sight, as corny as that was. No schoolgirl crush. She'd known that someday—

"Dixie, you have to know that I..." She dragged him to her, cutting off his words with a kiss. He swept her up in his arms, kissing her wildly, as he carried her to the deep leather couch in front of the fire.

He made love to her slowly in the firelight, kissing her as he removed each piece of clothing before he began a seductive trail of kisses across her bare flesh.

She arched against his mouth as he pushed aside her bra to suck one of her hard nipples into his mouth. Unlike him, she tore at his clothes, yearning to feel his naked body on hers.

"Dixie," he whispered as she tossed his shirt over the back of the couch. "We have all night."

She laughed, breathing hard as she reached for the buttons on his jeans, arching one brow as she met his gaze. "Then let's not waste a second of it," she said, and jerked his jeans open.

They rolled off the couch onto the braided rug in front of the fire, both laughing as they shed the rest of their clothing.

She pressed her naked flesh to his, taking in his scent, burying her fingers in his thick hair as she looked into his eyes. "Now," she said, "we can slow down." She met his mouth with her own, felt his hands cup her breasts, his thumbs teasing the nipples to hard, pleasured points before his fingers slid down her belly and between her legs.

He laughed and rolled her over onto her back. She arched against his fingers, then his mouth before she cried out in release. Then his body was back, warm and hard, as he fitted himself into her and began the slow sweet dance of lovers until they both cried out, clutching each other as the fire crackled softly beside them, the snow falling silently beyond the windows.

For a long time they lay in each others arms watching the fire, dazed and drowsy. Dixie couldn't remember being more content. That was one reason she was so surprised when she felt Chance pull away to get to his feet.

"Stay here," he ordered, then leaned over her and kissed her gently on the mouth before he dressed and went to the door. "I'll be right back."

WARMED BY THEIR lovemaking, she lay in front of the fire until she realized she was ravenous. She dressed and went into the kitchen to make them sandwiches. When Chance didn't come back, she began to worry. She missed him, and that reminded her that this was temporary. Maybe very temporary given that someone still wanted her dead. And now she'd involved Chance in it.

She was just finishing putting the sandwich makings away when she heard his footfalls on the deck. The next moment, the front door burst open and she caught the rich scent of pine as a huge pine tree was pushed through the door followed by a snowy Chance Walker.

He was smiling as he stood the tree up in a pot by the window. "I have no idea what we're going to decorate it with," he said, eyes shining when he looked at her. "I got rid of all my decorations."

She nodded, pretty sure she knew when that had happened and why. "Don't worry. We'll find something." She touched the prickly green bough, tears filling her eyes as she looked at him. "Thank you."

"It's Christmas," he said, his voice cracking.

CHANCE KNEW THAT no matter what happened in the future, he would never forget this night. *This* Christmas. Like the last one with his daughter, he would keep it always in his heart.

They made a huge batch of popcorn, eating some in front of the fire, stringing the rest on thread. They talked about religion and flying saucers and Bigfoot. They laughed and kidded. They kissed. And by midnight, the tree was decorated.

As they stood back and admired it, he had to admit, "I've never seen a more beautiful tree."

Dixie laughed. He loved the sound. It filled the cabin the same way her smile did, bringing a warmth that filled him to overflowing. He never thought he could feel like this again.

"I want to tell you about my daughter," he said after a moment. She nodded slowly. And he told her about a woman he'd been dating. "When she got pregnant I offered to marry her, but we both knew it wouldn't have worked. She moved in here, had the baby on Christmas Eve three years ago. I never thought I could be happier."

Dixie put her arm around him, knowing what came next.

"Her name was Star. She lived for just over three weeks. Her heart hadn't formed correctly." He fought back tears. "She was so beautiful."

Dixie took him in her arms. He buried his face in her hair. They stayed like that for a long time. When he pulled back he saw that she was crying. He thumbed away her tears.

"You know what our tree needs, don't you?" Dixie said, getting up to go to the kitchen.

He smiled, nodding as he saw what she planned to do.

He cut a star from the cardboard box their groceries had been in and she covered it with tin foil.

"Here," she said. "You can put it on the tree."

He shook his head and grabbed her, swinging her around as he carried her over to the tree to lift her up as she placed the star carefully on the top. The firelight caught it, sending the silvery light across the log walls of the cabin.

"Merry Christmas!" she said as he lowered her to the floor again.

He felt a well of emotion surge inside him as he pulled her to him. "Merry Christmas," he whispered against her hair, and kissed her.

Sometime during the wee hours of morning they fell asleep in each other's arms, Beauregard snoring softly in the corner as the fire burned down to embers and the snow continued to fall.

CHAPTER FIFTEEN

OLIVER STUMBLED INTO the house, half-drunk, sick to his very soul. He thought about sleeping on the couch, not wanting to wake Rebecca, but at the same time not wanting to have to face the rowdy kids in the morning.

Then he saw a note saying that the nanny had taken the kids somewhere. It was just him and Rebecca alone here tonight. The thought sent a shiver through him. Had she purposely sent the nanny and the brats away? Was she upstairs lying in wait for him because she knew?

The thought made him sick to his stomach.

He headed for the couch, planning to avoid her as long as possible. The phone rang.

He hurriedly snatched it up before it could wake her. Who could be calling at this hour anyway? "Hello?"

"Bad news."

Oliver's head buzzed as his heart pounded. "Ace?"

"The deal fell through. The money's gone. I've been trying to track the guys down all day. They blew town. I'm sorry."

"No." Oliver was shaking his head, thinking about how that money was going to save him. He was ruined. Worse than ruined. Even his name would be dragged through the mud. He'd be lucky to get out with the clothes on his back once Beau found out. "No."

"I'm sorry, man. You knew there was risk, right?

I mean, you can't expect to make millions with a few measly thousand dollars without there being risks."

"Two hundred and twenty-five thousand," Oliver said. "This can't be happening."

"I know what you mean, man. I put some of my money into this. That's why I'm leaving town for a while."

"What?"

"I owe the kind of guys who break your kneecaps just for the fun of it. You're lucky you don't owe any guys like that anyway."

Was he kidding? He owed everyone. And he'd lost more tonight. He was as good as dead. "You can't leave town. We have to find these guys and get the money back."

"Not happening. I'm out of here and I doubt I'll be coming back anytime soon. You might want to think about leaving town for a while." The line went dead.

"Ace? Ace!" He slammed down the phone, the sound echoing through the foyer. He leaned against the wall. He was totally screwed. There was no way out now. Nothing he could do.

He thought about the gun he kept in the nightstand beside his bed in case of a break-in. There was only one way out, he thought in his drunken, desolate state. Go up there, put the gun to his head and pull the trigger.

And if he wanted to be really considerate, he would take Rebecca with him. After all, this was all her fault. The thought buoyed him enough that he slowly pushed himself off the wall and began the long climb up the stairs to the master bedroom.

DIXIE WOKE SOMETIME in the night. She'd heard a sound outside the cabin. She closed her eyes, not wanting to get up. The cabin felt cold and here in bed with Chance, she couldn't have been more warm and content.

Beauregard let out a soft woof in the other room. Chance didn't stir. She smiled to herself, remembering their hours of lovemaking. Any other man would have been comatose.

Slipping out of the bed, she padded into the living room. The fire was little more than ashes, the room cold, at least by Texas standards.

She hugged herself as she moved to the window where Beauregard was staring out. He let out another woof, glancing over at her as if to say, "There's something out there."

"Right," she said, thinking it was probably a deer. Chance said there were often deer in his yard.

She put her face to the glass, cupping her hands to look out. It was still snowing, the sky light for the middle of the night. But still she couldn't see anything. If there was a deer out there, she sure didn't see it.

She started to turn away when she thought she saw a light. It flashed on for a few seconds off to her right, low on the mountain, and then was gone just as quickly. She stared into the snowy darkness until her eyes ached but she didn't see it again.

Even Beauregard lost interest. He dropped down to go back over to his spot next to the fireplace. She stayed a few more minutes, becoming convinced she'd just imagined it. Who in their right mind would be out on a night like this? And didn't Chance say there were no other cabins close by?

She got herself a glass of water, checked the door to make sure it was locked and went back to bed.

"Everything all right?" Chance asked sleepily as she crawled under the covers.

"Fine." Locked in the warmth of Chance's arms, everything *was* fine.

OLIVER CREPT INTO the master bedroom afraid to turn on a light. What he had to do was better done in the dark. He'd cried all the way up the stairs, stopping on the landing to sit.

He'd never felt more sorry for himself. He tried to imagine his parents at the funeral mourning over his grave. They would be sorry they'd treated him the way they had all of his life. Cold, uncaring snobs, that's what they were.

The bedroom was pitch-black—just the way Rebecca liked it. He silently cursed her as he stumbled in the general direction of the bedstand where he kept the gun, all the time imagining his parents breaking down at the funeral. They would be so sorry.

They'd never wanted him to marry Rebecca. They found her to be inferior in class. *But she's rich,* he'd said. They'd turned their noses up at Beauregard Bonner's new wealth as being crass just like him.

He hoped they'd feel guilty for the rest of their lives. In fact, he might write a suicide note telling them they were the reason. Why not?

He bumped into the bed and froze, afraid he'd awaken Rebecca. Not a sound came from the bed. He worked his way along the edge to the bedstand, opened the drawer and pulled out the gun.

Rebecca always slept on the left side.

He couldn't see her, but then he didn't really want to. Better just to get it done quickly.

He clicked off the safety, crying again. Not at the thought of shooting Rebecca, but at pulling the trigger on himself. He told himself this would save Rebecca the embarrassment of the divorce. She would thank him if she knew what he was doing for her. It wasn't like she would forgive him once she found out about the money. The cold-hearted bitch.

With his legs against the bed, he estimated the distance from where he stood to where Rebecca's head would be on her pillow. Aiming the gun, he braced himself. Two shots for her. One for him. Drunk and desperate, he decided he didn't have the energy to write a suicide note. Let his parents always wonder.

He closed his eyes and pulled the trigger. Boom. Boom. He opened one eye. He couldn't see Rebecca in the bed but there was no sound coming from her.

Knowing there was no turning back now, he turned the gun on himself.

BEAU BONNER GOT THE CALL early the next morning. At first he didn't recognize the voice. He had trouble making sense of the words the man was saying.

"What the hell are you talking about?" he finally demanded when he realized it was one of his pilots.

"Your jet, sir. It's gone."

"What do you mean, gone? Stolen?" Beau remembered that Mason had taken it. This was just a misunderstanding. "Mason Roberts took it—"

"No, sir. I'm talking about the jet you instructed me to fly to Montana today," the pilot said. "It was taken last night and I'm told it won't be back for several days."

Beau felt his blood pressure soar. "Who took it? Carl? That damned irresponsible cousin of his, Ace?"

"Apparently you gave your daughter Rebecca Lancaster permission to take it. She hired her own pilot."

"What?" He couldn't believe this. "Where the hell did she go with it?"

"According to her flight plan? New York City and possibly on to Paris."

Beau snapped off the phone, so livid he thought he might have a coronary. What the hell had Rebecca been thinking?

He groaned as he realized exactly what she'd been thinking. She didn't want to hear what he had to tell her. That was so like Rebecca. She'd never wanted to hear bad news. She preferred to pretend that everything was fine.

Beau cussed to himself. He should have gone to her house, made her listen. Well, at least in New York she wouldn't hear about what was going on in Montana. There would be time when she returned to tell her everything.

He felt as if he'd dodged the bullet yet another time and felt guilty for being relieved he wouldn't have to face Rebecca this morning. Christmas morning.

What now? He'd have to call Chance to tell him he wouldn't be sending a plane. With commercial flights booked solid this time of year, Beau knew there was little chance of getting Dixie back to Texas for Christmas now. Christmas, and he was all alone.

He had hoped they could all be together this Christmas like normal families. Were there normal families? He blamed himself for Dixie and Rebecca never getting along. He loved Rebecca with all his heart, but it had never seemed enough. Even as a child, she'd seemed incapable of being satisfied. He'd poured love into her, trying to make up for the father who hadn't wanted her. But Rebecca had proved to be a bottomless pit.

And then Dixie had come along.

Just the opposite of Rebecca, Dixie had been a willful, independent child who didn't seem to need anyone. He'd blamed that on her having to grow up without a mother from such a young age. But the truth was, Dixie was like him.

Beau had spent his life trying not to be like his father and yet he could see the similarities between Rebecca and Dixie, him and Carl. Carl had wanted their father's love desperately. Beau hadn't asked for it, knew he didn't deserve that kind of high regard, and often despised their mean domineering father as much as Carl.

Beau hadn't stayed on the farm out of love or loyalty. While everyone his age left to find good-paying jobs and adventure, Beau had stayed on the farm in Texas, knowing there wasn't any other place he'd be special except in his father's eyes.

And then a gusher came in a few farms away and his friends came back to work the rigs. Carl and Ace had returned to Texas along with Mason who'd been bumming around the country. Mason came to him, not just with stories of the places he'd been, but with an idea.

To scrape together all the money they had and have a test well dug on the isolated north forty of the farm so no one would get wind of it—especially Carl or Ace. Or Beau's old man.

He put his head in his hands. Rebecca had always believed that he loved Dixie more. Once she heard he wasn't her father, nothing would convince her otherwise.

The phone rang again. This time it was the police.

CHANCE CAME AWAKE slowly, fighting not to leave the warm contentment of the dream. He'd been so happy in the dream, happier than he could remember being.

He opened his eyes to find sunlight streaming into the cabin. For those first few seconds he thought he was alone—just as he'd been for so long.

Then he felt her beside him and closed his eyes tight to hold back the sudden rush of emotion. It hadn't been a dream. Beside him, Dixie stirred, her naked body warm and luscious next to his.

Opening his eyes, he looked at her, shocked by his feelings of just seeing her beside him, let alone the memory of their lovemaking. At that moment he would have moved heaven and earth to keep her beside him.

That thought made him carefully slide out of the bed and leave the bedroom. He found his clothing and dressed before building a fire and jotting Dixie a note. Beauregard bound up the moment the dog saw that they would be going outside. The snow was deep but Chance didn't take the time to shovel, Beauregard busting a trail ahead of him through a world of cold white.

He thought about taking the pickup, but decided to hike down the road until he could get cell phone service. The land lay in frozen silence. He stood in the deep snow, breathing in the scent of pine. He needed this time alone on this beautiful Christmas morning.

Bonner answered on the first ring. "Rebecca?"

"No," Chance said, frowning. "It's Chance."

"I thought it would be Rebecca." He sounded half-asleep. Or half-drunk. "She took my plane to New York or Paris. I don't know."

"The plane you were bringing to Montana today," Chance guessed, and swore under his breath.

"Mason has the other one. I don't know when either of them will be back. I'm trying to line up another plane."

"Beau, listen, this can't wait. Dixie and I found out some things about the man your wife had an affair with before she met you that I think you need to know. If you don't already."

KEEPING CHRISTMAS

Now it was Bonner's turn to swear. "I told you I don't know anything about him and I don't want to."

"You don't have a choice. I'm pretty sure he's the person who hired the two men who were trying to kill Dixie before she could unearth his identity."

"Are you sure this isn't just another of Dixie's—"

"Two men tried to run us off the road yesterday," Chance snapped. "The same two men Dixie says abducted her and ransacked her house looking for her research on her mother's family. The men are dead, but whoever hired them is still out there."

"Oh, my God," Bonner said. "Then it's true. Someone really is trying to kill her?"

"What the hell do you think I've been trying to tell you? And Dixie's aunt is dead, as well."

"My God. I was so sure—"

Chance tried to understand how Bonner must feel right now. Given the other tricks Dixie had played on Bonner, Chance could understand why he hadn't believed it. Mostly Bonner hadn't wanted to believe it. He'd have to share some of the blame if it were true since he hadn't been honest with Dixie when she'd come to him with the photographs.

"You think it's the man Sarah was involved with before me," Bonner said. "You have any idea who he is?"

"No, but from what we found out, he's someone who knows you. He used your name while he was living up here. Your wife's name was actually Elizabeth Sarah Worth. She changed it to Sarah when this man took her to Texas. By then, oil had been found on your farm." Chance hesitated.

"No," Bonner said, as if suspecting where Chance was headed with this.

"She changed her name to Sarah and went after you and your money."

"I don't believe it." But the tremor in his voice said he did.

"The man blackmailed her into doing it," Chance said. "It seems Sarah had a good friend in Idaho who she wrote to every week." He heard Bonner make a small, sad sound. "I assume you didn't know about Amelia McCarthy?"

"No." His voice was muffled.

Chance hated that he had to tell Bonner this over the phone. But the sooner Bonner had the information, the sooner maybe they could find the killer.

"In the last letter that Sarah sent, she said she'd fallen in love with you. She was happy. She said she could no longer live with the lies of her past and planned to tell you the truth."

Bonner sounded as if he was crying. "She never told me."

"The man had been blackmailing her, threatening to tell you. She was giving him money to keep him quiet. Apparently she was also afraid of him."

There was a painful choking sound on the other end of the line. "If you tell me that he—"

"Sarah's friend believed that the man killed her to keep you from learning the truth," Chance finished.

"My God," Bonner said.

"I'm telling you this because I think this man believes that once Dixie is stopped, the truth will never come out. He still has something to lose if you find out who he is. Do you have any idea who he might be?" Silence. "Bonner?"

Chance swore. Beauregard Bonner had hung up. He

tried him back, but the line was busy. He tried again, walking farther up the road. This time it rang and rang.

Just as Chance was going to hang up and try again, thinking he must have dialed wrong, he saw the footprints in the snow.

DIXIE WOKE TO a chill in the air. She felt in the bed for Chance only to find him gone. She knew he wouldn't have gone far, but still it filled her with a sense of loss. She didn't want to waste a second because eventually this would be over and they would go their separate ways. If they lived that long.

Hadn't she warned herself not to hope for more than what Chance could give her? She knew he'd been hurt badly in the past. It was no coincidence that his relationships were few and far between and little more than a few dates.

He liked living out here alone. He needed it. She understood the choice between living alone or being with the wrong person. Roy Bob Jackson had tempted her, made her realize that she wanted someone in her life. But it had never been Roy Bob Jackson—even if she hadn't found out he worked for her father.

No, it had always been Chance Walker.

She smiled as she remembered their lovemaking, regretting nothing. If this was all they ever shared, then she could live with that. At least, she hoped she could.

Rising, she tiptoed across the cold wood floor to open the bedroom door. Chance had a blaze going in the fireplace. She sniffed the air, hoping for the smell of bacon frying. And French toast, she thought. She always ate hers with brown sugar, honey and butter and had gotten Chance to try it years ago in Texas when she was just a silly kid with a crush.

She wondered if he still ate his French toast that way as she went through the living room picking up her clothing and putting it on as she moved.

But Chance wasn't in the kitchen. Instead she found a note stuck to the coffeemaker.

"Gone up the road to make a cell phone call. Be right back."

Did that mean there wasn't cell phone service in the cabin? She started the coffee and while it brewed, she found her purse and tried *her* cell phone which she'd turned off after talking to Amelia's sister-in-law, Rita McCarthy. The service was unreliable, but she did have a message. She played the message, surprised to hear Rita McCarthy's voice.

"After I talked to you, I got to thinking," Rita said. "I remembered something. Give me a call."

Rita had remembered something. About the man? Dixie went to the window and looked out, hoping to see Chance returning. But there was only his tracks and the dog's in the deep snow of the deck.

She moved to the bedroom window at the back of the cabin and peered out. She could see where he and the dog had walked up the road.

A thud toward the front of the house startled her. Maybe Chance and Beauregard had taken a different way back. Padding into the living room, she glanced out the front window again. No sign of anyone.

She jumped as a large clump of snow came sliding off the metal roof of the cabin to land in a pile just off the deck. Her heart was racing and for a moment, she reconsidered hiking up the road to find Chance. But what if he took another way back and she missed him?

It wasn't as if she'd get lost. All she had to do was to follow the road back. On impulse, she scribbled her note on the bottom of Chance's, that way he'd know where to find her if she did miss him. She was too impatient to wait for him to return. She had to know what Rita had remembered.

Tucking her cell phone into her pocket, she looked around for her coat and boots. Another thud outside. She glanced toward the window as she pulled on her boots and slipped into her coat.

As she opened the door, she felt the wind and heard the groan of the pines. Snow fell from a pine near the edge of the deck, startling her. Why was she nervous?

Because she had a feeling that in a few minutes she would know the identity of the man who wanted her dead.

CHANCE BENT OVER the tracks in the snow. Footprints. Snow had partially filled the tracks, making it hard for him to gauge the size of the boots that had made the prints.

It appeared someone had walked up the snow-filled road, then dropped down the side of the mountain.

He glanced back into the direction of his cabin, a good mile back and down another even less-traveled road flanked on each side by pines.

The tracks in the snow could be from someone going to one of the nearer cabins along the lake. Someone checking to make sure his cabin hadn't been broken into. This time of year all but his cabin was boarded up for winter.

"What do you think, old boy?" Chance said to Beauregard.

The dog's head came up at the sound of Chance's voice. There was snow on the mutt's nose from where he'd been sniffing the tracks.

"Yeah, that's what I was thinking," Chance said.

Heart in his throat, he dropped off the road, following the tracks in the new snow as quickly as he could along the steep frozen bank to the edge of the lake.

The snow was deep, the going slow. He had to wonder why anyone would have come this way. Why not stay on the road where the walking was easier?

He passed one cabin after another, following the tracks to where they picked up a second set. He stopped, surprised to see that these were older, possibly from last night during the storm.

The new footprints began to follow the older set.

Chance frowned. Beauregard was frolicking in the snow, sniffing the tracks and racing around. From here the tracks trailed along the edge of the pines, branching off to the south.

A blustery wind blew across the frozen lake to whisper in the pines along the side of the mountain. The snow-filled boughs swayed in the gusts as Chance hurried. There was only one other cabin about a half mile down a narrow private road. His.

He began to run.

DIXIE STEPPED OUT the front door of the cabin and paused to look off to the right as she remembered the light she'd thought she'd seen the night before.

Odd. Chance had said his was the only cabin down this road and yet there was something down there in the trees that certainly looked like a cabin.

She moved to the edge of the deck and peered over the railing through the pines. A boathouse.

Her heart began to beat a little faster. That's where she'd seen the light last night. But as she stared at the boathouse, she could see that the outside light wasn't on.

Because it hadn't really been a light. It had been smaller and had gone out, more like a flashlight beam. Her mouth went dry at the thought. Someone had been down there.

The hair rose on the back of her neck. She swung around, shocked to find no one behind her. She looked into the darkness under the snow-filled pines, positive that she'd felt someone there.

"You're just jumping at shadows," she whispered to herself, wishing Chance would return. It was too quiet. And yet she sensed she was no longer alone.

Her breath came out in white puffs as she turned to look back down the mountainside through the pines to the boathouse. She was trying to tell herself that she'd just imagined the light at the boathouse last night when she saw something in the snow.

Her blood ran cold as she saw the single trail of footprints that led up from the boathouse and around the cabin. Chance's? No, she thought, her mouth going dry, because there was no sign of the dog's prints with them.

Behind her, she heard the wood creak as if someone had stepped up onto the decking.

This time when she turned, she knew the person who'd made those tracks would be standing right behind her.

CHAPTER SIXTEEN

CHANCE RAN THROUGH the deep snow, breathing hard, his mind racing. Beauregard, thinking they were playing, had run ahead into the dense pines. He heard the dog let out a startled bark, then a yelp.

Furious with himself for not thinking to bring his gun, Chance shoved through the pine boughs, snow showering over him, and was struck hard. The blow glanced off the back of his head.

He could see his dog crouched down, hair standing up on his neck, a low growl emitting from his throat. Beauregard was staring at something behind Chance.

Bracing himself for whatever had been hiding in the trees, Chance swung around, ready to defend himself, but nothing could have prepared him for what he saw.

DIXIE COULDN'T MOVE. She couldn't turn around. The deck creaked behind her again, this time the sound so close she thought she saw a puff of frosty breath breeze past her on the wind. Fear paralyzed her because she knew what was behind her and she had no weapon. No hope.

"Dixie?"

She spun around at the sound of the voice, frowning in surprise, then smiling as she recognized the face. Her knees went weak with relief.

"Mason." She put her hand to her heart. It was beating a million beats a second. Of course her father would send Mason to get her. Mason, who always solved all her father's problems for him. "You scared me half to death. How did you find me?"

He smiled and shook his head. "I knew Beau had hired Chance Walker, so that made it somewhat easier." He glanced toward the cabin. "Tell me it's warm in that cabin. I hiked in last night, got turned around and ended up staying in someone's boathouse."

She realized that he was shivering even though he was wearing snow boots and a heavy, hooded coat and gloves. "Not exactly Texas weather, huh." She led him into the cabin, taking off her coat to toss more wood on the fire.

"Chance should be back soon," she said. "He's just gone up the road."

Mason stood by the door, looking cold, his hands buried in his coat. He was glancing around the cabin, silent, as if trying to figure out what to say to her.

"So my father sent you to take me back to Texas," she said.

"Actually..." Mason's gaze settled on her. "He doesn't know I'm here. I told him I had to go away for a few days on a business trip." He hadn't moved from near the door. He still had his hands deep in his coat pockets and he appeared to be watching for Chance.

She felt her first stirring of doubt. "Then why—"

"I thought if I came up here that we could discuss this little problem," he said, "and come to a satisfactory conciliation."

Her fear notched up a level as she looked into his eyes. She'd known Mason Roberts her whole life. He'd been at every birthday party, every family event.

He stood with the hood of his coat up, his face in

shadow. It was the way he was standing. Her heart leaped to her throat as she remembered the photograph of her mother and the man. The man had put his head down, avoiding the camera, his weight on one leg, shoulders angled away. He hadn't liked having his photo taken.

Just like Mason. She thought of what few photographs she'd taken as a kid at Bonner barbecues. Mason had always managed to be in shadow or partially hidden from view by the person next to him. Mason, a man who liked to work behind the scenes, not wanting to take credit, the problem-solver and Beauregard Bonner's closest friend and associate.

Mason was studying her, a half smile on his face, eyes wary. "Come on, Dixie. You and I have always been straight with each other. Let's not play games now. You know why I'm here, don't you?"

She stared at her mother's former lover. Rebecca's father. "You bastard."

"REBECCA?" CHANCE GAPED at the woman standing in the pines, a piece of tree limb in her gloved hands. He shook his head, thinking the blow to his head must have messed up his brain. "Rebecca?"

"Chance," she said in that breathless Southern accent of hers. "I didn't know it was you. I heard someone coming… Then I saw that big ol' dog."

All he could do was stare. It had been years and yet she seemed just the same. She was dressed in a suede coat with white fur, the same fur that was on her knee-high leather boots and her hat. She carried a large suede shoulder bag in the same color. Her blond hair curved around her perfectly made-up face as if she were going to breakfast at some fancy ski resort.

"What are you doing here?" he asked, wanting to

laugh. She was so Rebecca. So wrong for him. So not like her sister Dixie, who was so right for him.

"Daddy told me about Dixie," Rebecca said. "I was headed for New York to do some last-minute Christmas shopping and I decided to fly to Montana instead to try to get her home for Christmas."

He didn't know what to say. This was definitely the Rebecca Bonner he remembered. Jet-setter. Fashion plate. Privileged beyond belief.

"I tried to call," she said, and glanced at the dog who was still growling. "He isn't going to bite me, is he?"

"Put down the stick," Chance told her. Beauregard quit growling. "You just scared him."

"Not as much as the two of you scared me. I'm so sorry I hit you. But when I heard something coming, I thought it might be a bear." She smiled at him just like she used to so many years ago. The years had been good to her. He figured her money and the latest antiaging techniques and supplies hadn't hurt, either.

"Bears *hibernate* in the winter," he said, and rubbed the lump on his head, feeling a little dazed. "Why didn't you just follow the road?"

"I saw tracks coming down this way," she said. "So I followed them."

The second tracks. He glanced past her and saw that the footprints continued on down the shoreline—straight to his boathouse.

"Come on, we need to get up to the cabin," he said. "It's right up here."

Rebecca nodded and shielded her eyes to look up the hillside to the cabin. "I can't wait to see my sister."

"YOU *BASTARD!*" BLINDED by her anger at what he'd done to her mother and Rebecca, Dixie grabbed up the poker from the fireplace and came at Mason, hitting him across one arm and shoulder before he could get the gun from his pocket.

He swore as he wrenched the poker from her hands and shoved the barrel end of the gun in her face. "Try me," he snapped, his hand shaking with anger. "You think I won't pull the trigger? You're *dead* wrong."

"Oh, I know too well what you're capable of," Dixie snapped. "You hired two men to kill me and I know you killed my mother to keep her from exposing you." She wanted to fly at him again but knew he *would* shoot her.

"You're mistaken, Dixie. I didn't hire anyone to kill you. I prefer to take care of problems myself. I thought you knew that about me."

She saw pain in his eyes and desperation. He didn't want to kill her. She felt confused. Why had he come here if not to keep her from exposing him? Could she be wrong about him being a killer? Then how did she explain the gun he held on her?

"You were like family," she snapped.

He laughed. "Dixie, I *am* family. Haven't you figured it out yet? My father was Earle Bonner. Just because the son of a bitch denied me the same way he did Carl…"

She heard the bitterness in his voice. The jealousy she'd seen between him and Carl. It all made sense now. "That's why you pretended to be Beauregard Bonner in Idaho."

"Don't read more into this than is there. I just used his name," Mason said. "I love your father like the brother he is."

She smirked at that. "Is that why you killed the woman he loved, my mother?"

"Your mother died in a car accident. I would imagine

she couldn't face your father with the truth and found driving into the lake easier."

"That's a lie. She wouldn't have killed herself, not with two babies at home and a husband she loved," Dixie snapped. "Were you jealous because she fell in love with my father? Or was it only ever about money?"

"I made your father what he is today," Mason said. "I was the one who talked him into doing the test well on the farm. He wouldn't be anything without me."

"And you got rich right along with him."

He shook his head. "It's not the same. Beau's never understood that taking handouts from him isn't the same as being the man behind the fortune. It makes a man bitter."

"Especially if he's a thankless bastard," she said.

"Dixie, Dixie, why couldn't you have just left things alone?" Mason said in his conciliatory tone.

She heard a sound outside the cabin.

Unfortunately, Mason heard it, as well. He stepped to her, grabbing her arm as he shoved the gun into her side, shielding himself behind her as she heard the dog bark at the cabin door.

Chance. Her heart dropped. She opened her mouth to call to him, to warn him he was about to walk into an ambush. Mason clamped his hand over her mouth, the gun barrel now at her temple as he whispered, "Make a sound and the last thing your boyfriend will see is your brains blown all over his cabin."

CHANCE SAW BEAUREGARD sniffing at two sets of tracks on the deck. He motioned for Rebecca to hang back as he flung open the cabin door. Beauregard bounded in. Chance ducked and rolled, coming up behind the couch.

In that split second, as the door swung in, he'd taken

in the scene in front of the fire. His heart had dropped like a stone as he saw Dixie, the gun to her head, and Mason Roberts with his hand over her mouth. Her blue eyes were wide with fear and fury.

He came up from behind the couch just as Mason started to swing the barrel of the gun toward the dog. Dixie saw it, too, and made her move, just as Chance had known she would. She wasn't going to let Mason shoot the dog—or him. Chance could never have loved her more than at that moment.

As he leaped over the couch, Dixie elbowed Mason in the ribs and grabbed the wrist holding the gun. The shot went wild. The gun fell to the floor, skittering away as Chance tackled Mason and took him down, Dixie falling with them onto the floor in front of the fireplace.

It all happened in an instant. Chance got a choke hold on Mason, who seemed to instantly drain of fight. Chance had an age advantage, as well as self-defense training. But still it surprised him that Mason didn't seem to have the fight of a killer.

Dixie scrambled to her feet to find the gun Mason had dropped. Chance had the man down, but she wasn't taking any chances.

At the sound of a low growl, Dixie turned to look back at Chance. He'd completely neutralized Mason, who sat against the wall breathing hard, head down, looking beaten.

Chance reached to jerk Mason to his feet, turning as Dixie did to see what Beauregard was growling about.

Dixie blinked in astonishment. "Rebecca?"

She stood just inside the front door of the cabin. In her hand was Mason's gun, the one Dixie had been looking for.

"I thought I told you to call off your dog?" Rebecca said as she leveled the gun at him.

"Beauregard," Chance ordered. "Down."

The dog stopped growling, but like everyone else in the room kept his gaze on Rebecca.

"What are you doing here?" Dixie asked.

"Didn't Chance tell you? I came to see you, little sister."

Dixie knew that sarcastic tone too well. "How long have you known?"

Rebecca smiled. "I overheard Mother and Mason arguing. What was I?" she asked Mason. "Five? I heard you threaten to kill her if she told my daddy. I heard everything you said, including how you would take me far away so she would never see me again."

Mason was looking at her, a strange expression on his face.

"You said you would kill me, you didn't care about the little snotty-nosed brat, isn't that what you said?" Rebecca continued, the gun held steady in her hand, her voice calm, no emotion in her face.

"Rebecca, put the gun away and we can talk about this," Chance said quietly. "You don't want to do anything you'll regret."

She laughed. "Believe me, I'm not going to regret it. When I heard you were in Montana, I knew what you were doing," she said to Dixie. "All those years of keeping the secret just to have you planning to tell the whole world about me and my mother and my…" Her gaze shifted to Mason. "My *father*. You would love to destroy me, wouldn't you?"

"Rebecca, that's not true. I wouldn't—"

"Shut up!" She swung the gun so it was pointed at Dixie's face. "Daddy's little girl. You think I didn't know he loved you best? He knew I was some bastard's daughter. But you—" Her voice broke. "It doesn't matter. I always knew who I really was. What I really was. My own father hated me."

Mason made a sound of denial, but it was cut off by the boom of a shot from the pistol in Rebecca's hands. Wood splintered just over Mason's head.

Dixie felt Chance step up behind her, his hands on her waist. She knew what he planned to do, felt it in his touch.

"Rebecca," Chance said. "Give me the gun. You're not a killer."

She laughed. "Wrong, Chance. Who do you think hired the men to stop my sister? I'm my daddy's daughter." Her gaze moved to Mason. "My *real* daddy's daughter."

As Chance shoved Dixie aside and launched himself at Rebecca, she swung the barrel of the gun. Dixie heard the thunder of the shot as she fell, heard the sound Mason made as the bullet found its mark.

Rebecca got off only one more shot before Chance reached her.

Dixie heard his cry of pain and scrambled to her feet in time to see her half sister hit the floor, the gun still in her hand.

Chance swung around, a look of horror on his face as he dragged Dixie into his arms, shielding her from the sight of her sister dead on the floor from a self-inflicted gunshot wound to the head.

EPILOGUE

THAT SPRING WAS the longest of Chance's life. It had snowed every day for months after Dixie had taken the jet back to Texas to be with her father.

Chance had wanted to go, but Dixie said she needed some time alone and that her father needed her. For a while, Chance called her every day, then once a week, then once a month. He knew Dixie and Beau needed to heal and that they both blamed themselves.

Beau had managed to keep the real story out of the press. As far as the public knew, the holidays had been a tragic time for the Bonner family. A burglar had broken into the Lancaster home and killed Oliver Lancaster, husband of Rebecca Bonner Lancaster, while she was away on Christmas vacation with her sister Dixie in Montana.

While there, she was tragically killed along with Beauregard Bonner's closest friend and associate, Mason Roberts.

Only Chance knew that Beau had found an envelope with his name on it on his desk weeks later when he returned to his office. It was from Mason. A confession letter filled with painful apology and regret. In the letter, Mason told Beau he was taking the jet to Montana to try to protect Dixie from Rebecca. Mason feared that Rebecca was behind Dixie's abduction, faked kidnapping, and ultimately planned to have her killed.

Carl paid off Oliver's gambling debts, keeping that

part quiet from the press, and spent more time with Beau at the house. They talked a lot about Sarah.

Dixie had quit her job and taken Rebecca's and Oliver's three children and moved into her father's huge empty house. Beau had retired, selling Bonner Unlimited, and setting up trust funds for the kids. He'd realized, according to Dixie, that he had no need to make more money.

Instead he wanted to spend more time with his family. Dixie sent pictures of the kids with grandpa.

More times than he could count, Chance started a letter to Dixie, asking her to bring the children and come be his wife. But he always ended up tossing the half-written letters in the fire.

He'd thought about going to Texas and begging her to come back with him. But he couldn't ask her to leave Texas, her family and the only home the kids had known, as much as she wanted to.

One bright warm day in June, Chance took his fishing pole down to the lake, Beauregard bounding along beside him as they climbed into the boat and motored out to a favorite spot. He'd caught a few nice trout when he heard a commotion on the beach and looked back toward his cabin.

Over the winter, he'd remodeled it, adding a second floor to give himself something to do, as well as to put the memory of what had happened there far from his mind.

Now he stared toward the beach, his heart in his throat. When he'd built onto the cabin, he'd done it with the dream that maybe he could get Dixie and the kids to come up next Christmas. They could have a real Christmas with a larger tree. He'd even buy some decorations.

He knew that's all it was, a dream. He never thought

he'd see Dixie Bonner in Montana again, let alone standing on his doorstep.

But as he started the motor on the boat and turned the bow toward shore, he could have sworn that was her on the beach. There were three kids playing in the water along the edge of the lake.

Beauregard barked excitedly as Chance neared the shore. He cut the engine, staring at the woman standing near his boathouse. She had her eyes shaded against the sun, but even from a distance he could see that she was smiling. Her long legs were tanned, that not-so-scrawny behind was clad in white shorts, and he could make out a peach tank top beneath that wild mane of dark curly hair that fell past her shoulders.

She hesitated only a moment, then charged toward him, splashing into the water. Beauregard plunged in, swimming to her, making a yelping sound, excited at the sight of her.

Chance laughed, took off his shirt and dove in, swimming toward her as the boat floated lazily toward shore.

He caught her in chest-high water, pulling her into his arms. She was laughing and crying, kissing him, then pulling back to look into his eyes as if he was the best thing she'd ever seen.

"I got your letter," she said.

"My letter?"

"The one asking me to marry you, silly." She was grinning at him, mischief in her eyes.

"But I never—"

She kissed him cutting off the rest of his words. As she pulled back, she said, "But you know I would never accept a proposal unless it was in person."

"I recall." He looked into those amazing blue eyes. "Have you always known me so well?"

She grinned. "Since I was twelve and I fell madly in

love with you. It was just a matter of time before you asked me to marry you. That is why you added on to the cabin, isn't it?"

He laughed. "You know it." He glanced toward the edge of the lake where Rebecca's three children stood as if waiting. They looked anxious, almost afraid of what was going to happen next. "Do they know?"

Dixie nodded. "They're just waiting for you to make it official so they can go swimming in the lake at their new home. Oh, I should mention that my father and uncle Carl plan to buy a place across the lake. They want to be close to the kids. Including the ones you and I are going to have. Still glad you sent me that letter?"

He laughed. "Marry me, Dixie Bonner, and I promise to love you and those three kids and any others we might have until death do us part."

"Just like in the letter you meant to write me," she said with a grin.

"Just like in all the letters I did write you but just didn't mail," he said as he brushed her wet hair back from her face, wondering how he could be so blessed. "Well?"

She grinned. "All I can say is…it's about time, Chance Walker." She kissed him, then let out a whoop. On the beach the kids started clapping and cheering. Then they were all in the water, the sun beating down on them, the sky bluer than blue on one of those amazing Montana summer days.

He said a prayer for his daughter and gathered his family around him, already thinking of Christmas and the homemade tinfoil silver star he'd saved to put on top of the tree.

* * * * *

INTRIGUE

EDGE-OF-YOUR-SEAT INTRIGUE, FEARLESS ROMANCE

Use this coupon to save

$1.00

on the purchase of any
Harlequin Intrigue® book!

Available wherever books are sold,
including most bookstores, supermarkets,
drugstores and discount stores.

Save $1.00

on the purchase of any Harlequin Intrigue® book.

Coupon expires January 31, 2014. Redeemable at participating retail outlets
in the U.S. and Canada only. Limit one coupon per customer.

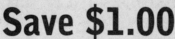

Canadian Retailers: Harlequin Enterprises Limited will pay the face value of this coupon plus 10.25¢ if submitted by customer for this product only. Any other use constitutes fraud. Coupon is nonassignable. Void if taxed, prohibited or restricted by law. Consumer must pay any government taxes. Void if copied. Nielsen Clearing House ("NCH") customers submit coupons and proof of sales to Harlequin Enterprises Limited, P.O. Box 3000, Saint John, NB E2L 4L3, Canada. Non-NCH retailer—for reimbursement submit coupons and proof of sales directly to Harlequin Enterprises Limited, Retail Marketing Department, 225 Duncan Mill Rd., Don Mills, ON M3B 3K9, Canada.

U.S. Retailers: Harlequin Enterprises Limited will pay the face value of this coupon plus 8¢ if submitted by customer for this product only. Any other use constitutes fraud. Coupon is nonassignable. Void if taxed, prohibited or restricted by law. Consumer must pay any government taxes. Void if copied. For reimbursement submit coupons and proof of sales directly to Harlequin Enterprises Limited, P.O. Box 880478, El Paso, TX 88588-0478, U.S.A. Cash value 1/100 cents.

52611171

5 65373 00076 2   (8100)0 11887

HIINC1113COUP

*Her target is tall, dark and dangerous…but now a vengeful
enemy is targeting them both. As the enemy lurks closer,
Eden Gray and federal marshal Declan O'Malley must fight
for a future they might not live to see.*

"I've watched you for the past two days, so I knew you take a
ride this time of morning before you go into work."

"You watched me?"

She nodded.

"Are you going to make me arrest you, or do you plan to keep
going with that explanation?"

"I'm a P.I. now. I own a small agency in San Antonio."

She'd skipped right over the most important detail of her
brief bio. "Your father's Zander Gray, a lowlife, swindling scum.
I arrested him about three years ago for attempting to murder a
witness who was going to testify against him, and he was doing
hard time before he escaped."

And this was suddenly becoming a whole lot clearer.

"He sent you here," Declan accused.

"No," she quickly answered. "But my father might have been
the reason they contacted me in the first place," Eden explained.
"They might have thought I'd do anything to get back at you for
arresting him. I won't."

He made a sound of disagreement. "Since you're trespassing

and have been stalking me, convince me otherwise that you're not here to avenge your father."

"I'm not." Not a whisper that time. And there was some fire in those two little words. "But someone's trying to set me up."

Declan thought about that a second. "Lady, if you wanted me to investigate that, you didn't have to follow me or come to my ranch. My office is on Main Street in town."

Another head shake. "They didn't hire me to go to your office."

"So, who are they?"

"I honestly don't know." She dodged his gaze, tried to turn away, but he took hold of her again to force her to face him. "After I realized someone had planted that false info on my computer, I got a call from a man using a prepaid cell phone. I didn't recognize his voice. He said if I went to the cops or the marshals, he'd release the info on my computer, that I'd be arrested."

"This unknown male caller is the one who put the camera outside?"

"I think so."

He shook his head. "If they sent you to watch me, why use a camera?"

"Because the camera is to watch *me*," she clarified. "To make sure I do what he ordered me to do."

"And what exactly are you supposed to do?" Declan demanded.

Eden Gray shoved her hand over her Glock. "I'm to kill you."

Will Eden and Declan be able to work together, or will their past get in the way?

Don't miss the edge-of-your-seat action in
JUSTICE IS COMING
by USA TODAY bestselling author Delores Fossen.
Available November 19, only from Harlequin Intrigue.

Catch a thrill with other

HARLEQUIN
INTRIGUE®
books

With **gripping** crime stories and page-turning suspense, Harlequin Intrigue will keep you **on the edge** of your seat and looking for more. Immerse yourself in a thrilling story of high intensity, lurking **danger** and hot protective **heroes.** Live in a moment of suspense with each book that is guaranteed to leave you **breathless.**

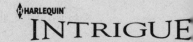